SLEEP WELL, MY LADY

Books by the author

The Inspector Darko Dawson Mysteries
Wife of the Gods
Children of the Street
Murder at Cape Three Points
Gold of Our Fathers
Death by His Grace

The Emma Djan Mysteries
The Missing American
Sleep Well, My Lady

Other Books
Death at the Voyager Hotel
Kamila

SLEEP WELL, MY LADY

MY LADY

KWEI QUARTEY

Published by
Soho Press, Inc.
227 W 17th Street
New York, NY 10011

Library of Congress Cataloging-in-Publication Data

Quartey, Kwei, author.
Sleep well, my lady / Kwei Quartey.
Series: The Emma Djan investigations ; 2

ISBN 978-1-64129-207-8
eISBN 978-1-64129-208-5

Subjects: GSAFD: Mystery fiction.
LCC PS3617.U37 S58 2021 DDC 813'.6—dc23 2020033010

Interior design by Janine Agro, Soho Press, Inc.
Map: © netsign33/Shutterstock

Printed in the United States of America

10 9 8 7 6 5 4 3 2 1

In memory of Careen Chepchumba
Let justice be done though the heavens fall

and

To Mama, who never got to see Emma #2

SLEEP WELL, MY LADY

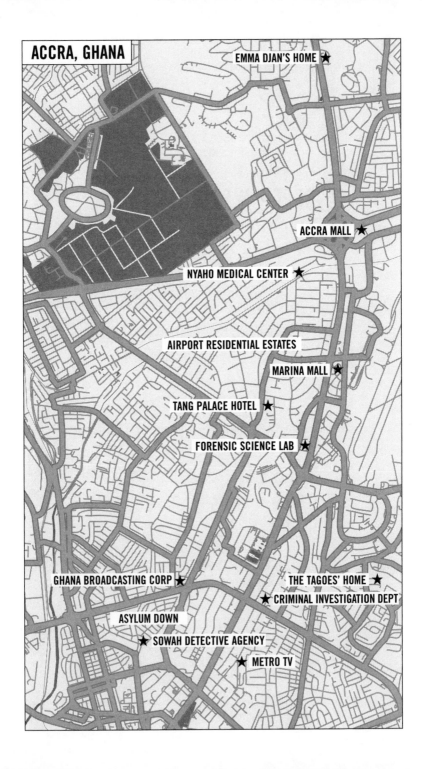

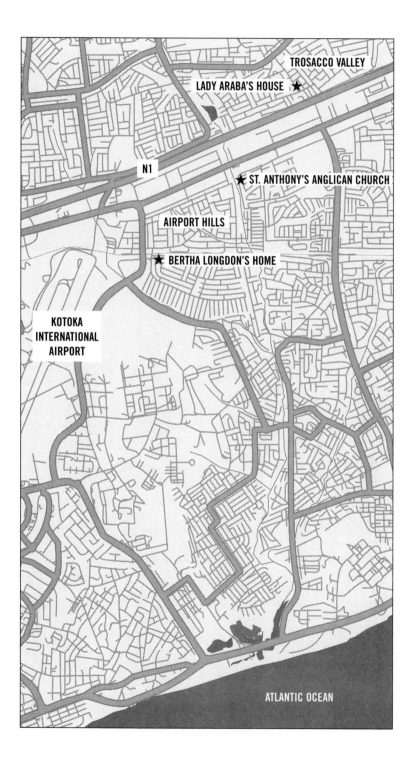

TROSACCO VALLEY

LADY ARABA'S HOUSE ★

N1

★ ST. ANTHONY'S ANGLICAN CHURCH

AIRPORT HILLS

★ BERTHA LONGDON'S HOME

KOTOKA
INTERNATIONAL
AIRPORT

ATLANTIC OCEAN

PART ONE

ONE

The day of the murder

IN THE LAVISH TRASACCO Valley, the Beverly Hills of Accra, no one would have anticipated a murder. The sprawling gated community was landscaped with neat hedgerows and palm trees lining its streets. Pink, yellow, and red hibiscus bushes dotted impossibly green lawns. Red and yellow bougainvillea spilled over the walls and fences.

Completed about a decade before, the Valley couldn't possibly fit any more buildings. However, east of it along the N1 Highway stretched acres of virgin land where the Trasacco Company had begun constructing several new gated complexes on what would be called Trasacco Hills.

The entrance to the Valley was a ten-foot-high wrought-iron gate with a sentry box where the security guards kept track of who went in and out. Peter, the veteran lead security guard, knew every resident by name and face, but all visitors needed to state their identity and destination, and their license plate number might be noted as well. Peter, forty-five, was older than his peers, some of whom were in their twenties. True, he was a tad overweight and could probably not outrun a fit young intruder, but the Valley's five-year security record was impeccable, with not a single instance of robbery, burglary, or carjacking. Peter was proud of that.

•   •   •

CHANGE OF SHIFT was between 6:30 and 7 A.M., giving Peter another fifteen minutes or so before he went home to his wife and kids. Another early bird in Trasacco Valley was Ismael, the head groundskeeper. With a small number of assistants, he kept hedges trimmed, grass mowed, and weeds cleared. Unlike Peter, he was wiry in build, but like the security man, he was friendly and smiled easily. He had a way with greenery. The elegance of the grounds was, for the most part, due to him. Today, he was to put in Blood of Jesus plants—eye-catching with their deep purple leaves and crimson veins that looked like streaks and splatters of blood—in select areas of the complex.

But before he did that, he had promised Lady Araba Tagoe, who loved decorating her palatial space with flowers and trees, that he would bring her a pair of planters for the upper terrace outside her bedroom.

It was a Monday—a fresh start to the week. Ismael went to the garden shed that stood at the end of Ruby Row next to a motion-sensor exit. From the shed, Ismael removed two large terra-cotta planters and carried them one in each hand to 401 Ruby Row.

For additional security, each mansion in the Valley had a remote-operated wrought-iron gate at the driveway entrance. Among the several different house types and colors, Lady Araba's was called "The Duke," painted orange chiffon with a red tile roof trimmed in white. A high-ceilinged portico formed the Duke's front entrance. As Ismael approached, Lady Araba's chauffeur, Kweku-Sam, was washing her Range Rover, which he did every morning before he took the boss out. Any driver worth his salt kept his employer's vehicles shiny and spotless—barely possible in Accra's dusty environment. Araba's second car was an Audi, but she preferred the Rover for its high profile and smoothness over rough roads.

"Morning, Kweku!" Ismael called out.

Kweku-Sam looked up from his work and smiled. "Morning. How be?"

"I dey, oo! Wassup?"

They slipped seamlessly into Twi instead of English. Ismael was from arid Northern Ghana, while Kweku-Sam was Akan, but Twi was their lingua franca.

"Where is the house girl?" Ismael asked. "Usually she's sweeping the yard by now."

"She traveled to her hometown for a funeral. Where are you taking those flowerpots?"

"To the terrace," Ismael responded. "Madam asked me to get them for her." He worked part-time at a plant shop in town.

"Okay," Kweku said, glancing at his watch. "She will be down in about thirty minutes. Today is a big day for her—the fashion show."

"Ah, fine." Ismael knew next to nothing about that kind of thing. It was a different world. The lives of Trasacco's residents were far removed from his own.

Ismael took a left across the green lawn with sprawling hibiscus, past the projecting bay window of the living room and the kitchen, then a right at the staff quarters to the rear of the house. On the second floor, Lady Araba's master bedroom occupied the west wing and opened directly onto a terrace via a framed glass door. Ismael already had a ladder leaning against the wall from the day before when he had been up on the terrace. It was tricky climbing up with a heavy planter in one hand, but he was accustomed to awkward maneuvers. At the top of the ladder, he reached over the decorative terrace wall and set down the first planter gingerly. He returned to the ground and did the same for the second planter before skipping over the wall into the terrace. Ismael loved it here. The shaded pergola, which Lady Araba had designed herself, was surrounded by explosions of color. Hanging ferns, blue plumbago, red ixora, yellow galphimia, and pink desert rose flourished. There wasn't any other homeowner in Trasacco who could boast of such plant glory. Ismael moved the planters to either side of the pergola.

Lady Araba liked symmetry and matching pairs. As Ismael went past, he looked toward the glass door and felt his stomach plunge.

HE SCRAMBLED DOWN the ladder, jumping the last four rungs to the ground. He ran around to the front of the house, shouting, "Kweku! *Kweku!*"

Kweku-Sam looked up from polishing off the Rover with a chamois. "What's wrong?"

"It's Madam," Ismael said, breathing hard. "Something bad has happened. Do you have a key to the house?"

Kweku-Sam shook his head. "No. But what has happened?"

"She's lying in her bed," Ismael said, "and there's blood. Take the car and bring Peter here. *Quick!*"

The Rover's tires squealed as Kweku-Sam gunned the engine.

INSIDE THE SECURITY booth, Peter had finished entering his summary of the night's activities into the logbook and was giving the morning report to the two security guards taking over duty. There wasn't much to report, as the shift had been quiet.

He looked up as Lady Araba's Rover came toward them at top speed. Kweku-Sam jumped out. "Peter, come! Ismael says something bad has happened to Lady Araba."

Peter frowned. "What is it?"

"I don't know. You just come, my brodda."

Peter dropped everything and got into the Rover. Kweku-Sam made a rubber-burning U-turn, and they took off back to 401, where they skidded into the driveway. Ismael was nowhere to be seen. Peter followed Kweku-Sam at a full run to the rear of the house.

"Ismael!" Kweku-Sam called out.

"I'm up here!" Ismael's head appeared over the terrace wall.

"*Chaley*, what's going on?" Peter asked.

"I think she's dead," Ismael said, voice shaking.

"*What?*"

"Do you have a key to get inside?" Ismael asked Peter.

"No, no, I don't." Peter started up the ladder. Kweku-Sam followed.

"Then I have to break the glass door," Ismael said, grabbing a metal patio chair from the pergola. By the time the other two men reached the terrace, Ismael was attacking the door with the legs of the chair. It splintered open on his second attempt, and he reached inside and pulled down the door handle. The other two men were right behind Ismael as he pushed the door open.

"*Awurade,*" he said. "Oh, Jesus."

Shades of white and cream were the color scheme of the room. The copious scarlet of the spattered blood on the carpet and bed was a jarring contrast. A bloody duvet covered Lady Araba's body up to her neck. She was lying on her back and might have simply been asleep, save that her face was bloated and gray. Her eyes, now milky white, were still open. So was her mouth. The pillow on which her head rested had a wide halo of dried blood.

Peter and Ismael stood staring, frozen. They heard a loud wailing sound and turned to see Kweku-Sam weeping as he rushed inside. Calling out his boss's name, he lurched toward the bed, but Peter grabbed him and held him back.

"Kweku," he said quietly, then more emphatically, "Kweku, there's nothing you can do. Madam is dead."

TWO

Twenty years before

ARABA HAD LEARNED TO sew by the time she was thirteen years old. Her Auntie Dele Tetteyfio was a seamstress who patiently taught her how to put together blouses, skirts, and dresses from scratch. Araba preferred the company of her doting aunt to that of her parents, Fifi and Miriam. Reverend Fifi Tagoe was a priest at the All Saints Anglican Church in Accra and an extreme disciplinarian apparently obsessed with the sin of fornication. Every other sermon of his seemed concerned with its evils.

In her early teens, Araba had only the foggiest notion what fornication meant. Was it having a boyfriend, or just hanging around boys? It might also mean having sex when you weren't supposed to. If that was the case, then Araba was not a fornicator. She didn't like boys much then, and certainly not enough to have a boyfriend. Boys were silly, empty-headed.

Reverend Tagoe wasn't a loving man in any demonstrable way. He didn't hug his children. Tagoe was a believer in the maxim, "Spare the rod, spoil the child." He kept a cane in his bedroom in case Oko needed a whipping, but rarely did he use it on his daughter.

• • •

LEANING AGAINST DELE'S chair, Araba watched her aunt hem a sleeve on her sewing machine, her fingers deft and precise while her feet pumped the pedal.

"Auntie?" Araba said. "What is fornication?"

Dele was a short, powerful woman with a stubborn mouth. Appropriately, she came from Bukom, a tough old part of Accra that continued to churn out a disproportionate number of professional boxers.

Dele held up a blouse to examine it. The fabric, a cotton blend with swirls of pale blue and fuchsia, was by Woodin— a well-known, upscale brand. "Why are you asking me that, Araba?"

"I always hear Daddy preaching to people not to fornicate," Araba said.

"And he hasn't explained it you?" Dele asked. "Or is it you don't understand the explanation?"

Araba shook her head. "He hasn't told me. If I ask him, he'll be angry."

Dele rested the almost-completed blouse to the side and turned to her niece. "When a man and a woman get married," she said, "they are supposed to stay together forever and only make love to each other. If the husband goes to be with another woman, or the wife goes to be with another man, then they have committed fornication."

"So, it's only for grown-ups, then," Araba said, relieved.

"Yes, my dear." Dele gave Araba a hug. "You won't have to worry about that for a long time. Now, sit here and do the sleeves. Let's see how good you are."

Araba executed it to her aunt's approval and smiled at her praise.

Someone knocked on the door, and Dele went to answer. Araba heard her father's voice and stiffened.

"Is she here?" Fifi asked Dele. His voice was deep and rich— perfect for preaching.

"Yes, she is," Dele replied. "Please come in."

Fifi did and saw Araba in Dele's sewing bay. Clothes were everywhere, and it looked like a jumble, but Dele knew exactly where everything was.

Fifi eyed his daughter. "You didn't tell me you were coming here," he said. "I was worried."

"Sorry, Daddy," Araba said in not much more than a whisper.

"It's not her fault," Dele said. "It's me who should have called you. I lost track of time."

Fifi grunted. "No problem. Come on, Araba. Say goodbye to Auntie. We have to go home for your bath and dinner."

"Bye, Auntie," Araba said. "Can I come back tomorrow?"

"I'll be here," Dele said. "But check with your father first."

Fifi guided Araba out with a light hand on her head. "See you later, Dele," he said, with not so much as a glance at his sister.

Araba didn't completely understand why her father and aunt didn't get along, but what she did know was that Dele always took Araba's side if it came to that.

THAT NIGHT, AFTER her bath and dinner, Araba waited for Mama to come up and tuck her in. To pass the time, she looked through her old dog-eared fashion magazines, examining the dress styles, the hairdos, the shoes.

Mama came in. She went by her middle name, Miriam, not her indigenous name, Yaa. She had a tiny waist and wide hips, the kind that always had men staring. But Araba had never seen her father show affection to his wife.

"Are you okay, love?" Miriam said.

"Yes, Mama." Araba put her magazines away. Her parents constantly checked her reading material to be sure there was nothing to encourage an interest in boys before she was old enough for that—eighteen, in her father's view.

Miriam sat at the edge of the bed and rested her hand near Araba's cheek. "How was Auntie Dele?"

"Oh, fine," Araba said. "She let me do a lot of sleeves and hems today."

"That's good," Miriam said, smiling sweetly. She had never appeared to have a problem with Dele, as far as Araba could tell.

"By the time I get to fashion school," Araba declared, "I'll already know a lot."

"Okay, well, we'll see," her mother said, smoothing Araba's covers. "You know Daddy wants you to have a job like . . . like—"

"Yes, I know," Araba said. "Like a nurse. Is that the only job in the world?"

"Now, now," Mama chastised gently. "He only wants the best for you."

"The best for me is what *I* want to do," Araba said.

Mama chuckled. "Well, you have a few more years before you know for sure. Things might change."

Araba played with her mother's gold wedding ring. "But I'll never change," she said. "I'm going to be a fashion designer."

Mama kissed her on the forehead. "All right, dear. Na-night, and sleep well, my love." She turned off the light, left the room, and closed the door quietly behind her.

LATER THAT NIGHT, the power went off. This time of year, it was hot and stuffy day and night, and without the air conditioner, Araba woke up sweating lightly. She threw her covers off and opened the windows to let some air in.

Her door cracked open, and she looked up to see the shadow of her father. He was a big, solid man. If you punched him, he probably wouldn't budge.

"Are you okay, Araba?" he whispered, coming into the room and shutting the door.

"Yes, Daddy."

"I'm sorry I couldn't come to say good night to you earlier," he said, sitting on the bed the same as his wife had done. "I was on an important phone call."

"Okay, Daddy."

"Give me a hug." He embraced her—he always did. "I love you, okay? God loves you too. It's a special love we have in the Lord, you understand?"

Araba nodded. "Yes. You're squeezing me so hard, Daddy."

"Ah, I'm sorry. My goodness, you're sweating. Why not let's change you into some dry clothes?"

He turned on the light and looked in her chest of drawers. "Here—a T-shirt and some panties." He dropped them on the bed. "I'll help you."

He took off her blouse. She flinched and shielded her developing breasts from him.

He laughed. "Come on, don't be shy. I'm your daddy."

She hurried to put on the shirt and turned away from him in bed as she put on her panties.

"You're growing so fast," he said. "Do the panties still fit you?"

"Yes, they're okay," Araba said, covering herself.

"I don't think so," he said, gently pulling the covers away. "Look at the hem—too tight."

"They're okay, Daddy," she pleaded.

"Right here," he said. "Too tight."

She caught her breath and held it, looking away as he slipped his finger under the lace edge of her panties. His breathing was irregular and sounded loud in the quiet room. It always did.

"You know I care a lot about you, Araba," he said. "These special little times we spend together are just for us and for God, right? It's not for others to know about because they won't understand. They'll say you're a bad girl, but I know and you know that you are good."

He pulled Araba's hand toward him to make her touch him, but she wriggled from his grip. Soon Araba became aware of the other sound—him stroking himself. She dared not look. She fixed her gaze elsewhere as Daddy spluttered and gasped—a strange choking noise pushed down against itself.

He stood up, kissed her on the forehead, switched off the light, and left without another word. Outside in the hallway, Araba heard him say, "What are you doing there?"

"Nothing, nothing." It was Mama, speaking timidly. "I thought I heard a noise, so I came to see if everything was okay."

"Well, everything is fine," he said tersely. "Go back to bed."

Mama's steps retreated, and then Araba heard Daddy going downstairs. Her parents did not sleep in the same room, let alone the same bed.

Araba brought her knees up to her chest, staring at the wall through the thick darkness.

THREE

The day of the murder

MONDAY MORNING WAS THE start of Accra Fashion Week, held this year at the garish Tang Palace Hotel in the South Airport Residential area. Before Araba's show at 10 A.M., a lot had to be done. Samson Allotey, Lady Araba's right-hand man, had arrived at six to begin setting up.

The models—sixteen in total—began to roll in at seven-thirty. Samson and a freelance helper Araba had hired for the day were going over the order of their appearances on the catwalk. The theme of the show this year was "We Too," a play on #MeToo to expose rampant but deeply buried sexual assault within the fashion industry. No one in this supposedly glamorous world liked discussing such a distasteful subject, choosing to pretend it didn't exist at all, but Lady Araba was dedicated to facing it down. Now that her eponymous line of women's clothing was gaining fame throughout West Africa, she intended to become an activist and influencer.

For this session, the models were to walk on in pairs—hence, "We Too"—to the end of the runway and return along each edge as stirring music blasted. Samson had the sequence in his mind, but as he got the women to do the first run-through, something just didn't look right, and he needed Araba. So did everyone else. She was the glue that held it all together. Her authority, her instincts, and her knowledge had a calming effect during the frantic preparation and inevitable last-minute emergencies before a show.

Now it was getting on to eight o'clock. Where was she? She ought to have arrived by now. The models were starting to have their makeup applied, and there would be last-minute fittings and alterations to their outfits—a button here, a slight hitch-up of a hem there. Araba was always present for that. She simply had to be.

Samson called her, and when she didn't pick up, he texted her. Fifteen minutes later, still without a response, he phoned Lady's brother, Oko, who had become a friend over the years.

"Hey, Samson," Oko said, picking up right away. "Wassup, bruh?"

"*Chaley*, have you heard from your sister?"

"We spoke yesterday, why?"

"She hasn't come in this morning to prepare for the show," Samson said, getting frantic. "She's normally here long before now. I've tried calling and texting her, but she's not answering."

"Let me try her," Oko said.

"If you reach her, tell her to call me as soon as she can, *please*. We still have a lot to do here."

OKO, A PROMINENT chemistry and physics professor, had been on his way to his first lecture at the University of Ghana and had almost reached the campus. Like Samson, he tried calling and texting his sister several times to no avail, so he tried his father, Reverend Tagoe, who was in a meeting at St. Anthony's Anglican Church.

"She's not answering her phone," Oko explained to him. "Neither text nor call, and Samson is getting desperate at the show because she should be there by now."

"I can go to Trasacco to see if she's there," Tagoe said. "Maybe she overslept or something."

• • •

THE REVEREND LEFT his meeting with his apologies—a "family emergency," he said, which was essentially true.

St. Anthony's is near the N1 Motorway via Achimota Road, and once Father Tagoe was past the chaos of the Accra Mall cloverleaf interchange, he made good progress to Trasacco Valley. He pulled up at the front entrance of the complex, where the guards recognized him at once as Lady Araba's father.

"Morning, sah," the guard said and waved him through. He looked nervous—or was that Tagoe's imagination?

As Tagoe turned left on Ruby Row and saw a crowd outside Araba's garden fence, he felt sick. A police officer stood at the driveway entrance. Beyond that point, an old Tata police vehicle and one of the newer Toyota Camry patrol cars were parked in the driveway.

Tagoe stopped the car abruptly and jumped out. The spectators' eyes turned to him as he ran to the gate, where the officer, a fresh-faced constable, moved to bar his way.

"What's happened?" Tagoe demanded.

"Who are you, please?" the constable asked.

"Reverend Fifi Tagoe. I'm Lady Araba's father."

"Okay, sir." The constable stepped aside.

Tagoe ran up the driveway and in through the open front door to the entrance hall. He heard voices from the second floor. The staircase was to Tagoe's right. Two men in conversation stood at the base of the stairs and turned as they saw him approaching.

"Who are you people?" he thundered. "What are you doing here?"

"Your name," one of them demanded as he reached them.

"Reverend Tagoe." He was hyperventilating. "Lady Araba's father."

The two men exchanged glances. One of them took a step toward Tagoe and put a hand on his shoulder. "I'm sorry, Reverend, your daughter was found dead this morning—"

"What do you mean, dead?" Tagoe said, raising his voice. "How can that be?"

He rushed up the stairs, screaming Araba's name. A crowd of people doing, it seemed to Tagoe, nothing but standing around staring into Araba's bedroom, had gathered on the landing. As Tagoe got there, a man blocked the doorway, preventing him from going inside.

But Tagoe could see a few people around Araba's bed, apparently taking pictures and videos. He also caught a glimpse of someone in the bed—and a lot of blood.

His vision went dark. The next he knew, he was on the floor in the hallway with people above him, shaking him and asking if he was okay.

"What happened?" Tagoe asked, confused.

"You fainted," someone said.

They began helping him up. He took two unsteady steps toward the room, but several people held him back and the door was now shut. "You can't go in, sir. They are collecting evidence."

"Who did this to her?" he said, beginning to break down.

No one responded, because no one knew the answer.

FOUR

Sixteen years before

AUNTIE DELE USED HER front yard to sell her outfits. She had three mobile racks of skirts, blouses, dresses, and gowns, and often a steady stream of women came in seeking her wares. Araba always looked forward to Saturdays when there was no school and she could help her aunt with retailing. By seventeen, Araba was blossoming into a fetching young woman, and customers constantly stole admiring—or jealous—glances at her.

Like her mother, Araba was fair in color, and her exceptionally fine skin had a silken sheen. Her waist was tiny, flaring out to buttocks that were at once muscular and bouncy when she walked. Boys hovered outside at Dele's front yard so they could peek at Araba. Sometimes they would walk slowly up the street and come back in the opposite direction five minutes later so they could look at her again. Dele kept an eye on them, saying nothing until they attempted to innocently wander into the yard to chat Araba up. That's when Dele yelled at them in caustic *Ga* to get lost.

Araba helped Dele's customers find the type of outfits they were looking for. There was a changing booth rigged up at the corner of the house, and there the customers could check the fit and style in the mirror. Araba quickly mastered saleswomanship. If the dress looked halfway decent on a potential buyer, she would praise and flatter. If, on the other hand, the customer didn't like it, she would be ready with an alternative. Because Araba was so stunning in her own outfits, women looked to her for approval. Dele loved having her around, and Araba loved being there.

Included on the different racks were many pieces that Araba had helped her aunt put together, and a few Araba had designed and sewn herself. She knew how to sketch her own designs, a precise skill people associated more with boys than girls. In fact, the only class Araba really enjoyed at school was art.

Now that women had begun to notice and purchase her outfits, Auntie Dele split the proceeds with Araba, which thrilled her niece and gave her a heady feeling of accomplishment. She loved Dele for that.

THAT SATURDAY EVENING, as Araba and Oko were watching TV at home in the living room, Father Tagoe came in and clicked off the set with the remote.

"I need to talk to your sister in private," he said to Oko.

Oko, who was twenty, got up and slouched out. Fifi took a seat on the sofa next to his daughter, who eyed him with anxiety. What was it now?

"How was your day with Auntie Dele?"

"Fine, Daddy."

"You enjoyed yourself?"

"Yes, I did."

"You like being around your aunt and helping to sell clothes."

Was that a question or a statement? Either way, Araba nodded.

"That's good," Fifi said, but something about his expression worried Araba. "Your mother tells me you've also been selling your own dresses there."

Araba hadn't shared this with her father because she'd sensed he would disapprove.

"Is that true?" Tagoe asked.

"Yes," she said.

"I see," he said, pressing his lips together. "From now on, you will hand over any money you make to me so I can donate it to the church, is that understood?"

Her eyes widened as she looked at her father in dismay. "But why?"

"Because I say so," he said sharply. "I am your father; you are living under my roof and you are not yet an adult. Where is the money you made today?"

Araba looked away sullenly. "In my room."

"Then go and bring it to me. All of it."

Head bowed, Araba rose and went up to her bedroom, where she had hidden her earnings in an envelope in a clothes drawer. On her way back to her father downstairs, Araba tapped on Oko's bedroom door. He was listening to music through a giant pair of headphones.

Araba pulled them off his head.

"*What?*" Oko said irritably.

"Daddy wants to keep all the money I make from selling my dresses," Araba said. "I don't want him to have all of it. Can you keep a portion for me?"

"Only if I get some," Oko replied sullenly.

Araba rolled her eyes. "Okay, okay. You can have a few *cedis*. But don't say a word to him about this."

"Whatever," Oko said, holding out his hand. Araba counted out about a quarter of the *cedi* bills and gave it to her brother with a warning. "Don't spend it, okay? I'm trusting you."

Oko grunted and put his phones back on. As she left the room, Araba gave a wistful backward glance, missing the days when she and her brother had been close. Once Oko had started boarding school at age twelve, the bond between them had weakened like a rusty old chain. Whenever Oko came home for the holidays, he was quiet and didn't communicate much except with his friends, who talked about girls all the time. Araba was amused by their boasts of getting this girl or that—most of it probably untrue. Despite his change in mood, Oko remained a brilliant student with As or A-pluses all down the line on his report card. He was a whiz at physics, chemistry, and mathematics, so much so that his teacher made him the unofficial tutor for the weaker students. Oko and his academic brain had no interest in Araba's budding taste for fashion, and the reverse applied: Araba couldn't care less about differential equations.

FIVE

Twenty years before

FRANCIS AUGUSTUS SEEZA HAD always been ambitious and competitive. He was a good student who always aced his exams. He founded a small school paper that chronicled events on campus, along with opinion pieces, short stories, and poetry.

After secondary school, Augustus entered the School of Journalism at the University of Ghana. While there, he interned at the Ghana Broadcasting Corporation, the country's equivalent to the BBC, to gain experience in broadcast journalism. He did everything—sitting in for people at the front desk, getting water for program guests, writing notes for the hosts. Augustus was very good. His strengths were his versatility and adaptability. He showed initiative where others frankly couldn't care less, and that made managers notice him. After Augustus graduated from university, the GBC offered him a job as a junior producer.

On one occasion, a prime-time radio host was held up by the monsoon-like floods Accra was experiencing that rainy season. The guest was in the studio, it was five minutes to airtime, and the station manager was in a state of panic.

"I'll do it," Augustus said matter-of-factly.

"What?" the manager said.

"I'll do the interview," Augustus said.

And so, he did—and a superb job he made of it. One hour of smooth, insightful conversation with the guest. Augustus's voice was a pleasing baritone that injected calmness into the most probing of questions—like giving quinine to someone in a spoonful of syrup. The regular host took over the second hour, but listeners began calling the station to ask about this Augustus "Caesar" who had sat in for the first half of evening drive time, and was that his real name?

Among those who heard Augustus that night was the Minister of Science & Technology, Adam Kyei. One of the richest people in Ghana, Kyei owned Metro Media, which had both radio and TV divisions. Kyei recalled meeting Augustus a couple of weeks back at GBC when they had planned a joint production on the plight of farmers in the drought-stricken Upper East Region of Ghana. Augustus had been accommodating, sharp, and quick-witted, and he had asked all the right questions.

Kyei lured Augustus away with a nice offer; competing with the government-run GBC was not difficult. Augustus came over to Metro without hesitation. With his university education and easy charm, he was poised to launch a successful career in journalism. At Metro, Kyei put Augustus in charge of two radio programs—the once-a-week *Politics Now* at noon, and an evening opinion and call-in show, *Ghana Speaks*. But Kyei wanted a flagship evening TV program to mirror its radio counterpart, a little later, in the 8 to 9 P.M. hour, when most people had gotten home from work, traffic allowing.

When Kyei thought the time was right, he pulled Augustus from radio and moved him over to TV, where he joined another producer on *Good Morning Ghana*. One day, Kyei took Augustus to a buffet lunch at the Mövenpick Hotel and asked him if he had any ideas about an evening show.

At that moment, Augustus was marveling at the amount of food Kyei had served himself. Kyei was fat and rich. He enjoyed food without limits.

Refocusing, Augustus said, "What I see in my mind is a show

where I talk to controversial or important people and ask them tough questions."

"Okay," Kyei said, chewing noisily with his mouth open. "Go on."

"Have you ever seen that BBC program *HARDtalk*? We need something like that. Where I, as the interviewer, don't let anyone, no matter how important he is, get away with anything."

"What would you call such a program?"

"*Tough Talk* comes to mind."

"That's not bad," Kyei said. "So, we would have politicians, performers, newsmakers, and so on."

"Yes, but the more controversial, the better."

"Of course."

"There is, however, one proviso I would ask from you, sir."

Kyei looked surprised. "What is that?"

"That we don't favor your political party in any way. Whether you're in power at the time or not."

Kyei stared at Augustus for a moment. "Okay. That's not a problem."

Augustus smiled, taking a sip of wine and looking at Kyei over the rim. "So, *Tough Talk* it is, then?"

WITH *TOUGH TALK*, Metro TV's evening viewership exploded. The show's debut episode was ironic in that Augustus's first guest was Kyei himself. The MP often appeared on his own station's programs. He talked a lot of bluster and braggadocio, but Augustus held on to Kyei's thrashing tail of sorts. Although the exchange wasn't acrimonious in any way, the questions and answers were sharply delivered.

Adam Kyei satisfied the "controversial figure" benchmark for *Tough Talk* because he was one. In the first place, as a minister of parliament, what was he doing owning a giant media company? His gruff answer: "But is it against the law? Do you think people in the three branches of government in the United States don't own businesses and property?"

"Doesn't make it right," Augustus returned evenly. "You are using the tactic of 'whataboutism,' sir, by deflecting the question to another target. Let's forget about the United States and concentrate on Ghana. Don't you think that your ownership of an information-disseminating institution might invite conflicts of interest?"

They argued about that for a while, and then Augustus segued to a second question: Why had Minister Kyei repeatedly demonized a young investigative journalist, Ahmed Hussein, who had been working on a story about corruption, only to be gunned down in the street?

Kyei bluntly denied any connection between his denouncement of Hussein and his subsequent assassination, even though Kyei had publicly revealed where Hussein lived and encouraged residents in the neighborhood to "take action against him" if they saw him.

After the show, Augustus sought reassurance from Kyei that he hadn't gone after the MP "too hard," which Kyei dismissed. "No, this is very good. These are the kinds of probing questions we want."

Over the next few years, Augustus went on to interview a string of personalities, both local and international, who fell into one or more categories: politically powerful and/or controversial, flamboyant entertainers and athletes, and trailblazers of all types. No matter who was in the hot seat, Augustus engaged with them in a way that captivated viewers. Most of the interviews ended on a cordial note, though a few concluded not in the best way—like the erratic manager of Ghana's Black Stars soccer team, who yanked off his mic and stormed off the set midway through the hour. Of course, all that made for great television and didn't bother Augustus in the least.

WHAT SOME SAW as Augustus's reassuring self-confidence, others perceived as conceited arrogance, particularly members of the old guard who had been around broadcasting for much longer.

But he was Adam Kyei's trophy, and no one could touch him. To balance out this resentment toward him was a certain admiration, even groveling. A good number of women at the station went googly-eyed in Augustus's presence, dressing to kill to attract his attention. He was good-looking with a ready smile of even white teeth and a habit of winking suggestively at these women, many of whom he ended up having sex with.

All that playing the field—well, most of it—came to an end when Augustus met his wife-to-be, Bertha Longdon, a woman a few years older than him and the daughter of Cyril Longdon, the owner of Longdon Shipping. Bertha was the only heir to Cyril's considerable fortune.

Augustus and Bertha's wedding was over-the-top, with three hundred guests in attendance. The first inkling Bertha had that something might be off was when Augustus got blind drunk in the final hours of the reception and had to be carried away by two of his friends, who recognized a disaster in progress.

SIX

The day of the murder

WHEN REVEREND TAGOE CALLED, Oko had just finished his chemistry lecture, and his mother, Miriam, had gone to a meeting with a community alliance trying to get old town Accra cleaned up and modernized.

Oko saw his father's name on the screen. "Yes, Daddy?"

For a moment, Oko thought his father was laughing, and he couldn't understand what he was saying. He realized then that Reverend Tagoe was weeping.

"Daddy, what's wrong?"

"It's Araba," Tagoe said, his voice cracking. "They found her body this morning." He gasped. "A lot of blood—"

"Stay right there," Oko said, his voice shaking. "I'm on my way."

A SHORT DISTANCE away from the front door of Araba's house, a detective questioned the Reverend after offering his condolences. His name was Sergeant Isaac Boateng, a tubby man in his early forties.

"Father Tagoe," Boateng said, "please, when did you last speak to your daughter?"

"Just last night," Tagoe replied, his brow creased and his eyes red. "It's Accra Fashion Week, so my wife and I called her just before nine to wish her luck."

"How did she seem, Father?" Boateng asked. "Did she appear to have any worries or fears? Was she upset about anything or anyone?"

"No, no, she sounded fine, even though she's been struggling to get over that man—"

That raised Boateng's eyebrows. "What man?"

"She was in a toxic relationship with—well, I'm sure you know of him. Augustus Seeza, the guy who used to be on Metro TV."

"Can you tell me more about that, sir?" Boateng asked. "I mean the relationship between your daughter and Mr. Seeza."

"It was abusive, and Mr. Seeza was, is, a drunk," Tagoe said bitterly. "Ever since his fall from grace, he became more dependent on Araba, who supported him financially and in every other way. We—the Tagoe family, I mean—confronted her and warned her to bring the relationship to an end. Araba tried her best, but every time Seeza got sick from drinking too much, he reached out to her and she came running."

"I see," Boateng said. "But I'm a little confused. I thought Mr. Seeza married that lady—the one who owns the shipping company. Or am I wrong?"

"Bertha Longdon, yes, you are correct. They are separated. I suppose at some point they'll divorce."

Someone called the Reverend's name. He turned to see his son running up to him. At thirty-six, he was stout with a broad, flat face and early baldness.

Father and son embraced briefly, and then Oko stood back, gripping his father's arms and looking squarely into his eyes.

"Can this be true, Daddy?" he said, voice quivering. "Is it true?"

"It doesn't seem real," Tagoe said, shaking his head.

"You saw her?" Oko asked. "You saw Araba dead with your own eyes? Where is she? I want to see her."

"They've taken the body, son," Tagoe said.

"*Why?*" Oko demanded wildly.

"The police didn't want too much decomposition to set in." Tagoe gestured to the detective. "This is Sergeant Boateng. In charge of the case."

"I want to know what happened to my sister, Mr. Boateng," Oko said, turning to the detective.

"Yes please, sir," Boateng said. "I can't say much at the moment. Hopefully, we will learn more after a postmortem is conducted."

"But you must have an idea, surely," Oko said forcefully. "I mean, how is it possible that my sister has been murdered in this supposedly secure neighborhood? Does that make sense to you? There are guards at the front entrance, and yet still someone was able to get into the house and kill her?"

Oko's voice rose and splintered, and he stopped talking to gulp down his emotion.

"Well, it may be your sister knew the culprit," Boateng said, "because there was no evidence of forced entry. Which is the one reason why I've been trying to find out from your father here if there's anyone who might have harbored ill will toward Lady Araba. He mentioned Mr. Seeza—that Araba was in a relationship with him?"

Oko's face clouded. "I tell you, the devil dwells in that man Seeza's heart. I won't tell you how to do your job, Mr. Boateng, but I would advise you to question him very closely."

SEVEN

The day of the murder

THE 37 MILITARY HOSPITAL in Accra is so named because it was the thirty-seventh medical unit built by the British Army in their now-evaporated empire. Government-run, the hospital is chaotic and lacks many of the facilities found in equivalent private institutions.

The ambulance took Araba's body to 37 Hospital, but she should have gone straight to the police mortuary, since her death was unnatural. After a furious argument between the 37 Hospital personnel and ambulance drivers, it was finally agreed that the Ghana Police Hospital was the correct destination.

Tagoe, wife Miriam, and son Oko committed the same error as the ambulance, going to the 37 Hospital morgue first before being redirected to the right place. When the Tagoes went in to officially identify Araba's body, they shuddered and averted their eyes from corpses stacked in piles for lack of space. The morgue was a distasteful place to be whether one was alive or dead. The place reeked, the sour, saliva-curdling smell of corpses mixed with the scent of the bleach used to mop the floors.

Tagoe and Miriam went in holding hands, but when the morgue attendant showed them where Araba lay on her slab, Miriam broke away from her husband, touched Araba's cold arm, and began to weep—not loudly, but so that each surge of grief rocked her entire body. She looked as if she might collapse, and Tagoe moved to her side to steady her. "I'm here for you, my love. Be strong in the Lord."

Oko stood a distance away. Tagoe looked at him, signaling for help. Oko came to stand next to Miriam, and she leaned against him with her head bowed.

The attendant watched as the Reverend launched into a soliloquy in steady, measured tones.

"He that overcometh shall inherit all things; and I will be his God, and he shall be my son."

"Amen," Oko and Miriam murmured.

Tagoe's voice rose. "But the fearful, and unbelieving, and the abominable, and *murderers*, and whoremongers, and sorcerers, and idolaters, and all liars, shall have their part in the lake which burneth with fire and brimstone: which is the second death."

"Amen," Oko and Miriam said, more strongly.

"In the Book of Isaiah," Reverend Tagoe continued, raising his right hand overhead, "the Lord says, 'so do not fear, for I am with you.'"

"Amen."

"Do not be dismayed, for I am your God."

"Amen."

"I will strengthen you and help you."

"Praise Him."

Tagoe concluded, "I will uphold you with my righteous right hand."

"Yes, Lord," Oko whispered.

Tagoe rested his hand for a moment on his daughter's right shoulder, then turned away to put his arm around Miriam and support her to the exit. Emerging outside, they breathed in fresh air with relief. Tagoe guided his wife to a chair, and she sat heavily, staring ahead in a daze. Suddenly, her expression turned to consternation, and she sat up straight. Tagoe turned to follow the direction of his wife's gaze and saw what—who—had caused this change in demeanor. Augustus Seeza was approaching the entrance to the morgue. An instant after Miriam spotted him, he recognized the three Tagoes, whom he had met on only a single occasion. His step faltered, and uncertainty crossed his face.

Miriam rose and walked toward him, her gait suddenly resolute. Augustus stopped moving. In fact, he took a step back.

"*You!*" Miriam said through clenched teeth. "You *murderer*. You killed her, and now you come to the morgue to delight in seeing her dead body?"

"No, *no*," Augustus said, looking distressed. "It isn't that. I was looking for you to express my—"

"Your what?" She grabbed the front of his shirt, clutching it in a fierce grip. "Your false condolences?"

Tagoe came up behind his wife. "Miriam—"

She ignored her husband and continued to address Augustus. "My daughter rejected you and you were filled with rage. So, you killed her, didn't you? *Didn't* you?"

Augustus shook his head, trying to shrink away from Miriam and take her hand off him. "*No!* I didn't do it. Why don't you look within your own family and find the real culprit?"

"What?" Her fists loosened. "What do you mean 'within my own family?'"

"Araba and I were reconciled again before she died," Augustus said. "Didn't you know that? Your husband knew. *He's* the one who was angry with your daughter for coming back to me."

Miriam moved back from Augustus as if a DO NOT TOUCH sign had materialized. She whipped around to her husband.

Tagoe was glaring at Augustus with narrowed eyes. "You are a liar, sir. I knew no such thing."

"No, *you* are the liar, Mr. Tagoe. Araba told me that she told Oko here, and Oko told *you*."

Oko got into Augustus's face with a warning finger. "Get out of here. You are not welcome."

Augustus's lip curled. He turned on his heel and walked away.

Miriam turned back to her husband. "Is what he said true? You knew Araba had gone back to him?"

Tagoe was indignant. "Of course not. Wouldn't I have told you?"

Miriam looked at Oko. "Did she tell you?"

Oko shook his head. "No." But he was dithering. "Well, she hinted at it once."

"*When?*" Miriam demanded, her eyes blazing.

"I don't remember exactly. Three months ago? Four?"

"*Four* months!" Miriam exclaimed. "And you said nothing?"

"I didn't want you to get more upset over it than you needed to. I tried to get Araba to see the light and turn herself around."

"When did you last see her?" Miriam asked pointedly.

"Why are you interrogating him?" Tagoe interjected.

Miriam looked surprised. "I'm not."

"Please," Oko said quietly. "Can we stop the quibbling? We're all very upset right now, so let's go home and cool off."

Miriam was visibly distressed. She pressed her palms to her tearful eyes. "Oh, God," she whispered. "Please rescue us from this nightmare. Let it not be true."

Oko exchanged a bitter glance with his father. Miriam was right. This was a nightmare.

EIGHT

Four years before

AUGUSTUS WAS THIRTY-EIGHT NOW. When he was twenty-nine, he and his wife, Bertha, had had their first child, a boy they named Benjamin. Three years later, they had a girl, Belinda. Because his last name was Seeza, Augustus had been inclined toward regal names like Athena and Apollo, but bowed to his wife's wishes for something more conventional. The name "Seeza" was originally from Northern Ghana. A Rashid Seeza had swung in on one branch of the family tree, and the name had kept going. Augustus's grandfather had christened his son Julius, and Julius in turn, continuing the play on the name, had named his son Augustus.

By the time Ben was nine years old, Augustus and Bertha were experiencing difficulties in their marriage. Augustus still loved the party life and seemed to be drinking progressively more heavily.

Bertha was torn, wanting to rein in her husband without smothering him. His constantly returning home late was insufferable, and his drunkenness was worse. On such occasions, Bertha wanted nothing to do with him. At the same time, she didn't want him straying to anyone else. She brimmed with suspicion, often texting Augustus and demanding that he prove in real time that he wasn't in the company of another woman. When he didn't answer, his most common excuses were that his phone was on silent, that his battery was low, that he just didn't hear her call or see her text, or that he was in a late-evening meeting.

But Augustus still managed to be a good father—a functioning alcoholic of a good father—which made it impossible for him to seem all bad to Bertha. In the moments he was so loving and caring to Ben and Belinda, she felt her heart go soft in her chest like a moist sponge, and everything would feel perfect until the next time she confronted him with an accusation.

Above all, Bertha was proud of Augustus's status as a premier broadcaster and one of the best TV interviewers around. She did watch him most nights, unless something unexpected came up. *Tough Talk* was a live program. The first take was the last, and anything could go wrong with no recourse or do-overs, like walking on a tightrope with no net. If something went wrong, it went wrong.

The night Augustus interviewed Lady Araba, Bertha had forgotten the fashion star was scheduled to appear. Belinda was already in bed, but Ben was still up, and he snuggled up to his mother on the sofa as she sat down to watch the episode. He was a real mama's boy.

The two of them watched as the fancy initial graphics and exciting music faded away and Augustus came on with his straightforward, "Good evening, and welcome to *Tough Talk*. I'm Augustus Seeza."

He really was that handsome in real life. Sure, the makeup made his face more matte than it was in reality—he, like most black men, had oily skin—but his complexion was genuinely that smooth. No filters needed.

"Tonight," Augustus said, "my guest is Araba Tagoe, most famously known as Lady Araba. She is an entrepreneur, a Ghanaian trailblazer who has quickly risen in the fashion world, a symbol of style and elegance. Welcome, Lady Araba."

Without a doubt, Araba was poised and beautiful, with long braided extensions gathered at the nape of her neck. Her tasteful pearl earrings made her look elegant but not showy. She wore an exquisitely fine white gold necklace with two sapphires and a ruby between them, and a cream-and-black outfit with a Ghanaian motif perfect for a TV shoot—one of her own designs, of course.

Augustus asked her about her background—the influences on her life, what had made her want to go into fashion—not an easy world, by any means.

"Mummy," Ben said, lifting his round face up at her, "do you know that lady?"

"Not personally," Bertha said, "although I do own some of her dresses."

"Oh," Ben said, returning to watching.

Araba spoke with an eloquence and intelligence that impressed Bertha. Augustus pushed her on being the daughter of an Anglican priest, and whether her choice of career had caused any friction with her family. Araba was frank and apparently truthful in her answer. Yes, there had been some "difficulties," but in the end, Father Tagoe had come to accept her as she was. After all, in the end, her father did love her.

"Nothing is as successful as success," Augustus said, "but what if you hadn't become the triumph you are now?"

"Then I wouldn't be on your show, would I?" Araba whipped back with a most disarming smile.

Bertha felt a twinge. Her heart skipped a beat, and her stomach did a somersault. For a moment, she thought she was imagining things, but as the program progressed, a chill settled into her very marrow as she became convinced that Augustus and Araba were flirting with each other on-screen. It was outrageous, offensive even. As the program entered its last fifteen minutes, she found her husband's interaction with Lady Araba too much to tolerate a second longer. She cast around for the remote and switched the TV off. Ben, who had fallen asleep, stirred and muttered something.

"Come on, sweetie," Bertha said. "Time for bed."

She picked him up, even though he was getting too heavy for her. Once she had put her son to bed, Bertha went to her own bedroom—she no longer shared one with Augustus—undressed, and took her shower. Clean and fresh, she got into bed with her latest novel. She intended to wait up for Augustus, who was usually back about an hour after the end of his show. Bertha dozed off for an unknown period and woke with a start as she heard the front door shut downstairs. She peered at her phone on the bedside table. *Past midnight.* She felt her throat tighten and her chest swell with a sick, enraged feeling. *He slept with that bitch Lady Araba.*

Bertha rose and went out to the landing. There, at the top of the staircase, she waited for her husband.

He started as he saw her. "Oh," he said. "You're still up?"

"I'm still up. Why are you so late coming home?"

"What do you mean?" Augustus stopped four steps down from her.

"Did you enjoy yourself?" she asked.

"Enjoy myself? Where? When?"

"You know exactly what I mean. With *her.*"

He finished the climb to the top and faced Bertha. "What are you talking about?"

"You had sex with Lady Araba, didn't you?"

"What? I did *not*! What gave you that idea?"

Bertha leaned forward slightly and sniffed. "Agh! I can smell her." Her face twisted with revulsion. "And you're drunk. Where did you two go to drink and have sex? To a hotel? Or to her house?"

"Bertha, stop. How do these things get into your mind?"

"You disgust me." She turned back to the bedroom but stopped before she entered. "I can't live with you anymore, Augustus. I'm moving out, and I'm taking the children with me."

NINE

Three years before

SOCCER GREAT ASAMOAH GYAN bought a three-million-dollar mansion at the top of a hill with a spectacular view of the Weija Dam west of Accra and not far from upscale West Hills Mall. The winding route to the home was by private access only, so you had to be the cream of the crop to ascend to Asamoah's palace.

Lady Araba was one of the select few who'd made the grade and received an invitation to an evening birthday bash at Asamoah's house. The bulk of the event was around the lit-up turquoise pool on the second-floor balcony, from where one could see the twinkling lights of the city of Accra miles away. A small cluster of partygoers hung out on the third floor, which overlooked the crowd around the pool. There was a lavish amount of food and plenty to drink. The music for the first part of the evening was with a live band backing Adina, one of Ghana's high-profile female performers, and then it was DJ Breezy who provided the jams at earsplitting volume. Where Asamoah lived, there were no neighbors to disturb.

Asamoah made the rounds and talked to Araba for a few minutes while she was in conversation with a group of three people she had joined. She had a little wine, then wandered into the large gleaming foyer adjoining the balcony. It was devoid of any furniture—just a vast empty space. From the center of this foyer rose a grand spiral staircase that looked like it went to heaven.

The noise of the party was somewhat behind Araba as she wandered into a room off the foyer. It was full of Asamoah's trophies, awards, and photographs, all bolted securely to the wall or locked away in illuminated glass cabinets. Araba was somewhat transfixed by a soccer shoe, presumably Asamoah's, cast in gold.

"Would you ever wear something like that?"

Araba turned. The voice behind her to her right belonged to a man she recognized at once. "Augustus Seeza! What a surprise!"

"How are you, Lady Araba?" he said, his tone like warm syrup. "Nice to see you again."

They embraced lightly.

"Let's see," Araba said. "Is it about a year since I was on your show?"

"Around that, yes," he said.

She smiled. "How are you?"

"Very well. I saw you from across the pool, but you weren't paying attention to me. I was gravely wounded."

She laughed. "Aw, so sorry."

He inclined his head with a grin. "Not a problem at all. Are you by yourself this evening?"

"Yes, I am."

"How could that be? There can't be any eligible bachelor in Ghana who would not want to take you out."

"That's not the question," she countered. "The question is whether there's an eligible bachelor with whom I want to go out."

"An excellent answer. In my line of work, I appreciate that. My next question is if I may show you around Sam's mini-museum. I know about pretty much all the items."

"Are you good friends?"

"Yes, although I also know him in a professional capacity. I interviewed him after the 2014 World Cup debacle, and in my opinion, it was one of the best interviews I ever did."

"I remember," Araba said.

"Are you a football fan?"

"I turn into one when it's the Africa or World Cup and Ghana is playing," Araba said. "Otherwise, only peripherally." She turned to a portrait of Asamoah done in charcoal. "I like this. I often prefer charcoal or pencil to color."

Augustus knew the history of the painting and whose work it was, as he did the details of each trophy. At length he said, "I hope I'm not boring you with all this football trivia."

"Not at all," she answered truthfully.

"Can I get you a drink?"

"I'm okay, actually."

"Then let me show you something." He put his head around the door to make sure the coast was clear. It was. He put his fingers to his lips while beckoning Araba to follow him. He led her to the opposite side of the foyer and up a short flight of steps, took a sharp left, and opened a door at the end of the staircase. They ended up on a small, solitary balcony far from the party crowd.

"Wow," Araba said. "The view's even more spectacular from here."

"Yeah," Augustus said, clearly pleased with himself. "It's one of the house's little secrets Sam let me in on."

"Nice," Araba said, gazing out. She thought she could make out sections of town by how bright the lights were. The older parts of the city, like Usshertown and Jamestown, were the "black holes" in the dance of lights. The evening was cool now, and somewhere from below, a flowering jasmine bush was sending up light dabs of perfume in the air.

"I would love to take you out one of these evenings," Augustus said. "May I?"

She gave him a sharp look. "I thought you were married."

He made a face. "Separated, now. Don't say you're sorry, because I'm not."

"Okay."

"My wife, Bertha, is crazy," Augustus continued. "Crazy with jealousy. She imagined time and time again that I was cheating on her. She even thought I was fornicating with *you*."

Araba pulled back her head sharply. "With *me*?" she asked in astonishment.

Augustus nodded. "The night I interviewed you, she became convinced I was having an affair with you—or planning to. She accused me of flirting with you on TV."

"Were you?" Araba asked with interest.

"Did you feel like I was?" Augustus said.

"Not in so many words."

"I would have *liked* to," he said, "but we can't do that on TV. Unprofessional."

"Yes," Araba said cautiously. "But a woman knows."

"You're saying my wife was right about my flirting with you?"

"Maybe," Araba said coyly.

"Oh, really," he said, facing her.

Araba laughed and looked out at the view again.

"So?" Augustus said.

"So, what?"

"When do I get to take you out?"

"You have your phone on you?" she asked.

He took it from his pocket, unlocked it, and handed it to her. Araba put in her number and gave the phone back. "There. Call me and we'll talk."

WHEN ARABA SPOKE to Augustus that night, she was open to romance. Her mind had often been in flux on the subject. Sometimes she was "looking for love," but other times, disillusioned by her choices of men out there, she simply couldn't be bothered.

She liked the fact that Augustus was separated, but she cautioned herself. In one sense, he was liberated and available, but separations weren't permanent in the way divorce was.

Augustus was gracious and smart. He had a good sense of humor. He was handsome. What was there not to like about him? In the first few months after Asamoah Gyan's party, he took her to the poshest places in town, many of which Araba already knew. She was not starstruck in any way, even when she met some of the country's most famous music, TV, and movie stars. Augustus paid for everything when he and Araba went out and seemed determined to impress her. When he took her to Paris for a week, she acknowledged that she *was* impressed. Yes, that was certainly memorable.

He preferred to spend time with Araba in her home rather than his. It didn't take long for Peter and the security team at the Trasacco's front entrance to recognize him and his car and wave him through with a smile. He tipped them generously, which made him a favored guest. They were courteous to him and discreet about his visits. At night, they were supposed to record the plate numbers of all visiting vehicles and cancel them out on their exit, but with the regularity of Augustus's social calls to Araba, sometimes staying overnight, they relaxed that requirement.

At times, Araba felt uneasy when she was out with Augustus at parties or clubs. Sure, they had fun, but as she watched him down all that hard liquor, worry began to stir. She didn't understand why he had to drink quite so much to have a good time, and after several months of seeing Augustus, she wasn't sure if their nights out were for the company and social exchange as much as the opportunity to drink.

After an all-night party one Sunday morning, Kweku-Sam pulled up to the Trasacco Valley entrance with Araba and Augustus riding in the back of the Audi. Sako the security man was on night duty, and he waved at them as they went through the open gate without slowing down much. Augustus had dozed off beside Araba, snoring lightly against the soft music playing. When Kweku stopped at the front door of the house, she roused Augustus. "Wake up, honey."

Augustus muttered something and sat up groggily while Araba went around to the other side to help him out of the car. He leaned against her as they made their way inside and draped himself heavily over her in the grand hallway. "Let's have sex," he slurred.

"I don't think you're in any state for that," Araba said firmly. "Come on, let's go upstairs. Hold on to the railing."

Augustus made it up to the top of the stairs with a valiant effort and from there made a beeline for the bedroom opposite, where he flopped onto the bed with a groan. Grunting with the effort, Araba pulled his shoes off and then began to tackle his shirt and pants. As she did so, he tried to pull her down to him.

"Honey, stop," she said. "Let me get you ready for bed."

His pawing at her became clumsier and more insistent. His breath was heavy with alcohol. He sat up for a minute, swung Araba down onto the bed, and got on top of her, muttering, "Let's have sex."

Araba had a sudden, horrifying flashback of her father, and with strength she didn't know she had, she pushed Augustus off her and slapped him across the face. He touched his cheek where she had hit him and looked at his palm in disbelief. "Why?" he said.

"You can sleep there or do whatever you please," she said, turning away. "I'll be in the other bedroom, and it will be locked, so don't bother."

Araba slammed the door behind her and walked across the landing to the second of four bedrooms. She locked herself in, undressed, put on a T-shirt, and got into bed. She switched off the light, but then heard Augustus behind the door begging to be let in.

"*Go away!*" she yelled.

A long silence ensued, and then she heard him padding back down the hallway.

Tears streamed down her face and plopped onto the pillow, her feelings lurching between fury and sorrow like a fitful pendulum. She loathed Augustus's behavior when he was drunk. He had just degraded her in the worst way. She thought of other men who had done the same to her, beginning with her father. What was it about her that made them do this? Why could she not be the successful woman she was without the assumptions about her sexuality? Men saw her as food ready to be devoured, and women said nasty things about her online—accused her of being a slut. That was baseless and arose out of pure jealousy. Araba didn't even *like* sex. It was overrated, not to mention painful sometimes. Most men didn't understand how to touch a woman the right way. They appeared to think their own pleasure was the center of the sexual universe around which women's heavenly bodies revolved.

ARABA CRIED UNTIL sheer fatigue dragged her into slumber. When she woke to the first signs of morning light, she sat up and rubbed her eyes, then looked around the room, wondering for a moment why she wasn't in her usual bed before it hit her. She dropped back into bed and covered her head with blankets, feeling profoundly dreadful. Last night's ugly episode with Augustus was triggering a new bout of melancholy. She had become aware of these spells of depression in her early twenties, but in retrospect, she realized that they had probably begun in her mid-teens. Sometimes they were so bad, Araba questioned her own worth. No one knew she was prone to depression. She hid it well and could function in spite of it.

She didn't want to get up this morning. She could work from home today. She started to doze off again, but woke to the sound of someone knocking at the front door.

Oh, God. Just go away, please.

But the knocking persisted. Annoyed, Araba put on her dressing gown and padded downstairs. She looked through the peephole to see who it was. Ismael. The guy just wouldn't leave her alone. He was a sweet man, but sometimes it was a little much.

Araba opened the door, and there he stood with a wide, tooth-chipped grin.

"Good morning, madam," he said. "How are you?"

She turned on her smile. "I'm good, Ismael. And you?"

"I'm also fine. Please, I brought you the plants you asked for."

He turned, knelt, and picked up a tray arranged with small pots containing some of the prettiest succulents Araba had ever seen.

"Oh, how lovely!" Araba said.

"Please, may I put them at the bottom terrace?"

"That will be fine. Thank you. Wait, let me get you a little something."

Araba trotted upstairs to the master bedroom where Augustus was still snoring, his clothes strewn all over the floor. She grabbed two twenty-*cedi* notes from her purse and went back down to hand it to Ismael.

He beamed. "God bless you, madam. Have a good day."

"You too, Ismael."

Araba returned to the bedroom, unraveled Augustus's shirt, pants, jacket, and undershirt, and hung them all up in the walk-in closet. Then she got into bed behind him and put her arms around him. He stirred slightly, turned over to rest his head against her chest, and fell asleep again.

TEN

Two years before

ARABA DIDN'T VISIT HER father and mother as often as she probably should. Their resentment over that was never expressed, but she was keenly aware of it. There were dark spots in her relationship with her parents, sores with scabs. Until the day Araba; her father, Fifi; and her mother, Miriam, decided to pull off those scabs and attend to what lay beneath, the wounds would go unhealed.

Today, her parents had summoned her home. She wasn't sure what the meeting was about, but she felt nervous and apprehensive.

She pulled into the front yard of the house. When she stepped out of the car, Fifi's two dogs ran up to her, smiling and tail-wagging. Oko's car was here as well, parked next to his father's.

Araba knocked lightly on the screen door to the sitting room. "*Ko-ko ko!*" she called out in traditional fashion and then entered. She felt the stuffiness and dimness of the place press upon her at once.

Fifi and Oko were sitting on the sofa. A soccer match was on, but Araba had the feeling they had been dedicating only half their attention to it. She couldn't see her mother, but heard pots and pans banging around in the kitchen and presumed it was Miriam.

"Hello, Daddy," she said, bending to kiss him on the cheek. He smelled a little musty.

"How are you?" he said, his tone neutral—no sign of joy. Araba's worry grew into distress.

Oko stood up and embraced her. "What's up, little sister?" But Araba thought he sounded strained.

"I'm good. How've you been?"

"You know—managing."

"Where's Mama? Kitchen?"

Oko nodded.

"Hi, Mama," Araba said, stepping into the kitchen and the delicious aroma of hot pepper soup.

"*Ei*, Araba!" she exclaimed, smiling.

Araba kissed her mother on the cheek. In her early sixties, Miriam was still very pretty and perfectly made up. She considered it her duty as a housewife, and her husband, the good Father, expected her to be well-dressed and coiffed at all times.

"Can I help?" Araba offered.

"Can you cut up the plantain and cassava?" Miriam said. "Then we'll put them on to boil."

"Okay." Araba waited until she and her mother were standing next to each other to whisper, "What is this meeting about?"

Miriam avoided her gaze. "Daddy's in charge of it," she said, and that was all Araba would get from her, because Miriam took the backseat wherever or whenever Fifi was involved, which meant practically every situation except cooking and managing the household. Even there, he had considerable control, since he gave her the spending money.

Miriam opened the rear screen door of the kitchen and yelled out for the house girl, who came running.

"When the plantain and cassava are ready," Miriam instructed her, "start making the *fufui*."

"Yes, madam."

"Okay, let's go and join the men," Miriam said to Araba.

Miriam sat between her husband and son on the sofa, which left Araba to sit facing them in one of the two twin chairs in the room. They were the base of the triangle, and Araba the apex.

Now she *knew* it was serious because Miriam rarely sat on the sofa. She was doing this so she could be opposite Araba, and Araba was certain Fifi had told Miriam to sit there.

They had turned the TV off now. The silence in the room was dense and uncomfortable. Fifi's chin was up, but his eyes were down, the pose he struck just before launching into a sermon.

"Araba," he began, "I have called this meeting out of our collective concern. Your mother, Oko, and I are worried about what is going on in your life. Yes, you are a grown woman who can make your own decisions, but as a family, when we see one of our own destroying his or her life, it's time for us to step in. I hope you understand that."

"Not really," Araba said without much energy. "What's causing you this concern?"

"Your involvement with Augustus Seeza," Fifi said. "This is a poisonous relationship for you. We hear stories—we even see pictures here and there—about his behavior in town. The drunkenness, the womanizing. This is not the correct environment or relationship for you."

Araba was silent.

"What do you see in that man?" Oko chipped in.

"He's an intelligent, talented person," Araba said, and realized at the same time how weak her defense sounded. She decided to go on the attack. "These reports you're hearing, you don't even know if they're true or not. Most of them are gross exaggerations at best. People are jealous of his success."

"You're telling us that Mr. Seeza does not drink to the point of inebriation?" Fifi said.

"Augustus likes to have his fun," Araba said evasively, like swerving around a pothole.

"And what about his finances?" Fifi demanded, glancing at Oko.

"What about them?" Araba asked.

"We've heard he's broke," Oko said.

"Augustus makes good money," Araba responded. "You know that."

"He also spends good money," Fifi shot back. "Who bought that red Jaguar he's been riding around in?"

Araba's face grew hot. They had her now. Fifi and Oko looked at her, waiting for her answer, but Miriam kept her gaze down, brushing away an imaginary loose thread on her skirt.

"Araba?" Fifi said. "Who bought the Jaguar?"

"I did," she said, facing them bravely.

"Oh, dear Lord," Miriam said softly.

Fifi sat back in his chair in disbelief. "*You* bought it."

"He's going to pay me back," Araba said.

"Come on, Araba," Fifi said sharply.

"Even you don't believe that," Oko added.

"Why are you attacking me like this?" Araba said, her voice rising.

"We're not," Miriam said. "Sweetheart, we're trying to *protect* you. The man is using you; don't you see? He's broke because he's frittered away all his money, and now you are his bank."

"And his cigars?" Oko asked.

"What cigars?" Araba said, feeling sick.

"He enjoys cigars," Oko said. "Who buys them for him?"

Araba was shocked, but tried not to show it. "Who told you about the cigars?"

"So, it's true, then," Oko said.

"Answer the question, Araba," Fifi said.

She shook her head. "No, I will not. Who told you about the cigars?"

"You don't need to know that," Oko replied.

His tone irked Araba. "Then I don't need to answer you either."

They all stared at her, and she stared straight back. It was a standoff.

"You also support his two children from his wife," Fifi said finally. "They are not yet divorced. What is the eighth commandment?"

Araba stubbornly kept her mouth shut.

"I'm talking to you," Fifi said to her, his voice keen and brimming with frustration.

Araba blinked her eyes slowly and looked to the side, a dismissive gesture she knew drove her father to distraction.

"Araba," Miriam chided. "Please don't disrespect your father like that."

"Don't mind her," Fifi said, curling his lip. "She knows the eighth commandment, 'Thou shalt not commit adultery,' because I taught her to recite all ten by heart. And First Corinthians says, 'Or do you not know that the unrighteous will not inherit the kingdom of God? Do not be deceived: neither the sexually immoral, nor idolaters, nor adulterers.'"

"Amen," Miriam said. "Sinfulness."

Oko cleared his throat and shot a glance at his parents. "Okay, look, I'm not sure the sinfulness thing is going to get us anywhere. Araba, we're proud of what you've made of yourself, but you're still family, and family cares when one of its members is going wrong. You're an amazing woman in so many ways, but here, you have stumbled. Yes, you have pride in your work and career, and rightfully so, but don't let your arrogance take over."

Araba's eyebrows shot up. "*Arrogance?* Are you seriously telling me that? In what way am I arrogant?"

"You can't see it," Oko said, "but we can. Look at you—scorn is written all over your face right now. Being rich doesn't make you the wisest person on earth, which is what you seem to think."

That last jab stung Araba. She felt tears rising but she wasn't going to let them see her cry. She stood up. "I'm leaving. You called me here just so you could tear me to shreds. You say a family must care when one of its members is going wrong, but this isn't about that at all, is it? It's only about *your* feelings, *your* fear of looking bad in the public eye, *your* false piety—"

"*Sit down!*" Fifi bellowed. "You will not leave this house before I say so."

Araba didn't leave, but she didn't sit, either.

"This is what you will do," Fifi said. "You will break off your relationship with Augustus. You will stop supporting him and any of his family members with immediate effect."

"Daddy, what happened to the love you preach about every Sunday?" Araba asked, finally looking at him again. "What if I love Augustus? Does that count for nothing?"

"This isn't love," Fifi retorted. "This is simply foolishness."

Araba's eyes locked with his. *Then what is love, Daddy? What you did to me when I was a little girl?*

For just a moment, her father's glare faltered. Araba snatched up her Gucci clutch and walked out.

ELEVEN

Two years before

AUGUSTUS HAD BEEN UP late drinking Wednesday night. On Thursday morning, he awoke with a sledgehammer of a headache. To get rid of it, he swigged down a bottle of beer and went back to bed.

His mind, heavy as lead, was drowned in alcohol and bewilderment. The previous evening, Araba had called him. He'd instantly felt something was wrong.

"Gus." Her voice shook. "We need to talk."

That was never good. "What's wrong?" he asked, terrified of what he knew was coming.

"I can't continue this with you," she said.

"What do you mean? Continue what?"

"It can't work—you and me."

"What do you mean, 'can't'? Don't say that. There's no such thing as 'can't.' We can make anything work as long as we really want it."

"I *used* to want it, but I don't anymore."

"*Why?*" he lashed out, his voice rising.

There was a short silence before Araba said, "The drinking has gone too far."

"But I can stop," he protested. "You know I can."

"That's what you always say."

"Are you calling me some kind of helpless alcoholic?"

"Not helpless—"

"It's your goddamn family, isn't it?" he said, furious.

"It's not."

"They've convinced you to dump me. That's what it is. I know them and I know you. If you think I'm going to just disappear from your life, you're mistaken."

"Goodbye, Gus."

After she'd hung up, he tried calling and texting her multiple times to no avail. Then he'd begun to drink. It was almost noon now, so he had a few hours before he was due at work. He weighed his options. He had enough time to sober up before the show, even if he had just a couple more beers.

At 5 p.m., Augustus walked into the Metro TV studios feeling a little unsteady, but he didn't think it was enough for anyone to notice. Tonight, he was to interview Chief Justice Angela Waters, Ghana's second woman to occupy the elevated position. She would be in at seven, and in the meantime, Augustus was to go over the approach to the discussion with Bob Agyekum, Metro TV's general manager. Waters was known for her unflappable personality and acerbic tongue, so Augustus would need to be on point, which, given his experience, shouldn't be too difficult.

Bob was a small man who moved in darts and stops—like a cockroach, Augustus always thought, but he was far from a pest. He was a good man. He looked up as Augustus came into the office.

"Hi, Gus."

"Boss, how goes it?" Augustus said, sitting heavily in one of the chairs in the room. He didn't feel so good. The headache was back.

"Fine," Agyekum said. "I wanted to go over some things with you before the interview. This one is important."

The two men sat next to each other to go over talking points.

The issue was the alleged rampant corruption in the justice system: judges at all levels being bribed to delay or frustrate court prosecutions, sometimes to dismiss cases outright. It was almost impossible to successfully sue a judge, because he or she would simply get the suit annulled by one of his or her colleagues.

Augustus was finding it difficult to focus on Agyekum's train of thought, or his own, for that matter. He grabbed a tissue from the box on the table, dabbed his moist forehead, and loosened his tie somewhat.

"Are you okay, Gus?" Agyekum said.

"What? Yes, I'm fine."

"So, what do you think of this approach to that particular question?" Agyekum asked.

Augustus panicked as he realized he didn't know what question Agyekum was referencing. "What's your own take?" he asked, playing for time.

"I think that rather than appearing to make our own allegations," Agyekum said, "we can quote the other sources of the accusations against the judicial system."

Augustus nodded enthusiastically. "I think that's good. Do you have some water in your fridge?"

"Yes," Agyekum said. "I'll get one for you."

In the short space of time that the producer's back was turned, Augustus allowed his eyes to close and he drifted away on a brief journey somewhere.

"Here you are."

Augustus started. Agyekum was in front of him, holding out a bottle of Voltic water.

"Thanks," Augustus said.

"You sure you're okay?" Agyekum asked him again, squinting at him.

"Yes, yes."

Agyekum went on to review Waters's history of judgments, suggesting there was a pattern favorable to the present government in power. "We should hammer that point home."

Augustus agreed and took a sip of water.

"I think we're all set, then," Agyekum said.

AUGUSTUS'S FATHER AND mother, Julius and Caroline, sat down in front of the TV set to watch *Tough Talk*. This episode was of great interest to Julius, since it was to examine—and probably attack—the judiciary system of which he had been a part for over four decades.

Chief Justice Waters looked like a combination of favorite aunt and stern university professor. She was highly respected among her peers and subordinates. Augustus began the interview with his usual direct style. After about ten minutes, however, his parents noticed something odd.

"What's going on with Augustus?" Julius muttered.

"I was about to ask the same thing," Caroline said, frowning. "Why is he leaving big gaps in the conversation?"

Julius frowned with puzzlement. "Like he's not all there."

As the program went on, Augustus appeared absent with intervals of the old lucidity. He made one comment that was in poor taste, and the cameras instantly snapped away from Justice Waters as her face registered consternation.

"Jules," Caroline said, turning to her husband in dismay, "is he *drunk*? You know he's had trouble in the past."

"But he got over it," Julius said, flipping a palm up. "He stopped drinking."

"It's an addiction," Caroline reminded him. "You never really get over it."

Julius blew out his breath in exasperation. "Okay, well . . . I don't know, then. I can barely watch this. If Bob is seeing it right now, he'll explode."

JUDGE JULIUS'S PREDICTION was accurate. It was a little past eleven o'clock the morning after the program when Agyekum called Augustus in. That was unusually early, so Augustus knew it wasn't good, but he wasn't sure exactly what it was about.

Agyekum got straight to the point. "Your interview with the chief justice last night should have been one of your best," he said. "Instead, it was the worst I've ever seen."

Augustus recalled snatches of the exchange, but not everything. He was unnerved. Had there been an issue? "I'm not sure I understand what you mean, sir," he said soberly.

"You don't understand?" Agyekum asked. "Or you don't recall?"

"Just tell me," Augustus said, going on the offensive, "what are you referring to?"

"To this," the boss said, bringing out his phone. He took a few seconds to bring up a video of the interview and passed the phone to Augustus, who began watching. Before long, it became apparent what Agyekum was talking about. It jarred Augustus to see himself so disjointed. It became so excruciating he handed the phone back. How should he handle this? Soldier through with blunt force, or apologize? He decided on a mixture.

"It's true, boss," Augustus said, "that I wasn't on point. One or two complicated problems have come up in the family, so I've been a little distracted of late. But, trust me, it won't happen again."

"I received a complaint from Madam Waters," Agyekum went on, "about your line of questioning—particularly the point at which you made a crass joke about the judges' white ceremonial wigs."

If anything warranted a joke, Augustus thought wryly, *the wigs were it.*

"I apologize," he said. "That was uncalled for."

"Last night, people detected a strong odor of alcohol on your breath," Agyekum said abruptly.

Augustus's eyes narrowed. "What? That's a lie! It's pure jealousy. People trying to bring me down because of my success."

"No one is trying to do that in any way, shape, or form," Agyekum said firmly. "Look, Augustus, I'll have to bring this matter to the Board of Trustees."

Anything to do with the board was usually bad, and an unexpected fear washed over Augustus. "So, what does that mean?"

Agyekum looked both frustrated and regretful. "I have to suspend you. Pending the board's decision. I'm sorry."

Augustus felt as if the ground had caved beneath him, plunging him into an abyss. He heard himself stammering feeble objections as his boss sat resolutely shaking his head to Augustus's every excuse.

"That's all," Agyekum said. "Go home to await the final decision."

AT 7:32 P.M., Araba's phone rang. She hesitated to pick it up when she saw Gus's name. Though she suspected she was inviting trouble, she did nevertheless. For a second, the voice was unrecognizable. "Gus? Is that you?" she asked.

"I'm suspended," he said, slurring his words. "Till further notice."

"Suspended?" Araba said. "Suspended from what?"

"My job, what else?"

"*Why?*"

"Did you see my interview on TV last night?"

"No," she said. "I missed it."

"I fucked it up," he said, sounding like he was about to cry. "It was a mess, and people said I was drunk."

"Were you?"

"I did have a little something—just some beer. But that doesn't mean I was drunk."

Well, if he hadn't been drunk then, he was now, Araba thought.

"Please help me," Augustus said. "I need you. Can you come over? Or I can come to you."

She stiffened in alarm. "No, no—please, don't do that. Stay at home; I'll drive to you."

AUGUSTUS WAS A mess. Eyes bloodshot, hair uncombed, clothes disheveled, and he smelled awful. Araba sat on the sofa with him and he cried into her lap. When he was quiet, she shook him and urged him to get up. "Go take a shower and you'll feel better. Then we'll talk."

While Augustus was in the shower, Araba scoured his cupboards and the fridge for any alcohol. He had mostly beer, but she found a couple of bottles of Hennessy and Jameson. She poured everything into the sink and dropped the containers into the trash can.

Looking somber but clean, Augustus emerged from the bedroom in a white silk dressing gown. He sat down heavily in a red leather swivel chair—his favorite in the lavishly decorated sitting room—and rested the side of his face in his palm.

Araba sat opposite him. "I've gotten rid of all your booze."

He nodded. "Good. Thank you."

"You need professional help, Gus," she said.

"I know. And I'm going to get it. But Araba, I need you in my life. You give me the strength to carry on. Please come back to me. *Please.*"

Araba was torn. One side was telling her to stand strong, the other to have compassion. "Gus—"

In a sudden move that startled her, he knelt beside her and took her hands. "I know I've been irresponsible and foolish. The drinking stops today. I promise you. The suspension from my job is the last sign I need to straighten out my life."

"And if you don't get your job back?" Araba asked. "Are you going to be able to deal with that?"

He shook his head. "I'll get it back, don't you worry. I'm going to write to the board and sway their minds before they even meet. I'm not going away. I've made a lot of money for the station, and they know that."

Araba hoped he was right. She wanted him to bounce back, and in that moment, she promised to help Augustus, to give him one last chance, regardless of what her family said.

PART TWO

TWELVE

Ten months after

AT THE SOWAH PRIVATE Investigators Agency, Emma Djan was bored. There was a pending investigation awaiting fresh information before she could get started. Apart from that, she didn't have a single new case, and neither did her three colleagues. In her downtime, she looked through pictures on her phone. A few weeks ago, Emma had discovered an abandoned box of old family photographs while visiting her mother Akosua in Kumasi. There were several hundred.

"Why have I never seen these before?" Emma had asked in astonishment.

"I forgot they were there," Akosua had replied with almost a shrug.

"Forgot!" Emma exclaimed in consternation, rummaging through the jumbled collection. "Mama, you can't just forget treasures like this."

"All right, dear," Akosua said.

Emma found this insouciance puzzling at first, but sifting through the photos, some of them faded by the passage of time, she realized that those of her father Emmanuel and his close-knit family outnumbered his wife's by far. From the little that Akosua had let on, Emma had gathered that her mother's childhood had been as fractured as broken glass. Perhaps looking at Emmanuel's cheery photos reminded Akosua of what she'd never had.

At any rate, Emma had carted the whole lot back to Accra with her and begun scanning and categorizing them. She wasn't even close to finishing, but not long after beginning the project, the difference in demeanor between her mother and father in the photos was plain. Papa was always grinning and animated for the camera. Mama was stiff and proper. Emma's parents had also been diametric opposites when it came to showing affection—her father very much a hugger and kisser, while Akosua wasn't comfortable with physical closeness. As an adult, Emma was somewhere between the two extremes. Emmanuel's doting on his daughter began the moment she'd been born. He'd spontaneously christened her "Emma," a shortened form of his own name. Confusion sometimes arose because the male name *Emmanuel* was often shortened to "Emma" as well, although pronounced "Im-MAH" rather than "EM-mah," the female form.

That Emma dearly missed her father was an understatement. He had been a homicide detective until the rupture of a stomach ulcer essentially bled him to death from the inside some seven years ago when she was twenty. All through her childhood and teenage years, she had been devoted to her father, often accompanying him to his Kumasi office at the Manhyia Division of the Ghana Police Service (GPS). There, without knowing it, she had absorbed much of the talk between detectives, having seen and heard them interviewing suspects and witnesses. While his colleagues sometimes used force to obtain a confession, Emmanuel's technique had always been quiet and coaxing to the extent of even appearing to empathize with a suspect. Emma had seen her father reduce the toughest criminals to tears as he slowly but relentlessly extracted the truth. The result was a girl who wanted very much to be like her father—a conscientious, driven homicide detective.

The oddest thing to observers either inside or outside the family was that Emmanuel had taught his daughter to do "boyish" things like playing soccer or swimming and diving in Lake

Bosomtwe. Akosua had never approved of that sort of nonsense. It was unladylike and inappropriate, from her perspective. "Why are you trying to make her like a boy?" she asked her husband.

"I'm not," Emmanuel replied. "But she can do things just as well as boys and she likes it, so why not?"

Had Emma's attachment to her father bred Akosua's resentment? Was that the reason she had never loved her daughter with the same warmth and enthusiasm that Emmanuel had? Perhaps in part, but besides that, Akosua had taken offense when Emma had left her in Kumasi to enroll in the police academy in Accra.

"There's an academy right here in Kumasi," Akosua had objected. "Why do you have to go to Accra?"

"The training school there is much bigger, Mama," Emma had told her, "and I have a better chance of becoming a homicide detective at CID headquarters."

"So you're just going to leave me here by myself," Akosua said pointedly. "You're trying to get away from me. I'm sure if your father were still alive, you would stay right here."

Emma had protested, although afraid it might be true. Nevertheless, she moved from Kumasi to Accra, looking forward to becoming a homicide detective like her father at the end of her police training. How naïve she had been. She quickly learned that she would have no say in where she would be assigned in the bureaucratic maze of the GPS, a top-down, undemocratic organization. Homicide? No, she was sent to the Commercial Crime Unit, a department that bored her to the point of despair. And then, only months into her job, Emma suffered a catastrophe that left her both shaken and abruptly fired from the GPS. There followed a period of her life with little direction, an aimless retail job at the Accra Mall and several opportunities for her mother to say, "I told you so." But then, by God's grace, Emma found the Sowah Agency, or the agency found her.

COMPARED TO MOST private detective agencies in Ghana, Sowah was relatively luxurious and well-resourced. Nevertheless, it was beginning to show some wear, and was in need of a new paint job and more electrical outlets to accommodate the multiplying electronic devices. Mr. Sowah's success was born of decades in the business, but his agency was not immune to the ups and downs of the economy, and now there was a market slump. Some clients, especially those overseas and new to the agency, refused to pay anything until they saw a formally written interim report that spoke to Sowah's reliability. Assignments came from all over, but those from Europe and the US paid the most.

With no fresh investigations and more downtime than usual, the group sat at their individual desks in the common office area and engaged in mostly inconsequential conversation, all the time aware that relaxed moments like these weren't good. Next to Emma was Walter Manu, the most senior employee at the agency, who had a graying beard and salt-and-pepper head of hair to prove it. He had a good track record, but in Emma's discreet opinion, he was rather full of himself. Pushed away from his desk because his generous belly prevented him from sitting comfortably close-up, he was complaining about his various in-laws. *And women are always labeled the gossipers*, Emma thought. At one point, in reference to his mother-in-law, Walter said, "You know how women are," then looked apologetically at Emma. "Present company excluded, of course."

Sorting folders on her desk, Emma made no comment. It wasn't worth the trouble, and anyway, her objections wouldn't change Manu's mind. He was too set in his outlook.

The other two detectives, Gideon and Jojo, were closer to Emma's age, more open-minded and easier to get along with. Jojo, small-framed and baby-faced, was almost thirty but could pass for nineteen. He often took undercover assignments posing as a teenager. On the other hand, Gideon, broad and solid as a brick wall, could appear older than his thirty-one years if he grew out his beard and dressed the part. Like siblings with a friendly rivalry between them, the two men constantly took verbal shots at each other.

Beverly, Sowah's always-well-turned-out assistant, came up to Emma and said quietly, "Someone here to see you."

Emma stood and followed Beverly to the foyer, where a woman sat waiting. In her late fifties, she was short and sturdy, with a face that announced she didn't tolerate rubbish from anyone. She rose to her feet as soon as she saw Emma. "Good morning, Miss Djan." They shook hands. "My name is Dele Tetteyfio."

Emma wondered how this woman knew of her. "Welcome. How may I help you?"

"I need to talk to you urgently."

Emma felt a small surge of anticipation. This could be a new job. "Please, come in."

At her desk, she offered the visitor a chair. Walter stopped his discourse, aware of Sowah's rule that idle chitchat in front of visitors and clients was a strict no-no.

Emma settled into her seat. "What can we do for you, Madam Dele?"

"Have you heard of Lady Araba?"

Emma searched her memory, retrieving the details quickly. "The fashion designer? Who was murdered a year ago?"

"Ten months. She was my niece."

"I'm sorry, madam."

"Thank you. You probably noticed that it faded from the news, but to me, it has never been resolved."

"They arrested someone, right?" Emma said, trying to recall whom.

"Yes," Dele said, "Araba's driver. On what basis, I don't know, but I'm positive he is innocent. This is the way the Ghana Police operates. They pin the crime on someone peripheral as a smoke-screen and claim the investigation is ongoing. Meanwhile, they have no interest in pursuing the case any further, the thing dies, and everyone forgets about it. That's why I'm here. I want the real culprit to come to justice."

"Okay," Emma said with a nod. "Madame Dele, can we discuss

this further with my boss, Mr. Sowah? He will need to hear about it, and I don't want you to have to repeat yourself."

"Okay," Dele said, with the slightest hesitation. "But . . . I would like it to be you in charge of the investigation. I read about you, and I have confidence in you."

Emma smiled. "Thank you, but first things first. Let's see if Mr. Sowah will even approve of me taking the case."

SOWAH WAS FREE and his door open. He welcomed Dele to his office with customary grace. Compact rather than small, he was wearing a crisp pale-blue shirt, a tie—always—and dark slacks. He was completely bald on most of his crown, leaving him with gray hair on the sides. He looked like a cross between a professor and a businessman. He asked Dele to take a seat on the scarlet leather sofa—the "hot seat," as it was called—while he and Emma sat opposite. Dele repeated what she had told Emma so far.

"I was following your niece's case in the media," Sowah said to Dele. "I know it dwindled from the public eye, but for you and the family, it must still be very much alive."

"It burns in my heart as if it happened yesterday," Dele said, thumping her chest so hard Emma almost flinched. "So much pain. No one loved Araba more than I did. Not her father nor her mother, not even her brother, Oko. Araba spent much more time with me than she did with her parents."

"I understand," Sowah said. "Now, if I remember correctly, the police arrested Lady Araba's driver."

"Don't mind the police," Dele said with a toss of her head. "They looked for a scapegoat and chose the lowest man on the totem pole—their usual MO. Kweku-Sam was Araba's faithful driver, and he wouldn't have killed Araba any more than I would."

"Who do you believe did it, then?" Sowah asked. "Have you formed an opinion about that?"

"Of course," she said, as if the whole world should already know. "Augustus Seeza."

"Seeza?" Sowah interjected. "The one with the radio show?"

"Yes, him. *He* should be the prime suspect, but the police and the judiciary have either sided with him or been paid off to let him go scot-free. Augustus is getting away with murder. His father is an influential judge, and I can see his hand in all of this."

"What do you have to support that belief?" Sowah asked, echoing Emma's own thoughts.

"Mr. Sowah, look," Dele said, her jaw setting. "You may or may not know that Augustus was once the highest-paid TV personality in Ghana. But he was a fool with his money—a big spender who lived beyond his means. By the time he started a relationship with Araba—after separating from his wife, Bertha, who, by the way, is also rich—he was already in serious debt. He saw an opportunity in Araba. People say women are the gold diggers, but not this time. Now, the second problem—Augustus is an alcoholic. The worse his debt became, the more he drank. The more he drank, the more ill-behaved he became.

"And yet, Araba stuck with him! At one point, she was giving him money so he could buy things for his two kids. Augustus was into expensive cigars, and she was getting him those as well—on top of all that, she bought him a shiny new Jaguar. It was too much. Her mother, father, and brother intervened and told Araba she had to put a stop to her relationship with Augustus and get him completely out of her life. She tried, but of course, he couldn't bear that. They went in and out of a toxic relationship. I believe Araba wanted to end all that, but he wasn't having it.

"Augustus had a spare key to her house. Even after Araba had told him to stay away, she never changed the locks as I advised her to. As far as I know, apart from the house girl, Augustus was the only one with a key to her home, which is important because the morning Araba was discovered dead, all the doors to the house were locked—the front door, the kitchen, the entrance from the garage, and the upstairs terrace. The detective who was on the case, Sergeant Isaac Boateng, confirmed that to me and said there were no signs of forced entry."

"What about the driver?" Sowah said. "What's his name again?"

"Kweku-Sam."

"Could he have had a key?"

"Possibly, but I doubt it."

"And, Madam Dele, did *you* have a key to her house?"

"I did not. I loved Araba, but her life was her own. I gave her that respect."

"I've failed to ask you what the official cause of death was," Sowah said.

"I've heard blunt force trauma to the head," Dele said, "and I've also heard strangulation. No one has shared the official report with me, not even my brother, Fifi." She shook her head in resignation. Emma thought that was interesting—family dynamics at play.

"At any rate," Dele continued, "about two weeks after Araba's death, I made an appointment with the head of CID, Madam Tawiah, to demand that they come out with the results of the DNA evidence, which I was informed were collected at the scene. You know what this woman told me? That she wasn't aware of any DNA in existence. Yes, the director of CID told me this. How worthless are these people?"

Sowah said, "That's a real shame. And you feel confident that if they *did* have such evidence, it would prove the murderer was Mr. Seeza?"

"Absolutely."

"I take it you disliked Mr. Seeza?"

"Intensely."

"What about Lady Araba's immediate family, though?" Sowah asked. "Any issues there?"

"Well, her father, Fifi Tagoe—my brother—is an Anglican priest. He was always very strict with his children, especially Araba, whom he watched all the time to be sure she stayed out of trouble. I think he was *too* strict, which is why Araba preferred to spend time with me when she was a child. I've run my clothing business for a long time, and that's where Araba learned the trade. Now Oko, Araba's brother, is very brainy and always loved school, unlike Araba, who clashed with Fifi over that."

"I see," Sowah said. "You are aware, Madam Dele, that if we take this case and solve it, the result may not be what you had in mind. If, for any reason, you're out to get Mr. Seeza, so to speak, you might be disappointed."

Dele sat forward and said, "If it wasn't Augustus who killed my niece, then so be it. But I don't believe I'm wrong."

"I hear you," Sowah responded.

"Very well, then. May I ask you a favor?"

"Of course."

"That if you take this case, Madam Emma here will be the investigator?"

"She will indeed be on the case. One other matter, though." Sowah extracted a sheet of paper from his left bottom drawer. "Please take a look at our fee schedule first, because that might ultimately be the deciding factor."

Dele looked over the document, which detailed the retainer and then the subsequent payments.

"Please, any chance of a small discount?" she said, looking up at Sowah with a coy smile.

"I can reduce the retainer by ten percent," Sowah said.

"That will be fine, sir. Thank you. Do I sign here at the bottom?"

Sowah already had a pen poised to go. Madam Dele signed.

THIRTEEN

Ten months after

KWEKU-SAM WAS THE COLOR of asphalt. Once, he had been quite thickset, but he now looked as if the fat had simply melted off. Remanded in custody for the murder of Lady Araba, he had spent the last ten months in the hell of the vastly overcrowded Nsawam Prison, 34 kilometers northwest of Accra.

In the morning, the prison guards released the prisoners to the yard, and beyond that, a large field. Meanwhile, the queue to the much-needed toilet was long. In Kweku-Sam's section of the facility, four toilets were available for over six hundred men. It often happened that three of the toilets were out of order, making the demand a case of impossible arithmetic. In the long line for the john, some inmates had "accidents."

Not too far from the toilets was an area for eating and washing. Breakfast was "porridge," which looked and tasted like cloudy water. Using a cup, a prison guard spooned the gruel into the tin bowls the prisoners brought with them to the serving line.

KWEKU-SAM HAD LOVED life as Lady Araba's chauffeur and all-purpose errand boy. He had been in her service for almost five years, and when he said "service," he meant it. He took her anywhere and everywhere, from the temperate hills of Aburi to the scorching desert of the northern regions. He kept her secrets, too.

He had never revealed her late-night trysts with Augustus Seeza to anyone.

Of the men Lady Araba had been involved with, Mr. Seeza was Kweku-Sam's least favorite. In his opinion, the broadcaster was loud, boastful, and overrated. And of course, in the days before the death of Lady Araba, he was an even worse drunk. That had worried Kweku-Sam, because Seeza had a violent streak.

Lady Araba spoiled Seeza. He had a taste for fancy cigars from a shop called Habana Vieja. Araba often sent Kweku-Sam there to buy cigars for Seeza, who never paid a single *pesewa* for them. Kweku-Sam didn't understand Seeza's power over her, and why she didn't see that the person who *genuinely* cared about her was the one who was with her the most: her chauffeur.

Araba and Seeza alternated homes when they spent time with each other. Kweku-Sam imagined that Seeza preferred Araba's house because it was bigger than his apartment in the affluent Airport Residential Estates.

When she fired her bodyguard, Kweku-Sam took over the role. Once, when Araba launched her second store at the West Hills Mall, a crazed fan ran up to her and tried to embrace her. Kweku-Sam wrestled him off and pushed him to the side. He then swept Araba away to safety as pandemonium erupted. Araba was shaken, but Kweku-Sam was there to reassure her.

From what Kweku-Sam picked up from Lady Araba's conversations, and he learned a lot that way, she'd had a partner in her company, Susan Hayford, whom Kweku called "Susan one hundred percent" because she always boasted she was "one hundred percent Fante." (Fante people always said that.) She and Araba had worked well together for about five years, but then Susan defected to form a competing fashion brand called Lady Pizzazz, which never rose to the level of the iconic Lady Araba.

On Lady Araba's last Sunday alive, Kweku-Sam took her to an early evening reception at the Villa Monticello Hotel for an American guy who was in town for Accra Fashion Week.

Kweku-Sam parked the Range Rover alongside the BMWs, Escalades, Benzes, Jaguars, and a Lamborghini. He put the seat back and lay back to doze off, jerking awake as his phone rang. Lady Araba said, "I'm coming down. I don't feel well and I want to go home now."

It was only 8:16. Kweku-Sam knew something was wrong. On the trip back home, he heard Lady Araba speak with three different sets of people on the phone: first, her assistant, Samson, who was tying up loose ends before the fashion show the next day. With Samson it was all business, but then Mr. Seeza called and it was an emotional and wrenching conversation—two, in fact. On Seeza's first call, Lady Araba said, "Don't come, Gus. This is not the right time and I can't deal with all this *wahala*. I have a full day tomorrow and I need rest. I can't see you right now."

His second call came only minutes later. Kweku-Sam saw it as harassment. Lady Araba became agitated, raising her voice. "*No*, Gus. I said no. Please stop calling."

As they arrived at Trasacco just before nine, Lady Araba chatted briefly with her parents, who called to wish her luck at the show the next day.

Kweku-Sam parked in front of Lady Araba's house and hopped out to open her door.

"You can leave the car out," she said. "Tomorrow morning, be here by seven to take me to the Tang Palace Hotel."

"Yes please."

Lady Araba had a chic gift bag from the reception. It was automatic that Kweku-Sam should carry it into the house for her. A good driver didn't allow the boss to bear any burden, no matter how small. Following her through the front door, he brought the package into the living room.

"Leave it there," she said, pointing to the marble-topped coffee table.

"Yes please." He put the bag down and hesitated before speaking. "Please, is everything okay, I mean with Mr. Seeza? If you like, I can stay a little while."

Lady Araba looked both surprised and irritated. "That's none of your business," she said crisply.

"Yes, madam. Sorry, madam." He knew he had stepped over the line.

"See you tomorrow," she said.

It was the last time Lady Araba ever said that, and the last time Kweku-Sam saw her alive.

FOURTEEN

Ten months after

SOME ASPECTS OF THE investigations at the Sowah Agency were best handled by the boss himself. With decades as a CID and then private investigator, he had formed and maintained a network of contacts he could depend on. That was the case with his old friend Cleophus Laryea, Deputy Commissioner of Police. They had been contemporaries at CID and would probably have been the same rank by now, had Yemo Sowah not chosen to leave the force. The Ghana Police Service's corrupt and lackadaisical approach to police work had left him unable to function in the way he wanted. Sowah felt bothered when cases simply languished on someone's desk for months to years with little to no effort put into solving them. Sometimes he felt as if he was alone in this disquiet and he realized he had only two options: he could get in line and become oblivious to the work that needed to be done, or he could get out.

For his part, Cleophus Laryea had survived the GPS with a combination of honesty and savvy. He was no angel, Sowah knew, but he was a cut above many. Laryea, unlike his friend, thrived on the strict hierarchical structure of the GPS, but he had a deep respect for Sowah and his eponymous agency. What police information Laryea could share with Sowah, he did. Otherwise he would either tell him that he was bound to secrecy or had nothing to disclose. Apart from Laryea, most police officers felt that communications between them and private detectives were a one-way street: the privates were expected to give information to the police, but not the other way around.

To get some background on the case Dele had brought to the agency, Sowah called Laryea. For a short while, they joked cordially with each other in *Ga*, their beloved indigenous language, which they regarded as the king of all Ghanaian tongues.

"How are you?" Laryea asked. "How is business on your end?"

"A little slow, my friend. We haven't had a new case in quite some time, although we have one now, and I wonder if you could help us."

"Let's hear."

"The fashion woman, Lady Araba, murdered about ten months ago. Do you know where the investigation has gone, if anywhere?"

"I know a little bit about it," Laryea said, "but not the most intimate details. I've heard two different stories: The first is that no useful evidence was taken from the scene. The second was that the crime scene was contaminated but one detective—his name slips my memory right now, but give me a few minutes—managed to salvage some evidence and send it to the forensic science lab."

"It should be possible to find out, right?"

"I can make some inquiries for you."

"I would be grateful. That forensic lab—it opened, what, about seven years ago? Is it fully operational?"

"Supposed to be," Laryea said. "It has an administrator, et cetera, so I assume it's functioning. Don't quote me, though. Ah, I've got it now. The name of the detective who perhaps collected evidence—Sergeant Isaac Boateng. But I believe he's no longer in homicide. He's been moved to another department, but I forget which. I'll follow up on all of this and get back to you in a few days."

"Thanks, Cleo. I appreciate it."

"Em, Yemo?"

"Yes?"

"Just my opinion," Cleo said quietly, "but this case steps into some sensitive areas because of Lady Araba's association with Augustus Seeza, the TV host. His father is a High Court judge who holds a lot of sway in the upper ranks of the police. Just a warning to tread lightly."

"*Maate*. I won't go any further than I need to. That's a promise."

FIFTEEN

The day of the murder

ALMOST IMMEDIATELY AFTER THE discovery of Lady Araba's dead body, Peter called his friend Detective Sergeant Isaac Boateng, who was the Crime Scene Unit leader at the Homicide Unit of the CID Headquarters in Accra. When his phone rang, he was standing at what he had hoped would be a crime scene. A woman in the town of Adenta had been stabbed to death just behind her house. About thirty minutes before that, the woman and her male neighbor, with whom she had had a running dispute over a small plot of land between their respective houses, were heard having a furious argument in which the man had made a threat on her life.

Shortly after the stabbing occurred, the victim's friends and relatives descended upon the neighbor's home accusing him of the murder, dragged him out of the house, beat him nearly into a state of unconsciousness, and then took him to the police station by taxi. The spectacle at the station was chaotic with all the shouting and crying. The inspector on duty returned with the family to where the victim's dead body had lain covered in blood from countless stab wounds. By that time, because a gawking crowd had formed, other relatives and friends had moved the corpse from its original location to a more private area within the house compound. They'd also covered the woman's body with a cloth to lessen the awful sight of her multiple jagged lacerations.

A person, so far unidentified, had thought of calling the CSU, a number that went straight to Boateng's phone. Meanwhile, however, after the investigating inspector had taken a few mobile phone photos of the victim, he summoned a police pickup truck to take the body to the closest mortuary. So, by the time Boateng arrived in the blue CSU van along with his photographer, Corporal Tackie, who also acted as the fingerprints man and the evidence technician, the body was gone and someone had washed away the victim's unsightly blood.

After Boateng had spoken to a relative and Tackie had snapped some photos of the scene, they returned to the van with resignation. Few Ghana police officers knew how to secure a crime scene. Worse, the public neither trusted the police nor knew anything about the science of forensics, a situation that for almost ten years now Boateng had hoped in vain to rectify.

Constable Gabriel, the CSU van driver, was leaning against the hood shelling and munching on groundnuts. "So, what's next, boss?"

Boateng shrugged. "Unsecured crime scene, body removed. Nothing we can do." He wanted to be annoyed, but he was too weary. The situation was all too familiar. "Let's go back to CID."

That's when his phone rang and he saw it was his old friend calling.

"Peter!" he said. "*Chaley*, wassup?"

"*Asem*, oo, *asem!*"

"What's going on?"

"Have you heard of Lady Araba?"

"Yeah," Boateng said. "The one they call queen of fashion? What about her?"

"Hm, this is serious. Somebody killed her last night."

Boateng raised his eyebrows. "Come again?"

"When Ismael, the groundskeeper at our Trasacco complex, went to put in some new plants on the terrace outside Lady

Araba's bedroom, he saw her lying in the bed with blood all over the place. I think she had been dead for some hours by that time."

"Is the body still there? What's happening?"

"Still in the house—the bedroom. I sent one of my guys to the local police station and he came back here with two officers."

Boateng felt a rising sense of excitement. Maybe *this* would be one of the few cases where he could make a mark. "We're on our way," he said to Peter. "But we're at Adenta right now, so from here to Trasacco will take some time. *Please*, I beg you, ask the officers to secure the crime scene, okay?"

IT TOOK THE team over an hour to get to Lady Araba's house. Several Tata police trucks and one shiny black BMW were parked in all directions in the driveway.

A constable stood at the front door while a couple of unidentified people hung around with no obvious role to play as far as Boateng could tell. The constable gave Boateng a brief salute and waved him and Tackie in. "They're upstairs to the right," the constable told them.

No one was at the bottom of the staircase, but multiple voices came from upstairs. Boateng peered up and began ascending, but Peter came running down before Boateng was halfway.

"So, what's going on?" Boateng asked.

Peter took Boateng's arm and brought him back to the base of the stairs. He lowered his voice. "The chief inspector from the Trasacco police station called his commander, who then called the Director-General of CID, Assistant Chief of Police, Madam Tawiah. The commander came first and she arrived after that. She came in saying she knew a lot about crime scene evaluation."

Boateng frowned. "Shit."

"She began touching Lady Araba's body, examining her for possible cause of death."

Boateng felt the blood leave his head. "*Touching the body!*" he exclaimed too loud.

Peter shushed him hastily, looking around to see if anyone

might have heard. "And then when I said I'd already called you," he continued, "the DG stepped back and said okay, then let's wait for the CSU to arrive."

"*After* she's contaminated the body," Boateng said bitterly. First rule of crime scene preservation: never let a senior officer near it. "Is she still there?"

"Yeah. Her and some other people—I'm not sure who they all are."

"But what are they doing?"

Peter shrugged. "Mostly just staring."

"What about next-of-kin?"

"No one has appeared yet. I had an emergency number to call, a Dele Tetteyfio, Lady Araba's aunt, but she hasn't responded so far."

Boateng nodded, turned, and with Tackie behind him, heaved himself up the stairs. He could feel he was putting on too much weight. Between work and early fatherhood, he didn't get to play soccer on the weekends anymore. Or he might just be making excuses for himself.

As he entered the room, he was partially aware of the handful of people standing around, but it was only Lady Araba's body on the bed that seized his attention. She lay on her back, covered by a bloody duvet, eyes open and staring at the ceiling. The color of her face, which was badly swollen, was an odd purplish-gray.

"Good morning, madam," Boateng said to the only woman in the room—the CID boss, Madam Tawiah. Tall and lean, she was sharply dressed in full uniform regalia. Her look was clean and prim.

"Morning," she replied, regarding him with skepticism. "Who are you?"

"I'm Detective Sergeant Isaac Boateng, please. I'm the CSU leader."

"Are you alone?"

"No, the photographer is here as well, madam." Boateng gestured to the doorway.

"That's all?" Tawiah asked, appearing puzzled.

Maybe if you top brass would stop chopping all the money, we could hire some more people, Boateng thought. "That's all we have right now, please," he said.

Tawiah nodded. "Well, anyway, I've already checked the body," she said with self-importance. "From what I can tell, she has suffered blunt head trauma to the skull. She has a wound on the left side of her head."

"Thank you for that information, madam," Boateng said. "Please, we can take over from here? If possible, I would like everyone to leave the room so that we may do our work."

"Yes, of course," Tawiah said. "This is a tragedy. Such a young and talented woman."

Boateng heaved a mental sigh of relief as everyone filed out. At least Tawiah wasn't going to be difficult. He had just begun to open his forensic kit when a commotion erupted downstairs, followed by pounding footsteps and a man's voice shouting, "Araba! *Araba!*" A man in great distress ran down the hallway, stopped just outside the door, caught one look at the body on the bed, and collapsed.

SIXTEEN

The day of the murder

NEWS OF LADY ARABA'S death spread like wildfire through the fashion gathering at Tang Palace that morning. Samson first heard about it from Oko Tagoe just as the show was about to begin. Samson considered canceling, but no, Araba would have wanted her show to go on. He didn't tell any of the models before they walked out onto the runway because he knew they wouldn't be able to hold it together. As it was, the show came off without any major hitches.

It was afterward that Samson gathered everyone to break the awful news. The women gasped and cried out. Several broke down weeping, while others stood shattered and numb. There were questions no one could answer, and to fill in for that lack of information, rumors began to fly. For the rest of the day, it seemed like everyone involved in Accra Fashion Week was phoning or texting about Lady Araba. It was on the news by midday, and wherever there was a TV, people crowded in front of it. Head of CID, ACOP Madam Tawiah, had taken the lead in providing what information she could to news outlets. With Lady Araba's mansion as a made-for-TV backdrop, a gaggle of eager reporters crowded around Tawiah, jostling for space as they shoved their phone mics in her face. She maintained absolute composure, even when the questions fired at her were somewhat asinine.

Have the police arrested a suspect yet?

"Not as such," Tawiah said. "It is very early in the process, so we will need some time."

Was someone else present at home with Lady Araba when she was murdered?

"If by that you mean someone besides the murderer, the answer is no."

Since the murder occurred just before Accra Fashion Week, do you suspect that a rival designer didn't want Lady Araba's show to come on?

"Possibly, but I don't know."

When do you expect to make an arrest?

"As soon as possible."

Is Augustus Seeza, the TV personality with whom Lady Araba had an affair, a suspect?

"I have no comment on that."

So, then he is a suspect?

"No comment. Next question."

Were DNA samples taken at the scene?

"Yes, I supervised that myself due to my extensive knowledge of crime scene management."

How long before you have the DNA results?

"It will be several weeks, at least. I will apprise you of any developments in that regard as far as I am able. Thank you, ladies and gentlemen."

Tawiah's bodyguard extricated her from the reporters.

SAMSON HAD BOOKED a two-night stay at the Tang Hotel for the convenience of being right where AFW was taking place. Susan Hayford, whose show was scheduled for the next day, was also at the hotel when the news hit. Almost at that moment, she received a call from Samson, who asked her to come up to his room.

When he opened the door to her, his expression was bleak. "You've heard," he said.

"Of course." Susan entered and Samson shut the door behind her. They embraced stiffly and briefly.

"I can't believe this is happening," he whispered.

Susan said nothing, turning on the TV broadcast of *Metro Midday News*. She joined Samson as he sat on the bed to watch. Like all men, he then took the remote and scanned through other channels. Several ran the same Q&A with Madam Tawiah, although they had slightly different commentary on Araba's life, achievements, and legacy.

Samson leaned against Susan. "I wish it was all a dream."

She put her arms around him. He wiped tears from his face and sniffled, but she remained silent, running her hands through his soft hair. Samson was the product of an Irish man and a Ghanaian woman. He had naturally lustrous black curls that made people stare. It was what had attracted Susan to him most when they had worked with Araba—before the fallout.

Samson pulled away from her, resting his face in his hands and staring at the floor. "I can't believe this is true. It just seems so unreal."

"When did you find out?" Susan asked.

"Araba's brother, Oko, called me this morning. Well, I called him first from Tang Palace to ask if he'd heard from her. I expected her to be in early for the show preparation and final rehearsal, but she still hadn't arrived a couple hours before start time, and I couldn't reach her by phone. Then Oko's dad, the Reverend, went to the house, and by that time there were already a lot of policemen and other people there. The gardener or something was the one who found her body."

"So, last night sometime," she murmured, looking down at her hands.

"Oh, my God," he said, falling back on the bed. "This is a nightmare."

"Stop it," Susan said abruptly.

He frowned and sat up. "What? *What?*"

"You resented the way she was treating you," Susan said, her voice like slick motor oil. "Now she's gone. So, what's all this drama about?"

"I don't wish death on anyone," Samson said sullenly.

She snorted, stood up, and went to the window. "I remember otherwise."

"What are you talking about?"

She turned around to look at him, leaning her plump body against the windowsill in a pose worthy of a fine sculpture. "We both wanted her dead, so stop being a hypocrite about it. Now everything can move forward. You'll take over the business and I'll buy you out. It's what we wanted, isn't it? I don't care how she died or who killed her. I'm just glad she's gone. Are you sorry about it now? Are you still in love with her?"

"I was never," he said, shaking his head emphatically. "I don't know why you're so jealous of her."

"I'm not," she snapped. "Ambitious whore. What do I care about her?"

"You must care, because you hated her," Samson said, sounding like a psychiatrist confronting his patient. "You wanted to kill her."

She moved from the window to look at him eye-to-eye. "*I* wanted to kill her?" she asked, pointing at herself. "*Me?* You're the one who hated her because of the way she worked you like a houseboy and wouldn't make you a partner when she was converting the business to an LLC. Don't try to pin her death on me, okay?"

"Don't blame it on me either!" he retorted.

They lapsed into a sulky silence for a while.

"Well, anyway," Susan resumed, "it's good you called Oko. If the police ask him any questions about you, he'll tell them that you asked him where Araba was. It looks better than if you hadn't."

Samson cleared his throat. "But last night—" he began.

"Last night, what?"

"We need to know what to say," Samson stammered. "I mean,

the police might ask where we were. They can't know about us sleeping together."

Susan rolled her eyes. "Those stupid police won't be asking us anything, and no one will ever know about us."

"Where did you go last night after you left me?"

"Home, of course. And where did *you* go?"

Samson's eyes shifted. "Nowhere. I was working on preparations for the show. Just like you."

Susan stared at him for a long moment and then began dramatically fanning her eyes as her eyes moistened.

"What's wrong?" Samson said.

Susan clapped her hands over her face, whimpered. Samson came to her, peering at her and trying to pull her hands from her face. "Hey, *hey*. What's going on?"

"Please, please don't lie to me," she said, her voice cracking. "Tell me the truth, did you see her last night?"

"What's *wrong* with you?" Samson said, his voice rising. "Are you going crazy? And what if I did? Who cares? Araba is dead now. She's gone."

"What about Saturday night? Did you sleep with her?"

Samson sucked his teeth and turned away in disgust to pick up his valise on the bed. "I don't have time for this. I'm going downstairs. Close the door behind you when you leave."

SEVENTEEN

Ten months after

AFTER SOME DIGGING, SOWAH located DS Boateng, who was now in the Domestic Violence and Victim Support Unit at the Ghana Police Regional Command on Kwame Nkrumah Avenue.

"I would like very much to meet with you," Sowah said after introducing himself.

"What is it about, please?"

"You spent some time working on the Lady Araba murder case, is that correct, sir?"

"Yes please—at the beginning, for a short while. But I'm no longer on it because I was transferred to DVU. Why do you ask?"

"My agency has been contracted to investigate the murder."

"Which agency is that?"

"Sowah Private Investigators. We're at Asylum Down."

"I see. If I may ask, who contracted you?"

"Lady Araba's Auntie Dele."

"Hmm," Boateng said.

"You sound worried," Sowah commented.

"I thought you detective agencies tackled only small-small cases like marital infidelity and so on?"

"It runs the gamut. Well, to be quite honest with you, the agency's cash flow has been negative for several months. I couldn't turn it down."

Boateng was silent for a moment. "I wish I could have talked with you before you accepted the case. I think you should leave this one alone."

"I'm interested to know why you say that."

"The politics around it. Sorry, but I can't discuss it right now."

"I understand. You're in mixed company, is what you are saying. Can we meet somewhere?"

Boateng hesitated. "I'll call you back."

"Okay—" Sowah was about to finish his sentence with, "When can I expect your call?" but Boateng had already gone.

If I haven't heard from him within twenty-four hours, Sowah thought, *he will hear from me.*

As it happened, Sowah didn't have to do that. In the afternoon, his phone rang, and he saw it was Boateng. The DS was ready to set up an appointment.

"Thank you, Sergeant Boateng," Sowah said. "I appreciate it. If you could come to our offices, that would be great, and you can meet my investigators as well."

BOATENG HAPPILY ACCEPTED a small bottle of Bel-Aqua water. In his ill-fitting shirt, he was sweating heavily from the punishing heat outside and looked like he could be wrung out like a wet rag. He had once been fit but lost all of it in a steady decline.

"Thank you for coming," Sowah said.

"It's no problem," Boateng said, wiping the corner of his mouth with the back of his hand after taking a gulp of water. "I'm willing to help you and your guys, but please, my coming to talk to you must never get back to the Ghana Police Service."

"I understand," Sowah reassured him. "You will be off the record. But before anything, are you at liberty to say what happened to you? You were investigating the Lady Araba murder, and then they moved you out to the Domestic Violence Unit?"

Boateng's jaw hardened. "Okay, I'll tell you. It was about four weeks after the murder. The investigation was slow, people were being evasive. As you know, in Ghana we don't like direct questions. Then I turned to the police forensic science lab to ask about the evidence I had submitted. There was always some excuse—the guy who was supposed to run the test was sick or had been traveling.

"Finally, one day, the administrator, Thomas, revealed in confidence that he had been asked to delay testing of the evidence. He wouldn't elaborate. And the next day, my senior officer told me I was off the case and being transferred to Domestic Violence. I didn't know what to say."

"They gave you no reason?"

Boateng snorted. "Do they ever give a reason? Two days later is when they arrested Lady Araba's driver. My friend Peter, who works at Trasacco as the head security officer, saw the chauffeur, Kweku-Sam, coming out of the house around nine o'clock on the night she died. Kweku says he had brought Lady Araba home from a party at that time. My belief is that the police used that as cause to arrest Kweku-Sam and charge him with murdering his boss."

Sowah raised his eyebrows. "If that's the sole criterion, it won't stand up in court."

"Well, it may never go to court. Kweku will just languish in prison without trial."

"Have you spoken with him?"

"Yes, sir. Look, the man didn't kill Lady Araba. I'm certain of that. The murder probably took place much later that night."

"To go back a little," Sowah said, "who called in the murder? How did it get to you?"

"It was Peter who called me. At the time, I was at the scene of another crime—which turned out to be a big disappointment—but went to Trasacco as quickly as possible in the CSU van. By the time I reached Lady Araba's house, several officers and personnel from surrounding police stations were standing around. The place was full of people who shouldn't have been there, including ACOP Madam Tawiah of CID."

"How so?" Sowah asked.

"Because she knows nothing about police work on the ground,

even though she pretends she does. Can you believe she examined Lady Araba's body before we arrived—supposedly to look for the cause of death? She wants to be the center of attention all the time. After the murder, she was on every TV and radio interview program possible. Do you know her background? For years she was with the Motor Traffic and Transport Division, and then someone imported her to CID in return for certain services I don't need to go into right now, eventually promoting her to director-general. I hear she's eyeing the inspector general of police position now."

"How badly contaminated do you believe the crime scene was by the time you reached it?" Sowah asked, staying on topic.

Boateng shrugged. "Bad. People were leaning against the doors and windows, they touched the bed Lady Araba was in, and we know that at least Madam Tawiah, if not more of them, touched the victim's body. There was a boot print on Lady Araba's white carpet, but we figured out it belonged to the constable who was standing at the front door of Lady Araba's house. We dusted for fingerprints and found several different ones. We were able to eliminate some as spurious, but not others. Finally, I found two strands of hair on Lady Araba's sheets and collected them as well."

"Well done," Sowah said. "I'm curious, though. You're both a detective and part of the forensics unit? How did that come about?"

"Ten years ago, the police service recruited me almost straight from university. It was part of a program to train police personnel in forensics, and they particularly wanted me because I had studied biochemistry. In 2011, the government got a loan from the EU to build a new forensic science lab, and by the end of that year they sent me for a three-month forensics course in South Africa. By the time I returned, the forensics lab was just about ready for use."

"And it's been a success since?"

"Yes and no. The problem isn't the equipment, it's the training to use it and the quality of the evidence sent to the lab. Not enough police personnel are trained to preserve the scene so that evidence can be obtained intact and suitable for testing. And that's just the start. Imagine a homicide committed in say, Tamale, Northern Region. The only forensics lab for the entire country is here in Accra. Who's going to collect the evidence in Tamale? Who knows how to do the proper chain of custody and the correct way to bring the evidence from there to here in a timely fashion?" Boateng looked despondent. "A lot of difficulties."

"But the potential is there, no?" Sowah suggested. "It seems the FSL did a good job of identifying the remains of the three girls who went missing a couple of years ago in Takoradi, not so?"

"Yes." Boateng grinned. "But it was me who did it."

"Oh!" Sowah exclaimed with a short laugh. "My apologies. I had no idea."

Boateng waved it away with a chuckle. "Of course. Not a problem."

"So, back to this case," Sowah said. "You feel Lady Araba's driver is the easy scapegoat, which is what Dele Tetteyfio also thinks. Who is, or was, your prime suspect?"

"Number one is Augustus Seeza. He's in a category all by himself because of his close and tumultuous relationship with Lady Araba. But him aside, I see two camps of plausible suspects. On one side, the Seezas—High Court Justice Julius Seeza and his wife, Dr. Caroline. On the other side, members of Lady Araba's own family—her father, Reverend Fifi Tagoe; her mother, Miriam; and her brother, Oko."

"They all had reasons for wanting Araba dead?" Sowah asked. "I mean, suggesting that a High Court judge could be involved in such a murder is a big deal."

"When it comes to human passions, we are all the same, whether a justice of the court or a guy who cleans toilets for a living."

Sowah conceded that with a nod. "What would be Justice Seeza's motive?"

"My sources told me that he and his wife felt Lady Araba almost cost Augustus his life. While in a relationship with her, he began to drink even more heavily and ended up being admitted to the hospital with a liver problem that nearly killed him. Just before that, Lady Araba had dumped him at the admonition of her family, but as soon as she found out how ill he was, she came rushing back to him. He was alcohol-free up until Araba was murdered, which apparently put him into relapse and right back to the hospital with some sort of ailment that left him deaf. Of course, Augustus's worsening alcoholism wasn't Araba's fault at all, but Julius and Caroline Seeza told me they felt she was a catalyst. To them, Bertha Longdon was the ideal woman for him.

"Likewise, the Tagoe family demonized *Augustus* as the problem—said he was a leech sucking Araba's lifeblood and money. They reprimanded her and told her to get away from him, but she kept going back."

"You interviewed the family, I suppose, Sergeant?"

"I did, yes, sir."

"What were your impressions?"

"Reverend Tagoe is very much the boss—quite a rigid man. He drives everything in the household and his wife and son fall into line."

Sowah nodded. "I see. Apart from speaking to the Tagoes, how did you get most of your information? For having worked the case for only a few weeks, you seem to know quite a lot."

"Some of it is from Peter, with whom both Araba and Seeza formed a bond over the years. The rest is bits and pieces I put together from other sources like Bertha Longdon, who was surprisingly cooperative. She was wounded by her separation from Mr. Seeza, but I found her to be quite open and honest."

"You've done well, Sergeant."

"Thank you, Mr. Sowah. Okay, now, to continue, some other things you should know. You might have heard that the entire house was locked from the inside. The security guard and the groundskeeper had to break in through the bedroom door to the upper terrace. They said it was locked, and so were all the other doors with no forced entry. Meaning what? That whoever left Araba last, presumably the murderer, had a key to at least one of the doors to the house. We know he didn't use Araba's, because her keys to the front and back doors were both hanging on a hook on the wall in the entry hallway. Whenever she returned home, she hung the keys on the hook. We know for sure that Augustus had a spare key, because it was Lady Araba who asked Peter to have an extra set made for him."

"What about Araba's relatives?" Sowah asked. "Could they also have had copies of the keys?"

Boateng thought about it. "Possibly, but I don't think so, considering her sour relationship with the family."

"Does Peter have spare keys to units in the complex?"

Boateng shook his head. "I don't believe so."

"But you've said that Lady Araba had Peter make copies of the key for Augustus Seeza," Sowah pointed out. "Peter could have kept one."

"It's a fair point. I don't have an answer except that Peter doesn't ring any alarm bells for me."

"All right, then," Sowah said. "Now, the question is: What's happened to your evidence from the scene—the prints, hair, blood, and so on? If they're still around, where do you think they are?"

"The DNA should be in the walk-in freezer in the Bio and DNA section of the forensic lab. The prints should be in the case file in their records department."

"What is the security setup at the lab?" Sowah asked.

"Surprisingly lax. There's no CCTV—at least not during my time there—and they still use old-fashioned keys, which of course anyone can duplicate. No keypad entry, retinal scans, fingerprint recognition—nothing modern like that."

"Strange," Sowah commented. "Do you, by any chance, have keys to the labs, or spares?"

Boateng pulled a regretful face. "No to both questions. They made me hand over my set on leaving."

Sowah nodded. "No problem. Did you deposit the DNA evidence in the freezer yourself?"

"Yes, I did. I was going to work on it during that week. But I never got to it before they transferred me out."

"I don't get why they would move you to Domestic Violence when you were so valuable for your forensic knowledge."

"I believe—even though I don't have concrete proof—that they didn't *want* me to start work on the evidence."

"By 'they,' you mean . . . ?"

"Powerful individuals who are trying to shield the murderer. There are any number of scenarios. Augustus's father, for instance, is a judge on the High Court. He could pull strings with the police to prevent his son from being implicated in the murder."

"Is it possible, then, that crime scene evidence has now been destroyed?"

"I hope not, but there is a good chance."

"That would be a terrible shame, not to mention a crime in itself," Sowah said.

"This is what happens when you eat where you shit," Boateng said. "The FSL is a section of the CID. We should *not* have police officers working at the FSL. This is a clear conflict of interest, don't you think, Mr. Sowah?"

"I do."

"If the FSL was an independent body, rather," Boateng continued, "it would be harder for someone in the CID to meddle with evidence."

"And that's what you're speculating," Sowah said, his eyes down. He looked up. "Somehow we have to find out if your evidence still exists or has been destroyed. That's the first step."

Boateng looked doubtful. "I wish you luck, but it will be tough. The FSL has something of a shroud of secrecy draped over it."

Both men were quiet for a while, thinking to themselves.

"Oh," Boateng said, as if waking up. "My apologies—I forgot something important. Miriam Tagoe told me that some of Araba's jewelry was missing."

Sowah raised his eyebrows. "Meaning?"

"Araba always wore a necklace with a sapphire and two rubies,"

Boateng said. "Or two sapphires and a ruby, I forget which. I'm told she seldom took it off. When her body was found, the neck-lace was gone, and so were other items from her jewelry drawer, which was left open."

"I'm confused," Sowah said, frowning. "This now becomes a burglary gone wrong? Makes no sense."

Boateng nodded. "I agree. I think it's the murderer's poor attempt to make it look that way."

Sowah suspired and leaned back in his chair. "So, we have the murder of a young, successful woman with a controlling family in a tumultuous relationship with a troubled, alcoholic TV celebrity who, so far, seems like the prime suspect but is certainly not the only one; a contaminated crime scene with a poor attempt to make the murder appear like a burglary and from which the evi-dence collected may or may not have been destroyed at the FSL as a result of meddling by a High Court judge and/or the upper police echelons, who have most likely deliberately arrested the wrong man, and an investigator—namely, you—removed from the FSL in order that someone, possibly Augustus Seeza, goes scot-free."

As Sowah stopped to recover a breath, Boateng smiled. "Well summarized, sir. Now, how do we—or should I say, you—make sense of it all?"

EIGHTEEN

Ten months after

TUESDAY MORNING, 8 A.M., the staff briefing at Sowah Agency began. Emma and the other three detectives sat at their stations facing Yemo Sowah, who was at the head of the group next to the whiteboard.

"Morning, everyone," he said. "We'll start with our new case, the unsolved murder of fashion mogul Lady Araba." He wrote *Lady Araba murder* in a rectangle at the top of the board. "She was murdered ten months ago, and the case was brought to us by Araba's Auntie Dele Tetteyfio, the lady who came in last week and spoke to Emma and me in the office. She was frustrated by what she thinks is police misconduct in the investigation, particularly regarding the arrest of Araba's yearslong chauffeur, Kweku-Sam, who Dele thinks is just an easy scapegoat and not a valid suspect. Dele thinks the driver had no good reason to kill his boss and believes others had much stronger motives to kill her niece.

"Lady Araba lived in Trasacco Valley, a guarded community where they keep careful track of who goes in and out—or are supposed to, at least. The story is that the groundskeeper, Ismael, was on the upper terrace of her house when, through the glass door of her bedroom, he spotted Araba's body lying in bed underneath a bloodstained cover. He notified Trasacco's chief security officer, Peter, and because all entry points to Araba's house were locked, the groundskeeper broke the glass door to get in.

"To make a long story even longer, police personnel, including the head of CID, contaminated the crime scene before a bona fide homicide detective and crime scene expert arrived—a man by the name of Sergeant Isaac Boateng, whom I met yesterday. He worked the case for about four weeks until his superiors transferred him out of homicide to the Domestic Violence Unit in Accra Central. Boateng shared what information he had with me, although he was hesitant at first. He is among the few officers with a science degree who was sent to a forensics training course in South Africa. At any rate, even though Lady Araba's crime scene was severely compromised, Boateng did get some prints and swabs of what he thought might contain DNA.

"Just like Dele, Boateng doesn't believe Kweku killed Lady Araba. I will try to get to Kweku-Sam myself to question him, but it will probably take a while to get permission from the director of Nsawam Prison. I'll handle that."

Emma had never interviewed a remand prisoner—which Kweku-Sam was now—but she knew that authorization to do so required wading through layers of bureaucracy thick as mud.

"Back to Dele," Sowah continued, "she states that Augustus Seeza, the TV celebrity, was in a turbulent relation with Lady Araba, and since he was with her the night she died—so Dele claims—she believes he should be the prime suspect, and that Seeza's father, who is a judge, pulled influential strings in the background to keep his son from being investigated."

Sowah scribbled *Seeza* on the board with a two-way arrow connecting it to *Araba*.

"But there are other possible suspects," he went on. "For instance, Seeza's parents, Julius and Caroline, either individually or together. Why? Because they despised Araba for, in quotation marks, 'ruining their son's life.' Augustus was—is—an alcoholic, but during his time with Araba, his drinking worsened significantly. At one point several months before Araba's death, he was hospitalized for an alcohol-related illness.

"Blaming Araba for Augustus's worsening alcoholism is moot, but people need someone to blame. Could Augustus's parents have been angry and bitter enough to kill Araba? Anything is possible. Meanwhile, the way Araba Tagoe's family felt about Augustus was the mirror image of how the Seezas saw Araba. They felt he was destroying her, and when it became apparent he was going broke and depended on Araba for his lavish lifestyle, they confronted her to try and get her to dump Mr. Seeza. She did bend to their will for a while, but after she learned Augustus was in the hospital, she came right back to him."

"Boss," Manu said, "how well or badly did Dele get along with the Seezas?"

Sowah shook his head. "No love lost between the Seeza and Tagoe families."

Emma spoke up. "So, Dele could even have an ulterior motive for coming to us—family squabbles, trying to get the Seezas in trouble."

"Maybe," Sowah said, "but I doubt she would pay that kind of money to an agency just for that. There are much less expensive ways to do it."

Gideon asked, "Sir, what about Araba's work? Could any of her associates have wanted her dead for any reason?"

"Good," Sowah said. "Araba's rival was a woman named Susan Hayford." He wrote her name on the whiteboard next to Araba's. "They were business partners until they fell out of favor with each other. Susan then founded Lady Pizzazz, a competing fashion line."

"Another 'Lady?'" Manu commented. "Not very original." He looked at Emma. "Do you know anything about Lady Pizzazz?"

Emma gave him a quizzical look. "No. Why are you asking me?"

"You're a woman, so you must follow fashion," Manu said, grinning.

"Walter, do I look like I follow fashion?"

The others laughed. Emma's wardrobe was quite basic compared to, say, the boss's glamorous assistant, Beverly. Emma did have one weakness, however: attractive purses, handbags, and clutches.

"Now," Sowah went on, "we come to the investigation as it stands. Araba's driver, Kweku-Sam, is accused of the crime. At about nine on the eve of the discovery of Lady Araba's body, which was a Monday morning, he had brought Lady Araba back from an event. We're not sure exactly when she was killed—late on the night before she was found, or very early that morning—but for simplicity, we'll refer to it as the night of her death.

"We know that Lady Araba's home was securely locked, windows and doors, and there was no forced entry apparent. If that means Araba knew her intruder, we're still left to explain how the murderer vacated the house and left it completely locked behind him. Obviously, we are looking for someone who had a copy of the house key, which Araba habitually hung on a hook on the wall by the front door, and which was still there when the murderer left. The police were quick to jump on Kweku-Sam as the prime suspect, even though it's unlikely he had a duplicate key. Boateng says he had nothing to do with that arrest and suspects it was a decision from on high. He even implicates CID Director-General Madam Tawiah."

"It's strange that whoever has the post of CID director-general," Walter observed, "there's always some kind of controversy or suspicion surrounding him or her. Why can't we have an untainted figurehead for once?"

"It seems almost to come with the territory," Sowah agreed. "At the same time, we should be careful how easily we accept Boateng's insinuations against Madam Tawiah, because he seems to have some personal feelings against her and how she got the position of the director-general of CID. He implied that she did some favors, so to speak, in return for being awarded the post."

Emma felt like asking why people always thought a woman in a high position of authority hadn't gotten there on true merit, but this wasn't the time or place to start that argument. Instead, she said, "Boss, the crime scene evidence that DS Boateng obtained, where did he send it? Who has it now?"

"Good question," Sowah said. "Boateng says he logged in the evidence at the FSL. He never got to check the prints against the database. Before he got further with anything else, they pulled him out and transferred him to DVU. It's as though they wanted him as far away from the lab as possible so he couldn't press for the analysis to be done."

"So then, Boateng's crime scene evidence should still be at the FSL?" Emma asked.

"If it hasn't been destroyed, then yes," Sowah said, "but has it been processed? If so, what of the results? If someone is concealing them or having them concealed, who and why? These are some of the initial questions to be answered. Secondly, what is going on at Trasacco Valley? We must get to know the people who were present for Lady Araba's life and death." He turned back to the board and began writing. "Let's talk about motive. Any suggestions? Oh, wait, before we start that, there's something I forgot. Boateng says the Tagoes let him know that some of Lady Araba's jewelry was missing from her dresser. So, I'll start with what I think is the least likely motive for the murder: burglary or robbery gone wrong. We'll have it up there just for completeness, but we'll probably strike it out very soon."

"I agree with you, boss," Manu said. "Unless something comes up in that regard."

"Walter, you and Gideon team up to interview the Seeza and Tagoe families undercover. Emma, you'll go undercover at the forensic lab, and Jojo goes to Trasacco."

Emma felt both excited and nervous about taking on an undercover assignment, which she had never done before.

As if reading her mind, Sowah said to her, "I'll coach you on how to conduct undercover work, since this will be your first time." He smiled, apparently reading the anxiety in her face. "Don't worry, you'll be okay."

"Thank you, sir." She felt relieved, but butterflies were still flitting back and forth in her stomach.

NINETEEN

Ten months after

EMMA WASN'T PRETENDING TO be nervous. She really *was* nervous. For this situation, it was perfect. Among her first lessons from Sowah about going undercover was that although she might be hiding her objectives, her behavior shouldn't entirely be an act.

She entered the grounds of the Ghana Police Forensic Laboratory. She was surprised there wasn't a security guard at the entrance, where a couple of guys sat by the gutter outside, either unconnected with the place or uninterested by who went in and out. The two-story building Emma was approaching was white with dark-blue reflective windows. She went up a flight of steps to the first floor, which was tiled from one end of the long corridor to the other. Several doors, all shut, lined the corridor, but one lab room could be viewed through a tinted window. The tall curved faucets reminded Emma of secondary school science experiments, but the impressive equipment on the counters did not. A tall metal cabinet stood at the end of the central counter, and on a shelf close to the window was an electronic scale. But where was everybody, or *any*body? She walked the entire length of the hallway and saw no sign of life.

Boss Sowah had warned Emma to look for CCTV cameras. She saw none along the ceiling or hidden in the corners. She went up to the second floor. There, she saw a large laboratory space similar to the one downstairs. She was about to sneak a picture with her phone when she heard a door open behind her. She jumped and turned around. A man in a purple shirt came out and started down the hall in the opposite direction without seeing Emma.

"Please, good afternoon, sir," Emma said.

The man turned around, eyebrows raised. "Yes? Can I help you?"

"Please, my name is Mary. I'm looking for cleaning job, please."

She hoped her clothes matched her persona—a black skirt with fraying edges and a white blouse with a brown stain on the collar. She was someone trying her best to be presentable with few resources to do it. She looked poor but earnest, and honestly, a year ago, those had been close to Emma's circumstances.

The man frowned. "Who told you we need a cleaner?"

She smiled sheepishly. "Please, no one, but I was passing this place and I thought maybe . . ."

He was still scowling, but now with some amusement. "My name is Thomas—I'm in charge here. Come into my office for a moment."

She followed him into the room from which he had first emerged. He sat down at his desk and pointed to a chair along the opposite wall. Emma sat accordingly. She noticed a chart on the wall behind Thomas comparing the number of FSL cases over the prior three years in the different divisions of DNA, Documents, Ballistics, and Biochemistry/Drug Analysis. The largest number of cases was in the last category by far.

Thomas apparently detected her gaze and glanced behind him. "What are you looking at?"

"Oh, nothing," Emma stammered, returning her eyes to him.

"You say your name is what?"

"Mary, sir."

"Okay, Mary," he said.

He was out of shape, but young in the face, which was nice-looking enough.

"Yes, sir," Emma said. "Thank you, Mr. Thomas."

She squirmed and he laughed. "You are funny. But I like you."

"Thank you, sir."

"We don't have any cleaning jobs right now," he said, and she saw his eyes stray to her knees, which she reflexively closed tight. "Where have you worked before?"

"Some hotels," Emma said vaguely, ready to make some up. "And also, people's houses. Inside and out."

Thomas nodded. "For how long have you been doing that?"

"Please, since I was sixteen."

"And you are how old now?"

"Twenty-two, sir." Emma felt uneasy under his gaze.

Thomas folded his fingers together in front of him. "I'll hire you on a trial basis. Every day Monday to Friday, you will mop the floors in the hallway and the offices, clean all the counters. Also, on Monday, Wednesday, and Friday, you will sweep the car park and the entrance steps. Do you understand?"

"Yes please, sir. Thank you, sir."

"We have some cleaning materials on the first floor that you can use. If you need anything more, let me know." Thomas stood up. "Come with me and I will show you everything."

Emma followed him as he exited the office to his left. He stopped briefly to point in both directions. "You will mop all the hallway, okay? Take care to clean the corners."

"Yes please."

Thomas walked on. "After that, you will come to this laboratory. This is Lab One. Lab Two is downstairs. It's supposed to be the other way around, but they labeled it wrong." He shrugged and pulled a bunch of keys from his pocket. "You will have a key to enter."

Emma stepped in with him. The room was capacious and quite cold with the air conditioner on. Four long counters, two abreast with ample space between them, occupied most of the room, but several side tables projected from the outer edges of the room. At intervals along the counters were large pieces of equipment Emma had no idea about, but they looked complicated and expensive.

"You mop the floor, eh?" Thomas instructed. "Then you clean the counters very well. The mornings after your cleaning, I will come and inspect to make sure you have done a good job. If not, I sack you."

"Yes please. It will be well, sir."

Thomas smiled at her in an odd way. "We will see," he said. "You wipe the instruments and machines only on the outside. We used to have a special kind of spray for them, but we don't anymore. Don't open any of these instruments, and don't touch anything you're not supposed to. Look at this one. You see this dial? You must be careful not to move it or change the settings, you understand me."

"Yes please."

Thomas showed her some more instruments without explaining their function. In any case, at this point, Emma wouldn't understand much of what he said. She knew she must have appeared overwhelmed and intimidated because in fact, she was. She felt nervous, out of her depth, and underlying all that was a concern about Thomas. Why had he just hired her if he hadn't originally been looking for cleaning services?

"When will I start please?" she asked him.

"Tomorrow at five-thirty in the evening," he said. "By that time, most of the employees will be gone or leaving."

Emma had an impulse to ask where the employees were now, but she suppressed it. Thomas might find it odd or impertinent.

"Mary, first, you sweep the car park before it gets dark," Thomas continued, "and then you will come inside and clean everything like how I told you. You have to wear shoe covers, okay?"

"Yes please," Emma said.

And he smiled inscrutably at her again.

TWENTY

Ten months after

FOR JOJO, GETTING A job at Trasacco Valley took more effort than Emma had had to exert at the FSL. Initially, Sowah and the team thought Jojo could try posing as a freelance security guard looking for work. But the risk was relatively high that there would be no position available, in which case Jojo would be turned away and all options shut.

It was Manu who had come up with an idea: "I was looking at the Trasacco website this morning. They've just begun a new phase of construction they're going to call Trasacco Hills. Those construction sites always need a hand, even if it's unskilled work. Jojo could offer to do odd jobs and so on."

Jojo turned up at the job site the following morning. Trasacco Valley, which included Lady Araba's home, was a completed property, and since there was no further construction there, Jojo would have to make do with working at the adjacent Trasacco Hills, which now looked much like the Valley must have ten years ago—solitary houses materializing on rough, unpaved, slate-gray soil among clumps of hardy shrubs.

As Jojo approached the building area, he paused as he realized the sheer size of Trasacco's projects. The company owned vast stretches of land between here and the N1 Motorway, and yet in Jojo's estimation, still less than ten percent was being built upon.

But that would only be temporary as the leading edge of the homes moved forward steadily like an oncoming tide. One day in the future, Jojo imagined, every plot, every space on all this territory, would be taken up with homes.

For now, the buildings were in varying stages of construction, from the laying of a foundation to painting the exterior of a completed building and everything in between. Excavators and bulldozers moved back and forth, incessantly droning against the diesel engine blasts of the trucks hauling dirt away.

Workers were too busy inside and out of the homes to pay much attention to Jojo, and he wasn't quite sure where to start. He picked out two men standing off to the side. One was dressed dapperly in a dark suit and tie. The other, a shorter man holding a tablet in front of him, was wearing a checkered shirt and khaki pants.

Jojo approached tentatively, hovering as the men talked so earnestly with each other that they failed to notice him. He waited for them to finish their conversation, which seemed to go on forever. Then the taller, suited gentleman said, "Okay, Edinam, we'll talk, eh?"

They shook hands and the guy in the suit left. The other one, Edinam, was preoccupied with an image on his tablet.

"Please, good morning," Jojo said. He was wearing a backward baseball cap, distressed jeans, a dark-blue T-shirt, and scuffed trainers.

"Yes?" Edinam said impatiently, with a look at Jojo that translated to, *Who are you, and why are you bothering me?*

"Please, my name is Jojo," he said, removing his cap out of respect.

"Eh-heh? And what?"

"Please, I'm looking for a job."

"What kind of job?"

"I can do anything."

Edinam looked him over. "Are you strong?"

"Yes please," Jojo said with a good-natured laugh. "I can help the workers lift and carry, I can collect the *bola* and scrap metal—anything at all."

Edinam grunted, and then appeared to be lost in thought as he watched two workers at one house having an awkward time passing a large plank of wood up the scaffolding.

"Okay, maybe we can use you," he said. "I will talk to someone. Give me your phone number and I'll call you this evening. You say your name is Jojo?"

"Yes please."

Jojo didn't want to jinx his luck, but when he returned home in the evening, he was feeling confident that Edinam would take him on, and he was right. At 10:11 p.m., Edinam called to say, "You start at six tomorrow morning. Don't be late. You work twelve hours, I pay twenty-five *cedis* a day. Good night."

JOJO WASN'T LATE. He had bunked with a brother in Tema, much closer to Trasacco than where Jojo lived. That way, traffic was less of an unknown getting to work.

Jojo arrived so early at the construction site that no one else was around yet. He hung around, texting, 'gramming, and surfing on his phone. Closer to seven, a thick-bellied man arrived and looked at Jojo with an *Are you lost?* expression.

Jojo introduced himself. "Good morning, sir."

The man stared at him for a moment, and then his puzzlement dissipated. "Ah, yes, you're the one who will be helping us, eh?"

"Yes please."

"I'm Solomon," he said. "Okay, come with me. Let me show you what you'll be doing."

It was a collection of odd jobs, as Jojo had expected—helping to carry 2x4 planks and cement blocks, carting picks and shovels around, moving and supporting ladders, picking up scrap, trash, and empty paint cans and other biohazards, all at the command of practically everyone else: Jojo, come here, go there, bring that, take this, and so on.

The homes in Trasacco Valley, technically known as Trasacco

Phase One, were all valued at upward of a million dollars, including the late Lady Araba's mansion. Rows or clusters of those houses had names like Royal Gardens or Mahogany Row. That was where Jojo *really* needed to be. On the map, Trasacco Hills appeared somewhat close to the Valley, but in fact, there was no seamless way to go back and forth between the two. At the end of his first day at work, Jojo went home trying to think of a legitimate excuse to get from Trasacco Hills to the Valley.

THE NEXT DAY at work was hotter than the one before. By lunchtime, Jojo was pouring with sweat. He had drunk two full sachets of water to quench his thirst, and now he was famished. Solomon told Jojo about a good chop bar on Valley Road, somewhere near the entrance to the Valley complex. Jojo had barely an hour for lunch, so he trotted down a path that eventually led to the road and made a left. He found the chop bar, ate a quick meal of *red-red*, and sauntered over to the entrance to the Valley, which was an off-white seven-meter arch with a double wrought-iron entry framed with fluffy palm trees and trimmed hedges. Two sentry posts were present on either end of the arch.

A uniformed, fifty-five-ish security man in dark slacks, a light blue top, and a reflective lime-green vest was sweeping a few leaves to the side to keep the driveway spotless. Jojo ambled over in his friendly manner (he couldn't help it—that was the way he'd been born) and said hello. The other man replied with a smile. Jojo had that effect on people.

"*Ete sen?*" Jojo said.

"*Nyame adom,*" the other replied, putting the broom aside.

They introduced themselves. The security man's name was Peter, evidently the one Mr. Sowah had described. He was the boss for the first twelve-hour shift today, but sometimes he did the second graveyard shift. They stuck to Twi for the conversation.

"I am working at the Hills," Jojo told him. "Even, I just started yesterday."

"Oh, fine. You are welcome to Trasacco."

"*Medaase*. Your job, is it tough?"

Peter turned his bottom lip inside out contemplatively. "Not as such. Anyway, I like it. I've been doing it for a long time. This is the best post I've ever had."

"Yeah, I like security jobs," Jojo said. "For some time, I was a guard at the Barclays Bank on Ring Road." That wasn't true.

"Ah, okay." Peter showed interest. "We don't have any openings here right now, but maybe something will come."

Peter was distracted momentarily by one of the other guards asking a brief question, then returned to Jojo.

"Okay, then please, Mr. Peter," Jojo continued, "if you have any job for me, can you call me? Because I will love to work here."

Peter seemed impressed and exchanged numbers with Jojo.

"*Ei*," Jojo said, staring past the other man with admiration at the luxuriant complex beyond the entrance—palm trees at regular intervals, neat sidewalks flanked by low hedges and flowering shrubs, bougainvillea spilling over the walls of the residences. "I'm sure these houses will cost more than one hundred thousand dollars."

Peter laughed hard at that and called out to his colleague what Jojo had just said, which set up another round of laughter.

"Or am I wrong?" Jojo said, smiling sheepishly.

"Jojo," Peter said grinning, "these houses sell for over one million dollars."

"*One million!*" Jojo appeared stunned—well, he *was* stunned in any case, but he made his disbelief even more dramatic. "But is it Ghanaians living here, or only white people?" he asked.

Peter shook his head. "There aren't that many white people—Ghanaians, mostly. They have money, oo. Like some of these rap singers, musicians, football players, people like that."

"Wow," Jojo said in awe. "So, like if I live here and I want to sell my house, plenty of people will come to buy?"

Peter made a derisive noise with his lips. "They will come like a flowing river! They are rich and ready to spend money anytime, just like that."

"So, no empty house right now?"

Peter hesitated. "There's one, but because the lady who lived in the house died, no one wants to buy. They are afraid of ghosts."

"Ah, okay," Jojo said in his wide-eyed innocence. "Is it some old woman who died?"

Peter shook his head. "No, not some old woman! Do you know Lady Araba?"

Frowning, Jojo shook his head slowly. "I don't think so. Who is she?"

Before Peter could respond, a car pulled up and he leaned in toward the driver's window to ask the purpose of their visit. He nodded and waved them through before turning back to Jojo. "Yes, Lady Araba, she was, em, this thing, whad'you call it—fashion designer." His expression clouded. "Somebody killed her in the house. Almost one year now."

"What!" Jojo said. "*Here* in Trasacco?"

Peter nodded.

"And so, have they caught the one who killed her?" Jojo asked.

"The police say it was Lady Araba's driver."

"So, if they can't sell the lady's house," Jojo said, "what will happen?"

Peter shrugged. "I have no idea."

"Like if I have the money," Jojo said gleefully, "I will buy it. I'm not afraid of ghosts."

"Okay," Peter said with a snort. "We will lock you in that house one night and then we will see if you can really stay inside by yourself."

The two men laughed, but Jojo thought the challenge, even made in jest, might prove useful. There was only one problem: he really was afraid of ghosts.

TWENTY-ONE

Ten months after

A LITTLE PAST 5 P.M., Emma began sweeping the FSL court-yard, car park, and driveway, gathering the trash in small mounds before combining it all in a large plastic sack, which she took out to large metal bins outside the compound for collection later in the week. That over, she went to the cupboard on the first floor to get the cleaning supplies. As she backed out, grappling with a long-handled broom, a mop, bucket, and industrial-strength detergent, she started as she bumped into someone behind her. She spun around to find Thomas in her space.

"Oh, it's you, sir!" she exclaimed, touching her chest and releasing a sigh of relief.

"Sorry," he said. "I scared you?"

"Oh, no," Emma said, "it's okay, sir."

Thomas wasn't moving, and Emma found herself partially wedged between him and the cupboard. "I'm now going to clean the verandah, please," she said awkwardly.

"Follow me first." He turned. "I have a meeting with someone in about thirty minutes. I want you to tidy up my office before he comes."

"Yes please," Emma said, following him down the hallway with the cleaning stuff. "I will do that."

He unlocked his door and took a seat at his desk. "Carry on. I'm just doing some work here."

"Yes please," Emma said. "Please, I'm going to fetch water and come."

She returned with the bucket half filled and began to mop the tiled floor, aware that Thomas's eyes were on her. Emma was desperately uncomfortable.

"There's a spot here that needs cleaning," Thomas said, indicating the corner closest to his desk.

"Yes please." She approached, expecting him to vacate his swivel chair and give her some space to get by.

Instead, he wheeled back only a few inches. "You can pass," he said.

Facing him, she squeezed by, her jeans brushing against his pant legs. He was slouched in his chair with his legs apart. Emma's face grew hot as she tried maneuvering in a space that was too close.

"Please, can I—"

"Can you what?"

"I want to clean it well, so if you can—"

"If I can move?" Thomas laughed and stood up. "Okay, if you say so, Madam Mary."

He sounded mocking. He leaned against the wall and stared, and Emma wished to God he would stop.

"Are you schooling?" Thomas asked.

She squeezed out the mop. "Schooling?"

"Yes," he said. "Are you taking some online courses or attending classes in the daytime? You seem very smart. I'm sure this isn't all you can do."

Emma had gone over this with the rest of the team. The consensus had been that "Mary" should appear vulnerable but motivated. "Please, I want to make some money before," she said, "and then next year I will go for classes to enter college. I didn't finish senior high."

"I see," Thomas said. "Why?"

Emma avoided his gaze. "Please, I got pregnant."

"Ah," he said knowingly. "How old is the child now?"

"She's now five, please."

"Oh, nice. And the father, where is he?"

Emma shook her head. No verbal answer was necessary.

"Okay," Thomas said. "Then I wish you luck."

"Yes please. Thank you."

"I see that you work hard," he commented.

She smiled. "Thanks."

He looked at his watch. "Okay, finish up."

Emma wiped the side tables down and tidied up the few old magazines lying around. Someone knocked on the door and opened it. He was bespectacled and short, very dark in color, with receding hair and a weak jaw. He carried a briefcase and was dressed in a polo shirt, light blue jacket, and dress slacks.

"Kingsley!" Thomas said. "Come in. How are you?"

"I am blessed, thanks be to God. And you?"

They shook hands and seated themselves next to each other as Emma was collecting her stuff. The visitor, Kingsley, paid little or no attention to her.

"You can go now, Mary," Thomas said.

"Yes please. Thank you."

Emma moved out, deliberately leaving a rag behind out of sight on the floor. She pulled the door behind her but didn't shut it all the way. Her ear to the small gap between the door and the jamb, she eavesdropped.

"How was the trip from Cape Coast?" Thomas asked.

"It was fine, thanks. How far with your negotiations with the minister?"

"One moment. Let me shut the door well. Why didn't the girl close it?"

Emma heard Thomas's footsteps, jumped back, and moved away, bending over the bucket to appear busy in case her boss looked out into the hallway. He didn't. Emma leaned the broom up against the wall and returned to the door. All she could hear was muffled sounds. She knocked lightly and opened.

"Yes? What is it?" Thomas said, irritated.

"Sorry, sir," Emma said. "Please, I left a cleaning rag here."

"Okay, hurry up. You are disturbing us."

She located the rag and began to leave as the two men returned to conversation.

"He's saying they have to cut the grant to our forensic lab at UCC," Kingsley said, sounding frustrated. "At most, then, we will produce six graduates this year."

"Where do they go on graduation? Do you place them?"

"We try to. In any case, they all end up in one of the private DNA labs in Accra and Kumasi. They mostly do paternity testing. But Thomas, it's of the utmost urgency that we try and get some of our graduates into the police force as forensic experts."

"We've talked about it. It's a slow process. CID is always stretched thin. The Ministry of the Interior would have to give us a lot more money for us to bring on officers as forensic experts. You know the private labs must pay these people four or five times the salary we offer. Why should they come here? There's no incentive."

"That's why I say, privatize the FSL."

Thomas looked uncomfortable.

"You too, why?" Kingsley said, showing amusement and irritation at the same time. "You'll be okay. They'll find another position for you. You're not going anywhere."

"I know, but . . . well, you can't expect me to start promoting privatization, can you? That's like chopping my own leg off."

The two men laughed, obviously relieving some of the tension.

Emma left the room, and as she pulled the door shut quietly, she heard Kingsley say, "We are both being strangled, my friend."

She felt an itch to eavesdrop further, but she had the jitters that she might get caught. She instead swept the verandah on the first floor, then proceeded to the second. Midway through cleaning and mopping the corridor, she heard a vehicle start up, then a second. Looking down from the window, she saw that both men were departing.

• • •

WHEN THOMAS HAD first shown Emma the ropes in the first-floor lab, she had unobtrusively looked for CCTV cameras and had seen none. Now, as she unlocked the door and entered, she satisfied herself that she hadn't missed any hidden security cameras, even if it was rather unlikely those would be here.

At the door, she slipped on her gloves and shoe and hair covers and began working on the first of the countertops, which were all made of a beige-colored Formica. With a diluted bleach solution, Emma wiped down the surfaces carefully, avoiding touching the instruments, as Thomas had instructed. One of them, about the size of a large desktop printer, had a red upper section and a lower panel of multiple LED lights and switches designated with the words ELECTRONIC GAS PRESSURE CONTROLS and other things Emma didn't understand. The instrument was called SRI 8610C GAS CHROMATOGRAPH. With her phone, she took a photograph quickly, even furtively. A part of her felt she was being watched.

There was more: a HIGH-PERFORMANCE LIQUID CHROMATOGRAPH and INFRARED SPECTROPHOTOMETER. Emma took photos of them as well. At the end of the counter was a sink and tap, both of which she thoroughly scrubbed and rinsed.

Forgetting about the cleaning for a moment, Emma went around the lab's periphery, where there were work and washing stations, rows of different-colored chemical bottles, and microscopes—huge, double-barreled instruments nothing like the small ones Emma remembered from school biology. She looked for the manufacturer—Zeiss, which she presumed was German.

On another of the counters was a glass chamber the size of a small fridge labeled CYANOSAFE. Inside the chamber were hooks and what looked like clothespins hanging from thin metal bars. Emma peered at a plastic cup hanging from one hook. That looked interesting. She took a photo.

At the end of the lab was a door labeled FORENSIC BIOLOGY/ DNA. Emma tried it, but it was locked. She peeped through a small window in the door. There, too, lots of instruments and devices. She could just make out the label on one of them—7500

REAL-TIME PCR. To the right side, Emma could see a large, solid door, at the top of which were the words: FREEZER: NO UNAUTHORIZED ENTRY. She had a feeling this was where she needed to be to check on the existence, or lack thereof, of the DNA from Lady Araba's crime scene. The only question was how.

TWENTY-TWO

One year before

DURING THE TWO WEEKS after Araba had told Augustus she wanted nothing more to do with him, he turned in desolation to the bottle. The sun had just set one Saturday when he began to feel terribly ill. His stomach was aching. He must have had a fever, because he felt like his face was on fire. When looked at his reflection in the bathroom mirror, he gasped at how dreadful he appeared. Was he imagining it, or had the whites of his eyes really turned yellow? Was he hallucinating? A rush of nausea enveloped him. He fell to his knees and threw up ghastly material that looked like a slurry of coffee grounds.

I'm dying, Augustus thought. He felt so awful he almost wanted to. He crawled to the bedroom and climbed up on the bed, where he lay very still. His breathing was rapid and shallow, with a grunt on every exhalation.

He had to call someone. The first person who came to mind was Araba, even if she'd told him to stay away from her. Where was his phone? He realized he'd left it in the sitting room and dragged himself out of the bed, holding onto the walls and furniture to steady himself.

Araba answered only after two attempts to reach her. "Gus, we agreed you wouldn't call anymore," she said.

"I know," he said hoarsely. "But I'm sick. I've been throwing up, and I think I have a fever. Araba, please—I need help, and you're the only one I can depend on. I've got to get to a hospital."

There was a pause, and then Araba relented. "Okay, wait there. Kweku and I will get to you as soon as we can."

"Thank you," Augustus said. "You're an angel. I love you."

To MAKE IT easier to get into the vehicle, Araba had Kweku-Sam drive the Audi instead of the high-profile Range Rover. Augustus needed their help to get to the car, his balance precarious. Araba had never seen him look so sick. His eyes were bloodshot and yellow at the same time. She didn't know what that meant, but he was obviously in bad shape.

She checked him into Nyaho Medical Centre, the best hospital closest to them. Several heads turned to look at Araba as she entered behind the nurse's aide pushing Augustus along in a wheelchair. While the staff attended to him, Araba went to the payment office to settle the requisite minimum fee.

Once Augustus was checked in, he was placed temporarily in the intake ward for monitoring. Araba sat and waited in the hallway, watching nursing staff, aides, lab techs, and physicians both young and old going back and forth. After almost two hours, a staff member popped out to say Araba could go in to see the patient.

Augustus was hooked up to an IV and heart monitor in a spotless, oddly empty ward. A public hospital would've had patients in every bed, busy as a beehive with people running about in unspecified chaos.

Augustus seemed to be sleeping as Araba came to his bedside, but he must have sensed her, because he opened his eyes.

"Hi," he said weakly.

"How are you feeling?" she asked.

He smiled wanly. "Like shit run over."

She gently took his hand. "Did the doctor come in?"

"Yes. She looked like she was sixteen. That's when you realize you're getting old."

Araba pulled up a chair and sat next to him. "Does she have any of the blood tests back?"

"Yes," Augustus said, "but even before that, they knew what was wrong: alcoholic hepatitis."

"That sounds serious."

"It is," Augustus said, turning from his back to the side. "She said my liver is twice the size it should be, and if I continue drinking, one day it will stop working altogether."

"What happened, Augustus?"

"It was . . . it was after you'd told me you wouldn't see me again. I went to pieces and started drinking nonstop. I'm not blaming you; I'm just telling you what pushed me over the edge."

"I get that, but you need to take responsibility for your own actions too, and I don't think you are."

"I can," he said, "but I need you by my side."

"No, you need to attend Alcoholics Anonymous," she countered. "I can't help you, but they can."

He pulled her down to his cheek. "Araba, you can help me just by being there for me. Please. I'm begging you."

Araba sighed. "This is your last chance, Gus. I can't afford to drop everything just to take you to a hospital every time you go overboard."

"I promise you, I really will stop drinking. Having you there will ground me."

"All right," she said.

Augustus's eyes moistened, and he squeezed her hand. "Thank you so much," he said.

"Promise me you'll go to those AA meetings."

"I do, and I will. I'm going to be sober from now on."

They gazed at one another for a moment.

"My parents will be here soon," Augustus said.

"You called them?"

"I didn't want to, but sooner is better than later. They'll probably hear about it eventually. Everyone is such a blabbermouth in Accra."

Araba clicked her tongue. "It won't be long before a whole bunch of people know I brought you in."

"Give me a kiss," he said, and she kissed him on the lips.

"I'm sorry," he whispered. "Please forgive me for everything I've put you through. I love you, Araba. I really do."

After a while, their mood lightened, and they began to watch a fun Nollywood movie on Araba's iPhone. Holding hands, they laughed at the antics of a clueless villager trying to find love in the big city. In the middle of that, Augustus received a text from his mother that she and Julius were almost there. He showed the message to Araba, and they looked at each other with the same question in mind. Should Araba be there when Augustus's parents arrived, or should she leave before that?

"Stay," Augustus said firmly.

"Are you sure? I don't want any trouble."

"I won't allow it," Augustus said fiercely. "We've decided to stay together, and that's *our* decision. I'm an adult, you're an adult. No one, not even our parents, can force us to do otherwise."

WHEN JULIUS SEEZA and his wife, Caroline, entered Augustus's room and saw Araba, they froze, their faces turning dark as a thunderstorm sky.

"What in God's name are you doing here?" Caroline snapped.

"Mama, Papa," Augustus said calmly, "please sit down and we can have a civilized discussion."

"Civilized discussion," Julius repeated in disbelief. "Civilized discussion? Just yesterday you were promising to turn your life around, and here you are with the same old detritus that has pulled you down in the first place—"

"Pulled him down?" Araba interrupted. "Justice Seeza, it's me who has buoyed up your son time and time again. The terrible effects of his upbringing under you and your wife made him turn to the bottle—that is what I have been saving him from over and over."

"*What?*" Julius said.

"Everything from your mouth is rotten, Lady Araba," Caroline said, her face twisted with contempt. "When you speak, all we smell is garbage. You are a bitch of the highest order. Get your claws out of my son or you will be sorry, very sorry—mark my words. I will not take insults or abuse from you after the havoc you have wreaked in my son's precious life. The reason he is here in this hospital is *you*—"

"Mama, that isn't true!" Augustus said, sitting up straighter in bed. "You can't blame this on Araba or anyone else, for that matter. I take full responsibility."

"She poisons you," Caroline said, her face bitter as bile. "She fills your head with propaganda and turns you against those who love you the most. That conflict is what is eating you alive, and it's why you've been drinking. The first step to take to conquer this affliction is to wash yourself of the past and leave behind everything and everyone that has been to your detriment. That includes her."

They stared at each other, opposing armies at an impasse.

Then Araba, cool as watermelon, said, "I'm not going anywhere."

"You will regret saying that," Julius said, pointing at her. "Come, Caroline. We are leaving."

At the door, Caroline turned and addressed Araba for the final time. "There is a special place in hell for people like you. I hope you get there very soon."

TWENTY-THREE

Ten months after

JOJO PEEPED INTO THE window of the Trasacco Valley security booth and greeted Peter with an ebullient smile. "Good afternoon, boss."

Peter looked up. "Hey, Jojo! Come in."

Jojo went through the open gate under the arch and around to the booth, where the interior space seemed less than Jojo had estimated looking from the outside. Peter was filling out some papers on a clipboard. They shook hands with the traditional terminal snap of the fingers.

"How be?" Peter said.

"By His grace, my brotha. How are you doing?"

"I'm blessed, Jojo. You know, God is good."

"For sure. Today my boss said there's no work this afternoon, so I'm going home early."

"Oh, okay," Peter said. "I'm going to the other side to check the back gate. You can come with me if you're not in a hurry."

"Not at all."

Peter let one of the other guys know he would be back in a bit, and Jojo walked alongside him as he took the road straight ahead. Jojo glanced behind and noticed two CCTV cameras mounted on a mast to the right side of the gate.

The roadway was perfectly paved, lined by a low trimmed

hedge, on the other side of which the grass was green and well-tended. Beyond that, the fences enclosing each property were topped with flowering bushes of bougainvillea or hibiscus. Towering over all of these were palm trees planted at regular intervals.

"How you keep the place fine, oo," Jojo praised Peter. "The grass and everything."

He smiled. "Not really me. Our landscaping master is Ismael. Maybe we'll meet him on the way."

"Okay, cool. And the house where the woman died, which one is that?"

"It's near the back gate where we're going. I'll show it to you."

They walked for a while without saying anything, Jojo looking around in admiration of the huge homes painted vibrant sun yellows, subtle olives, or sky blues with white trims, rust reds, and even lily pinks. *The kind of money one must have in a place like this*, he thought.

Jojo heard a mechanical drone in the near distance. He saw the source of the noise as they turned the corner down a new block of houses. Ahead, a man wearing goggles was shaping a shrub with a powered hedge trimmer.

"That's Ismael," Peter said. He called out, "*Ayekoo!*"

Ismael turned, grinned, and switched off the trimmer. "*Yaaey!*"

"How goes it?" Peter greeted him.

"I dey oo," Ismael said, grinning.

He was sweating heavily. He was wiry and strong, around thirty, and seemed friendly. He had a tribal mark on his right cheek and a chip in one of his front teeth that slightly marred an otherwise easy smile.

"Meet Jojo," Peter said. "He just started working at the Hills. Jojo, this is Ismael, the best gardener in the world."

"Oh, don't mind him," Ismael said bashfully to Jojo, laughing. "You are welcome here."

"Thanks," Jojo said. "But in fact, I have to agree with Peter—how you make the place is very nice. Congrats."

"Thank you, thank you. You know, I like my job very much."

"But do you do everything by yourself?" Jojo asked. "Because the place is big."

Ismael smiled. "Not everything. I bring in other guys sometimes, when there's a lot to do. In the rainy season, the weeds grow very fast."

That season had already begun, but the weather hadn't cooled down as much as expected. Jojo mopped his forehead with his handkerchief. "Will you also be working at the Hills when they're ready to start planting?" he asked.

Ismael seemed doubtful. "I'm not sure. Maybe, but no one has told me anything about it. They might use a contractor landscaper."

"Ismael is a Trasacco employee from the early days," Peter explained, "but now they do things a little differently—they use more third parties."

"I see," Jojo said.

"Where are you going now?" Ismael asked Peter.

"To check on the back gate. Have you seen if it's working today?"

Ismael shook his head. "It's not, but I think yesterday it was okay. I'll go with you."

Carrying his hedge trimmer easily in one hand, the groundskeeper joined the other two men on their walkabout.

As they reached the rear side of the complex, Peter said to Jojo, "We're having too many problems with the back gate. It's supposed to have a vehicle sensor so it opens as the car approaches and the person can leave the complex."

"Why do you have a rear gate?" Jojo asked.

"Good question," Peter said. "Personally, I would get rid of it. They wanted it so people deeper inside the complex have an easier, faster exit by using the back, because the front gate is a little far for them. But sometimes the sensor doesn't work, and the gate itself is always getting stuck. They keep repairing it, and then it just breaks down again." They were in front of the notorious gate now, which, like the front entrance to the Valley, was made of wrought iron painted black, though not as high. Jojo deduced from the chain and motor housing at about calf level that the gate was the sliding type.

Peter knelt at the motor box and opened it with a key to peer at the device's innards. He pressed a button, and the gate slid to the right rather sluggishly all the way to its end point. When Peter pressed another button, the gate started back in the other direction and looked as if it was fully functioning until it stopped a little past halfway.

Peter shook his head in disgust. "There it goes again. This time, I think it's the chain." He leaned over to the rear side of the box and fiddled with the chain to no avail. "I'll disconnect the box and we can manually push the gate shut."

Jojo and Ismael helped him. Without the mechanical advantage of the motor, the gate was quite heavy.

When they were done, Peter said, "I will put an out-of-order sign here."

Ismael nodded. "Yes."

"And then the residents will come complain to me that they don't like the gate to be locked," Peter said ruefully.

"Is that so?" Jojo said.

"Oh, yes," Peter said, using his hand to flick off sweat from his forehead. "They don't think about their safety, just their convenience. But when someone gets into the compound and commits a crime, they come to complain again. We never win. They treat us like shit."

Jojo was surprised by this flash of anger from Peter, who otherwise had seemed laid-back and not easily flustered. This aspect of his work, his treatment by the Trasacco residents, was obviously a sore spot. Had Lady Araba treated him that way?

"Like when Lady Araba was murdered," Ismael said, almost under his breath.

Jojo looked at him. "Come again?"

"The residents here—and Lady Araba's family too, by the way—say it's security's fault that someone was able to kill her,"

Ismael explained, "because the murderer must have entered the complex through this back gate."

"Was it giving trouble at that time too?" Jojo asked.

"No," Peter said, "it was fine. But still, people tried to blame us by saying, even if the gate was closed, we should have been doing a better job of patrolling the place."

"And what about the front entrance?" Jojo asked. "Did anyone come through that evening who might have killed Lady Araba?"

"A little before nine that night, Kweku brought her home in the SUV," Peter said, "and by nine-twenty he was leaving on foot. After that, we had a few residents returning home up to about midnight, and after that it was quiet."

Jojo gestured to the CCTV on a mast about a hundred meters away. "Did the CCTV cameras pick up anything?"

"The cameras were working, but the DVR wasn't recording," Peter said. "It's an old machine that was here already when I started to work for Trasacco. It's still there in the security room, but we have a new one now."

"How was she like?" Jojo said conversationally. "I mean Lady Araba."

Ismael glanced at Peter, who spoke first. "She was a good woman. Better than all the other people here put together. Not so, Ismael?"

He nodded. "Yes, it's true. Very nice woman."

"And beautiful?" Jojo said coyly.

"Wow, I tell you, brother!" Peter said. "When you see her in real life, eh? You will be amazed! The skin, the hair, the shape of the body. She was truly blessed."

"And she loved plants and flowers too," Ismael said. "That's one thing I liked about her."

Peter shot him a sly glance and winked at Jojo. "This guy loved her."

"Me?" Ismael said in exaggerated consternation. "Not me, oo! You, rather!"

The two men went through a cycle of mock accusations and

denials. *It was a good question though,* Jojo thought to himself. Had either of them had a fatal attraction to Araba?

Peter's phone rang and he walked off to take the call. "*Chaley,* I'm going back to the front, okay?" he told the other two.

"Okay, boss," Jojo said, smiling brightly. "Thank you, eh? Maybe I'll see you tomorrow."

"The whole thing pains him," Ismael said, watching Peter walk away. "I think he still kind of blames himself for Lady Araba's death. He feels that, somehow, he could have prevented it. For me, the issue is this stupid automatic gate. I like Peter, but, come on, you just have to be tough and go to the Trasacco people and tell them, *no,* we should lock the gate permanently, and then we won't have any issue of people sneaking in."

"I see what you're saying," Jojo said. "You're right."

"Yes, of course I'm right," Ismael said fiercely, but a slight smile crept to his lips.

"So, it was you and Peter who discovered the body?" Jojo asked, sensing an opening now that they had exhausted the subject of the gate.

"Yeah," Ismael said, taking a seat on the grass along the curb. "This is how it happened. I will tell you."

Jojo sat next to him.

"Like I said," Ismael began, "Lady Araba liked plants and flowers. She knew I worked at a garden shop, and so she asked me to bring two flowerpots to put on the terrace outside her bedroom, and then after that I was going to plant something nice for her. Monday morning by seven o'clock, I took a ladder and climbed it to her terrace. It was when I was arranging the flowerpots that I saw through the window she was there on the bed." Ismael shook his head. "It was a terrible sight. She was lying on her back across the bed with plenty of blood around her head. Her face was like . . . it was swollen." Ismael formed the shape of a ball with his hands.

"So, I ran back down to the front, where her driver, Kweku-Sam, was waiting for her to come down, and I told him to go and fetch Peter quick. When Peter arrived, I asked him if he had a key to the house and he said no, so I broke the glass door to get inside."

"When you got inside the room, were you afraid?" Jojo asked.

Ismael shook his head. "Naw, but seeing her like that shocked me."

"Did you touch her?"

"Yeah." Ismael held Jojo's gaze. "She was cold—not like ice, but you get me."

"Yes." Jojo looked around. "Is Lady Araba's house like any of these ones?"

Ismael shook his head. "No. Come, I'll show you the place."

The two men walked side by side in relative silence. Jojo was aware of birds twittering, a sound often missed in Accra. He felt as if the air here was as clean and clear as Wli Falls. Did rich people breathe separate oxygen from everyone else?

"Here is her place," Ismael said, pointing.

From the rear, Lady Araba's house was the fourth on their left. It was pale orange with a red tile roof. White columns framed the front entrance portico from the ground to the second floor. The two-car garage was on the far right. Projecting outward was a large bay window divided in three.

Two cars sat in the tiled driveway—a Hyundai SUV and a glistening emerald-green sports car of a type Jojo had never seen before. Two people were emerging from the front door—a young Ghanaian woman and a forty-five-ish-year-old balding white man with a carelessly trimmed graying beard.

"I think someone is trying to buy the house," Ismael said. "I know the woman. Her name is Rita—she's a realtor with Trasacco who brings people around to see the place. Lady Araba's family has been trying hard to sell it."

As the woman talked with the man, she caught sight of Ismael and beckoned to him. Jojo followed him as he went up to them. Indeed, the white man was interested in making a purchase, but he had a question for the groundskeeper: Would Ismael be able to replace the grassy lawn with succulent plants? Ismael said, yes, of course—no problem.

"Good," the man said.

"Anything you want to change," Ismael said, "just let me know."

The man smiled at him for the first time. "Thank you."

"You are welcome, sir."

Rita thanked Ismael as well, and then began showing the man the garage after remotely opening the door.

Jojo lowered his voice to ask Ismael, "Where is the room where the woman was killed?"

"It's upstairs at the back. You can't see it from here."

"Can we go there?"

"By all means."

They changed direction, passing the big bay window, through which Jojo could see expensive and luxurious furniture.

"That's the living room," Ismael said.

"Wow," Jojo said. "Where I live with my family can fit inside there five times."

Ismael made a face. "You see, oo," he said, expressing the cruel irony.

The kitchen, which they passed next, seemed unnecessarily large in Jojo's humble opinion, but then, if you could afford to buy all that space, why not?

They turned the corner.

"The storeroom is there," Ismael said, pointing, "and these are the staff quarters."

On their left, a flank of fully grown trees and a tall hedge would prevent an intruder from being spotted.

"Did the lady have a houseboy?" Jojo asked.

"House girl," Ismael corrected him. "Amanua."

"And she didn't hear anything?"

"She wasn't here. She was back in her hometown for a funeral at that time."

"The killers must have known their way around the place," Jojo said.

"Yes," Ismael said soberly.

Jojo noticed he didn't comment on the reference to more than one killer. "So, what do you think really happened to Lady Araba?"

"*Chaley*," Ismael said, dropping his voice as if other people were around, "her life was a disaster—I mean, the people around her. That man, Augustus Seeza, her so-called boyfriend—drunk all the time. And they used to fight sometimes too."

"Did you ever see or hear them fighting?" Jojo asked.

"One time," Ismael said. "When I was taking Lady Araba some flowers, they were near the garage shouting at each other."

"You said you were taking her some flowers?"

"Yeah. Like I said, she liked them, so I used to bring her some from my shop."

"Ah, okay. That was nice of you."

Ismael smiled, but said nothing. That moment felt odd to Jojo.

"People say Augustus Seeza killed Lady Araba," Jojo said. "What do you think?"

"It's him," Ismael said. "The man was jealous because people said the lady had more than one lover."

They paused as they reached the kitchen terrace at the rear side of the house.

"More than one lover?" Jojo asked. "Like who?"

"Peter says Araba's assistant was fucking her too. He used to come here at night sometimes."

"But then maybe the assistant might have killed her," Jojo pointed out.

"Anyway, that's true," Ismael conceded. "But I still think it's Augustus, and they will never get him or send him to prison because he's an important guy and his family has money. I'm sure they paid the police to arrest Kweku-Sam."

"You don't think Kweku killed her?"

Ismael made a disdainful sound with his lips. "Not at all. To me, he was the most loyal person in her life. But you know, this is how the Ghana police do. They find some guy who can never pay for a good lawyer and then tell the public he is the guilty one. Then they send him to prison and that's the end of it." Ismael dusted his hands symbolically. "Let's go."

The backyard wasn't as spacious as the front, but it was just as pleasant, with shrubs and bushes Ismael had kept pruned and shaped. At the garden terrace, Jojo recognized that the living room at the front of the house wasn't visible from where they stood. Instead, Ismael explained, they were looking at the dining room and "family" room. A few meters on, he pointed upward. "You see? I carried the flowerpots up the ladder to the terrace. That's when I saw her."

Wondering what emotions were going through Ismael's mind, Jojo contemplated him for a moment, then returned his attention to the terrace. Even ten months after the crime with the house now empty, he wanted to get inside for a feel of the place, but he felt it would be too much at this point to ask Ismael or Peter. Later, perhaps.

And then Jojo had an idea.

TWENTY-FOUR

Ten months after

Friday just before 6 p.m., Emma got her cleaning supplies ready to work on the first-floor lab. She filled her mobile bucket with water, added some bleach, and picked up the mop. She was about to pass Thomas's office but paused when she noticed he hadn't left for home yet. His door was about one-quarter open and Emma saw him standing by a small desktop refrigerator reading a document. Emma wondered what Thomas kept in the refrigerator.

At that moment, he turned and almost caught Emma staring before she looked quickly away and bent over to appear busy with the mop.

"Emma?"

She straightened up. "Yes, sir?"

"Anything wrong?"

"No please. I'm going to clean the lab now."

"No, wait—clean my office first."

"Yes please."

Emma dipped the mop, wrung it out, and entered the room with the bucket. Thomas sat askew on one corner of his desk, and as she passed, he grasped Emma's waist and pulled her to him.

"I saw you looking at me," he said softly. "You like me?"

The bucket was just behind Emma's right foot. She moved her

heel back and up, tipping the bucket over. Water gushed onto the floor.

Thomas jumped away. "Shit."

"Oh!" Emma cried. "Sorry, my boss! Let me clean it."

He looked annoyed as she feverishly got to work mopping up the mini-flood. "Hurry up and finish," he said crossly, leaving the room to stand in the hallway.

"Yes please."

She mopped as quickly as she could, left the office with another apology to Thomas, hurried to the nearest washroom, and locked it behind her. She shuddered as a wave of revulsion washed over her. Although Thomas's unwanted advance didn't come close to the attempted rape she had experienced a year ago, it was enough to bring the traumatic memory flooding back.

What should she do? Realistically, she should relay this episode to Sowah, but because he eschewed putting his investigators in danger, she knew he would pull her off the case. And then what? He would give it to one of the guys. Oh, no. This was *her* assignment. She would handle this and see it through.

Emma splashed her face with cold water, patted dry, squared her shoulders, exited the bathroom, and went to the lab to begin her cleaning.

Emma finished up, left the lab, and prepared to go upstairs to the second floor. As she did so, Thomas stepped out of his office ahead of her, turned right down the hall away from Emma, and went to the washroom—the same one Emma had just been in. Thomas had left his door open—or halfway, at least. Emma glanced in and saw several items out on the counter beside the mini-refrigerator and wondered if that was where they'd come from.

What were they?

Emma's elementary school teacher used to say, *She who hesitates is lost.*

With a glance down the hall, Emma quickly entered the office and went straight to the counter where the objects lay: four small paper envelopes and a medium-sized paper bag. Still cold from the refrigerator, they were evidence bags containing various items. Each had a label filled out with handwritten information: case number, investigating officer, victim, date and time of recovery, and who had released the evidence to whom and when. The investigating officer was DS Isaac N. Boateng, and the victim was Araba Tagoe.

Emma heard the washroom door open again, and Thomas's footsteps as he returned. Heart racing, Emma pulled her phone out and snapped a picture of each of the evidence containers, replacing them more or less the way she had found them, then turned and ran for the door. Thomas couldn't be more than a few steps away—she wouldn't make it.

They almost collided in the doorway. Both stopped, their gazes locked. Emma's stomach dropped. Thomas's chin lifted and his eyes narrowed in suspicion. "What are you doing here?"

Emma still had a dust rag in her hand. She waved it at him. "Please, I forgot this in your office."

"That's the second time you've done that." He looked her up and down. "What is that in your hand?"

"My phone, please."

"Why? For what?"

"Oh—just my friend texted me," she said, her face hot.

"So, you're texting while working." Thomas looked at her with scorching disapproval. "I don't like your behavior, you hear me? You are not performing well at all. Have you completed your work for today?"

"Yes please."

"Then put all the supplies away and leave. Don't come back."

TWENTY-FIVE

Forty-eight hours after

AFTER TWO DAYS OF explosive media coverage of Lady Araba's death, Dr. Caroline Seeza was distressed by the vitriol heaped on her son. On GhanaWeb.com, a news outlet and troll factory, she saw some of the foulest language and most outrageous accusations she had ever seen directed toward Augustus.

A scenario popular with the website's readers was that Augustus was a philanderer, and when Araba confronted him, he flew into a rage and murdered her. They called Augustus a drunkard, murderer, piece of shit, wife abuser, ignorant broadcaster, liar, AIDS spreader, and an adulterer. On the opposing side were some who were certain that Araba had been seeing one or more men besides Augustus, and so he killed her out of jealousy. They sided with Augustus, going as far as calling Araba an *ashawo*—prostitute—who had gotten what she deserved.

But there was other nonsense as well—claims, for example, that since Augustus had grilled so many government officials from both parties on his show, the murder must have been politically motivated. GhanaWeb wasn't a bastion of advanced thinking.

Caroline, obsessing over this on her laptop in the bedroom, started when Julius came up behind her.

"What are you reading?" he asked.

She quickly clicked another tab, pulling up a medical website. "Nothing much. Just the usual stuff."

He put his hand on her shoulder. "I hope you're not reading that GhanaWeb rubbish. I told you to stop that. It only makes you upset."

She turned to him in earnest. "I simply hate what they're saying about Augustus."

"Ignore it!" Julius said heatedly. "These are idle, empty-headed people with nothing better to do all day than spread lies and gossip. They aren't worth your time. We know our boy didn't do it, and that's all that matters."

"Of course—*we* know that, but . . ." Caroline sighed, looking distressed. "What are the police saying? I mean, do they consider Augustus the prime suspect because of his history with Araba? I don't want them coming after him and making him suffer for something he didn't do."

"No one is coming after Augustus," Julius said quietly. "I can guarantee that."

Caroline raised her eyebrows. "Really? How?"

Julius brushed the question aside. "I've taken care of it. Don't worry yourself for another minute."

He departed the room, leaving his wife staring at the door in his wake.

The previous day

DIRECTOR GENERAL POLICE Madame Tawiah received Justice Julius Seeza in her office on the fifth floor of the CID Headquarters building on Ring Road East.

"How are you, sir?" she said, smiling. "It's been such a long time. Please, have a seat. Would you like some water?"

"Thank you very much, but no."

Julius and Tawiah had come to know each other over the decades as she testified in his court as the arresting officer in various criminal cases. He had seen her rise steadily through the ranks. Now, she was the first woman ever to have attained the position of director-general of the CID. He could see her artistic touch in the huge office: plants in all four corners of the room, furniture that went well together, paintings, and the carpet—flourishes that her male counterparts could never have come up with.

Julius sat gingerly. His arthritic spine was giving him hell. "I don't think I've had the chance to officially congratulate you on your auspicious promotion to director-general," he said, getting as comfortable as he could. "Very well done. I have the utmost respect for you."

"Thank you, sir. I appreciate that so much. And please, how is Madam Caroline? Is she still practicing?"

"Oh, yes," Julius said, with a light laugh. "You know my wife won't stop working until it's physically impossible."

Tawiah smiled. She had always looked rather desiccated to Julius, but her laugh was delightful, like the tinkle of crystal. "God bless her. Please, give my regards to her."

"Thank you, I will. What I came to see you about, Madam Tawiah, concerns the murder of Lady Araba."

"Yes, of course. Terrible affair."

"As you are aware, my son Augustus was closely involved with Lady Araba for approximately three years before her death, and I'm sure you've heard innuendo being cast around that he might have been involved in her killing."

Tawiah tut-tutted with disapproval. "All unjustified talk, sir."

"Of course, I'm aware." He paused. "I wonder, and of course this may be very sensitive information, but to your knowledge, has there been any official police interest in my son?"

Tawiah was firm. "No, sir. That kind of thing would have come under my radar."

"Thank you, Director-General. That's good to hear."

"As a matter of fact, if you could keep this confidential, we already have the prime suspect in custody—Lady Araba's chauffeur. He was seen exiting the house that night, and we now have a signed confession. What I'm hoping is that the DNA evidence submitted will help us finalize the case against him."

Julius felt a pang in his chest. *DNA. What DNA?* "Ah, I wasn't aware that potential DNA evidence was collected," he said.

"Yes, we have one guy, DS Isaac Boateng, who helps us with these things."

Julius gave her a less potent version of the look for which he had long been famous. It could vaporize lawyers in their tracks. "With respect," Julius said, "I would be careful about the DNA submissions. As you no doubt know, I have tried quite a few cases in which such evidence was involved, and, unlike what we see on TV, DNA is not always a helpful or definitive answer, especially if the evidence falls into inexperienced hands. You say this Boateng man is good?"

"He has a chemistry background, and we sent him on a forensic training to South Africa."

"And how many forensic DNA samples has he handled since then?" Julius asked.

"Well—I don't have the exact number, but by now he should have done at least . . . thirty? To be honest, I can't say for sure, but last year the FSL did fifty-one cases, and Boateng oversaw many of them, including the Takoradi missing girls case."

"Thirty?" Julius said critically. "That can hardly be described as extensive experience in the field—certainly not for a complicated case like this, Madame Tawiah. I'm not casting any aspersions, and I don't want you to feel that way, but from my legal experience, these DNA issues that can get so complex, a person with less than at least a hundred cases under his belt is not ready for prime time."

"Well, certainly you have more knowledge of such things, sir," Tawiah stammered deferentially.

"My concern, you see," Julius said, wincing slightly from the effort of moving forward in his seat, "is that the DNA found in the home will almost certainly include Augustus's DNA mixed in with the assailant's DNA. And there you have a very confusing situation that might unjustly implicate Augustus. A false positive, in a way."

"Although from what I understand," Tawiah said, "the contaminant can be told apart from that of the assailant based on their respective volumes—"

"Maybe so, but that also depends on how reliably these pieces of evidence were collected and the circumstances—"

"Oh, I was there," Tawiah said.

Julius was startled. "Director-General—you were there? I didn't know that."

"Yes, and I watched him collect the evidence. From what I could see, he did a good job, but I do take your point regarding the contamination."

"Good, I'm glad you do. Thank you for that."

"What I can do for you," Tawiah said, "is talk to the administrator of the Forensic Science Lab, Mr. Thomas, to ask him if anyone has begun analysis on the physical evidence."

"What I would like to say, Madam Tawiah," Julius said, "is that it's my fervent wish that the evidence at the FSL is never analyzed."

"Oh," Tawiah said blankly. "Sir, that might be difficult, since we already have the evidence in hand."

"I feel it would not be advisable," Julius said more sharply. "After all, we all have a past, not excluding yourself."

"I beg your pardon, sir?"

"Coming to CID straight from MTTU? I know the people in high places who facilitated that move. I'm not exactly saying there was a quid pro quo. You would know more about that than I."

Tawiah sat very still, a look of consternation creeping to her face.

"Nevertheless," Julius continued brightly, "congratulations are still in order, and I was just contemplating this morning how I've never sent you a congratulatory gift on your taking this post. But I can certainly make up for it now—many times over, of course."

"Yes, sir," she said, her voice strangled. "Thank you, sir."

"Well, I must go now," Julius said, carefully rising. "If my arthritic back will allow me."

"Oh, let me help you," Tawiah said, standing up. "Are you okay?"

Julius waved her assistance away. "It is all well, Director-General. Thank you very much for your time."

"I can at least see you out, sir."

Before heading to the door, Julius stopped at Tawiah's desk to lay a crisp, thick envelope on the corner, the international language of dead presidents on green. He'd bet that someone like Tawiah would have a dollar account, so this neat packet would be a nice top-up. It was a kind gesture on Julius's part.

TWENTY-SIX

Ten months after

ON MONDAY MORNING, EMMA'S revelation that she had brought some potentially valuable information with her from last Friday's undercover operations and that she had also been sacked brought respective cheers and jeers.

"How did it happen, Emma?" Sowah asked.

She began by relating Thomas's unwanted touching, which brought exclamations of disapproval. Now that Emma wasn't returning to the FSL, she felt that Sowah should know about it. He seemed to be withholding comment on the episode for now.

"Okay," Sowah said to her. "Tell us what you found."

She began part two of the story—how she discovered Thomas's open door and saw the evidence bag and envelopes on the table.

"So, I went in there and took pictures as quickly as I could," Emma said. "I tried to leave before he got back, but I was too late. Seriously, I was in hot water! I pretended I had accidentally left a rag in the office, but I don't think he believed me. Here are the pics, boss."

She handed the phone to Sowah, who sat down on a free chair and studied the photos intently for several moments. He nodded. "Okay everyone, come and take a look."

The investigators gathered around him.

"First image," Sowah said, "is of a small paper envelope with a label stating that the contained evidence is two strands of hair taken from Lady Araba's bedsheet. There's also a chain of custody form with the date and time the hair was collected—the third of July last year at . . . not sure I can read it—is that 10:11?"

"I think so, sir," Emma said.

"And it's signed by a Corporal Tackie, evidence tech," Sowah continued, "with his rank and ID number, et cetera. Seal is intact, as I said, so no one has tampered with it. Next it was handed over to Kobina Thomas, the administrator at FSL, at 3:31 that afternoon, and that's the end of the CoC."

"So that means . . ." Jojo said uncertainly.

"That Tackie took the evidence directly to Thomas," Sowah said, "and that Thomas was the last one to receive the evidence, which he still has in his possession. If, for example, he then sent it to the lab to be analyzed, we would see a third entry with the date, time, and person receiving. If that person then sends it on to someone else again, we will see another name, and so on. This is proof that no one has analyzed this piece of physical evidence."

"So, the question is, why?" Manu said.

"Exactly," Sowah said. "Now, the next one . . ." He fumbled with the phone's screen. "Which way do I go on this thing?"

"Oh, let me help, sir," Emma said, smiling, but not too much. She swiped left for him.

"Thanks," Sowah said, then read off the evidence form. "The next two paper envelopes are both blood swabs. Same thing—no one on the CoC beyond Thomas. Therefore, all of these are in his custody and have gone no further than him."

"Why would he withhold them?" Gideon said.

"Better question is who *told* him to withhold it," Sowah said. "It's unlikely that he's doing this of his own accord."

"Or, sir," Manu chimed in, "it could be as simple as he's waiting for an officer to be assigned the job while everyone else has just forgotten about it."

"Laziness," Jojo said.

"Or plain disorganization and incompetence," Sowah said.

"Worse things have happened in the Ghana Police Service, but if they have accused an innocent man who is now languishing in prison at the mercy of forensic evidence that hasn't been analyzed, that's criminal in and of itself. I'll talk to DCOP Laryea again. Maybe he can find out something for us. Anything else, Emma?"

"Yes please. One other thing to mention. A man called Kingsley from the University of Cape Coast visited the lab while I was there. From what they discussed, it looks like they're both being squeezed by a lack of government funding. The private DNA labs are doing much better."

"Oh, that must have been Attah Kingsley you saw," Sowah said. "I know him somewhat. He runs the forensic program at UCC."

"He appears to want them to privatize the FSL," Emma said.

"I'm sure Thomas didn't like hearing that."

"He didn't seem to, no. Their conversation made me wish the UCC could run DNA evidence on behalf of the FSL."

Sowah grunted. "That would mean getting an order from CID. Not going to happen."

Emma sighed with some despondence. "You're right, sir."

"Anything else for us?" Sowah asked.

"No, that's all, sir. Thank you."

"Well done. And remember—don't hesitate to call on any of us if you ever feel like you're threatened or in danger. We are here for you. We know you can take care of yourself, but as a woman, you face some additional hazards, okay?"

Emma nodded. "Yes, sir. Thank you, sir."

But she had a lingering, uncomfortable feeling that she hadn't done well on her first undercover assignment. The goal had been to curry favor with Thomas in a way that she could coax the information out of him. Had she been overeager and ended her mission too soon? Perhaps she might have discovered more if she had stayed longer. On the other hand, had she been fawning over Thomas, he might have perceived her as open to his advances. For now, she shelved her disquiet, but she intended to think it over some more.

Sowah turned to Jojo. "What do you have for us?"

Jojo talked about his growing friendliness with Peter and his introduction to Ismael, the gardener. "It seems both of them admired Lady Araba," Jojo said. "Whether there was something beyond that, like lust or unrequited love, I can't say."

"*Ei*, Jojo!" Gideon said, grinning wickedly. "Where from the big words? You say what? Unrequenching love?"

Jojo sent Gideon a look that could kill as the room dissolved into laughter. Even Sowah couldn't hold it in. "Okay," he said, regaining composure. "Settle down. Jojo, don't mind them. Unrequited love is a legitimate motive for murder."

Jojo stuck his tongue out at Gideon. "See?"

"Jojo, please continue," Sowah urged him.

"Ismael took me around to Lady Araba's house," Jojo went on. "The family are trying hard to sell it, but few people want to buy a house where someone was murdered. We went from the front of the place, past the staff quarters to the back, where Lady Araba's upstairs bedroom is. I wanted to ask if we could look inside, but I think that would seem strange—what do you think, boss?"

"That level of curiosity might seem a little out of place, I agree."

"But I think there's another way we can get an investigator into the house," Jojo said.

"Oh, really?" Sowah said with interest. "How?"

"While we were there, we ran into a realtor called Rita who was showing the house to an *oburoni*. Rita is one of Trasacco's employees. What about if we call her—or anyone at Trasacco—and tell them we're interested in buying a home in the Valley? Then we send somebody down there to have a look at the house. Since only Lady Araba's is for sale, that will be the one she'll show."

"Send someone like who?" Manu asked, askance.

"Emma," Jojo said.

She looked at him in surprise. "Me?"

"Yes, you. Imagine you arrive there all dressed up, in a nice car with a driver. You can pose as a rich businesswoman or something like that."

"Brilliant, Jojo," Sowah said at once.

"Wow, the brain is working today," Gideon muttered. Jojo ignored him.

Sowah looked at Emma. "I like the idea."

"We should do it," she said, at first surprising herself with her quick response, but then realizing what was driving her: she wanted to improve on what she considered her disappointing first undercover performance.

TWENTY-SEVEN

Two months after

FOR WEEKS, THE MEDIA had relentlessly circulated their innuendo and speculation that Augustus had killed Lady Araba, despite the lack of evidence. Meanwhile, he hadn't been able to keep his job at the station, or get any other job, for that matter. Unemployed, Augustus was now living in an apartment in upscale Roman Ridge, but Julius was paying for it. Augustus *said* he was keeping up with his AA meetings, but Julius had his doubts. He had been making it a daily habit after court to check on Augustus. In the end, he really did love his son.

Julius parked the car and went up the steps to the second floor, where he knocked on Augustus's door. No response. Julius knocked again, louder. Silence, until he heard someone inside say, "Who is it?" in a barely audible voice.

"Gus? Are you there? It's Papa."

"Papa, help me." Augustus sounded like a little boy.

Julius had kept a spare key for exactly such emergencies. He unlocked the door and entered. There on the kitchen floor was his son curled up into a ball.

"My God," Julius said, kneeling beside Augustus. "What's going on? Talk to me."

"My stomach," Augustus said, tears squeezing out between his clenched eyelids.

"*Awurade*," Julius said as he looked up at the kitchen counter and saw the empty beer bottles. "Why did you start drinking again. You foolish, foolish boy!"

"Sorry, Papa," Augustus said. "I couldn't help it." He began to moan with pain.

"We have to get you to the hospital. Wait for me here, okay? I'm going for help."

"Am I dying?" Augustus asked, voice shaking.

"No, you're *not*. Listen to me. You're not dying, you hear? Wait here."

JULIUS THOUGHT IT best to take Augustus to the Nyaho Medical Centre, where his medical record was already on file from the previous visit. Two nurses worked quickly to check Augustus over while Julius told them how much his son had been drinking. Then there was an hour's wait for the physician. Meanwhile, Julius called Caroline at the clinic. She dropped everything and summoned her driver to take her to the hospital.

THE NEXT MORNING, after a long, torturous night in which Augustus had been injected with morphine for pain relief, he was awake but drowsy as one of the junior doctors came in to examine him, review his vital signs, and adjust his medications.

Julius and Caroline had been at Augustus's bedside until late the night before, and they returned at seven in the morning. The senior doctor on duty arrived a little later. He had an air of both authority and weariness.

"You have had a severe episode of acute, alcohol-induced pancreatitis, sir," he said to Augustus. "One of the worst I've seen in my career. You're lucky to be alive."

Augustus lowered his eyes, chastised. Julius stared at him with a mixture of alarm and pity. Caroline kept silent, but anyone could see she was anguished by the news.

"Please, Doctor," Augustus said, barely audibly, "am I still in danger?"

"Yes, everything of yours is in danger, Mr. Seeza," he responded crisply. "Your liver, pancreas, stomach, and your life. If you don't stop drinking, you'll kill yourself. We will observe you for a few more days. You'll begin a clear liquid diet later today."

When the doctor had left, Caroline turned to Augustus.

"I know what you're about to say," he whispered.

"This was a sign," she said. "God has spared you this time, but the next occasion, you may not be so lucky. Do you understand what I'm saying, dear?"

"I don't need a lecture," he said.

"Oh, but you will get a lecture," Julius barked, making Augustus snap to attention. "You speak to your mother with such disrespect after she and I have been here for hours watching over you? Do you even deserve that? Drinking yourself almost to death, ruining your career? What is wrong with you, boy? Did we bring you up to be a failure? Eh?"

Augustus closed his eyes wearily. "No, Papa. You didn't."

"Then straighten your life up. After you leave the hospital, you will not touch another drop of alcohol, do you understand?"

"Yes, Papa," Augustus whispered.

An uncomfortable silence followed, and then Julius put on his reading glasses and opened the newspaper he had brought with him. He folded it back at the politics page—everything was politics, really.

Augustus cleared his throat. "I'm going to turn my life around, okay, Papa? I promise you."

"I hope you mean it," Julius said, "because your mother and I will not continue to rescue you."

"Yes, sir." After a moment, Augustus said, "please, can I get my phone? I left it at the house—I think it's in my bedroom."

Caroline looked to her husband for an answer. He lifted his eyes for a moment over the top of his glasses. "Send the driver to get it," he said, returning to the paper. "When he returns, we'll leave so Gus can get some rest. We'll be back in the evening."

•   •   •

EARLY ON THE morning of Augustus's fourth day of hospitalization, Julius received a call from the attending physician. It was a Sunday.

"Sorry to inform you, sir, that your son has taken a turn for the worse," the doctor said. "We've had to admit him to the intensive care unit."

Julius stiffened. "What's the matter?" he asked, his voice shaking.

The doctor hesitated. "His blood pressure has dropped, and he's developed a high fever. He appears to be septic—"

"What exactly does that mean?" Julius demanded.

"I would prefer not to discuss it over the phone, sir. Please, if you can come to the hospital as soon as possible?"

Julius ended the call and walked downstairs to his wife's bedroom, tapping on the door. "Sweetie? Are you awake?"

He heard a muffled voice and opened the door. Caroline was still in bed. She lifted her head to squint at him. "What is it?"

Julius stood at her bedside. "The doctor called. Augustus is sick. We have to go."

WHEN THEY ARRIVED at the ICU, a nurse led them to Augustus's bedside. Caroline gasped. Augustus, attached to an oxygen mask and a confusing array of wires and tubes, was surrounded by digital instruments that flashed and beeped. His once-imposing frame was now so small and vulnerable. His eyes fluttered open, appeared to fix on his parents for a moment, then drifted closed again.

Caroline gently took her son's hand—the one with no IV catheters inserted—and lovingly cradled it. Her eyes swam with tears. "Augustus? It's Mummy. Can you hear me? I'm right here with you. You'll be okay."

His eyes didn't open this time. Caroline looked up at Julius and choked. She didn't cry, at least not out loud. Abruptly, she switched into her professional mode and began to examine the hanging IV fluids and the data on the instruments. To be honest, much of the modern technology and medications were beyond her scope, but no one needed to know that. She went to the nurses' station at the center of the unit.

"I'm Dr. Caroline Seeza," she announced with importance. "Where is my son's physician? I need to see him *immediately*."

"Yes please," one of the nurses said. "I've already called him. He told me to do so as soon as you arrived."

THE DOCTOR, AN intensive-care specialist, went deep into conversation with Caroline just outside of the ward, and they both fell into medical terminology while Julius stood by quietly. After the doctor left them, Julius asked Caroline, "What does it mean that Augustus is 'septic?'"

"It means the infection has spread throughout the body," she said.

"And it's dangerous?"

"Of course it is!" she responded with an unexpected flash of irritation. "He could die."

"But why is it happening?" Julius said, clenching his fists.

"He's an alcoholic, Julius! What else?"

"Yes, I know that, but—"

"He was already in a state of immune suppression, and along comes an inflammatory condition like pancreatitis, what do you expect to happen?"

"I'm not a doctor," Julius protested, his voice shaking. "There's no need to talk down to me."

Caroline sighed and dropped her head. "I'm sorry."

To her shock, Julius covered his face with his hands and began to weep. "Oh, Augustus," he said. "Augustus."

Caroline glanced furtively around, but no one was watching them. She pulled her husband closer and put her arms around him. "Shh, it's okay," she soothed him. "He's going to pull through. We all will, okay?"

ON HIS FOURTH day in the ICU, Augustus began to turn around. His vital signs were stable, and he was much more alert.

His mother had been at his bedside as much as the hospital's strict visiting hours would allow. Sometimes she read a book, interrupting herself to check her son's monitors. At other times, she dabbed his face with a cool, moist washcloth. She questioned the nursing staff's every move and made them check every day that Augustus wasn't developing any bedsores. If there was one thing Caroline knew, the patients who received the best care were the ones with the most vigilant family members.

The per diem rate of a private ICU stay was staggering, one most ordinary people couldn't afford. Furthermore, the patient and family members themselves were responsible for purchasing the medications, either at the pharmacy attached to the medical center or some other pharmacy in town, many of them surprisingly well stocked. For Caroline, things were much easier. She could get or order most of the supplies at a heavy discount from the pharmacy at her own clinic.

On the sixth day, Augustus was ready to be transferred to a step-down unit, where he would begin physical therapy the following day. He had lost almost a third of his weight by then, his muscles devoured by illness and inflammation. His legs looked like matchsticks, and the roundness in his face was gone, leaving it gaunt. He had begun to eat, but what he took in was far below his urgent calorie requirements. His recovery would take months.

On the morning of the seventh day, his nurse, Mabel, came to his room with an injection. "Good morning, Mr. Seeza," she said. "How are you feeling today?"

He looked at Mabel with raised eyebrows. "What did you say?"

"I said, 'Good morning, how are you?'"

"I can't hear you. Speak up, please."

She raised her voice. "Good morning."

He nodded, but looked confused.

Mabel frowned. "Can you hear me, sir?"

Seeza stared blankly at her. A shiver ran down her spine. Something wasn't right. She hurried out of the room and found one of the senior nurses, who said, "What do you mean he can't hear you?"

"Either he can't hear me or something else is wrong," Mabel said. "I don't know."

Looking skeptical, the senior nurse joined her back to Augustus's room. He was sitting almost upright against his pillows gazing ahead in an unfocused way.

"Is everything okay, Mr. Seeza?" the senior nurse asked, lightly placing a hand on his shoulder.

He looked up at her.

"Mr. Seeza?"

"I can't hear you."

The senior nurse was baffled. She fiddled around in her pockets, found her cell phone, and switched on the flashlight to peer into Augustus's ears. She saw nothing blocking the auditory canal. "Hello, sir!" she shouted into the left ear.

He looked at her, but not as if he were responding to her voice. He seemed perplexed.

The two nurses stood staring at him for a moment.

Panic grew in Augustus's eyes. "What is wrong?" he shouted. "What's happening?"

The senior nurse tried to sign that he should stay calm, but it was difficult to convey that message. She left the bedside and beckoned Mabel to follow her out of the room.

"What's the matter with him?" Mabel said.

"I don't know," the senior nurse said, pulling out her phone again. "I'm calling the doctor. Mr. Seeza has either gone deaf or crazy."

TWENTY-EIGHT

Ten months after

SATURDAY WAS MARKET DAY for Emma. She was shopping for cocoyam leaves, salted fish, eggs, and yam for tonight's *kontomire* dinner with her boyfriend, Courage. They had been dating for a year; the relationship was up and down, but mostly good.

Having finished shopping for the essentials, Emma went to her favorite kiosk in the market, Abena Style. Abena, the owner, sold women's clothing and fashion accessories. Emma's visit wasn't all pleasure this time, as she was getting ready for her undercover assignment at Trasacco Valley, which meant putting together an outfit in keeping with a sophisticated, well-to-do woman. Working backward, she started with a coral purse she immediately fell in love with. Purses were her Achilles heel.

After looking at dozens of styles, Emma decided on a denim top with a ruffled hem and puffed sleeves, plus a high-waisted blue and coral print skirt that picked up the color of the purse. But there weren't any matching shoes that Emma liked, so Abena, the consummate businesswoman, called an associate in the same market and asked her to bring over some shoe samples to the shop. She had a coral pair that matched the purse, but it was the navy-blue pumps that eventually did the trick.

Emma expressed the almost obligatory consternation at the price of all the merchandise, and then the haggling battle began.

The final victory went to Emma as she put the skirt back on the rack with the words, "Okay, maybe next time." In the retail world, "next time" meant "no time." Emma got her price and all was well.

EMMA BEGAN PREPARING *kontomire* by mid-afternoon. The kitchen with its stove and mini fridge led directly into the sitting room. There was a matchbook bedroom and bath adjoining that, but as small as it all was, the place was a step up from where Emma had lived during her former life as a police officer. She would always be grateful to have joined the Sowah Agency.

Courage walked in at 8:05 P.M. "Hello, love." He put his arms around Emma.

"You're late," she said, slipping out of his embrace.

"What, no kiss?" he asked.

Emma gave him a light one on the cheek and Courage laughed. "I know you'll give me a nice long one later," he said, flopping on the sofa and reaching for the TV remote. Courage, who was a tad overweight, was almost always in a good mood. His face was round and open, and he seldom frowned. In civilian clothes, he appeared friendly and approachable, but was much more serious in uniform. He was a member of the Panther Unit, the Ghana Police SWAT team.

When the food was done, Emma and Courage served themselves from the kitchen and sat at the dining table. The fluffy white yam contrasted with the dark greens bathed in golden-red palm oil. Courage attacked the *kontomire* like a starving man, which he certainly wasn't.

"What are you working on right now with Prof Sowah?" Courage asked her, using his favorite honorific title for her boss. "By the way, how is he these days?"

"Very well," Emma replied, thinking that the *kontomire* was especially delicious, if she did say so herself. "I think he's relieved we finally have a new case after so many months without anything showing up. It's an unsolved murder."

Courage, eating the traditional way with his right hand and

munching with gusto, said, "Wow, so you guys are taking on murder now? I thought you were all about catching cheating husbands and wives."

"Sowah's hand was forced, I think," Emma said. "Our bank balance must have been dwindling."

Courage nodded. "So, what's the case?"

"You remember the murder of Lady Araba not quite a year ago?"

He frowned. "I'm not sure. Who was she?"

"The fashion designer. She had her own line of clothing."

"Oh, yes. Now I do. She was found dead in her own home—in the bedroom?"

"Right."

"They arrested her houseboy or something."

"Her chauffeur, actually. But from what we know, no physical evidence ties him to the act."

"When does the Ghana Police ever have physical evidence?" Courage said unkindly.

"Believe it or not, in this case they do," Emma said. "Potential DNA and fingerprints."

Courage raised his eyebrows. "Really? Who told you that?"

"I saw it myself. Where's my phone?"

Emma found it in the kitchen and pulled up the pictures she had taken in Thomas's office. "See? The evidence is in the custody of the FSL administrator, and it appears no one has tampered with it, but why hasn't anyone tested it? And why did they get rid of DS Boateng, who collected this, before he could run the tests himself?"

Courage looked up at Emma. "How did you even get these photos?"

"Undercover," she said cryptically.

Courage made a face and shook his head. "Emma, be careful." He sighed. "You know, sometimes I feel uncomfortable about your work. You're messing around with potentially dangerous people."

"Isn't your job dangerous as well?"

"We have *guns*, remember? You have no such defenses."

"Hm," Emma said neutrally.

Courage sucked up some stew with relish, his lips gleaming with palm oil. "I think someone has prevented the evidence from being processed any further."

Emma had finished eating and went to wash her hands in the kitchen. "It's very frustrating," she called back. "Someone is getting away with murder."

When she returned, Courage said, "And so, who is this exceptional police officer who recovered evidence from the crime scene?"

"DS Isaac Boateng. Familiar?"

Courage shook his head. "No."

"They suddenly took him off the case and transferred him from Homicide to Domestic Violence."

Courage grunted. "What did I just tell you? Suppression of evidence."

He cleared the table and went to the kitchen to wash the dishes—that was their agreed-upon arrangement. Meanwhile, Emma found one of her favorite Nigerian soap operas to watch.

When Courage was done, he returned and settled on the couch with Emma lying against him as they watched TV. But her mind wasn't entirely on the program. She sat up, turning down the volume with the remote. "Let me ask you something," she said to Courage. "How many different ways could DS Boateng's evidence at the FSL be interfered with?"

"Many," Courage said. "First, Thomas, the administrator, for whatever reason, could claim that the evidence was too contaminated and therefore he can't or won't release the findings. Or he could say the evidence is blank."

"What do you mean, 'blank?'"

"I'll give you an example. A couple of years back, this Lebanese guy was accused of raping his house girl. She reported it to the police, and the lab at the police hospital the girl was taken to recovered and documented sperm from her. When they took the specimen to the FSL, the FSL claimed there was zero sperm. So, either the evidence was preserved incorrectly so that the spermatozoa disintegrated in transit, or someone at FSL was lying."

"Do you know anything about Thomas?" Emma asked. "Is he trustworthy?"

"I don't know a lot about him," Courage said, "but I hear he's a yes-man—does exactly what his superiors tell him."

"So, if, say, the CID director-general told Thomas not to analyze the evidence, he would obey, no questions asked."

"Exactly."

"What's your impression of Madame Tawiah?"

"Nobody likes her," Courage said bluntly. "She doesn't deserve the post, and she's too arrogant to admit or realize it."

That went along roughly the same lines as what DS Boateng had expressed. "But is she honest?" Emma asked.

Courage looked skeptical but said, "To be fair to her, I don't really know."

"What about the new inspector general of police?" Emma asked. "Would he also have interfered directly or indirectly with the evidence for any reason?"

"I doubt it," Courage said. "From what I hear, his style is very hands off. He delegates everything to his deputies and otherwise keeps his distance. They do all the work. He's more of a titular head. Most people don't even know what he looks like."

Emma grunted and gave an ironic smile. "I don't either."

"You see?" Courage said.

"And Justice Julius Seeza?" Emma asked. "Doesn't he hold sway over the IGP?"

"That I'm not sure, but definitely over Madam Tawiah."

"Why is that?"

"When Seeza was a district court judge and she was an officer in the field, he presided over many of her cases. She was in awe of him."

"So, if he came to her," Emma said, "and told her to prevent the evidence from being analyzed, you think she would comply?"

"Yes, I do. Tawiah may be incompetent, but she knows how to curry favor and with whom. I know the last director-general did some terrible things, but at least he maintained some independence."

Emma gave him a look and felt her lips and jaw set. "Independence, huh? I see."

Courage's expression changed to concern as he saw her expression turn morose. "What's wrong?" he asked.

Emma shook her head and remained mute as her eyes moistened.

Courage moved closer and put his arm around her. "My God, did I say something wrong? Talk to me."

Was now the time to tell him? She had kept it from him for over a year now.

"Emma, please," he said. "What just happened?"

She stared at the floor without seeing it and Courage wiped away the tears on her face with his fingertips. He shook her gently. "Baby, what's going on?"

She took a breath. "I didn't tell you this before. I've been waiting for the right moment, but it never seemed to come—or I haven't been ready. It's about the former director-general of CID."

"Yes?" Courage said quietly.

"As you know, the Ghana Police Council removed him from office after he confessed publicly to assaulting and raping new female recruits."

"Right. He still hasn't been prosecuted."

"And probably never will be," Emma said with a hint of bitterness. "When I started at CID Headquarters, they assigned me to the Commercial Crime Unit, which I hated, so I asked if I could transfer to homicide. DCOP Laryea sent me up to see the D-G about my request."

In a monotone, Emma told Courage the rest: how the director-general had trapped her in a small, closed room; his sudden violence and attempt to rape her, and how she had escaped. When she was done, Courage stared at her without blinking for a moment, then got up and paced the room twice. He stopped in the middle of the space and growled, clenching and unclenching his fists. "I swear," he said, "if I ever see that man, I will kill him."

"Courage," Emma said, with a hint of reproach in her tone.

"I'm serious." He bunched up his fist and Emma saw his eyes shift to the wall closest to him. She jumped up to Courage's side and grabbed his hand. "Oh, no—not that," she said sharply, pulling his hand back down. "Why do men always punch walls when they're mad? All it does is break your hand, and for what?"

All of a sudden, Courage's demeanor changed, and a choking sound came from his throat as he pressed his eyes with his fingers to try to stem the flow of tears. Emma would never have expected this reaction, and it was her turn to put her arm around his shoulders. "You okay?"

"I'm sorry, Emma," he said, his voice quivering and breaking.

"Why, Courage? Why do you say that?"

"Because I've made sex jokes in front of you before, and now I realize it must have hurt you—"

"No, no," Emma said, in turn breaking down.

Embracing each other in the middle of the room, they were a crying mess of a couple. When they had regained their composure somewhat, Courage said, "I just wish you had told me. How could you hold it in all this time?"

Emma led him by the hand the few steps back to the sofa. "It's one of those things you can't talk about before you're ready. Sometimes . . . sometimes, women feel shame over it."

"Do you?"

Emma shook her head. "Not anymore, but I did for a while."

Courage gently squeezed her hand. "Do you want to talk about it now? I'm here if you need me."

Emma did want to talk, and now, far from ashamed, she felt a great unburdening of her soul.

TWENTY-NINE

Ten months after

NOT MUCH MORE THAN a hundred meters away from the CID front entrance, the University for Development Studies owned and ran a guesthouse. They also served a very good breakfast in the restaurant on the ground floor. This was the venue Sowah had chosen to meet with his old friend Cleo Laryea. From the many unoccupied tables, they selected one in the back corner.

After going through their litany of old jokes and ordering their respective meals, they got serious.

"So, Cleo," Sowah said, lowering his voice a step, "about the Lady Araba murder case we're working. We now know that DS Isaac Boateng did submit fingerprint and DNA evidence from the crime scene to the FSL administrator, Mr. Thomas."

"And they did the testing?"

"No, they didn't," Sowah said, "but the evidence is apparently intact and still in Thomas's custody."

"How did you find that out?"

"I won't detail it, but we've been investigating," Sowah said cryptically. "The question is, why the delay? In a couple weeks, it will be eleven months since Araba's death. Is someone preventing the evidence from being examined? Is Thomas himself withholding it for some reason, or has someone pressured him to?"

Cleo was coating a chunk of white bread with a thick layer of butter. "You want me to find out, is what you're saying," he said with a smile.

Sowah smiled back. "Well, yes, that's what I was driving at."

Cleo let out a low groan. "Sowah, you are killing me, oo!" he said in mock agony. "This is a political minefield. Are you trying to get me sacked just before my retirement?"

"Oh, never," Sowah protested, grinning. "Besides, no one can sack a legend like you."

Cleo almost snorted tea out of his nose, and the two men had another round of laughter.

"You're the master of flattery," Cleo said, wagging his finger. "Well, I'll see what I can do, but it will be a tightrope walk. For one thing, Madam Tawiah doesn't like me much."

"Come on," Sowah said confidently. "Everyone likes you."

SOWAH KNEW BOB Agyekum from way back when. In their respective roles as private investigator and TV station manager, their paths had crossed, and each of them had on occasion asked the other what they knew about some rumor or whisper around town. Still, they hadn't seen each other in quite some time, and they had a lot of catching up to do when Sowah dropped in for a visit at Agyekum's Metro TV office.

Both of them were grandfathers now, so they spent some time extolling the achievements and capers of their grandchildren. Agyekum enjoyed laughing at any good story.

And then it was down to business.

"I'm looking into the Lady Araba murder," Sowah said.

"Ah," Agyekum said, leaning back. "What aspect of it?"

"A family member brought the case to us. She's not satisfied with the way the police conducted the investigation, if you can even call it that."

"I've been wanting to do an investigative report on it, but the problem is conflict of interest, since Augustus was once an employee of the station and has been implicated in the murder.

I mean, he hasn't been charged with anything, but many people still believe he did it."

"May I suggest something?" Sowah asked. "If you broaden the topic and make it not just about Lady Araba, but also about how CID investigates homicides and the role of the police forensic science lab, then there will be less of a conflict—or at least the perception of one. The question to frame it around is: What is the true level of expertise that the Police Service has in forensic analysis? We have a crime lab, yes, but for all that expensive equipment, is it being used to capacity or not? They have police officers doing the work. Isn't that an opportunity for more corruption?

"We've had some high-profile cases recently, like the four murdered teenagers in Takoradi. DNA studies were certainly used successfully for identifying the Takoradi girls, but what of the others, like J.B. Danquah, the MP killed four or five years ago? What part, if any, did DNA play in that case? Reportedly, the crime scene was badly contaminated, particularly by senior officers. We have a forensics lab, but if people don't know how to secure a crime scene or collect evidence from it, what's the point? If you could get Madam Tawiah on your new *Tough Talk* episode, it could be a great discussion."

"Yes, but there's a problem."

"What's that?"

"You know, of course, who owns this station," Agyekum said.

"Minister of Science & Technology, Adam Kyei. Yes, of course. Why do you ask?"

"He's related to Madam Tawiah—sibling or half-sibling, I'm not sure which, but I don't think he would appreciate his sister grilled on *Tough Talk*."

"Oh," Sowah said, making a rueful face. "I didn't know Kyei and Tawiah were related."

"Let me ask you something," Agyekum said. "You mentioned available DNA—do you know if there is such a thing in Lady Araba's case?"

"A trained police officer—one of the few—a guy named Isaac

Boateng, took DNA and fingerprint evidence from the crime scene and submitted it to the FSL. As far as we know, the evidence has not been submitted for testing."

"Is it possible the evidence has been destroyed?" Agyekum asked.

"At last check, it was in safe custody at the FSL."

"You know that for sure?"

"Yes, I have photos."

Agyekum looked intrigued. "Really. Can I see?"

"Yes, you can, although you can't *have* them. Before I show you, may I ask you a few questions?"

"But of course."

"From your perspective, what's the story of Augustus Seeza's downfall and his ups and downs with Lady Araba? Was he forthcoming to you about her?"

"To some extent, yes, because when he started his downward spiral, I forced him to tell me what was going on. He and Bertha were at each other's throats and he became depressed. I suspect he was drinking more heavily at that time, but not to the point that his performance was adversely affected. I think he got over it quickly, and he entered a period of about a year of sublime performance on TV. At that point, I didn't know he had started to see Lady Araba until a reporter snapped a photo of them together at Sky Bar in Osu. I can't say I was surprised. He was an incorrigible womanizer. The office romance at this station alone, God help us. At one point, it seemed he was messing around with at least three women on staff. The tension in the station was suffocating."

"And as far as you know, did Augustus continue his philandering when he was with Araba?"

Agyekum folded his fingers together. "I don't believe it compared with how he behaved with Bertha. I think it was genuinely a good time for both Gus and Araba until Bertha wedged herself between them. She dogged and harassed them both on Instagram and Facebook, went on radio programs and made wild, scandalous claims about Augustus and Araba. She sent a photo to Augustus of Araba supposedly hanging out with a rapper at a club, but it turns out it was a Photoshop job, and Araba had never even been there.

"At any rate, the seeds of suspicion Bertha sowed began to grow in Araba's mind, and she started questioning Augustus at every turn—sometimes calling him several times a day while he was at work. So, then he felt under siege from both women, and the drinking came back with a vengeance. It was during that time he conducted the now infamous and disastrous interview with Chief Justice Waters. That's when we suspended him, and then the night he didn't show up for work on time when he was supposed to resume the show, we sacked him." Agyekum sighed. "It was not a pleasant experience. I wanted to give him more chances, but Kyei said no. Full stop."

"Seeza's condition worsened even further after the dismissal," Sowah commented. "Am I correct?"

"Yes." Agyekum looked regretful. "I don't feel good about it at all. And because he took a turn for the worse, Araba went back to him even after she had supposedly disowned him at the behest of her family."

"Do you have an idea of how the relationship was going after she came back to him?"

"It was, what, a good eight months together again before she died?" Agyekum said. "I think he was up and down, but the eve of the murder, Augustus was definitely depressed."

"Did he ever direct any threatening language at her? Or express it to you?"

Agyekum shook his head. "No, he was just despondent. Listen, I know there's been a lot of talk in the press about how Gus is probably guilty and getting away with murder, but in my opinion, he was basically a good man who fell from grace at the hands of alcoholism and, in some ways, just plain bad luck. Is he a somewhat pathetic man now? Sadly, yes. But a murderer? I don't think so."

"Well, perhaps you're right," Sowah said, reserving his doubts.

He stood up. "Thanks for your time, Bob. It was good to see you again."

"Hey, wait!" Agyekum said indignantly. "What about the pics you were going to show me?"

"Oh, yes," Sowah said with a laugh. "Almost forgot."

"Sure," Agyekum said dryly.

Sowah obliged and let his friend have a good look.

"This is important," Agyekum said. "Thank you for sharing this."

They walked to the entrance together. As they shook hands and Sowah prepared to depart, he placed his hand on his friend's shoulder. "Think about my idea, would you?"

"About interviewing Madam Tawiah? I'll look strongly into it, but I can't guarantee anything."

THIRTY

Eleven months after

WALTER, WITH GIDEON BEHIND him, knocked on the solid black gate of the Tagoes' house on Ndabaningi Sithole Road in Cantonments, a particularly nice part of town where homes constructed decades ago were mixed in with modern, expensive high-rise apartments that ruined the view for their one- and two-story neighbors.

Dusk had fallen, and already the street lights were on and houses were lit up as if Ghana had all the energy in the world and no deficits to worry about. Cantonments residents almost never experienced the rolling blackouts that the Electricity Corporation foisted on other neighborhoods for the simple reason that Cantonments people actually paid their bills and wouldn't put up with blackouts, in any case.

A dog barked from behind the wall and a woman's voice yelled, "Heh! Shut up!" The owner of the voice opened up the gate. "Yes?"

"My name is Busia," Walter said. "We are expected."

"Oh, yes," the woman said, opening the gate wide. "Please come in, they are waiting for you. I'm Esi, the housekeeper."

She had a worn face, but her expression was open and welcoming. The dog growled at the newcomers but ran off with its tail between its legs as soon as Esi shooed it away. "Busia" and Gideon, whose name was "David" for the purpose of this visit, followed Esi along a stone path lined with low-profile lamps. Off to the side were two SUVs and an Infiniti Q50. Like other priests and pastors in Ghana, Tagoe was rolling in money.

When they got to the front porch full of patio chairs and a parakeet in a hanging cage, Esi asked the two men to wait there while she informed the Tagoes their guests had arrived. As they stood looking around at the comfortable surroundings, Walter reflected that Father Fifi Tagoe had not initially seemed open to the idea of the two "journalists" conducting an interview, but something must have changed his mind, because he had called back later to say he was okay with it.

The front door opened, and a woman, very slim in a two-piece print outfit, came out. She looked as if she had just arrived from the hair salon and was heavily made up.

"Mr. Busia, is it?"

"Correct. Good evening, madam. You must be Mrs. Tagoe. This is my assistant, David. He'll be taking some notes, if that's all right with you."

"Yes," she said. "No problem. Please come in."

The sitting room was spacious, the furniture solid—*the way they used to make it*, Walter thought. A man who could only have been Fifi Tagoe was in a large armchair with his feet up on a large, classically designed leather pouf from northern Ghana. He was reading a newspaper, spectacles halfway down his nose and his head tilted back to get that sweet spot on his bifocals.

"Good evening, Father," Walter said, offering his hand. "Busia, and my assistant, David."

Tagoe looked over his glasses at them. "Oh, was it tonight we were supposed to meet?"

"I reminded you, dear," Miriam said with a little laugh.

"Fine," the Reverend said. He waved vaguely at the chairs in the room. "Please, have a seat."

Miriam offered Walter and Gideon water, which they declined. She sat in the chair closest to her husband, facing their guests.

Fifi took off his glasses and rested them on the table beside him. His wife leaned over and put them in a case she had magically produced. He gave her a quizzical look, and she said, "You know you're going to forget where you put them, dear. I'll hold on to them."

"Yes, all right."

He smiled at the two men. "My wife always knows where everything is."

"Mine too, sir," Walter said, glad for this chance to break the ice.

"So, what is this visit about again?" Fifi asked.

"Well, as I mentioned on the phone, sir," Walter said, "I'm a Web-based freelance journalist. I write articles about topics I believe are of general societal interest and rooted in the human experience, as in the case of your daughter, for which I must express our condolences."

"Well, thank you for that. We know she is now in paradise and being watched over by our Lord."

"Amen," Walter said.

"To which church do you belong?" Tagoe asked.

"The Church of Pentecost," Walter replied.

"Ah, very good." Tagoe looked at Gideon. "And you, young man?"

"Action Chapel," he lied. In fact, he was a rare Ghanaian who didn't attend church—at least not regularly.

"So," the Father said, "what is your mission today?"

"Sir," Walter began, "I find the story of your daughter tragic, but it also seems to me that many things have been said about her that may or may not be true. So, what better way than to ask you, the parents, a little more about her life? Anything at all that facilitates our getting to know the late Lady Araba better. I'm looking for nothing salacious or sensational—just honest."

Tagoe nodded slowly. "We appreciate your effort, then. I think the first thing I will say—and my wife can add her observations—is that God truly blessed our daughter with talent. She was a wonderful woman—to me, she will always be my little girl, of course."

"I understand she has a brother?" Walter asked.

"Yes. Oko is her beloved brother. He should be here in a little while."

"By the way," Walter said, "how old was Lady Araba when she died?"

"Thirty-three, almost to the day." He looked at his wife. "In fact, we had just begun to plan a nice party for her, not so?"

"Yes." Miriam smiled warmly. "What Father Tagoe is saying about Araba is true. She was truly blessed, not only with talent, but to have been brought up in a loving home with the Lord looking out for her all the time."

Gideon had begun taking notes in a composition book.

"Please tell us a little bit about the day you learned of her terrible death," Walter said.

"The call came from Oko a little after eight that morning," Tagoe said. "I was at St. Anthony's Anglican Church in a meeting. He told me Samson, Araba's assistant, had phoned him to ask if he had heard from Araba, because everyone was waiting for her at the fashion show. Oko had tried to reach Araba without success. I excused myself from my meeting and rushed to Trasacco Valley as quickly as I could, but the traffic was terrible, and it was past nine by the time I arrived. There was a big crowd around the place—the police and I don't know who else. I lost control of my emotions. I remember everything as if it was a dream. They tried to stop me from entering the bedroom, but I could see inside: people hanging around the bed, taking photographs of my daughter in her nightgown lying in her bed in a pool of blood. What happened then, I don't quite recall, but I was told I fainted, and when I regained consciousness, people had carried me back into the hallway and were fanning me, trying to revive me. I couldn't remember what had just happened."

Father Tagoe looked away, his reddened eyes misting over.

"I'm very sorry, sir," Walter said quietly. "I can only imagine what a terrible experience it must have been."

Tagoe took a breath. "I didn't tell my wife right away.

Something in me kept saying that Araba couldn't possibly be dead. It's strange how the mind works. I was clinging to a thread of hope that it was somehow a mistake. But of course, it wasn't, so I made the most painful and difficult call to Mrs. Tagoe that I ever have."

Walter looked at her. "You must have been devastated, madam."

"It was too much to bear. I don't . . . I don't even know how to describe what I felt as my driver brought me to Araba's house."

"Understood," Walter said, nodding appreciatively. "When was the last time either of you spoke to your daughter?"

Tagoe looked at his wife. "We talked to her on the phone the evening before, to wish her luck with her big fashion show the following day. We were both here at home."

"Please, at what time was that?"

"About nine, honey?" Tagoe consulted his wife again.

"Yes," Miriam agreed. "She was returning from an event."

"Were you planning to attend the show on Monday morning?" Walter asked, glancing at Gideon to make sure he was writing all this down. He was, furiously.

Miriam smiled. "No. She wanted us to, but we had some schedule conflicts that prevented us."

That seemed odd to Walter. What kind of schedule conflict would prevent at least one of them from attending their daughter's big event?

"Did she seem normal when you spoke with her?" Walter asked.

"She was positive and excited about fashion week," Miriam said.

"Did she always appear happy?"

"Absolutely," Tagoe said.

"Oh, not *appear*, Mr. Busia," Miriam said somewhat sharply. "She *was* happy."

"Father," Walter said, "people always talk about the very special relationship between father and daughter. How would you describe the bond between you and Lady Araba?"

The instant Walter asked that, he noticed Mrs. Tagoe's gaze drop ever so slightly. Up until then, she had kept her eyes steadily on her husband with a look of deference and admiration.

The Reverend, on the other hand, didn't skip a beat. "She was the apple of my eye, Mr. Busia," he said. "When she was born, it changed my life forever in the best way imaginable. Yes, she meant everything to me, and now that she's gone, it's like a part of me has been removed. Sometimes I still can't believe she's no longer with us."

"When did she first indicate her interest in fashion?"

Tagoe cued his wife, who said, "Very early in her life. She always looked at fashion and beauty magazines, and she used to draw women clothed in her own designs."

"That's fascinating," Walter said. "It was very much in the blood, then. And when did she become active in that world?"

Both Father Tagoe and Mrs. Tagoe began to answer at the same time, but Miriam quickly shut up to let her husband answer.

"My dear sister, Dele, is a seamstress," he said, "and she took Araba under her wing, teaching her many design and sewing techniques."

"Did that in any way trouble you, Father?" Walter asked.

"Come again?"

"I mean, fashion is such a different world from that of religion and being devoted to the service of the Lord."

"That is true," Tagoe said, "but if that was my daughter's calling, then so be it. My only duty was to make sure that she didn't become caught up in certain evils of the fashion world."

"Evils of the fashion world?"

Walter and Gideon turned at the new voice. A stout, balding gentleman had just entered.

"Ah, welcome," Tagoe said, breaking into a smile. "This is my son, Oko."

"Hi, Daddy, Mummy. Are these the journalists you told me about?"

"Yes, that's them."

Walter and Gideon stood up to shake hands, and Oko pulled up a chair.

"What was I saying?" Tagoe said. "Ah yes, the evils of the fashion industry. You know, vanity, lust, greed, ungodliness, and so on. I felt I should protect my daughter from those iniquities, but, well, she was an adult in her own right. Would you agree, Oko?"

"Yes, of course," he said. "She was a very smart woman. People often didn't give her credit for that just because she was so beautiful, and I thought that was very unfair."

Miriam smiled. "Oko was so protective of her."

"Always helped Araba with her homework, isn't it, Oko?" the Reverend said. "Very patient with her."

Oko looked self-conscious. "Well, I did my best."

"Oko topped the Senior Secondary Certificate Exam in his year," Tagoe said, beaming. "The entire country."

"Wow," Manu said. "Congratulations, sir."

"Please, let's talk about Araba, not me," Oko said, his abashment rather disarming.

Miriam took the cue. "Well, what I was also about to say," she said, "is that the paramount goal—the Reverend and I—was to bring up a girl in an atmosphere of love, which ultimately flows from God."

"Araba went to church regularly?" Walter asked.

Tagoe was a little rueful. "Perhaps not as often as I would have liked, but regularly enough."

"I understand," Walter said. "Now I would like to ask a rather sensitive question, and I hope you won't find it objectionable. If so, please let me know. What was the nature of Lady Araba's relationship with TV personality Augustus Seeza?"

Tagoe looked bothered for the first time. "The media has made too much of this, in my opinion," he said, a knife edge creeping into his tone. "My daughter may have strayed slightly from the right path, but the focus should rather be on Mr. Seeza. Araba had a good heart and a tendency to put others before herself, sometimes to her detriment. Mr. Seeza is a case in point."

"Do you believe that arresting Lady Araba's driver, Mr. Kweku-Sam, was warranted?"

"Perhaps they know something we do not," Tagoe said, "but the Kweku-Sam my wife and I knew was not a monster. The person who killed my daughter *is* a monster."

Miriam, who had been quiet for a while, nodded and said, "He is. And that person is Augustus Seeza."

"You seem very certain, madam," Walter said, maintaining his courteous tone.

"He had every motive," Miriam said. "She had broken her ties with him, and he became furious. For all we know, that drunkard was intoxicated and out of control when he killed our little girl, but whichever way you look at it, he's a murderer." Her voice splintered on the last word.

"Yes," Walter said softly. "I'm so sorry, madam."

"Araba was a very good and blessed person," Tagoe said. "I didn't say perfect, I said *good*. And those who cast aspersions upon her have evil motives in their hearts."

Walter looked at Mrs. Tagoe, who said, "What my husband says is true, and whether on earth or in the fire and brimstone of hell, the murderer *will* one day come to justice."

THIRTY-ONE

Eleven months after

EMMA WAS TO MEET Rita at the entrance of Trasacco Valley at nine on Thursday morning. Sowah had hired an E-class Mercedes and a driver for a day at an undisclosed but no doubt hefty fee. Emma waited for the driver in the lobby of the African Regent Hotel. At seven-fifty, he texted her that he would arrive soon, and several minutes later, he called to say he was parked out front. Emma left the lobby through the main entrance, where she saw a gleaming, dark-blue Benz waiting for her. It was a stunning machine.

Emma walked up with confidence. For this assignment, she was Melody Acquah.

"Good morning, Madam Acquah," the driver said as he opened the right rear door for her to get in. He was young and thin, resembling a small boy. "My name is Jordan."

"Morning," she replied with a nod.

Emma got in. She had the clothes, now she just had to act the part. In real life, she would have gawked at the impeccable tan leather upholstery, the wood trim on the dashboard and along the doors, the overwhelming number of buttons, but now she behaved as if she had been born into such a privileged world.

Jordan took off, and Emma experienced the extraordinary power propelling them forward so smoothly. She sat back and took a relaxed pose, discovering very quickly just how easy that was to do in a vehicle like this. Now she understood why Benz drivers and passengers always appeared smug. It was because the car *made* you feel that way. Before long, that self-importance crept into your face and your every gesture. You believed you were superior to the rest of the world, which you probably weren't.

"Please, madam," the chauffeur said (she granted him that title, rather than just "driver"), "you said Trasacco Valley, is that right?"

"Yes. Correct."

"Please, is it the Valley or the Hills?"

"The Valley," she responded, impressed that he knew the difference.

Emma's phone vibrated, and she saw it was Mama. *No*, she thought. Now was not the time to engage in conversation with her mother, who always had a long catalog of things to tell Emma.

As anyone could have predicted, morning traffic was intolerable, but they made it to Trasacco only a few minutes past nine. At the entrance, one of the security guards bent down to the window to glance inside. She wondered if he might be the Peter they'd heard about from Jojo. The guard saw Emma, stepped back, and waved the car through. Emma looked back to check if anyone was taking down their license plate number, but that didn't appear to be the case. The guard hadn't asked what their business was there either, and she wondered if they had grown careless about security. Had that benefited Araba's murderer that night?

Rita had instructed them to park in one of the four spaces reserved for visitors who, like Emma, were there for their realtor to take them around. Emma didn't see another vehicle there yet, so the chauffeur stood in place with the air conditioner running. Just as she was wondering how late Rita would be, a silver SUV with a man in the driver's seat pulled into the space next to them. A woman whom Emma presumed was Rita emerged from the passenger side.

"I think this is the lady I've come to meet," Emma said to Jordan. "I'll get out now."

"Yes, madam."

Jordan hurried around to open Emma's door and she exited with what she hoped was the self-assurance of a wealthy woman.

"Melody Acquah?"

"Yes, good morning. You must be Rita." They shook hands. "You may call me Melody."

"So nice to meet you, Melody. I must apologize for being late—had to drop off the kids at school, and then traffic—well, you know the story."

"Of course," Emma said. "No worries."

"Come along," Rita said, opening the rear door of the SUV for Emma. As Rita buckled up in the front passenger side, she introduced her driver as Frank.

"We'll drive around the estate a bit," Rita said to Emma, "and then I'll show the property you're interested in."

Frank, who had evidently been to the Valley multiple times, took rights and lefts, twists and turns as Rita narrated, pointing out the different styles of house. Emma made only one- or two-word comments as Rita talked.

All worth well over a million dollars, none of the houses was for sale except Lady Araba's Duke home. The family, desperate to get it sold, had chipped at the price until it had lowered to less than 500,000 dollars. Emma reasoned that was a bargain. Why, *she* would buy it if she had that kind of money, ghosts be damned.

"And here we are," Rita said as Frank pulled in at a driveway. Rita pressed a button on the remote in her hand and the gate slid open slowly, after which Frank drove up to the entrance of the house and the two women got out.

"This is the official entry to the home," Rita said, leading Emma to the portico and front door. Emma looked up and saw the ceiling soared to the second level of the house.

Rita used an ordinary key to get in—nothing fancy like a key card. She shut the door behind them, and Emma noted it was the type of dead bolt with a thumb lever on the inside. A flip to the right locked the door. From the outside, it would only engage with a key.

"The staircase to the right takes us to the upper floor," Rita said, "but let's see the lower first."

The place appeared immense to Emma, and she couldn't get over having both a living room and a so-called "family room." The furniture was clearly expensive—leather and beautiful fabrics.

"The living room opens onto the garden terrace," Rita said, pointing to the view of the garden through the bay windows. "There's a table out there for get-togethers."

"Do you mind if I take some pictures?" Emma asked.

"But of course. Not a problem."

They moved along to the kitchen, where Emma fantasized about cooking up to four separate meals at the same time on all that stovetop.

"Right, we can go upstairs now," Rita said, leading Emma back down the corridor toward the stairs. "How are you liking it so far?"

"I'm impressed most by the family room and the view of the garden," Emma said truthfully.

"Ah, yes, through those bay windows," Rita said. "That's one of the things I really love about the Duke design. If you don't mind removing your shoes, as there's white carpeting upstairs."

They went up the carpeted steps. Unlike the first level with tile and stone floors, the second floor was entirely carpeted in light blue on the landing.

"A little to the left is the first bedroom, which is the master," Rita said as they got to the landing. "Please, come in."

Emma loved the space and light of the master bedroom, the airiness created by the high, vaulted ceiling. The carpet was a light cream, almost white. On either side of the room was a window. A glass door opened onto the infamous bedroom terrace.

The bed looked like a picture out of a magazine: a white-and-blue checkered spread, white pillows, and three bright blue cushions arranged largest to smallest. *So, there was where Araba's body had been found*, Emma thought.

Two low-profile armchairs with a white-and-blue floral print faced the foot of the bed on either side of the room.

Emma nodded approval—not too eagerly, she reminded herself. She snapped a few photos. "I'm curious," she said, turning to Rita. "You advised me that a violent death occurred in the house. Where and when did it happen?"

Rita looked distinctly uncomfortable. "Yes, almost one year ago now. The owner was murdered sometime during the night. That morning, the gardener came onto the terrace outside to do some work and spotted the owner lying deceased on the bed. Have you heard of Lady Araba?"

"Yes, of course! It was *here* she was killed?" Emma feigned shock. "I didn't realize. I knew she lived in one of the estates in town, but I had no idea it was here. Oh, goodness."

"Does it trouble you? I mean, in terms of potentially buying the house?"

"Well," Emma said, hesitantly, "I must confess it's a little disturbing."

Worry flitted over Rita's face. Emma imagined she had shown the house to several people who had balked about buying it on seeing the "murder bedroom." She wondered if the white man from last week was still interested, then laughed inwardly. As if she could buy the house in his stead.

"It does lead me to ask about the security here," Emma said. "How was someone murdered when there are three—or is it four—guards available?"

"Well, from what I can gather," Rita said, "it's because the murderer was probably someone very familiar with the security guards; they let him in without thinking anything was strange. The other possibility is that the rear gate wasn't operating, or someone climbed over it or otherwise got in. But I can assure you the security team does a great job." Rita switched subjects hastily. "Would you like to see the bathroom?"

They moved into the master bathroom, which had a huge shower stall, tub, marble-top his-and-hers vanity, and an oddly shaped toilet Emma had never seen the likes of. She looked around. All this space was almost shocking. The fixtures gleamed. She thought of the tarnished, worn-down taps at her house.

They wandered out of the bathroom back into the bedroom.

"Please, may I inquire what you do for a living?" Rita asked Emma.

"Import-export business. I'm partnered with my father."

"Ah, I see." Emma thought she saw a knowing gleam in Rita's eyes. Domestic-international trade was full of opportunity, loopholes, bribery, and corruption, and it could certainly make you a lot of money, especially if you had been at it for a long time—which, presumably, Emma's fictitious father had been.

"How is it working with your father?" Rita asked, smiling.

"I'm his only child," Emma said sweetly. "He dotes on me. In fact, it will be him buying the house for me."

"Wonderful," Rita said, her face shining.

"I love the layout," Emma said, looking around the room. "I wonder what it looked like when Lady Araba lived here."

"Lady Araba's bed was in the same position, but we changed the actual bed. For obvious reasons. Also, the carpet, of course."

"I understand," Emma said. "Please, may I see the terrace?"

"Oh, yes!" Rita said with enthusiasm. She felt uneasy in the bedroom, Emma suspected.

Like downstairs, the door had a dead bolt and opened from the inside with a hand-turned lever matching the white trim of the door. Emma and Rita stepped out onto the terrace. The sun was scorching, especially after the air-conditioned room behind them.

The area was smaller than the garden terrace downstairs. In the shade of a well-crafted pergola, four wicker chairs surrounded a circular central table. A flowerpot stand with several shrubs and flowering plants stood on either side of the pergola.

Emma walked to the edge of the terrace, which was guarded by a decorative wrought-iron railing. The view from here was spectacular. Between and among the palm trees, she had a

bird's-eye view of many of the other residences. Rita joined her
at the railing.

"How do you like it?" she asked.

"It's nice. So peaceful." Emma turned around for a different
view of the terrace and immediately noticed she was perfectly
reflected in the glass door and that she couldn't see through into
the bedroom. Why was that? With the interior darker than the
brightly lit terrace, the glass behaved as a mirror. Emma took a
couple of pictures, walked back to the door, and got close to it.
Still, her reflection partially obscured how much she could see
inside. At night, with the light on in the room, the mirror would
"reverse."

"Anything wrong?" Rita said from behind Emma.

"No, nothing. Does the glass have a coating on the inside?"

"That I'm not sure," Rita said, "but I believe it comes tinted."

"I see," Emma said.

"Is that a problem for you?"

"Just making sure someone can't see into the bedroom from the
terrace."

"I understand."

Emma knew Rita might have found it odd, but she cupped
her hands around her eyes and peered into the room through the
glass. And then she noticed something even stranger. From where
she was standing, the head of the bed was outside her view. That
meant something Ismael had told Jojo couldn't possibly be true.

THIRTY-TWO

Eleven months after

THE LAST ITEM ON Rita's list to show Emma was the garage, which had more than ample space to accommodate two cars. One of its doors led into the downstairs corridor. The door had a deadbolt lock, but what if Lady Araba wasn't accustomed to locking it behind her on entering the house once the garage was shut? What if the killer—and now, Emma was fairly or unfairly visualizing Ismael, though she'd never seen him—had hidden behind or underneath one of the two cars as Lady Araba pulled into the garage in the other that night? If she'd gone inside, closing the door but not locking it, then he would have access to her bedroom. He could have strangled Araba to death and left through any door in the house, locking it behind him. But Emma was stumped again—he would still need a key to do that. All the doors had been locked.

Emma must have looked pensive, because Rita smiled at her and said, "Thinking it over?"

"I am," Emma replied. "I do like the home. What I'll do is get in touch with you in the next two weeks, as soon as my father returns from Frankfurt. He's there on business."

"Of course," Rita said. "Very good."

"Thank you so much for showing me around."

"It's my great pleasure. Let me take you back to the front entrance."

Before they got to the SUV, Emma noticed a man watching them from outside the driveway. He turned away and walked off. As they drove back, Emma spotted the same guy crouched on the sidewalk, digging a hole in the soil with a trowel. Rita lightly pumped the horn and the man looked up, waving back with a grin.

"That's Ismael," Rita said. "He's the one who's kept the landscaping looking so good all these years."

Must talk to him, Emma thought. She might never be back, so this was the time.

At the gate, Emma thanked Rita again, and they proceeded to their respective vehicles.

"Please wait a few minutes," Emma said to Jordan.

"Yes, madam."

Emma improvised a quick plan. If she went back into the estate in the Mercedes, it might provoke some pesky questions on the way out and perhaps even jeopardize coming back here if she needed to. But what if she befriended one of the guards? Now was a good time to see just how serious they were about security.

She got out and approached the nearest guard. "Hello, I'm Melody Acquah."

"Yes, madam."

"Your name, please."

"I'm Peter."

"Peter, I want to go back to look at the streets around the house Rita was showing me," Emma said. "She didn't have a chance to walk me through them all."

He nodded. "No problem. Madam Rita knows you, so it's fine."

"Thank you, Peter." Emma slipped him a twenty-*cedi* bill.

His eyes brightened several-fold. "God bless you."

Emma returned to the car. "Let's go," she said to Jordan.

She directed him to the spot she had seen Ismael planting and found him patting the soil around a seedling. "Stop here, please," Emma said.

She alighted and walked the few steps back to Ismael, greeting him by name. "I'm Melody, how are you?"

"I'm fine, madam." He couldn't shake hands because his were soiled, so he offered his right wrist.

"I saw you as I was leaving and I wanted to come to greet you," Emma said. "I've heard so much about you—how good you are at your work."

Ismael's face lit up with a smile, and he gave a laugh that was both self-conscious and pleased. "Thank you very much, madam."

"Rita has been showing me house number 401," Emma said.

"You want to buy?"

"Yes."

"Oh, fine, fine," Ismael said, looking happy. "Then you are welcome in advance, Madam Melody."

He certainly is charming, Emma thought. "Please, Ismael, I wanted to know whether you—I mean, if I buy the house— whether you will be able to bring me some new and different plants."

"No problem, madam. I can do that." He hesitated. "Please, number 401 . . . that's the house . . ."

"Where Lady Araba died? Yes, Rita told me."

"But you are okay to buy it?"

"Yes, it doesn't trouble me," Emma assured him. "Why? It seems you are worried."

"Not at all, please," Ismael said, smiling with some embarrass-ment.

"What are you planting there?" Emma asked. She wanted to ease the pressure off him, at least temporarily.

"That one is begonia," Ismael said.

"I heard Lady Araba loved flowers."

Ismael nodded. "Madam Rita told you?"

"Yes," Emma said. "When we went to the terrace and I saw all the plants there. Are you the one who took them to Lady Araba?"

"Yes." Ismael's gaze dropped for a second and he patted around a seedling. "I used to bring her some from my business."

Emma saw something in his face and eyes. "It's paining you, Ismael? About Lady Araba."

"Yes please."

"Me too," Emma said. "You know, I admired her. Are you the one who saw her that day? Dead, I mean."

"Yes please."

"Oh," Emma said, shaking her head in regret. "Terrible."

Ismael nodded. "I broke the glass door to enter. Lady Araba's face was so swollen." He seemed to shudder. "It looked horrible. Then I called security."

"Sorry," Emma said again.

"Oh, you don't worry," Ismael said. "I'm okay."

"Good," Emma said, flashing him a smile.

"Please, madam, I have to go to the other side of the estate."

"Of course." She passed a ten-*cedi* bill to him. "Thank you for your good work, Ismael, eh?"

He beamed. "God bless you, madam."

Emma watched him as he walked away. The "dash" she had given both Ismael and Peter was just in case she had to come back to ask them further questions. An appreciative gratuity could buy people's silence, but it could also loosen tongues.

THIRTY-THREE

Eleven months after

AT THE NEXT MORNING briefing, everyone was on time except Walter, who came running in with an apologetic look. After making a few routine announcements, Sowah got down to the case.

"Let me bring you all up-to-date with what I've learned from my visit to Bob Agyekum at Metro TV," he said. "As you're aware, he and I have known each other for a long time." He stood and walked over to the whiteboard, which still bore the web of suspects in the case.

"Bob brought a couple of things to my attention. One is that Augustus's relationship with Bertha Longdon, his ex-wife, played a big role in his behavior. Even when they were separated, Bertha either couldn't let him go or was crazed with jealousy over his being with another woman—or both. She harassed and stalked Araba and Augustus, mostly on social media, where she insinuated that Augustus had always been a philanderer and still was, even after getting together with Araba. That made things rocky for him, and it appears to be the point at which he started drinking heavily again, leading to his dismissal from Metro TV. The bottom line is that Araba had a powerful enemy in Bertha, and we must look at her too."

Yet another angle. The room murmured.

"It is now imperative that we talk to Augustus. Walter, I think you can pose as the same sympathetic freelance journalist you were with the Tagoes. Call DS Boateng for his phone number."

"Okay, sir," Walter said.

"Now," Sowah continued, "we still have the issue of the crime scene evidence. If the DNA or fingerprints match any of the people we've been considering, we could have a breakthrough. So, I'll keep nudging DCOP Laryea on this. I'm hoping he can make some headway with Director-General Tawiah."

"To get FSL to do it?" Gideon asked.

"Yes."

Which reminded Emma of something. "Boss, I've been wondering about Lady Araba's postmortem. We don't know what they found. We don't even know who did the autopsy."

"Oh," Sowah said. "Yes, you're right. That slipped my mind. I can ask Laryea for help on that as well. Now, Emma, it's your turn to tell us about your visit to Trasacco."

"Okay, boss, but first, I want to thank you for the rented Benz."

A cheer went up from the others, who promptly began to tease her.

"Lady Emma, fashion icon!"

"No, it's Princess Emma rather."

"Is that so?" Gideon said, looking awestruck. "Then we must bow to her!" He jumped up and executed a showy, ridiculous bow. Emma struggled to keep a straight face.

"No, seriously, Emma," Jojo said, "you dey take selfie for Benz inside? Come on, make you no lie."

"Okay, yes," Emma confessed. "I did."

"And you've been hiding it from us?" Jojo said in mock consternation. "Let's see. Come on, show us!"

Emma feigned reluctance in pulling out her phone. She located the photos and first showed the boss, who smiled and let it pass around to exclamations of admiration.

"Can I be your husband in the Benz next time?" Jojo asked, winking at her.

Emma couldn't hold her laughter in any longer.

"Okay," Sowah said, finally. "Back to work. By the way, Emma, I agree—the Benz suits you."

"Thank you, sir."

More cheers and laughter. "The boss approves."

Sowah turned to Emma. "Don't mind them. Go on."

Emma described her tour of what had once been Lady Araba's home, down to the kinds of locks on the doors and windows and all the access points, front to back. Emma felt the garage was important to consider as a possible means of entry into the home.

"As you climb the stairs to the second floor," Emma continued, "you see the master bedroom ahead a little to your left. Wait, I have some photos you can all look at." She fiddled with her phone as the others came around to her desk. "In the bedroom, you can see how the bed is arranged in relation to the door that opens onto the terrace. Here we are on the terrace, which is facing the back of the house. This railing is where Ismael leaned his ladder against to come onto the terrace. So, from the railing, I took a picture of the terrace door. The glass has a tint, so it acts like a mirror. Even when I got close, it was hard to see inside. Jojo, Ismael told you it was around seven in the morning that he went to the terrace, not so?"

"Correct."

"And I was there between nine o'clock and nine-thirty, so the sun was brighter than at seven o'clock, but not *that* much. The glass would still be like a mirror. So, my question is, how did Ismael spot Lady Araba in the bed unless he put his face right up against the glass door? Why would he do that? Unless something or someone tipped him off to do it, or he's a Peeping Tom?"

"Oh, I see what you're saying," Jojo said slowly, light dawning.

"Go on," Sowah said to Emma.

"Lady Araba was known to wake up around five in the morning, when it's still dark outside," Emma said. "With the lights on in the room but off on the terrace, what she can see outside is limited. It's the exact reverse of the situation during the day, right? Someone can observe her from the terrace without being seen."

"You mean Ismael was watching her?" Walter interjected. "And then what? He went in and murdered her? What's his motive?"

"I have an idea what it might be," Emma said, "but I want to finish this part first. Let's say Lady Araba neglected to lock the terrace door. Late at night, Ismael could get up to the terrace with his ladder, open the door quietly, attack Araba, and strangle her to death. When he's done, he arranges her in what we can call a 'normal' sleeping position, under the covers.

"Around seven in the morning, when Ismael goes up to the terrace with the planters, he already knows Lady Araba is dead. He raises the alarm to Peter while pretending the terrace door is locked. So, he smashes the glass to get in, already knowing what he will find. The story he tells everyone is that he happened to see into Araba's room at seven and see her dead."

Jojo applauded, but Walter looked skeptical, while Sowah and Gideon appeared neutral.

"And what about motive?" Walter asked.

"Ismael told me Lady Araba loved flowers," Emma continued, "and how he always brought her special ones from his garden shop. What if the real reason he kept bringing flowers to Araba was that he was in love with her? And if she spurned him when he professed his love to her? Well, that can become intent to kill."

"These are excellent thoughts," Sowah said. "They still leave us with one question, though. If Ismael is the killer, why, then, would he want to be the one who 'discovers' the body?"

Emma blew out her breath. "You're right, boss. That's a good question."

"I know!" Gideon said, snapping his fingers. "He wanted to return to the scene of the crime. Certain killers either enjoy reliving the murder or just feel compelled to see it again."

Sowah smiled and pointed his index finger at Gideon. "Gold star for you."

"Oh, no," Jojo muttered, slapping his forehead. "He's going to be boasting about this all day."

Gideon stuck his tongue out at him and grinned.

"Walter," Sowah said, turning to him, "you and Gideon visited the Tagoes last night, correct?"

"Yes, boss," Walter said. "It was a strange experience."

"How so?"

"Gideon and I talked about it after we left," Walter said. "There's a kind of tension in the air between the Father and his wife, but even before we get to that, I noticed how heavily made-up Mrs. Tagoe was—almost what they call 'pancake,' is that the word?" He looked at Emma, but she said nothing. She wished Walter would stop assuming she knew everything about all things female.

"Why did you think it was strange, Walter?" Sowah asked.

"Well, I use my wife, Beatrice, as a frame of reference," Walter said, "and maybe this isn't a valid thought, but Beatrice has levels of makeup. At home just relaxing and not doing anything, she may have none. Going out shopping, or maybe when friends come over, the makeup is moderate, but when we're going to a special event, she's in maximum makeup mode, if I may call it that. To me, that's how Mrs. Tagoe was."

"Okay," Sowah said slowly, "so, what are you driving at?"

"What crossed my mind was physical abuse," Walter said. "Disguising her bruises."

"Oh, really!" Sowah exclaimed, taken aback. "That didn't occur to me."

"Perhaps Mrs. Tagoe was planning to go out later," Emma said.

"I don't think so," Walter said. "Without the husband?"

"Why not?" Emma asked.

Walter shook his head. "He wasn't dressed up at all to go out, and I don't get the feeling she's the kind of woman who would go somewhere and leave the hubby at home."

Emma gave a little snort and then realized too late that it sounded derisive. On the one hand, Walter was getting on her nerves, but on the other, she wondered why she was taking this so personally.

"Okay, let's come back to that," Sowah said. "You mentioned tension between the Father and Mrs. Tagoe?"

"When I asked about Father Tagoe's relationship with Araba," Walter said, "Mrs. Tagoe seemed uncomfortable, and at a few other points, I felt like she wanted to say something but wouldn't dare in front of him. The Father laid on the piety thick, and she seemed to follow his example just because she felt she had to. Something was simply not right."

"Where do you position Father Tagoe in a hierarchy of suspects?" Sowah asked.

Walter thought about it for a moment. "Despite the strange feeling I got there, honestly, I don't think we were looking at a killer."

"What did you think, Gideon?" Sowah asked.

"I agree with Walter. He's religious, and I think he may be a hypocrite as well—like so many priests—but I couldn't see any motive."

"In summation, then," Sowah said, "it looks like Ismael has floated somewhat to the top of our list of suspects? Rather closer to Augustus Seeza. Does everyone agree?"

But no one in the room enthusiastically endorsed that either.

"Boss, I don't know what to think," Jojo confessed.

"We still need to talk to Seeza," Walter pointed out. "Maybe we can get a better perspective then."

"Yes," Sowah said, "but Jojo, you will go back to Ismael, and push him this time to come out with whatever he's hiding from us."

"Yes, boss."

"Okay," Sowah said. "Meeting over. Well done, all of you."

THIRTY-FOUR

One month before

IN THE LATE AFTERNOON light, Bertha was the vision of love-liness as she welcomed Justice Julius Seeza to the sprawling living room of her Airport Hills mansion. Elegant and tall, her skin even fairer than Lady Araba's, Bertha possessed an aura of dignity and self-assurance. She was a full-figured, strongly built woman who wore her weight well.

The house girl brought in some refreshments—a small platter of Danish butter cookies, Star beer for Julius, and tropical punch for Bertha, who did not drink.

"How are you faring?" Julius asked her, pouring his beer.

Bertha sighed and gave an ever-so-slight smile. "By God's grace, I'm managing—even though I still feel the pain."

"I'm sorry," he said. "Caroline and I miss you. We always loved you. We still do, and I hope you know that. My parents knew yours so well and for such a long time that you've been like a daughter to us and will always be."

Bertha smiled sweetly. "Thank you. I miss you too, Papa. Was Mama Caroline unable to come with you?"

"Honestly, she doesn't know I'm here. She plans to visit you, but I wanted to warn you in advance about what she intends to ask you. She constantly talks about the possibility of you and Augustus getting back together again, and she has a plan. She's thinking along the lines of a truth and reconciliation process."

Bertha laughed. "What is this, Rwanda?"

Julius smiled only slightly at the poor joke. "The point is, Mama wants you and Augustus to meet, sit down in our presence, and express what you've been through on both sides. All the pain. And don't forget, Mama Caroline and I have *also* suffered through all these troubles."

"I don't see the point of a truth and reconciliation mission—or whatever you want to call it—when Araba the temptress is still hanging around. Honestly, Papa Julius, I detest that woman."

"And I can understand that," Julius said. "Look, Araba will eventually fall by the roadside, or I should say, will be dropped there. Her family has been pressuring her to cut herself off from Augustus, and if you got back together with him, she would see that there's no point in continuing the charade. Bertha, dear, Araba is not a permanent fixture here. You, Augustus, and your marriage are."

A brief silence fell between them, and Bertha spoke. "How is he—Augustus?"

"He's doing well," Julius said with enthusiasm. "He's been alcohol-free for almost four months straight now and returning to his normal self. I'm very proud of him."

Bertha nodded. "I'm glad for you. And him." She nibbled on a cookie and sipped some juice before resuming. "If I were to consider ever reuniting with Augustus, he would have to be stone-cold sober."

"And we're going to make sure of that," Julius said. "We are paying for his rehab program, and I think he's going to do well."

"That's promising, Papa Julius."

"Yes, it is," Julius said. "Bertha, it's been a bumpy road, but we are finally in control at the steering wheel. What you and the kids and we too have been going through is unsustainable, and we won't allow it to continue? Okay? You have my word on that. So, what do you say?"

Bertha held Julius's gaze in hers. "If Augustus can stay sober *and* push Lady Araba away once and for all, then yes, I am open to truth and reconciliation."

THIRTY-FIVE

Two days before

THE ANNUAL ACCRA FASHION Week, sponsored by NIVEA, was at the Tang Palace Hotel. It was already Saturday night, meaning Lady Araba and Samson had less than two days to nail down every detail for a flawless runway performance Monday morning. The so-called rehearsal earlier that day had not gone well. Four models hadn't shown up, so Araba either needed to find replacements or change the sequence and timing of appearances so their existing models could appear on the runway multiple times. So far, two new models had pledged to show up early the next morning and have the outfits altered to suit their body type.

The caterer for the event had run into a technical problem at the last minute and had threatened to back out until Samson got on the phone and yelled at them, threatening to expose them as unprofessional on social media.

In the Airport City office, Araba pored over the models' names and walk-on times, allowing for the possibility that they would be two short. Samson popped out to find something to eat and returned with food and good news. Diamond, one of their standby models, had just called him to say she could fill in.

"*Yes!*" Araba said, pumping the air in triumph. "Thank God. Just one more now."

"You should eat," Samson said, plonking a large plastic bag of food down on the table.

"What did you get?" Araba said, not looking up.

"Jollof rice."

"Okay," she murmured. "I'll have some a little later."

"No," Samson insisted. "You eat right now. You know how you are before events. You get tense, starve yourself, and are on the verge of collapsing on the day of the show."

Araba acquiesced and opened the bag.

Samson cleared his throat. "Lady Pizzazz is everywhere on the 'gram and Facebook saying how she's going to have the greatest show on earth."

Araba rolled her eyes. "Please. It's all talk."

"They say she has a new line based on traditional clothing from Northern Ghana."

"I don't give a damn. It could be from the Sahara Desert and she couldn't keep up," Araba said. "Come on, let's finish this."

She and Samson worked for another hour.

"The music is set up?" Araba asked him.

He nodded. "Yes. DJ Breezy is confirmed."

"Good." She sat back for a moment and stretched her arms above her head, only to wince and grab the back of her neck.

"You're tense," Samson said. He stood behind her and began to massage the sore spot.

Araba moaned with relief. "That feels so good."

"I want to help you de-stress," he said. "Your muscles are so rigid."

He worked on her neck and shoulders in silence for a few minutes, then bent to kiss her on the neck.

"Samson," she said. "No."

"Sorry," he whispered. "I couldn't help myself."

"I'm your boss," she reminded him sternly.

"Yes," he said, nuzzling her ear. "The most beautiful boss in the world."

He moved his fingers to Araba's collarbone, gently caressing her until she stood up and slipped out from his grasp.

"You have to control yourself," she said sharply. "I don't like this."

"The times we were together, you liked it," he reminded her.

"I know," she said wearily, "but that was a mistake. For both of us. Let's move on."

He said nothing in response, but looked at her the way a hungry animal eyed food snatched from under its nose.

"I'll see you back here tomorrow morning," she said, packing up for the day. "We still have a lot to do."

"Okay, boss."

FINALLY AT HOME, Araba took a shower, then took to the sofa in the living room in her nightgown. Amanua, the house girl, came in to ask if Araba needed anything more. She would be leaving early Sunday for a funeral. Araba dismissed her for the night and switched on the TV in time to catch the latest episode of *Real Housewives of Atlanta*. After a while, she began to feel drowsy and decided to call it a day.

Her phone buzzed. Samson had texted. She opened the message and saw: **Sorry about earlier. It won't happen again.**

Araba texted back: **It's all right. Let's just move forward.**

THIRTY-SIX

Two weeks before

JULIUS AND CAROLINE SEEZA joined forces to stage an intervention with their son. He had been sober for longer than any recent stretch. They sat him down in the dining room, where they faced him from the opposite side of the table.

Caroline began. "We're proud of you, Augustus." She had never called him "Gus," which she found to be crude. "You've been clean for almost five months, and for that, you deserve praise. In view of that, your father and I want you to consider getting back together with Bertha again."

Augustus, freshly shaved and looking better than he had in a long time, suddenly appeared weary. "I think that ship has sailed," he said dully.

"No," Julius said quietly. "It has not. Look, I've spoken to Bertha, and she's willing to try a truth and reconciliation process. This could really work."

"You have two dear children," Caroline pressed. "You owe it to them, if no one else—*especially* your son, Ben. No child should grow up with an absent parent. This will negatively affect them for life."

"So, will their seeing Bertha and me in a constant state of hostility toward each other," Augustus said.

"We're not talking about abruptly bringing the two of you

together under one roof," Caroline said. "This is a process—a marathon, not a sprint, and we speak of truth and reconciliation because it's one of the best ways to bring peace between two parties. Little by little, you and Bertha will iron out the difficulties and find ways to resolve the challenges that the two of you have been facing and lay the groundwork for a solid future."

Augustus averted his eyes to stare at the table in front of him. He seemed to be mulling over the points his parents had made, but he suddenly buried his face in his palms. "I just wish I could forget about her," he groaned.

Caroline frowned. "About whom?"

"Araba, of course!" he said, almost angrily. "What is it about her, that I can't get her out of my system? This is like torture."

Almost at the point of weeping, Augustus began to hyperventilate and become overwrought. Caroline got up, came around, and put her arms around him. "We're here for you, my love. We will help you get through this. You're not alone."

THIRTY-SEVEN

Eleven months after

DCOP Laryea had scheduled an end-of-day meeting with Director-General Madam Tawiah, who was running behind. Finally, after six in the evening when the sun was setting, Tawiah was ready to receive him in her office. Laryea came in and took a seat in one of the comfy chairs in this now tastefully furnished room. Unlike her predecessor, she seldom stayed behind her desk when speaking with her senior officers. She sat a comfortable distance from Laryea.

"How can I help?" Tawiah asked.

"Please, it's regarding the Araba Tagoe case—you know, the lady murdered almost a year ago."

"I remember," Tawiah said. "What about it?"

"I've had an inquiry from an old friend of mine, Yemo Sowah, who runs a private detective agency. Lady Araba's aunt brought the case to him because she was dissatisfied with the way we've handled the case."

"Dissatisfied in what way?" Tawiah asked skeptically.

"Although Araba's driver was arrested for the crime, Dele believes that Augustus Seeza, who was in a relationship with Lady Araba, is the prime suspect."

"I'm well acquainted with Dele Tetteyfio," Tawiah said. "She came to see me weeks after the death of her niece, and I listened duly to her concerns, but as I told her, we have a full confession from the lady's driver, Kwesi—or was it Kweku?"

"Kweku, madam."

"He tried to steal Lady Araba's jewelry, and she caught him in the act. He panicked and murdered her. We have the complete confession from Kweku. Case closed."

She knows confessions can be false, Laryea thought. *I know that too, and she knows I know.* "Please, what would be wrong with using the DNA evidence to bolster the case against the driver?" Laryea asked. "We have an officer who can perform it—DS Isaac Boateng, whom I'm sure you know."

"I do," Tawiah said. "But, in this case, the DNA evidence may only confuse the picture. You see, because Augustus Seeza was frequently in her house, his DNA is likely to be present in the evidence."

"But only in traces, surely, madam? I think they can tell—"

"We want to avoid any confusion," Tawiah interrupted. "It's not worth the chance that we may imprison the wrong person."

Typical nonsensical obfuscation, Laryea thought.

"Furthermore," Tawiah continued, "I question the motivation behind Boateng going for training in South Africa. I won't mention names, but he persuaded someone it was a good idea, and off Boateng went."

"Oh," Laryea said blankly. "I wasn't aware. But that doesn't say anything about his competence to process the DNA. After all, he handled the case of the missing Takoradi girls, and that wasn't easy. He should be up to the task of this case."

"Just be aware, between you and me, that we were having behavioral problems with Boateng."

"How so, madam?"

"Some mental instability."

Laryea found this odd. "Please, is that the reason Boateng was moved from Headquarters to the Tema division?"

"*I* transferred him," Tawiah said. "He was overstepping his bounds in the Lady Araba case. He was biased against the Seeza family, harassing them unnecessarily. It seems he had an axe to grind."

"Then, madam, what about contracting a reliable third party like Professor Kingsley at CCU or one of the private DNA labs in town? Then we will have an unbiased evaluation."

Before Tawiah could answer, there was a knock on the door, and a man with an egg-shaped bald head entered. Laryea recognized him at once. Adam Kyei, the Minister of Science & Technology and owner of Metro TV.

He didn't look at Laryea, only at Madam Tawiah. "Are you ready?" he barked.

She laughed at him, then smiled at Laryea. "My brother. I must go now, because he has no patience."

Laryea rose. "Of course, madam. Good evening, sir."

"That's DCOP Laryea," Tawiah informed Kyei, as if he cared.

"Ah," Kyei grunted. "Good evening."

Laryea stood up. "Okay then, Madam Tawiah. I'm taking my leave. Thank you for seeing me."

"You're welcome. Take care."

As Laryea shut the door behind him, he was assembling a theory in his mind. Seeza and his Metro TV owner Kyei had been close and still were, despite Seeza's downfall. To protect the network and the *Tough Talk* show from bad press, Kyei may have asked his sister, Tawiah, to stop the crime scene evidence from going any further than administrator Thomas's office. Laryea found himself weighing this hypothesis against the other, equally credible alternative that it was Judge Julius Seeza who had had a hand in stopping the march of justice in order to protect his son.

THIRTY-EIGHT

Eleven months after

SEVERAL DAYS AFTER SPEAKING with the Tagoes, Walter Manu finally secured an interview with Augustus on the pretext of being a freelance journalist writing an in-depth feature on the famous TV anchorman. Gideon was to be Walter's "photographer."

Julius Seeza's home was the venue of the interview. Unemployed, Augustus had sold his apartment and was living with his parents. The house was large, as could be expected for a well-off doctor and judge. With Gideon beside him, Walter knocked on the front door. A young man in a *batakari* opened it after a few seconds.

"Good morning," Walter said. "I'm Busia, this is David, my assistant. Mr. Seeza should be expecting us."

"Wh—which Mr. Seeza?" The man had a pronounced stutter.

"Augustus." Walter said.

"Okay. Please c—come in."

He asked Walter and Gideon to have a seat while he went to get Mr. Seeza.

After a brief while, it wasn't Augustus who appeared. It was Julius, who didn't seem wildly excited to see the two visitors. "Morning," he said dully. "You're the guys from the newspaper?"

Standing, Walter introduced Gideon and himself by their aliases. "I'm a freelance journalist, sir."

"Have a seat, please," Seeza said, taking a chair himself. "So, you don't know yet where your article will appear?"

"That's correct, sir, but several websites both here and abroad almost always publish my work."

"We can conduct the interview in my study," Julius said. "I'll take you there in a moment, but before we proceed, I have a favor to ask of you."

"Yes, sir."

"Due to his illness, Augustus has suffered severe sensorineural hearing loss, which has been devastating to all of us, but to him especially. We are in the process of raising funds for a cochlear implant, for which the doctors say Augustus is eligible, but which is an extremely costly procedure. I need you to make that very clear in the interview and where any donations should be sent."

So, there's something in it for them, too, Walter thought. "Of course, sir," he said. "It will be my honor to do so. I've always been a great fan of Mr. Seeza's." That much was true.

"I appreciate that," Julius said, a hint of a smile appearing like the sun peeping through the clouds. "Please come with me, gentlemen."

They followed him down a dim hallway to a musty room with a formidable old wooden desk and bookshelves laden with large law volumes.

"Have a seat," Julius said. "I'll be just a few minutes." At the door, he turned. "One other thing. I will not allow you to question Augustus about anything to do with Araba Tagoe."

As soon as he left the room, Walter muttered, "Oh. That's not good."

He exchanged a glance with Gideon, who said, "What are you going to do, then?"

"Don't worry. We'll talk around it. He might even bring her up."

They sat looking at the framed awards, qualifications, and photographs of Julius Seeza with prominent international figures present and past hanging on the walls.

"Wow," Gideon whispered. "Impressive."

Voices, one of which was a woman's, emanated from down the hall. The two male Seezas appeared in the doorway first, and Caroline brought up the rear. Holding on to Julius's arm, Augustus walked with a cane, his gait awkward and unstable. He swayed as if being buffeted by gusts of wind, almost certain to fall were it not for his cane on his right and his father on the left. With each step, Augustus looked down at his feet as if to make sure he was planting them correctly.

"Almost there," Julius murmured encouragingly as he guided his son toward a large brown leather armchair. Augustus sat down with some effort and a short groan.

Walter felt a jolt of dismay. This man didn't remotely resemble Augustus Seeza, host of the brilliant *Tough Talk* program Walter had watched for years. He was much leaner, and where he was once clean-shaven, he now had a patchy gray beard, appearing to have aged twenty years. Walter hoped he was successfully hiding his shock.

"Good morning, gentlemen," Caroline said. With her teal-colored stethoscope draped around her neck, she was dressed in a fetching yellow pants suit over a white silk blouse. She wore pearl earrings and a necklace to match.

Walter and Gideon rose in deference. "Morning, Doctor," they said, almost simultaneously.

"Oh, please, sit," Caroline said. "I'm leaving for the hospital now, so I won't be able to stay. I just want to say that in welcoming you to our home for this interview, we expect a tone of respect and civility over this sensitive matter. My son is recovering from a serious illness, and so I would ask you to be as brief and to-the-point as possible, so as not to tire him out too much."

"Yes, of course, Doctor," Walter said. "We will see to that."

Caroline nodded. "Very good." She rested her hand on Augustus's shoulder for a moment and smiled at him. "I'll come back at lunchtime and we can eat together."

Gideon found Caroline Seeza attractive. "Please, Doctor,"

he said. "Do you mind if I take some pics of you and your son together? It will promote the cause."

"Of course not," she said sweetly. She kneeled down beside Augustus and flashed a brilliant smile as Gideon snapped a few.

"Thanks, Doctor."

Once she had left, Julius grabbed a pen and legal pad from the desk and settled into a seat next to his son. "He can read lips a little," Julius explained, "so, when asking a question, look directly at him and enunciate your words, but *please* do not shout in the expectation that he will hear you any better. I will help by writing down the questions he doesn't understand, but he will respond verbally in the normal way. I know it's tedious, but this is the only way it can be done."

"Yes, sir," Walter said. "No problem." He looked at Augustus. "Thank you for allowing us to speak to you, sir."

"You're welcome." His voice was raspy, like sandpaper—nothing like his booming, melodic baritone from before.

"Do you mind if my photographer takes a few photos while we're talking?"

Augustus looked at his father, who pointed at Gideon and mimed using a camera.

"Yes, no problem," Augustus answered.

"How have you been feeling, sir?" Walter asked.

Augustus cued his father to transcribe the new question, which he did quickly on the pad.

Augustus replied, "Well, we take it day by day. Physically, I'm broken, but emotionally, I'm recovering, and I thank God for rescuing me from the hell I was living in."

"When you say 'hell,' sir, what do you mean?"

Augustus leaned toward Julius to see the scribbled question. "For years, I was in Satan's grip—drinking heavily, even while I was working. Now I'm in recovery, alcohol-free for six months."

"Congratulations, sir. I'm sure it wasn't easy. How long had you suffered with this before you turned it around?"

"For twenty years, I have been a functioning alcoholic. About two years ago, it became much worse."

"What do you believe triggered that?"

When Augustus saw the written question, he shrugged. "Many things. Mostly marital issues."

Aware that Julius was watching closely, Walter asked, "Please, sir, can you expand on that a little bit?"

"I was stuck between two women, both of them wonderful in their own way. I was cruel to them both."

"If I'm not mistaken, sir, you were married to Bertha Longdon?"

"That is correct."

"And the other woman you're referring to?"

Julius interrupted sharply. "This is an area I warned you to avoid, Mr. Busia."

"But, sir, your son brought it up himself," Walter pointed out.

Augustus was watching the back-and-forth closely and must have figured out what was going on. "Papa," he said keenly. "I'm not a child, so please don't try to censor the questions. If I don't wish to answer something, I will make it known."

Walter was glad to see a flash of the old Augustus Seeza. Julius scowled and went into a wounded, resentful silence.

Gideon was moving around them quietly taking pictures.

"I'm sure you're aware that Lady Araba and I were in a relationship," Augustus continued to Walter. "It was the stress of being caught between Bertha and Araba that pushed me toward the bottle."

Not exactly taking full responsibility, Walter thought. On the other hand, women *could* be ruthless and nagging. The constant calls, the stalking, the unfounded jealousy—Walter understood all that. It had been a long time since anything of that nature had been part of his life, but before his marriage decades ago, he'd had his share of "women problems."

"How were you able to stop drinking?" Walter asked.

Augustus studied Walter's lips. "Come again?"

Walter repeated it more slowly.

"Only by the grace of God," Augustus responded. "He pulled me from a destructive fire. Let me tell you something, Mr. Busia.

After my hospitalization for acute pancreatitis, the Lord spoke to me. He said, 'Augustus, if you don't relinquish alcohol forever, you will die.' And I listened to Him."

"We thank God," Walter said with approval. "Please, I know this is a sensitive topic, but if you don't mind telling me when you stopped drinking in relation to the death of Lady Araba?"

"Why is that important?" Julius interjected, flipping up his palm.

Augustus saw the gesture and put a hand on his father's shoulder. "Papa, relax. I'm not afraid of these questions. Please, I beg you—write what he asks."

Julius did. Augustus read it and returned the notepad to Walter. "I'll explain everything to you; I have nothing to lose and perhaps something to gain. A little less than a year after Bertha and I separated, I met Lady Araba at a party, and we began an affair."

Augustus continued, "For several months, I felt relentless pressure from both Araba and Bertha—jealous attacks and bitter accusations. For relief, I took to drinking. One night at the station, I was drunk. It was obvious during my terrible interview with Chief Justice Angela Waters, following which I was suspended and then fired. Soon after, Lady Araba told me to stay away from her, but I knew it was at the behest of her family, particularly Fifi Tagoe, the so-called Reverend, one of the greatest hypocrites I have ever encountered. But I digress. The day I was hospitalized with alcoholic hepatitis, I called Araba out of pure desperation, and she came down to see me. I vowed to her I would never drink again. Both of us cried that day and decided to make things work.

"I was true to my word over the next six months. I grew strong again, gained some weight, and had one of the happiest times of my life with Araba. We went to church together every Sunday and prayed to the Lord to give us strength. And then, just like that, she was gone. Dead."

Although instinct alone was no reliable indicator, Walter thought Augustus's anguish seemed real. Was it also true that, during the months leading up to Araba's death, the couple had been together in blissful harmony?

"After her death," Augustus said, "I turned back to alcohol. The last time I ever drank, I barely escaped death. It was also during that hospital stay, which lasted weeks, that this deafness attacked me out of nowhere. They say they don't understand how it happened, but I do. It was God's punishment. How many times in church had I promised Him that I wouldn't drink again? Lies. I didn't hold up my end of the bargain. By His grace alone, God is giving me one last chance. The media have cast doubt as to whether I've truly found God, which I have, but I can't force anyone to believe me. They also continue to insinuate that I murdered Lady Araba. I didn't, but I'm certain of who did."

"Who?"

"Father Fifi Tagoe."

Walter's eyebrows raised. "Her father? That's a bold accusation to make."

"And when I tell you why I say it, you'll understand," Augustus said. "Araba held a deep secret practically all her life. When she was a young girl, her father, the Most Reverend Tagoe, a so-called man of God, sexually abused her."

Walter started. "Excuse me?"

"Araba's father abused her for years, starting when she was six or seven and for years until she left home in her late teens."

Walter, stunned, exchanged a glance with Gideon.

"Very few people know about the depression she suffered as a result of what that man did to her," Augustus went on. "She described it to me in horrible detail—the way her father would come into her bedroom and violate her after Miriam had gone to bed."

Walter was staggered. "When did she tell you?"

"Well into our relationship. Over a year."

"Did anyone else know?"

"Her Auntie Dele might have," Augustus said, "but it's not something you share with many people, and holding something like that inside you for years can make you sick. Araba was often plunged into deep depression, even without obvious cause. It was the weight of that awful secret, and once she began to realize that, things improved. We never discussed if or when she would go public with this, but I knew she was moving in that direction. When one of the organizers of fashion week decided to make the theme "We Too," Araba took it as a signal that it was time.

"Araba was scheduled to be interviewed live on a special Monday-night edition of *Tough Talk* for the start of fashion week, and that was when she intended to expose her father. She confronted him about this ahead of time, but he denied ever abusing her. He then tried to stop her from moving forward with her plan, but Araba's mind was made up. Now, you tell me, Mr. Busia, as a priest, how would you feel if you had built your entire career, even your identity, on piety, and someone was on the verge of exposing your sin and wickedness to the world? Think of the shame."

Walter agreed with what Augustus was implying. It was a strong motive for murder. But not proof.

"Now, Mr. Busia, are you finished?" Julius said. "My son is tired. That's all the questions he can take for now."

THIRTY-NINE

Eleven months after

TO GET AHOLD OF Kweku-Sam at Nsawam Prison, Sowah posed as a university professor interviewing murder suspects. After visiting the prison administrator with a small "donation," permission was granted. A semi-private area of the prison yard was the chosen venue for the interview. Not far away, a guard kept a languid eye on the prisoner and the "professor" sitting opposite each other.

Kweku-Sam was rail thin and didn't look well.

"How are you?" Sowah asked just the same.

"I'm fine, thank you." His voice was low and listless.

"I appreciate you meeting me here today."

Kweku-Sam kept his gaze down. "Okay, sir."

"My name is Professor Chinery. I am interviewing prisoners charged with murder and awaiting trial."

"Yes please." Kweku-Sam looked up, fresh hope creeping into his lifeless eyes. "Please, can you help my case?"

"I can't promise you that, but let's pray for the best. Okay?"

"Yes please."

"How are you surviving here?"

Kweku-Sam shook his head. "If one of those guys doesn't kill me, then the food will. I can't even tell you how terrible everything is. Every day I wonder: Will I die here?"

Sowah felt sympathy for him.

"Has anyone told you why you're here?" Sowah asked.

Kweku-Sam shrugged. "They say I killed her. That I went to steal her jewelry and I killed her."

"Lady Araba, you mean?"

"Yes please."

"And did you?"

"No please."

Tears were suddenly streaming down Kweku-Sam's face. He wiped them away before he spoke again. "Madam was a good woman. When my boy was sick and we took him to the hospital, she helped me and my wife because the cost was too much. I'm grateful to Lady Araba for everything. Why should I kill her?"

"When did the police arrest you?" Sowah asked. "And what did they say to you?"

"The last time I saw her was that Sunday, the night before they found her dead," Kweku-Sam said. "Around seven that evening, I took her to a party and brought her back home at about nine. Her assistant, Samson, called her once while we were on our way out, and Mr. Seeza also called her twice. He asked if he could come see her, and she said no, she wouldn't let him in. She was very annoyed."

Sowah thought about that for a moment. Walter had reported from his interview with Augustus that his relationship with Araba had been wonderful up to the time of her murder, but this story didn't support that.

"What happened after that?" Sowah asked.

"I brought Madam home and helped her take her bags inside the house, and then I left."

"So, was that around nine-fifteen?"

"Something like that."

"Did anyone see you leave?"

"Sako—one of the guards."

"Did you speak to him?"

"Not so much. I just told him I was going home and I'd see him in the morning."

"And then you went home?"

"Yes, I took a *tro-tro*."

"Can someone confirm it?"

"You can call my brother to ask him. He lives with me, and we were at home together that night."

Sowah took the number down before continuing. "Now, Monday morning, what happened?"

"I came to take her to the Tang Hotel for the fashion show. First, I washed the car, and I saw Ismael there too. He was going to put some flowerpots up at her door behind the house. I thought Madam would come down by seven-fifteen, but she didn't. Then Ismael started shouting to me that I should go and call Mr. Peter. I returned with Peter and we went to the roof and Ismael broke the glass and we saw the madam lying in the bed." Kweku-Sam stared at the ground, seemingly in a daze.

"What happened after?"

"When the police arrived, they detained all of us and we went to the police station to write our statements of what we were doing and where we were Sunday night to Monday morning, and then they let us go. Maybe two days later, they came to question me again because I had written that I was inside the house with Madam to carry her things from the car. They kept asking me what I did after. Said maybe I tried to rob her and killed her, or that I hid in the house and tried to steal from her later." Kweku sighed. "They took me to CID to question me more. They worked in shifts to interrogate me all day and night. When one officer went home, another one came. They didn't let me sleep. They kept saying, 'Just sign this paper, and we'll let you go to bed.'"

"Did you read it before you signed it?"

Kweku looked uncertain. "I think so. I don't remember."

Sowah nodded. "Okay, I understand. Let me ask you something. Who do you think killed Lady Araba?"

With no emotion on his face, Kweku said, "Mr. Seeza. And Peter helped him."

"Why should they do that?"

"They are good friends. Mr. Seeza gave Peter money all the time. That Mr. Seeza is a madman. A nasty drunkard who treated Madam very badly." Kweku shook his head, bitterness written on his face. "She wanted to get away from him, and he got angry."

But to Sowah, Kweku's assessment did not build a solid case. Kweku-Sam was convinced that Peter and Seeza had killed Lady Araba, but that was all he had—the conviction. As passionate as he was in that, he had not produced a single solid piece of evidence to back it up.

FORTY

Eleven months after

Doctors in government hospitals all over Ghana were on strike for better working conditions and benefits. Emergency services were sharply curtailed.

One subset of physicians couldn't care less about the strike and refused to join under any circumstances: the Cuban doctors in Ghana, participating in Cuba's decades-old program of "medical internationalism." Cuba sent out thousands of its doctors every year to parts of Latin America and Africa.

This ended up working in Emma's favor. She showed up at the Police Hospital mortuary with a reasonable facsimile of a Citi-FM Radio ID badge and showed it to one of the attendants, a wizened man who looked like he must have worked there forever. His work badge said FOSTER.

"Good morning, boss," Emma said, flashing her most brilliant smile.

It must have been catching, because Foster returned a big-gapped grin. "Morning, madam."

"I'm from Citi-FM news. Is any doctor on duty today?"

"Yes, madam. Do you wish to talk to her?"

"Yes, please."

"Okay," he said. "Please, I'm coming." He disappeared into another room.

To Emma's right was a refrigerated storage room in which she could see dead bodies piled onto gurneys and even on the floor. This sight, combined with the smell of decomposition and form-aldehyde, made her feel ill. She held her breath for a moment, but she couldn't sustain that for very long, eventually giving up and breathing in the fumes.

Foster returned. "Please, she says if you can wait in her office. She will come when she has finished her case."

He led Emma through a pair of swinging doors. Straight ahead was the autopsy room, but thankfully Foster made a left and took her into a small office. The smell still permeated, but was less intense.

Emma looked around. There wasn't much to it: a plain, rick-ety, wooden table piled with medical files, a more-or-less tidy desk, an open cupboard with a couple of white doctor's jackets on coat hangers, a battered gray file cabinet, and a bookshelf filled with large forensic pathology textbooks. From the post-mortem room next door, she heard the thud and bang of bodies being thrown around onto and off gurneys, the whine of the skull saw, and other noises she could not and did not care to identify.

After about thirty minutes, the door burst open and the doc-tor appeared. She paused for a moment to yank off her mask and surgical cap, which she dropped into the trash can in the corner. Emma had not pictured her this way. Probably not more than five years older than herself, the woman wore her auburn hair down to her shoulders.

Emma stood up.

The doctor looked at her matter-of-factly. "Hi," she said, with a heavy *H*. "Doctora Jauregui. And you?"

"Oh, em, Jasmine Ohene. Citi-FM news."

"Ah, *bueno*."

They shook hands. Jauregui pulled out a chair and sat down opposite Emma with her legs stretched out. "So, you wonder why I'm working when all the Ghanaian doctors are not? You're not

the first to ask. What can I say? I'm *Cubana*. We never stop working. In my country, we cannot strike, you know?"

She smiled briefly at Emma before sweeping up her hair into a
bun in one deft movement.

"Actually, Doctor," Emma said, "I'm doing a Citi-FM story
about a murder case that the police haven't been able to solve, and
I was wondering if the postmortem report might be here."

"I see." She bounded from her chair, crossing the room to the
file cabinet in a couple of steps. "I can check if the autopsy was
done here. What is the name of this person?"

"Tagoe, Araba," Emma said, her jaw almost dropping. Had it
been a Ghanaian doctor, he would have plied Emma with a thousand questions and instructed her to write a letter to the hospital
director for permission to see the report. Was Dr. Jau . . . however
her name was pronounced, really willing to show it to Emma
immediately?

Jauregui pulled open the second cabinet drawer, which had
neatly arranged folders in hanging files. Her fingers ran through
the tabs like a sprinter on a track. "You know, when I came here
one year ago, *Dios mio*, you should have seen what a disaster this
place was."

"Really?" Emma said.

"All over the place," Jauregui said, waving her free hand in a
circle. "Big mess! I worked three days straight to get the place back
in order." She went back to the drawer, muttering letters as she
riffled through the folders. "Ah, here! Lady Araba Tagoe."

Emma's heart jumped for joy.

Jauregui slammed the drawer shut with a well-placed back kick
and returned to the table stacked with files, which she transferred
to her desk. She lightly tossed Araba's file onto the table and
dropped herself into a chair. "So, what is it you want to know
about her?"

Emma sat down as well. "We are producing a radio program
about the life and death of Lady Araba. We are curious about her
death. No one seems to have the details about it."

"The police have a suspect?"

"They've arrested someone," Emma said, "but we don't believe he's the culprit."

"Hm," Jauregui said, shaking her head. "Ghana police. I don't even know what to say. Anyway, I remember this case. I did it myself."

"Oh," Emma said, thrilled. She had instantly liked the doctor, and something about her straightforward manner inspired confidence.

Jauregui flipped open the file. "Bring your chair over. I'll explain everything."

Emma did so, scooting beside the doctor, eager to learn.

"So," Jauregui began, "this is the police summary: 'The deceased was discovered lying in bed by one Ismael Cletus, followed by one Peter Sarpong, blah, blah . . . deceased was positioned with head on a blood-soaked pillow, the bedcovers were neatly placed over the corpse . . . blah, blah . . . No murder weapon was found.'"

Emma noticed DS Isaac Boateng's name and signature at the bottom.

"Next page, my report. At top, deceased name, address, age, case number, and so on. So, let's continue. 'Body is that of a normally developed black female, appearance consistent with stated age of thirty-three years. Length is 1.7 meters. The body is cold and not embalmed. Lividity is present at the dependent portions of the body, and rigor mortis is also present.' Do you know what lividity is? It's when the blood settles in the parts of the body that are closest to the surface the body is lying on." Jauregui flipped a few pages forward. "Here is the photo. You see? The blood settles around the back area because she was on her back. 'Rigor mortis is also present.' That is, the body muscles start to turn stiff after two to four hours and can stay like that for longer. You understand?"

"Yes, Doctor."

"*Bien.* We continue. 'Laceration at the left parietal scalp'— the side of the head— 'due to blunt force trauma is ragged and measures 8.3 centimeters, penetrating to the skull table, with associated secondary contusion noted 90 degrees to the laceration. No skull fracture is noted.'" Dr. Jauregui went to the next page. "Next injury is in the neck region. 'Externally, a double ligature mark encircles the neck in the horizontal plane at the level of the larynx and upper trachea. Minimal hematoma is identified in the subcutaneous tissues and neck muscles. Internally, fractures of the hyoid bone or trachea are absent.'"

Jauregui glanced at Emma, who shook her head and laughed.

"Doctor, I'm completely lost."

"Let me show you. There is a bone high in the neck—put your fingers here on my neck. You feel it? That is the hyoid. During manual strangulation, this bone can crack or break, because the killer usually faces the victim and puts direct pressure on the front of the neck. But in a ligature strangulation like this case, the killer is *behind* the victim pulling the ligature tight around the throat."

"So, that squeezes the windpipe and she can't breathe?"

"Ya, but that's not the main factor causing the death," Jauregui said with a little smile. "It's that the ligature blocks off the arteries in the neck and therefore no blood or oxygen gets to the brain."

"Oh, I see," Emma said, startled that she had been under the wrong impression for so long.

"Now let's look at the photos," Jauregui said, turning several pages to the first image. "To start, this is a general picture of the bedroom where the body was found."

Taken from the doorway, the photograph showed a portion of the room and the bottom one-third of the blood-splattered duvet that covered the lower portion of Lady Araba's body. Unlike the sparse environment the bedroom had been when Emma had seen it, in Lady Araba's time, it had been filled with paintings on the wall, a dresser with a porcelain vase of fresh flowers at either end, two matching armchairs, and a decorative shelf with a silver vase on one side.

The next image showed Lady Araba in full, lying on her back with her head on a blood-smeared pillow. Emma was shocked and saddened by how profoundly death had changed Araba's appearance. Her face was swollen and congested. Her eyes and mouth were open with her tongue protruded slightly. *Who could have slain Araba in this brutal way?*

Jauregui went to the next set of pictures. "Here, we see at the far side of the bed the blood spatter on the white carpet, and more on the bedcovers. There is a large pool of blood here, about halfway across the bed, and a smaller amount on the pillow. So, how I see it, the assailant hit Araba with a blunt instrument this side of the bed and she fell, but she was still conscious at that point. She got on the bed to try to crawl to the other side, but before she could make it there, the killer also climbed on the bed, maybe even on top of the victim's back, looped the ligature around the victim's neck, and tightened it until Araba was dead."

Emma nodded soberly. "How long would that take? Before death, I mean."

Jauregui tilted her head. "You will lose conscious by fifteen seconds, dead by three or four minutes. But the pressure on the neck must be constant, so it is not as easy as in the movies. It's hard work to strangle someone."

Emma shuddered inwardly as she visualized such a murder in progress. "Doctor, can you tell if it's more likely to be a man or a woman who did this?"

Jauregui shook her head. "Impossible to say."

"Please, what about the ligature? You said it was double?"

"Well," Jauregui said, "it appears to be something like two strips of wire close together, or two tubes or a double tube made of *plástico* or rubber?"

"Why use two ligatures?" Emma wondered aloud. "Double the force?"

Jauregui considered that a moment. "Same total force on the throat, but a double ligature puts half the pressure of a single ligature on the killer's hands, making it a little easier for him or her." Spotting Emma's momentary puzzlement, the doctor added, "Pressure equals the force over the area to which the force is applied."

"Ah," Emma said. "I got it." Her memory of high school physics was only a faint glimmer.

"Now," Jauregui continued. "Let's look at the blood pattern. It shows she was lying across the bed as he was strangling her. You see all this blood on this side of the bed? This is where she died, but then, he moves her—look at the bloody drag marks—to lay her on the back and put her head on the pillow. Finally, he covers her with the duvet."

Emma nodded. "Why do you think he changed her position on the bed?"

"This I'm not sure about," Jauregui said, "but here is what I believe: from everything we see here, there is much anger—a crime of passion. Maybe the murderer didn't plan it. It was spontaneous. And then, the killer realizes the terrible thing he has done and he feels remorse, so he repositions her body and covers her; and so now, in his mind, she looks acceptable. We call this 'undoing.' A lover or close family member. They feel shame and try to symbolically reverse the homicide."

"Please, Doctor, could it also be that another person—not the murderer—found Lady Araba and wanted to 'undo' the murder, as you call it?"

"Yes," Jauregui said, nodding vigorously, "that also happens, and sometimes the family doesn't want the police and the media to see their loved one in such a degraded condition."

Emma thought of the people in Araba's life who might have had such love-hate feelings toward her. The person who most fit that profile was Augustus Seeza. Even Auntie Dele came to Emma's mind. But what motive would Dele have? Jealousy? Or was it possible Dele demanded money from Araba because of the part she had played in her niece's success as a seamstress, then designer? That didn't seem likely to Emma. Returning to the present, she said, "One other thing, Doctor: the family says Lady Araba always wore a necklace, which was missing along with some other jewelry."

Jauregui shook her head. "There wasn't any necklace on the

body. Let me check the detective's report to see if he found one at the scene." She quickly scanned DS Boateng's detailed report. "Nothing here. What kind of necklace?"

"To be honest," Emma admitted, "I don't have a good description. All I heard was it was a necklace with rubies and sapphires or something like that, along with some other jewelry snatched from Araba's dresser."

"Oh, I see," Jauregui said with interest. "It's possible someone noted that down in the police docket. I'll be at the CID Headquarters tomorrow morning to give a class to the CSU techs, so I'll ask one of the officers to get the docket for me. But meanwhile, I have an idea."

She rose to her desk, returning with a loupe magnifying glass through which she peered at three autopsy photos of Araba's neck. She spent several minutes and then finally looked up at Emma with a shake of the head. "I was hoping to see something like the impression of a chain into the skin of her neck, but no, nothing."

Jauregui passed the loupe to Emma, who was pleasantly surprised by the collegial gesture. She spent a few seconds looking for an elusive necklace-print, and then shook her head. "No, Doc. But how do you expect me to see something you haven't?"

The women laughed. "You never know," Jauregui said lightly and stood up. "I have to get some work done, but if you want to spend more time here looking at the photos, you can."

"Sure, Doctor. Thank you. Oh, em . . . may I take pics?"

Jauregui shrugged. "Take them or don't take them. All the same to me." She winked at Emma and left the room.

Emma smiled and began snapping pictures of everything in the record, which she presumed was a violation of some kind, but as long as she had Doctor Jauregui's tacit permission, Emma wasn't bothered in the least.

She stared at the image of the white duvet tarnished with scarlet blood spatter, a symbol of Araba's life rapidly waning and then suddenly over.

Emma caught what appeared to be a tiny glint of metal amidst the blood near the foot of the bed. She examined it through the magnifying glass. It certainly did seem to be a small metallic object partially obscured by a bloodstain. What was it—a piece of jewelry? Emma doubted it.

She looked up as Dr. Jauregui returned with a stack of paperwork. "Doctor, I see something here, and I wondered if you noticed it too?"

Jauregui put her folders aside and looked at the object through the magnifying glass. "I have no idea what that is. Let me see if there's any mention of it in the report."

Jauregui went over the notes and photos again, but she found nothing that addressed the mysterious item. She shrugged. "I don't know. It may not be important. But I'll check if there's any mention of it in the police docket when I'm at CID tomorrow."

"Thank you, Doctor," Emma said, somewhat lost in thought. "Could the piece of metal be part of the weapon the killer used?"

Jauregui looked skeptical. "Too hard to tell. But I believe I know what the weapon was."

"Really, Doctor?" Emma asked eagerly.

"Look at this picture—see how neat it is? Araba likes everything in matching pairs—two armchairs of the same type, two identical bedside tables, two bouquets of flowers, and so on. But what here is not a matching pair?" She looked at Emma. "Don't think too hard. Just imagine you are inside the room looking around."

Emma gave it a try. Her face began to turn hot. She felt as though she was back in high school taking an exam and Jauregui was her teacher, awaiting the correct response.

"Oh," Emma said. "I see it. The silver vase."

Jauregui applauded. "*Felicidades*. Yes, it is on top of the shelf in this corner. At the other corner? Nothing. Why should that be? Well, as I said, a crime of passion. In a rage, the offender grabbed the vase on impulse, hit Lady Araba at the side of her head, and then strangled her on the bed. It's just a theory."

"Thank you for sharing it," Emma said, beaming at her. "Thank you for everything here today, Doctor. I've learned so much. And now I know we should be on the alert for a silver vase identical to this one. It could connect us to the murderer."

FORTY-ONE

Eleven months after

THERE WAS SO MUCH to discuss at the next morning's briefing, it was more like a summit. Emma had set up the whiteboard and erasable markers for the boss.

"I'll begin," Sowah said. "Day before yesterday, I interviewed Kweku-Sam and came away with certainty that he did not kill Lady Araba, even though he admitted to signing what could be a confession. He left sometime past nine the night of the murder and went home. I confirmed with his brother, who lives with him, that he was back about thirty minutes after that. There would not have been time to commit the murder and return home within that time. Furthermore, Kweku had no motive to kill his boss. He was obviously devoted to her, she seems to have treated him well, and he had a steady job. Because Kweku had written a truthful statement that he went into Lady Araba's home to carry some items in from the car for her, they seized on that as his opportunity to kill Araba. The officers questioned him to the point of exhaustion. At that point, I imagine he was ready to sign anything or too fatigued to realize what he was signing."

The detectives murmured their disapproval, even though this type of police behavior was no surprise to them.

"What did Augustus tell you, Walter?" Sowah asked.

"According to him, Father Tagoe sexually abused Araba for several years."

Exclamations went up around the room.

Walter nodded. "From when she was six years old. According to Augustus, the abuse stopped only after Araba left home in her late teens."

"Wait, wait," Sowah cautioned quietly. "People say all kinds of things for all kinds of reasons. Please continue, Walter."

"Augustus said Araba revealed this to him a year or so into their relationship, and that, unknown to many people, Araba was sometimes severely depressed as a result of the trauma. But with her family relentlessly pressuring her to dump Augustus, she was probably depressed about that too. Anyway, he claims she had decided to conquer her past by confronting her father with the abuse, then exposing him on *Tough Talk* the Monday night of her fashion show, in keeping with the 'We Too' theme of Accra Fashion Week."

"That could be a powerful motive for Father Tagoe to kill his daughter," Sowah said.

Emma thought about what Dr. Jauregui had said about Araba's murder: anger, an unplanned crime of passion, and then deep remorse. Emma could perfectly well visualize Father Tagoe having a heated argument with Araba in the bedroom, his fury spilling over into a total loss of control. Emma also thought it was in keeping with his character for the Reverend to move and cover his daughter's body to purify the scene.

"Emma—your turn," Sowah said, interrupting her thoughts.

She told the group about the lively Dr. Jauregui. Emma's description of how she jumped up and went searching for Araba's file with no questions asked brought exclamations of admiration and approval.

"Then she went through the full record with me," Emma began. "Lady Araba died of two injuries. First, a blow to the left side of her head knocked her down but didn't kill her. The doctor said from the blood pattern that Araba then scrambled onto the bed and tried to crawl away, but the killer climbed on top of her and strangled her to death with some kind of ligature. I have some pictures to show you."

"Wow, Emma," Gideon said approvingly. "You are good!"

It took some time for Emma to go through all the images with her colleagues while explaining the findings as depicted by Dr. Jauregui.

"She also said that after this violence, the killer might have wanted to sanitize it," Emma continued, "to make it look like Araba was simply asleep. This points to someone very close to her. The doctor also believes the murder wasn't planned, but a crime of passion."

"Family, associates, or close enemy," Walter added.

"Okay, good work, Emma," Sowah said, walking up to an empty spot on the office whiteboard. "Let's use those categories to go over the possible suspects," Sowah said. "Family—two columns, the Tagoes and the Seezas. Under Tagoe we have the Reverend; next the mother, Miriam; the brother, Oko; and Auntie Dele. Anyone else? Are there siblings we don't know about? Emma, you're to check that when you see Dele next, and that's going to be soon.

"Let's go through each of the Tagoes," Sowah continued. "This family has some issues, no joke. Motives? Start with Father Tagoe."

"If it's true he molested or assaulted Araba and she threatened to expose him publicly, he would have wanted to silence her," Emma said.

"What if Araba was bluffing and wasn't really planning to tell the world?" Jojo asked.

Sowah shrugged. "The effect is the same whether she meant to carry it out or not, but that is a good point. What about Oko and Miriam?"

"The way I think of it," Jojo said, "Araba's threat could have been a motive for them too, but to kill her? I think they would be likely to go to Araba and reason with her instead. And anyway, we don't even know if Oko and Miriam knew about Araba's plan to expose her father."

"True," Sowah said. "All right. And the Seezas, Julius and his wife—what's her name again?"

"Dr. Caroline," Emma said. "We know how much the Tagoe family detested Augustus, and I don't think Justice Julius and Dr. Caroline were happy about Araba being involved with their son, either."

"I agree," Sowah said. "So, they would have some motive to get rid of Araba, although I must say, even if Justice or Dr. Seeza did that, it probably wouldn't bring Bertha and Augustus back together."

"Yes, sir," Emma said. "I suppose it's a matter of which situation they hated more: Augustus with Araba, or him without Bertha."

"Could be equally detestable to them," Sowah commented. "Moving on: Araba's associates."

"Samson, Araba's assistant," Emma said.

Sowah wrote the name down and paused. "Wait a minute. Have we talked about him? Emma, did you speak to him?"

"No, sir."

Sowah looked at the others and drew a blank. "What, no one? All this time, and no one has thought about interviewing this man? He was expecting Araba that morning for the fashion show, and she never showed up. Didn't you think he would be a useful person to speak to?"

Everyone in the group became shifty-eyed, muttering excuses.

"Guys," Sowah said, "I can't give you instructions for *every*-thing. We have so many loose ends that need to be tied up, and where are we? Nowhere." He suspired. "Emma, I'm assigning you to Samson."

"Yes, boss," she said. After that scolding, what else could she say?

"Who else was connected to Araba?" Sowah asked.

"Bertha Longdon," Gideon said.

"Motive?"

"Araba took her man."

Sowah smiled slightly as he wrote that down. "Well said."

"What about the lady who used to work with Araba's business partner?" Walter said.

"Good," Sowah said. "Susan Hayford was Araba's direct competitor."

"*And* her enemy," Jojo said. "She never could reach Araba's level, so sheer jealousy is a motive. Boss, I still can't see a family member killing one of their own. As far as I'm concerned, Ismael is the one. How did he know Lady Araba was lying murdered in her bed unless he put his face right up against the glass door to see into the room?"

"You asked the question, now get the answer," Sowah said crisply. "Go back to Trasacco *today* and get the man to talk. I don't care how you do it, just do it. And don't come back until you do."

Jojo gulped. "Yes, sir."

"Walter, you've posed as a journalist to the Tagoes already, and now you must go back to Father Tagoe to ask him about this accusation of sexual abuse. It won't be easy. I suggest an indirect method."

"Sure, no problem."

"Also," Sowah continued, "find a way to interview Augustus Seeza again without his parents present. We want to know just how much they hated Araba, maybe establish a firm motive."

"Yes, boss."

"Emma, it's also time for you to speak to Dele again and find out if she knew her brother was abusing Araba."

"Okay, sir."

"The two outstanding are Bertha Longdon and Susan Hayford," Sowah said. "I'll see if I can reach out to contacts who know Bertha. Oh, Emma, it's just occurred to me that Samson might have information about Susan."

"Sure, boss."

Sowah looked around. "Any questions?"

There were none, but just as he was about to leave the room, Emma remembered the small metal item she had spotted in one of the crime scene photos. "Sorry, sir, one other thing," she said hastily.

Sowah turned. "What is it?" he said, a tad impatiently.

Emma explained what she had noticed and showed the boss the corresponding crime scene image.

Sowah nodded. "Okay, good. Follow it up." He seemed unimpressed, and Emma, who had been patting herself on the back for picking up on a potential clue, felt disappointed.

Sowah left the room and the team exchanged glances. The boss did not appear to be in the best of moods.

Emma stood in place for a few moments, kicking herself as she realized that she hadn't done what she should have the day before. Now she called DS Boateng, and when he didn't pick up, she texted him instead. Twenty minutes later, he called back.

"Emma, how are you?"

"I'm good, sir. I hope you are well? I called regarding something I noticed on the crime scene photos. It looks like a piece of metal near the foot of the bed on which Lady Araba's body was lying. I wonder if you recall anything like that."

"A piece of metal?" He paused. "Oh, yes, yes! You are right. I had forgotten. I couldn't figure out what the thing was, but still, we retrieved it, and the evidence tech photographed and bagged it. If I recall correctly, there was blood on it, but just like all the other evidence, I never got the chance to analyze it for DNA."

"Please, do you think the evidence tech might still have the photograph?"

"Of course! As a matter of fact, I think I have it too. He usually forwards all the photos to me. Hold on one second, please, and I'll see if I can find it."

Emma waited a while, staring at her fingernails and wondering if she should have a manicure done, for a change.

Boateng returned. "I can't find it right now," he said, "but I know I have it. I'll send it as soon as I locate it."

"Thank you very much, sir." She couldn't wait to see it.

FORTY-TWO

Eleven months after

EMMA FOUND AUNTIE DELE in the early evening, locking up the dress shop for the day.

"I was just thinking about you today," Dele said. "Welcome. Come with me, we can go upstairs to talk."

Her home sat directly over the shop. On entering the living room, Emma observed the place was quite cluttered—two sofas, six chairs, a cross-legged desk, wooden masks and brass statues on top of the furniture, a muddle of dresses in progress slung over the back of one of the chairs, unpaired shoes on the floor, and paintings occupying every possible space on the walls. The place smelled stale.

"Sorry about the mess," Dele said casually. "I'm doing a home makeover. Trust me, it won't look like this in a couple weeks. Would you like something to drink?" Dele asked.

"Water is fine, thank you."

"Oh," Dele said, disappointed. "Nothing stronger?"

"No, thank you," Emma said, smiling.

"Teetotaler?"

"Yes."

"All right then," Dele said. "Water it is."

She yelled for the house girl, who came running. Dele told her to bring bottled water, two glasses, and a Star beer.

"Yes, madam," the girl said.

"Please, have a seat," Dele said, waving vaguely at the furniture. The choice was Emma's, so she took an armchair draped in a cover cloth with a bright Ghanaian print.

After the drinks arrived, Dele said, "So how far are we with the case, Emma?"

"At our meeting today with Mr. Sowah, we discussed a few things. Before I approach this subject, please understand, Auntie Dele, that I don't want to cause any discomfort to you, and I would prefer never to ask this question. I come to you with respect and a commitment to find out who killed your dear niece."

"Okay," Dele said slowly, now wary of what might be coming.

"Recently," Emma said, "we've heard that your brother, Fifi, might have sexually abused Araba as a child and teenager. Do you know anything about that?"

Dele's self-assured mien collapsed before Emma like a monument severed.

"Who told you that?" she asked, her voice shaky.

"Augustus Seeza. He said Araba had told him."

"He is a liar!" Dele said, leaning forward and back again as if her spine was momentarily failing her.

"Please, why would he make that up, Auntie Dele?"

"Because he wants to implicate the family in something disgusting. That's all."

Dele folded her arms and stared at the floor.

Emma let some moments pass. "Auntie Dele," she said softly. "I beg you. You came to us for help, now I need your help in return. We can't move further if we don't have the truth."

Dele remained in the same position for a while, and then released a long, loud sigh. "What's the point? We've been living the lie for so long, we Tagoes."

"Auntie, when did you find out?"

"When Araba was seven or eight." Dele shook her head and shuddered. "I could tell something was wrong from the way she was behaving. And one day, when I was helping her bathe, she kept shielding herself down there. When she finally allowed me to look, I saw she had been hurt."

Dele seemed to cringe.

"Auntie, did you confront your brother?"

She shook her head. "How? Me, a girl, and younger than him?" Without weeping audibly, tears streamed down her cheeks and dissolved in her lap. "But I tried to protect her however I could. I would often have her stay the night at my house, even if Fifi objected. And now she's gone. I'm so sorry, Araba."

In the room's silence, Emma could hear Dele gulping down further tears. "Auntie, you didn't tell anyone?"

"No," she whispered. "I couldn't shame the Tagoe family. I think I was trying to protect Araba from that shame, too."

"Yes," Emma said. But she was dismayed by Dele's lack of action.

Dele looked up at her. "Do you think less of me now?"

Emma shook her head. "No, because I can understand the pain of such a secret in the family."

"A terrible stain."

"Auntie, do Miriam and Oko know?"

"We've never discussed it, but I'm certain Miriam does. As for Oko, I'm not sure."

"Please don't be offended, but did you come to us at the agency to protect your family from disgrace? To shift the blame elsewhere?"

"Oh, no!" Dele cried. "That's not it at all. I just want them to get that bastard Seeza for murdering my niece. I *know* he did it. Those last days were hell for Araba. He was tormenting her to stay with him, but she wanted to break away. That's why he killed her."

"Augustus tells us they were very happy together in their last days. Lady Araba visited him at his home on the final Saturday afternoon before her death, and she seemed full of life."

Dele shook her head. "That can't be true, because I was receiving distress calls from her all the time in the two weeks preceding her murder."

Emma frowned. Who was lying, Dele or Augustus?

Dele abruptly stood up and announced she was getting another beer. "Do you want anything more?" she asked Emma. "How about some Malta? Come on, live a little!"

Emma smiled. "All right, then."

"Good, I'll be right back."

Emma leaned back in her chair as she wrestled with the contradictions the case was sending up: Augustus's claims versus Dele's, Kweku-Sam's versus Augustus's. She felt an uncomfortable lump in her chair and reached behind her to feel a cylindrical object under the chair cover. When she pulled away the cover, she saw a portion of a metallic object between the top and bottom cushions. Working it free, she pulled it out. It was a silver vase identical to the one in Araba's bedroom.

WHEN AUNTIE DELE returned with a tray of Malta and more beer, Emma was on her feet, staring at the vase.

Dele stopped. "My God, where did you find that?"

Emma pointed. "In between the cushions. I was sitting on it."

"Wow!" Dele put down the tray on a flat surface she somehow managed to find. "Do you know how long I've been searching for that? Thank you so much, Emma."

"It looks like the one Araba had in her bedroom," Emma said.

Dele gasped in surprise, then laughed. "How did you know that? So, you have been doing a good job on the case. You are right. I bought them in Italy when I lived there long ago. It was a set of three, so I gave two to Araba and kept one."

"One was in the crime scene photographs. But the second of the pair was missing."

"Well, that isn't it," Dele said. "This one is mine."

"It's beautiful," Emma said, moving closer to a floor-standing lamp to examine the vase in detail. On an improbable whim, she also looked for any traces of blood, especially at the base, but the ornament was spotless.

Emma handed it back to Dele with a smile. "But Auntie, keep it somewhere safe. It's too nice to be buried inside a chair!"

"You are right," Dele said, shaking her head. "Sometimes I'm quite absentminded. I'll put it here on the shelf, next to my masks."

As Emma took her leave, she wondered if she had been over-cynical in looking for blood on the vase. Auntie Dele couldn't possibly have played a part in her niece's murder—could she?

FORTY-THREE

Eleven months after

JOJO AND ISMAEL BROKE for lunch at the same time and walked to Clara's Chop Bar to have a full lunch of *fufu* with groundnut soup and *banku* and okro stew. On the way back, Jojo said, "*Chaley*, can you show me the place where you saw Lady Araba dead?"

Ismael thought about it for a moment. "Okay, but don't tell Peter, okay? Otherwise big trouble for me."

"No problem, bruh."

Peter wasn't on duty, and the junior security men naturally felt more relaxed and apt to overlook minor details like writing down visitors' license plate numbers. Ismael and Jojo stopped to josh and laugh with the guards, one of whom asked where the two guys were going.

"To check some plants down there," Ismael said vaguely. "So, we talk later."

He and Jojo headed to the gardener's supply shed at the end of the Ruby Row cul-de-sac. Ismael extracted an aluminum ladder, which he hoisted onto one shoulder and carried as if it were a feather. His wiriness belied his pound-for-pound strength, making Jojo think of Lady Araba's murder. Ismael could very easily have overpowered her.

At the rear of Araba's home, Ismael planted the ladder and secured it. "You go up first," he said to Jojo. "I'll hold the ladder."

Jojo ascended, and Ismael followed him onto the terrace. The sun was intense, but the elevation afforded a cooling breeze.

"Oh, nice!" Jojo said, looking around.

"Yeah," Ismael agreed. "Before, when Lady Araba was around, she had all kinds of plants and flowerpots. More than this."

"The ones you brought to her?"

Ismael nodded.

"And she bought them from you?"

"Yes."

"Then you made plenty money from her, oo!"

Ismael laughed. "Not so much. Usually I charged her half of what people normally pay."

"Ah, okay," Jojo said with approval. "What about Valentine's Day?"

"Come again?"

"Like, on Valentine's Day, I would bring hundreds of flowers to such a beautiful woman."

Ismael grinned sheepishly. "Yeah, like, one time I did. She was happy."

The two sat down with their backs against the wall, which gave them some shade.

"When was the last time you saw Lady Araba?" Jojo asked

With a slight hesitation, Ismael said, "Sunday evening."

"Okay. Do you normally work on Sundays?"

"No, I don't. I . . . I just came to get something."

Jojo knew Ismael was lying, but he left it for the moment. "What was she like as a person?

Ismael shrugged. "To me she was a good woman. Not everyone thought the same."

"Is that so? Why?"

"Like sometimes, she was annoyed that the back gate wasn't working. She said, like, what kind of security is this that some-one can enter and leave without being seen? So, one day she was annoyed with Peter. He tried to tell her that they were waiting for some parts for the gate opener."

"And Peter was annoyed with her?"

Ismael turned his bottom lip out. "To be honest, I don't know. Peter will never show you what he is thinking. But you see, Lady Araba really cared about the place. The other residents?" Ismael made a rude sound with his lips. "They could care less. Some of them just go in and out in their cars and they don't even greet us. Lady Araba always did."

"I was watching some of her YouTube channel," Jojo said. "She looked beautiful. Is that how she was in real life?"

"Oh, for sure. Even better than that. Looked nice, smelled nice—everything."

"Nice melons?" Jojo asked, cupping his hands in front of his chest.

Ismael looked at Jojo in feigned shock. "*Ei!* Are you like that?"

"Oh, come on!"

They laughed.

"The melons, bruh," Jojo said. "As for that one, I can't resist."

"What about the ass?" Ismael said.

"What man don't like ass? Between ass and melon," Jojo said slyly, "which one do you like?"

"Big ass," Ismael said, forming the shape with his hands. "Those ones that shake when the woman walks."

"Lady Araba had it like that?"

"Well, hers was not too much big—it was correct for her size. Just nice."

Jojo lowered his voice conspiratorially. "You saw her naked, bro?"

Ismael giggled nervously. "*Chaley,* stop."

Jojo gave Ismael a playful shove. "At night, you can spy on her."

"Like how?"

"Like through the glass," Jojo said casually.

Ismael frowned. "I'm not like that."

"Oh, I'm just joking with you," Jojo said, laughing. "Why do people say she liked too many men?"

Ismael sucked his teeth. "Stupid people. What do they know?"

"Then tell me the real story."

"It's because she was beautiful, so women were jealous of her, and the men who couldn't get her became frustrated. That's what happened to Seeza at the end. He wanted Madam Araba back, but she didn't want him anymore."

Jojo needed to get to the heart of the matter and wouldn't leave before then. He rose and went to the terrace door, putting his forehead against the glass and cupping his hands to see inside. Ismael joined him and did the same. Without the reflection, he could see into the spacious room with the bed and two armchairs. Otherwise, it was bare.

Jojo looked at him. "Why were you here at Trasacco on that Sunday evening? I mean the real reason."

Ismael turned and leaned against the wall next to the door. "I'm shy to tell you."

"My brother, you can trust me."

Ismael stared at the ground. "You were right. I used to come and watch her sometimes."

"Lady Araba?"

"Yes. I wait until dark, then get the ladder and come up here."

"Okay," Jojo said. "Go on."

"She had curtains over the door—the thin kind you can see through. In the nighttime when she pulls the curtains and the light is on inside the room, if I'm out here, I can see her, but she can't see me. Sometimes she would take her shower and come into the room naked."

"You saw her body. She was beautiful."

"Yes . . . I wanted to stop doing it, bro, spying on her, but I couldn't help myself, you understand?"

"I get you, my brother. It's tough for us men to control ourselves."

"Yeah."

"So, how often did you do it?"

"Sometimes in the night before she slept, but other times early in the morning around five because that's the time she used to wake up and it's still dark outside. That Sunday evening, I came here not knowing she was out, but by that time, my wife texted me to come home, so I left, but I was feeling some kind of way."

"Like, strange," Jojo prompted.

"Yes. Like I needed to see Lady Araba. When I got to work around five, I saw the light was on in the bedroom, so I came up to the terrace. I looked inside the room and saw her."

A thought flashed through Jojo's head. *He killed her.* But why?

"She was dressing to go to work?" Jojo asked.

"No, no," Ismael said with a touch of impatience. "You don't understand. She was dead already."

Jojo started. "What?"

"She was lying naked across the bed," Ismael said, his voice cracking. "Blood was all over the bedsheets."

"What did you do?"

"The door wasn't locked," Ismael continued. "I went inside. She was lying there just like that, and it was so pitiful. I was afraid to touch her. When I did, the body was completely cold—you know, the AC was on. But I couldn't leave her like that, Jojo. No one should see her like that. I put her under the covers with her head on the pillow so she looked like she was sleeping. I just wanted her to rest in peace. And then I left."

Jojo said nothing for a while. He put his hand on Ismael's shoulder. "*Chaley*, tell the truth. Was it you that killed her?"

"I didn't kill her, bro. She was dead when I came."

"And you didn't tell anyone about finding Araba dead until daylight," Jojo said, more a statement than question.

"Yes, of course. Because people will ask me how I came to be outside Lady Araba's room at that time of the early morning. For sure the police will arrest me. So, I waited until seven that morning and came up to the terrace again. I pretended I saw Lady Araba through the window by accident, called Kweku-Sam to fetch Peter, and made like the door was locked and that I had to break the glass to get in."

"Because if they knew the door was unlocked," Jojo said, "they would be suspicious of you."

"Yeah." Ismael raised his hands and let them drop limply to his sides. "So, now you know. I told you because I've been wanting to tell someone who I can trust, and I trust you. I didn't kill Lady Araba myself, but I felt so much shame—as if I was part of her murder."

"I understand," Jojo said. "Thank you."

"Thank you too." Ismael smiled, the first time in quite a while.

He could be lying, but Jojo had nothing to the contrary, and he believed the man.

"The question now," Jojo said, "is who killed Lady Araba."

"Like I said, Mr. Seeza, of course," Ismael said promptly. "And Peter helped him."

FORTY-FOUR

Eleven months after

MIRIAM GREETED WALTER, SEEMING neither happy nor sorry to see him. Once again, she was fully made up on an early Sunday evening. Walter took in the long scarlet dress and the pumps to match.

"Please, have a seat, Mr. Busia. Father Tagoe told me you called earlier to ask if you could visit us again. I'm sorry, but he's running a little late."

"No problem at all. Thank you very much." Walter sat and looked at Miriam intently. "Please, how are you doing, madam?"

"By God's grace, thank you for asking. How is the article about my daughter going? I didn't hear from you, so I was worried you had already sent it in for publication. You remember I asked if I could look it over before you do that—just so there are no major errors, you know."

"Yes, madam. Well, I can say I've been making progress, but I had one or two other questions to ask you, if you wouldn't mind. When the Reverend arrives, I can get his perspective as well."

"Of course."

Walter took out the same notebook he had used the first time he'd interviewed the Tagoes. "Madam, today I wanted to expand on a few points about Araba's childhood. She was born here in Accra, I suppose?"

"Yes, of course. Osu, to be precise."

"Nice. How was she as a little girl?"

Miriam laughed with a toss of the head. "Curious about everything."

"Is that so?" Walter said, smiling. "I can just imagine. Maybe that's where she got her entrepreneurial spirit?"

"I'm sure that's the case," Miriam agreed.

"Now, madam, I know that last time you mentioned you had no problems with Araba wanting to be a fashion designer. Was that always the case?" This was the same question, in slightly different wording, that Miriam had been about to answer when her husband had cut her off on Walter's first visit.

"It could cause some friction at times," she said. "For instance, my husband wanted her to go into one of the professions, but Araba said no way. And you know, she was right. She knew where her abilities lay. She wasn't as academically inclined as her brother, Oko, was, and I think it was brave of her to admit that to herself and look for her own strengths."

"But, at least initially, Father Tagoe had misgivings about her choice."

"Perhaps so," Miriam said evenly, "but ultimately, Araba was a Daddy's girl. She meant the world to him. She also looked up to her older brother, who was so caring of her, looking out for her and so on. We all did that for each other, really. The love of God and family has always ruled our home. In the end, it's love that triumphs, isn't it, Mr. Busia? God's love, especially, always wins."

Her words were reminiscent of a sermon—a bit sanctimonious, perhaps, but then, she was a reverend's wife.

"Yes, always. You've painted a beautiful portrait of your daughter and the full Tagoe family," Walter said. "As I've said before, I'm truly sorry for your loss."

"Thank you. We still feel the pain of it, especially my husband, who doted on her so much, but in Romans, we read, 'O the depth of the riches both of the wisdom and knowledge of

God! how unsearchable are his judgments, and his ways past finding out!'"

"Amen. I can see that it's your deep faith that keeps you going."

"It is, Mr. Busia."

"Madam, I want to discuss something that I have heard, and which I feel you should have the chance to refute, given its distasteful nature. You should always have the right to rebuff anything that could tarnish the reputation of your family."

Miriam appeared wary but curious. "What is this about, sir?"

"I mean no disrespect here," Walter went on, "and I beg your forbearance as I say this. There has been an allegation that Araba was sexually abused as a child."

Miriam went rigid as stone. Her eyes, fixed on Walter, emptied of expression as if her soul were leaving her body. Walter stayed silent and waited.

She recovered, suddenly cold. "Who told you that?"

Walter didn't answer, and she didn't press.

"Sexual abuse?" Miriam said, her strength of tone returning. "*No.* Not in this house watched over by the Lord. Why would someone say that?"

To Walter's alarm, she covered her face with her hands and began to weep uncontrollably. Walter stood up. "I'm sorry, madam. I didn't mean to cause you any pain."

Walter heard a car door slam, and his head whipped around as someone called out, "Miriam?"

Fifi Tagoe. It was the worst possible timing.

The Reverend entered the room and stopped. "What's going on?"

"Good evening, sir," Walter said.

Tagoe advanced, looking from his wife to Walter and back. "What's happening? What did you do to her?"

"We were talking," Walter said, "and I said something that upset her. I'm sorry, sir."

Tagoe knelt beside Miriam, who was now attempting to collect herself. "What's wrong, sweetheart?" he said softly to her. "Are you okay? What happened?"

She shook her head but didn't respond. Tagoe helped her up. "Let's go to the bedroom so you can lie down, okay?"

He escorted her out. A door shut, followed by muffled voices. Walter thrust his hands in his pockets, blew out a breath, and weighed the situation. Had he just advanced the case or taken it several steps backward? Why had Mrs. Tagoe reacted so dramatically? Was it that she had become overwhelmed with the truth of her daughter's sexual abuse as she knew it to be true, or was it a lie so shocking that she felt wounded?

Walter heard footsteps returning and he began another round of apologies as Tagoe reentered the room.

"Please, take your seat," he said icily.

They both sat down, and Walter waited. Tagoe lowered his head and Walter realized the man was praying.

Tagoe brought his gaze back eye-to-eye. "You've just asked my wife whether I sexually abused my late daughter, is that correct?"

"Sir, the allegation has already been leveled, and I was giving Mrs. Tagoe a chance to respond."

"Well, the answer to your ridiculous question is *no*. But beyond that, you've demonstrated how tactless and vicious you and the rest of the media are. We are still grieving the loss of our daughter, and you come here and bring up such a revolting idea? What is wrong with you?"

"It wasn't my intention to inflict pain, sir."

"Well, then perhaps you shouldn't be conducting interviews at all. This is unacceptable. As of this moment, I am disallowing you to publish anything about my daughter. If you do, I will sue you. I hope I'm making myself clear."

"Yes, sir. You are."

"Do you think something like that would ever go on in this household, where the Lord makes his presence known to us every hour, minute, and second of the day?"

Walter said, "Sir, I had to follow up on the accusation. You have the right to deny or refute it."

"Where did you hear this lie? Or rather, who is slandering my family? I demand that you tell me."

Wary of what Tagoe might do with the information, Walter decided not to oblige. "I'm sorry, sir. I won't reveal my source."

He remained silent as the Reverend glared at him.

"That's all right," Tagoe said finally. "I already have a very good idea of who is responsible. You've been speaking to Augustus Seeza and his father, isn't that correct? They are dishonorable lowlifes, and you shouldn't believe a word out of their mouths."

Walter wouldn't allow himself to be thrown off track. "Father, if you please, let's disregard the Seezas for a moment and concentrate on your family. We have a very moving account of a gifted young woman, your daughter, who suffered trauma as a child and, had she not been murdered, would have shared it with the public because she wanted to lift the scab off a deep wound no one dares touch, especially in this country: the sexual abuse of children, and moving beyond that, sexual assault within the fashion industry. We cannot address the problem if we don't admit to it. I admire Araba for her courage. Now, you too, as a man of God, have the opportunity demonstrate some of that same bravery and inspiration in admitting your wrongs."

Tagoe leapt up and lunged at Walter, who tried to scramble out of his chair to avoid the assault. He didn't quite make it, but nor did the Reverend's blow hit its intended target. The wild swing of his arm threw him off balance and onto the floor.

At that moment, Miriam appeared in the room and began screaming. "*Stop!* Stop fighting!"

"What is going on here?"

Walter turned at the voice. Oko, who had just entered the room, was gaping in astonishment.

Tagoe scrambled to his feet, shouting, "*Get him out!*"

Walter backed away hastily. "What have you done?" Oko asked. "Did you hit my father?"

Walter squeezed past Oko. "No, he tried to hit *me*," he said. "I think it's best I take my leave."

FORTY-FIVE

Twelve months after

EMMA FOUND SAMSON ALLOTEY'S office at the Marina
Mall. Emblazoned at the entrance in a looping font was the name
Lady Pizzazz.

When he opened the door, Emma had to make an effort not
to stare as she silently acknowledged that he was one of the best-
looking men she had ever met. He wore a tapered, blue-black
shirt with the top button open to reveal a fine gold chain, and his
black-and-white striped pants were as snug as his top. He even
smelled good.

"I couldn't hear you too clearly on the phone," he said as he welcomed her in. "You said you're at the Ghana Journalism School?"

"Yes please."

"Have a seat—any chair is fine. And your name again, please."

"I'm Pamela Kumson."

"Pamela," he repeated. "Beautiful name. Well, as you know,
I'm Samson. Nice meeting you. Oh, would you like some water
or coffee?"

"No, sir. Thank you very much."

In contrast to her appearance as Melody Acquah, Emma was
dressed quite casually in a pink-and-black track suit that shaved a
couple years off her age. Samson sat down opposite her in a sleek
chair with no arms. His physique matched his biblical name.

All the desks in his office were thick, solid glass. There seemed to be no drawers or papers anywhere—just laptops, and a lot of them.

"So," Samson said, settling in, "how can I help you today?"

"Thank you for seeing me today. My professor has assigned me a project in which I must take a real-life news story and write an in-depth investigative report as if I had been the original reporter on the case. I chose the murder of Lady Araba as my topic, and I know you were her trusted assistant."

"That's correct," Samson said gravely. "And if she were still alive, I would have remained so. It was a great loss to me, to everyone."

"My condolences."

"Thank you."

"How did it come about that you moved to work with Lady Pizzazz after Lady Araba's death?" Emma asked.

"Formerly, both Susan Hayford and I were managers for Araba. After her death, the family began fighting over her will—I don't know the details, but the company became tied up in the litigation as well, and I was out of a job. Susan had a position available in her younger enterprise, so I made the logical move."

"Understood. May I ask you some questions? If you don't know the correct answer or you are not sure, then you can just say so, please. Or if they are too personal, just let me know."

"Absolutely," he said. "No problem. Fire away."

From her backpack, Emma took out a pen and a ringed notebook, which she opened on her lap. "When was the last time you saw Lady Araba?" she asked Samson.

"It's been almost a year now," he said. "It was the Sunday evening before our big show during Accra Fashion Week, which was . . . just a second, the exact date is on my calendar." He picked up his Galaxy phone, scrolling with one hand. "Yeah, the third to seventh of July. So, the second of July was the last time. We were at a party, welcoming a few of the dignitaries who had arrived for the events."

"What was Lady Araba's mood like at that time?"

"She was always tense before a show," Samson said, "but this time, it seemed worse than usual. I asked her if something was wrong, but she just shook her head. It wasn't even nine o'clock and the party was barely getting started when she said she wasn't feeling well and left."

"And that was the last time you spoke to her, sir?"

"In person, yes, but I called her while she was on her way back home to make sure she was okay and get last-minute instructions for the show." Samson paused, shaking his head in regret. "I didn't know that would be the last time I ever heard her voice."

"And please, what time did you leave the party yourself?"

"Just before eleven. I went straight back home to sleep, because I had to be up at four in the morning to prepare."

"Okay, thank you, sir. And in the morning, what happened, please?"

"I was expecting Araba in by about seven-thirty, so as it neared eight o'clock, I got worried and tried calling her. There was no response, so, next, I tried her brother, Oko. He said he hadn't seen or heard from her, but he would try to get ahold of her. We had to go on with the show at ten without Araba, and just before it began was when I got the terrible text from Oko. It was hard holding it together through the entire show, but I didn't want our models to realize anything was wrong until it was over. Though the news wasn't public yet, I did my best to keep them off their phones, and we were down a model, so they were busy, in any case."

"I'm sure you miss her very much."

"Yes, I do."

"What was she like to work with?"

Samson smiled. "She was so brilliant, it was hard to keep up with her sometimes. And hardworking, too. She had great plans."

"Do you think someone wanted to stop her from carrying out those plans?" Emma asked.

"By way of killing her?"

Emma nodded.

"Well," Samson said, turning up his palm with a shrug, "it's possible. But if you're thinking Susan had something to do with it, I'd like to disabuse you of that notion. The media tried to portray Susan's separation from Araba as acrimonious, but it wasn't. They parted on good terms."

"Still," Emma said, "Susan became Lady Araba's competitor, with a company name that seemed almost purposefully close to the original. Now her biggest rival is conveniently out of the way."

"Susan knew the implications of her move," Samson said. "As a matter of fact, you can ask her right now, because here she is."

He got up to open the door for a woman laden with brand-name shopping bags, which she handed over to Samson. "You can put them in my office for now."

Susan was short and plump, with a kinky-curly wig, over-the-top eye makeup, and lashes. She looked at Emma. "Who is this? The new employee?"

Emma jumped up. "Oh, no, madam. Good morning. I'm Pamela. I'm a student."

"The one I told you was coming," Samson told Susan. "Remember?"

"Not exactly," Susan said. "Anyway, welcome, Pamela. Are you at the fashion school?"

"Journalism school," Samson called out from the inner office, where he was setting down the bags. He came back out. "She's working on an assignment about Lady Araba."

Susan frowned. "Lady Araba again. Why won't people let her rest in peace? What is it you want to know, Miss Pamela?"

"Please, madam, we were just discussing her untimely death."

Samson returned to his chair. "Pamela has pointed out that it must be convenient for a competitor in the fashion business having Lady Araba gone so they could gain market share."

Susan grunted and made a face. "Someone like me?" She pulled over a chair, sat down, and kicked off her pumps, which had left a deep imprint in her puffy feet. "Look, I'm flattered that anyone would think I have the guts to literally kill for success, but I don't. I'm not that cold-blooded."

"You wouldn't have to do it yourself," Samson pointed out with a one-sided smile. "You could always hire someone."

Susan laughed. "What for? Waste of time. I'd rather beat my competitors on the runway. I love competition. People think I had ill feelings against Araba—why? Because they have nothing better to do all day than sit around on their asses and spread false gossip. The truth is, Miss Pamela, it is always family, family, family. Love and hate. You want a real story? Go to her family members and talk to them. Dig deep, and you'll find a lot of dirt underneath what seems to be a nice, clean surface."

FORTY-SIX

Two weeks before

IT WAS ALMOST 6 P.M. on a Sunday, and Father Tagoe's post-service duties were finally over. He went through the side door off the chancel and took a left to pass behind the church to the sacristy, the repository for the vestments, chalices, missals, and all other accoutrements of the Anglican sacrament. It was quiet, everyone having gone home.

Tagoe hung his cassock among the other vestments in the opened rickety closet, which badly needed repair or replacement. As he donned his civilian clothes, he heard a light tap on the exterior door. It opened a second later.

"Araba!" he exclaimed. "To what do I owe such a wonderful surprise?"

She was dressed in sleek white pants and a checkered red-and-white blouse. Without makeup, she had a fundamental, immutable beauty. Tagoe attempted to embrace her, but she seemed stiff and unwilling.

"Come in, have a seat," he said, sensing something was wrong.

They sat in chairs near the vestments closet.

"How are you?" he said, smiling. "Business is good?"

"Good enough," Araba said. She was staring at him in a way that made his blood run cold.

"What's wrong, my love?" he said. "You look . . . off."

"Daddy, it's time we talked."

"I'm here."

"I need to heal," Araba said. "I've been walking around wounded for too long."

"Yes. It's never too late to turn to the Lord. He will always accept you."

"This has nothing to do with religion or God," she said. "Best leave those out."

"Then what, Araba? I'm not following."

"We've both buried it," she said. "We tried to erase the memory, but it's like a dead body at the bottom of a river. Eventually, it will rise back to the surface. That's what's been happening over the past couple of years."

Tagoe's heart began to thump.

"You remember when I was a little girl?" Araba said.

"Of course! The apple of my eye, then and now."

"When I think about growing up, I was six, and then all of a sudden, I was seventeen, eighteen. Didn't you ever wonder how those years flew by so quickly?"

"Yes, even now," Tagoe said.

"Well, for me, many of those years are lost because I've done everything I can to block them out."

"Araba." His voice shook slightly. "What are you talking about?"

"Have you done that too, Daddy? Do you ever feel guilt or shame? I felt shame, but not until later. First, I thought it was normal, because you told me that what you were doing to me was part of God's love. Then I was confused by the pain it caused me. And finally, when I realized it was wrong, I thought it was my fault, that I should have done something to stop it. That's when the shame set in."

Tagoe shook his head, seemingly mystified. "My love, I don't know what you mean. What has happened to you?"

"What's happened, Daddy, is that you took away my rights to my own body. But now I'm taking them back. Almost every night when you came to tuck me in, you touched my breasts and my vagina. I was still a little girl. Do you remember that?"

"You're making this up," Tagoe said, his voice rising. "None of this is true. I don't know why you're saying it."

Araba's eyes narrowed. "So, even now, you're denying it. Making me suffer the consequences of *your* actions. But I won't accept that this time."

At an impasse, they stared at each other for minutes in dead silence.

"You forced me to touch your private parts."

Tagoe's face went hot. He moved to the edge of his seat with his teeth clenched. "How dare you use such disgusting language in this holy place."

"Then I should ask you how you *preach* in this holy space about the sins of the flesh—lust, fornication, pornography, self-defilement—when you defiled your own daughter in the worst way."

Tagoe rose and walked to the door, which he opened wide. "Leave," he said, switching to *Ga*. "You are not the daughter I raised. You are a disgrace."

Araba got up in silence. As she passed her father in the doorway, she stopped and turned to him. "You should know something. The theme at this year's Accra Fashion Week is 'We Too,' and in two weeks, I will be on a special edition of *Tough Talk*. It's then that I will talk about the sexual abuse I suffered at your hands. The whole world will know."

FORTY-SEVEN

One week before

SUNDAY MORNING, ARABA PAID an unexpected visit to the family home and found her mother chatting with Oko on the sitting room sofa.

"Araba!" Miriam exclaimed, rising from her chair to give her daughter a hug. "How nice to see you, my dear!"

"Hi, Sis," Oko said, smiling. Araba pecked him on the cheek.

"We just finished breakfast," Miriam said. "Would you like some?"

"Oh, no, Mama, thanks," Araba said, choosing a seat opposite the other two.

"Are you planning to join Oko and me for the ten o'clock mass?" Miriam asked eagerly. "Your father will be administering the Holy Communion, and I know he would love to see you there."

"Not today," Araba said.

Oko scrutinized her. "Are you okay? You seem uneasy, or nervous."

Araba was. Now that the moment had arrived, she felt shaky. "I have something to say."

"Oh?" Miriam said. "What's happening?"

Araba's eyes were down. "What's happening is I'm finally moving forward."

Oko half frowned, half smiled. "Moving forward? How is that?"

"For years, I've lived with depression. Sometimes it gets very bad."

"Well," Oko said, "you're moody sometimes, but I always thought it was a by-product of your genius." He smiled, trying to make it a joke, but Araba didn't play along.

"I didn't know what the cause was until about two years ago, when I began having strange dreams and waking up with memories that had been buried."

"Memories." Miriam stared at her daughter, puzzled. "What sort of memories?"

"Of a man's hands touching my body without consent."

Miriam gaped at Araba.

Oko pulled back his chin. "What?"

Araba looked at her mother. "You knew, didn't you? That he molested me for years, starting when I was six and continuing until I left home."

Oko looked from his mother to his sister and back. "What's going on? Araba, what are you talking about?"

"Mama always came to tuck me in at night, and later, once she had gone to bed, Daddy would come to say good night. But that wasn't all. He used to touch me and masturbate in front of me. He raped me."

Miriam jumped up and hurled herself at Araba, who shielded her face from her mother's blows.

"*Mom!*" Oko cried, grabbing her and pulling her away. "What are you *doing?*"

Miriam broke away and went to stand at the window, breathing unsteadily with her arms folded and her back to her children.

Oko was in shock. "Araba," he said, "is this some sort of joke?"

"Do I look like I'm joking?"

Oko sat down, his elbows on his knees and his head in his hands. "No," he groaned. "This can't be."

At the window, Miriam, palms to her face, was weeping. It was a terrible sound.

Oko went over to her. "Mama." He tried putting his arms around her, but she pushed him away. Oko raised his palms, then let them drop in a gesture of helplessness. Araba stayed where she was, unmoved.

Oko looked at her again. "I mean . . . how can it be true? *Daddy* did that to you?"

Araba nodded. "Yes."

"There's no way. *Our* father?"

"None other than Reverend Fifi Tagoe."

"How could you not tell me?" Oko looked devastated. "I would have done something."

Araba looked down. "I was only six when it started, Oko. And what could you have done?"

There were tears in her brother's eyes. He seemed to shift his focus to Miriam, taking her by the arm and guiding her to the sofa. "Come, sit."

"Can you get me some water?" she whispered, eyes closed.

"Yes, of course," Oko said.

Araba stood. "I'll get it."

When she returned from the kitchen with a glass of water, Miriam was leaning back on the sofa, staring at the ceiling.

"Mom," Oko said. "Here, have some water."

She took a few sips and rested the glass on a side table.

"Are you feeling better?" Oko asked. "Mom, answer me."

Miriam nodded. "I'm fine."

"Is this true? What Araba is saying, is it true, Mom? I want to know the truth. Did you know? No, of course not, because if you'd known, you would have stopped it, right? I'm right, aren't I?"

Miriam didn't respond, so Araba did. "She knew."

Oko's head whipped around. "How could you know that?"

"She used to come around in the hallway," Araba said. "Maybe she thought about stopping him, but she never did. My door didn't close completely, and she almost got caught once when Daddy left my room."

Appalled, Oko asked Miriam, "Is it true?" When she didn't

respond, he muttered, "Jesus," and got off the sofa to pace the room with his hands on his hips. He stopped to stare at his mother, who had resumed crying.

Oko lost his temper. "Oh, stop, *please*! You don't get to cry now. What about back then?" He went to Miriam and put his face right up against hers. "Did you try to stop it?"

"I should have!" she cried out. "I know I should have."

"But you didn't," Oko said, pulling away. "Oh, God. I'm going to be sick."

He ran to the kitchen, and Araba heard him retch, then run the tap. "Araba," he said. "Can I talk to you in here for a second?"

She joined him. He leaned against the sink, head down, arms crossed. Araba waited.

"Have you confronted Daddy?"

"I have. I went to talk to him last Sunday."

"What did he say?"

"He was furious. Claimed I was making the whole thing up."

Oko stared at her. "Look, is there any chance that . . . I'm not trying to devalue what you're saying, but is there any chance you're misremembering? Or . . . I don't know."

"No, Oko," Araba said. "I know what happened. And look at Daddy and Mama's reactions."

"Sis, why not come to me first so we could team up and approach them in a more delicate way? Why so brutal?"

"A *delicate* way? To talk about how I was raped as a child? Would you even have believed me, Oko?"

"Of course, I would! I would have even when we were kids."

"You barely believe me now," Araba said. "Oko, you were perfection in Daddy's eyes—a brilliant student and all that. You looked up to him with such admiration, and you still do. There's no way you would've believed me when we were children."

Oko broke down and wept, but briefly. "I suppose you're right. What are we going to do now?" Before she could answer, he rushed on. "Araba, we must heal as a family. This is like a cancer on us."

"Daddy will have to admit what he's done before we can start to heal," Araba said, "but he continues to lie. What *I* am going to do is move forward on my own to help others who've been through this. I want to prevent this hell from being inflicted on other women and girls who believe they have to be silent. I must speak out publicly. I have enough of a platform now that my words will carry weight. It's a new lease on life, Oko. I already feel cleansed, like a load has been lifted."

Oko regarded her with a new wariness. "Wait a moment. You don't mean you're going to air this out in the media?"

"That's exactly what I mean."

Oko was aghast. "You're going to talk about *Daddy* doing this to you?"

"I can't do this halfway," Araba said. "Everything must come out."

"Araba, *please*," he whispered fiercely. "Let's think this through. Think of his reputation, his profession. For God's sake, please don't be so hasty."

"This may seem hasty to you," Araba said, "but for me, it's been a long time coming."

FORTY-EIGHT

Twelve months after

WHEN WALTER AND GIDEON returned to the Seezas', only Augustus was home, sitting on the back porch reading a large book titled *Africa: A History*. He looked up in surprise as the houseboy brought the visitors through.

"You again," Augustus said, looking surprised. "I wasn't expecting you."

"Good morning, sir," Walter said.

"Bring two chairs," Augustus said to the houseboy.

Walter and Gideon sat down when the chairs arrived. The backyard was pleasantly green and shady with a border of shrubs around it.

"How may I help you?" Augustus asked them. He looked better than when they'd last seen him, having put on some weight.

To save time and effort, Walter had pre-written the interview questions on a legal pad. As Augustus began reading them, there was a rustling sound to his left and he looked up, turning his head as a man came into view, dragging a bunch of dead tree branches behind him. He got to work cutting them with his machete into more manageable pieces.

"Wait a minute," Walter said, exchanging a dumbfounded look with Gideon. "Did you see that?"

"I saw it," Gideon replied.

A slow smile came to Walter's face. "Mr. Seeza, you can hear. You're not deaf at all, are you?"

Augustus looked confused. "What did you say? Please write it down."

Walter shook his head. "No, no. It's too late, sir. You've already exposed yourself. The sound of those dead branches came *before* your gardener appeared."

"I can read your lips now," Augustus said. "What you're saying isn't correct. I saw him from the corner of my eye."

"Impossible," Walter said. "Not from that angle. He was in your blind spot. That's why you turned around."

Walter and Gideon stared in silence at Augustus, who became increasingly flustered.

"Call Citi-FM," Walter said to Gideon. "Tell them Augustus Seeza has been running a scam. Just think what the thousands of donors to his recovery fund will say."

"Yes, boss," Gideon said, fishing for his phone.

"No, no, *wait!*" Augustus said. "Don't do that, please. I'll tell you everything, but please don't call the radio stations."

"You're a fraud, sir," Walter said, his voice tightening with anger. "Have you no shame?"

Morosely, Augustus looked away. "It wasn't my idea," he said finally.

"Whose, then?" Walter snapped.

"My parents. They more or less forced me," Augustus said, whining now. "My time in the hospital, especially intensive care, cost us thousands. My father's a judge, yes, but that doesn't mean he has all the money in the world. The fees needed to be paid. My mother told us she knew of nerve deafness as a rare complication of pancreatitis, for which the only cure is a costly cochlear implant."

"Go on," Walter said.

"So, we did some YouTube videos showing me in my situation, and set up the fund."

Augustus seemed to wither under Walter's glare.

Gideon wrote on his pad and passed it to Walter, who read it, nodded, and said to Augustus, "You said you were struggling for money. Mr. Seeza, were you the one who stole Araba's jewelry?"

"Oh, please!" Augustus exclaimed in disgust. "I would never do such a thing."

"Really?" Gideon said sarcastically.

"If you were in the course of stealing the jewels that night," Walter said, "but Araba woke up and caught you in the act, there easily could've been a struggle, and even if you hadn't planned to, you could've ended up killing her."

"What?" Augustus cried. "Why would I kill the woman I loved for a few pieces of jewelry? You're out of your mind."

"You tell us the truth, or we call Citi-FM," Walter said.

Augustus denied it repeatedly, though pleading with them not to call. Neither Walter nor Gideon trusted the man, and for good reason. He had lied before.

And then Justice Julius Seeza emerged from inside onto the porch.

"Papa!" Augustus stammered. "You're back early."

"Yes," Julius said, approaching. "What are you two doing here?"

"Conversing with your son," Walter said. "Without having to write anything down for him because, all of a sudden, his hearing is back. It's a miracle!"

Augustus cast his eyes down. "They know, Papa. There's no point in continuing the charade."

The elder Seeza let out a gasp.

"So," Walter said to him, "your son tells us your wife invented this scam, which you went along with in order to pay his hospital expenses. You, Justice Seeza, a High Court judge taking part in an illegal act; your wife, a doctor, engaging in medical fraud—"

"But you don't understand," Augustus interjected with a sudden flash of anger. "It's not about that! My parents have cared about me, given me unconditional love and drained every single one of their resources for me despite all my many failings. And whatever you may say about my mother, she has supported me and defended me through all of this without reservation and without the kind of criticism I was handed day and night from Bertha Longdon and Araba Tagoe, in whose eyes I could do nothing right."

Augustus stopped, looking away sullenly. Perhaps he had said too much.

"You did bear quite a grudge against Araba, then," Gideon said pointedly.

"Look, I didn't mean it that way," Augustus snapped.

"Why don't you tell the truth for once?" Walter said. "When we last spoke, you told us that you and Lady Araba were together and happy in the six months before her death, but that's not exactly true, is it? For weeks, the relationship was stumbling on rocky ground, and we know that as Lady Araba was returning from a party on that Sunday evening, you called her not once, but twice, harassing her and pressuring her to let you see her that night—"

"Who told you that?" Augustus snapped.

"—but she didn't *want* you to come over, right?" Walter continued. "That must have angered you, did it not?"

"All right, yes!" Augustus barked. "We were arguing that night after a couple of bumpy weeks. So what? We still loved each other."

"So, you lied to us," Walter said.

"How dare you interrogate him like this!" Julius bellowed. "Why all these probing questions that are none of your business? Please leave now. We don't ever want to see you again. And if you write anything disparaging about any member of my family, I will see you in court."

FORTY-NINE

Twelve months after

JOJO RELATED TO THE team how he and Ismael had gone up
to the terrace outside Lady Araba's bedroom. "I asked him about
Lady Araba, trying to get him to admit that he'd lusted after her,
but he just said he used to bring her flowers from his shop, sometimes at a discount but also as gifts. It seemed like he cared about
keeping her reputation intact.

"I brought up Araba's beauty, which he seemed happy to talk
about, and I finally asked if he had ever seen her through her window. I could see he wanted to tell me something. That's how it is
sometimes—you just want to unburden yourself on whoever is willing to listen. Ismael then told me the truth. He used to climb up to
Lady Araba's bedroom when it was dark outside to watch her."

"Aha!" Gideon exclaimed. "Emma was right."

"He confessed to doing this either late at night or before dawn,"
Jojo continued. "That Monday morning, he got to Trasacco
around five and went to spy on her. The light was still on in the
bedroom, and lying across the bed was Lady Araba's corpse with
blood all around it."

There was a unified outburst from the room.

"Wow," Gideon said. "What did he do?"

"He tried the door," Jojo said, "and it was open. Lady Araba—
or somebody else—had left it unlocked."

"The murderer, maybe," Walter said.

"It could be," Jojo agreed, "but anyway, Ismael went into the room, and for sure Araba was dead. He says her body was cold. It pained him to see her that way, and I think this was because, in fact, he really did love the woman. Seeing her body defiled and just left there to rot away was deeply offensive to him, so he moved Araba into a sleeping position, put her head on the pillow, and covered her with the duvet."

"What then?" Gideon asked.

"Well," Jojo said, "let me pose the question to all of you: What would you do next?"

"Report it immediately," Emma said.

Walter smiled. "I knew you would say that."

"Why, Emma?" Jojo asked.

She shrugged. "Because it's the right thing to do."

"But not the *best* thing," Gideon said. "Where is Lady Araba's body going to go again? It's less than one hour before daylight. Whether they find her at five, or six, or even eight o'clock, what difference does it make?"

"But it might make a difference in the calculation of time of death from the body temperature—" Emma tried.

Her colleagues drowned her out with their objections.

"You'll even be lucky if the Crime Scene Unit even has a thermometer to get the core temperature of the corpse," Jojo said, laughing.

"The way I see it," Gideon said, "it's a matter of self-preservation. If you go and report this to the police now, they'll hold you for questioning and might well accuse you of the murder, because what are you doing snooping around Lady Araba's bedroom in the dark? If I'd been in Ismael's shoes, I would have done what he did."

Jojo nodded. "Me too."

"That is, assuming we believe him," Gideon added, "which, by the way, I don't."

"I do," Jojo said. "I was there talking to the guy."

"There's no proof he's telling the truth," Gideon said.

"No proof he isn't," Jojo shot back.

"The story he told is ridiculous," Gideon declared.

"How is it ridiculous?" Jojo said, gesticulating.

"Are you done with your report, Jojo?" Sowah asked him quietly.

"Yes please. That's all, sir."

"Well done. I think the story is credible. But now, let's hear what Emma has been up to. You went to meet with Samson Allotey at Lady Pizzazz?"

"Yes, sir. And later, Susan Hayford arrived."

Emma gave the full story, ending with Hayford's admonition that Emma pursue Araba's family members.

"That could be Hayford trying to shift suspicion away from herself," Gideon observed.

"Yes," Emma said, "but I didn't feel like she had anything to do with Lady Araba's murder, even if the motive was quite strong. Susan talked about relishing competition with Lady Araba, not wanting to eliminate it."

"I think women would prefer to make their female rivals suffer," Walter put in, "rather than killing them."

"Oh, is that so?" Emma said in mild amusement.

"Yes," Walter said with certainty. "Much more satisfying. And I agree, actually."

"What about Samson, Emma?" Sowah asked, shifting the subject.

"Well, again, I don't see how much he would benefit from killing his boss," she said. "Wouldn't it be better to stay with Araba's successful company than to join Susan Hayford's less-established one?"

"But you never know," Jojo said. "Hayford or Samson might not have done anything as individuals, but sometimes when people get together, they feed off each other and can get up to all kinds of bad things."

"I hear you," Emma conceded.

"Thank you, Emma," Sowah said. "Now, Walter and Gideon, your turn. What happened yesterday with the Seezas?"

Walter led off with, "First of all, Augustus Seeza is not deaf."

The others said, "*What?*"

"We sat outside on the porch with his back to the garden," Walter explained. "Without thinking, he reflexively turned to see something that had made a noise behind him. It was the gardener. He'd heard him coming before he saw him."

Walter and Gideon bathed in the glory of their discovery for a moment.

"Augustus claims the hospital fees during his illness left his father completely broke," Gideon said, "so they looked for a way to make some money."

Jojo made a rude noise with his mouth. "Justice Seeza isn't broke, he's greedy—all his millions are in banks abroad."

"But how did they come up with this strange deafness story?" Emma asked.

"It was Caroline Seeza's idea," Walter said. "She had knowledge of an obscure connection between Augustus's illness and loss of hearing, and it's hard to challenge that kind of medical knowledge."

"This family seems incapable of any honesty whatsoever," Emma said, almost wearily.

"The question, though," Jojo said, "is if they're capable of murder, and my answer is yes. My money is still on Augustus."

Emma raised her hand. "One other thing, boss. Remember I told you I saw a small metallic object on Lady Araba's bed in the crime scene photos?"

"You did?" Sowah asked, looking momentarily blank. "Okay, okay—I recall, now. What of it?"

"I called DS Boateng, and he said, yes, they had spotted it and submitted it with the rest of the evidence. Fortunately, he had a couple of photos of it, which he has now sent to me, and I'd like to show them to all of you."

While the others came closer to look, Emma opened up her phone to the images of the object taken from different angles. It was a bloodstained metal band about a centimeter wide. End on, it took the shape of a "ω" and measured about nine centimeters in total length.

"What is that?" Gideon said.

"I don't know," Emma replied, "but to me it looks like a clasp or clip to hold two things together—like the ligatures used to strangle Lady Araba."

"Ah," Sowah said, thoughtfully. "Not bad, Emma."

"On the other hand," Walter said in bored tones, "it could have nothing to do with the murder itself."

"Manu, it has blood on it," Emma said pointedly. "You're going to overlook that?"

"I didn't say we should overlook anything," Walter replied crisply. "Just that we can't attach too much significance to every little thing."

"Well," Sowah interjected, "if we suppose for a moment that Emma is correct, this metal clip, or band, or whatever it is, doesn't look like it was made at home by the murderer to hold two ligatures together. It looks like he repurposed it from something else—but what?"

Emma racked her brain, but came up short.

"Is it something to fasten electrical cables together?" Jojo suggested.

Sowah snapped his fingers and pointed at him. "For wiring a house, for example."

Gideon, the office's electrical and electronics wizard, said, "I've never seen a cable fastener like that before, and I've done a lot of household wiring in my time."

"Show-off," Jojo muttered.

Emma zoomed in and out on the image showing one side of the metal clip. "Are those engraved letters I see where the layer of blood is very thin?"

"Yeah, maybe," Gideon said, peering at it.

Walter disagreed. "Your eyes are playing tricks on your brains," he scoffed.

"Well," Sowah said with a sigh of resignation, "obviously, we're not going to solve this right now. The main issue is that we have something from the crime scene with someone's DNA all over it. How can we get it tested with Thomas and Madam Tawiah standing in the way?"

FIFTY

Twelve months after

EARLY IN THE AFTERNOON, Doctor Jauregui called Emma. "I just returned from my lectures to the CSU guys at CID, and I also checked the police docket for the Lady Araba case. You were right that the family claimed some jewelry pieces went missing from Lady Araba's room, including the necklace that she wore habitually. The police accused Kweku, the driver, of the theft as well as the murder, but they didn't find any such jewelry when they searched his living quarters. For the record, they officially concluded Kweku had already sold off the alleged jewelry for personal gain."

"Convenient scapegoating," Emma said grimly. "The infamous MO of the Ghana Police."

"Unfortunately, you are right about that," Jauregui said. "I have some other news for you, though."

"Yes, Doctor?" Emma said, eagerly.

"The metal object at the crime scene that we couldn't identify. I think I've found it."

"You have?"

"Yes, it's not at the FSL. According to this record, it's at the CID property room."

Emma raised her eyebrows. "The property room? Should it be there?"

"No, it should have gone to the lab," Jauregui said. "Otherwise, how was it to get tested for DNA?"

"Then how did it get to the property room, I wonder?" Emma said.

"Exactly the question I had, so I called DS Boateng and asked him. At first, he was mystified, and then he figured it out. Everything they took from the crime scene was divided in two piles—the evidence that was to go to the FSL in one pile, and regular belongings in the other—things like her phone, purse, and so on. Corporal Tackie, the evidence tech, took the evidence to the FSL, while one of the constables took the ordinary belongings to the CID property room, but someone must have accidentally put the metal clip, which was in a paper envelope, in the wrong pile, and so it was unknowingly signed out to the property officer."

"Ah, I see," Emma said. "That must be the explanation. Is the seal on the bag intact? No sign of tampering?"

"Everything is correctly sealed," Jauregui said. "I will send you a photo."

"Thank you, Doctor." Emma felt a growing sense of excitement. "Somehow we have to get that piece of evidence and have the blood DNA-tested."

"I would have signed it out myself," Jauregui said, "but I'm not a police officer, so it's not allowed."

"I understand, Doctor," Emma said. "No problem. We don't want you getting in trouble. You've already gone far beyond the call of duty. Thank you."

After ending the call, Emma ran down the hall to Sowah's office. "Sir?"

He looked up over his glasses. "What's up?"

Emma dropped into the scarlet sofa, which was beginning to show its wear. "I just heard from Dr. Jauregui, who was at CID this morning. She discovered that the mystery object we were looking at this morning wasn't sent to the FSL as it should have been. Instead, a police constable accidentally submitted it to the CID property room."

"Really?" Sowah sat up straight. "Then we have to get hold of that evidence."

"Yes, sir."

The boss leaned back in his chair to reflect for a moment. Then he cast around his desk, muttering, "Where did I put my phone?"

"In the drawer, sir?" Emma suggested.

Sowah found it there. "Thank you. How did you know?"

Emma merely smiled.

Sowah dialed someone and waited with the phone to his ear. "Cleo! How is life, my friend? Oh, you know, we are surviving like anyone else. The case? Well, to be honest, we have been stalled, but we might have a breakthrough that I'm hoping you can help us with."

Sowah detailed Dr. Jauregui's discovery of what was a potentially useful piece of evidence from the crime scene. "We can't let it sit there, Cleo," Sowah said urgently. "In fact, I would argue that we are morally obligated to get it tested for DNA . . . Okay, maybe that's a bit dramatic, but you know what I mean. And we can't let this get into Thomas's hands, or it will likely suffer the same fate as the other pieces of evidence."

Nodding and murmuring agreement at intervals, Sowah listened to what Laryea was saying on the other end, which Emma tried without much success to gauge.

"Yes, of course," Sowah said at length. "You're perfectly correct, but how can we allow this miscarriage of justice? An innocent man is in jail for this."

He paused again as Laryea said something, and then there was another back-and-forth exchange. Finally, Sowah said, "Thank you so much, Cleo. I appreciate your help." He ended the call, and turned to Emma. "I had a tough time persuading him to get involved, but he finally relented."

"What is he going to do, sir?"

"He's going to sign the evidence out of the property room himself."

"Wow. And then?"

Sowah shook his head. "I don't know. He didn't say."

BACK AT HER desk, Emma sat pondering as she doodled absent-mindedly on a page in her composition book. She felt as though she and the team were wandering around lost in a forest. The blood on the metal clip might reveal something new, but if it had only Araba's DNA on it, they were back at square one.

What was the crux of the difficulty they were having? It was that they had been unable to place anyone at the scene of Lady Araba's murder at around the time it was likely to have occurred—probably between nine-thirty Sunday night and five o'clock Monday morning. Peter had said it had been quiet the whole night at the front gate, so the consensus was that the murderer must have used the rear gate to gain entry. *Why* hadn't the surveillance cameras worked?

"Gideon?" Emma said.

He was glued to his cell phone screen. "Yes, Emma?"

"Have you ever worked with security systems?"

Gideon looked up. "What kind of security systems?"

"Like the one at Trasacco Valley. Peter said the DVR they were using for the CCTV surveillance was old and he didn't think it was working well, but has anyone really checked it? It could just be that Peter doesn't know how the thing functions. I mean, what if there really is surveillance footage available from the night of Lady Araba's murder and we've overlooked it all this time?"

"Yeah, you're right," Gideon said thoughtfully. "Well, I haven't worked on security systems as such, but before I came to the agency, I did do repairs at a friend's electronic shop in my neighborhood. What are you thinking?"

"Could you or your friend take a look at the machine? Jojo can ask Peter."

"It's not a bad idea," Gideon said. "Where's Jojo? *Jojo!*"

"Mm?" The languid reply came from the makeshift staff room around the corner.

"Can you come here for a minute?"

"I'm eating."

Gideon shook his head and muttered, "He's always eating. Come, Emma, let's talk to him about it."

Jojo was digging into a full bowl of yam and *kontomire*. Emma couldn't imagine eating such a heavy meal in the middle of the afternoon. She sat opposite Jojo at the table. "We have a mission for you."

Jojo grunted, his mouth too full to say anything.

Emma explained her idea and Jojo paused the banquet for just a few moments to think about it. Then he nodded and continued his meal. "I'll talk to Peter about it tomorrow."

"Why not save some time and call him when you're done?"

"No problem," Jojo said, chewing noisily. "I'll take care of it. Now, go away and let me finish my lunch."

HIS BELLY FULL, Jojo discussed with Gideon how to frame the DVR matter before putting in the call. Peter was home on his day off. Jojo kidded with him briefly, and then got to the point. "I was talking to a friend of mine about the old DVR you had been asking the management to replace before Lady Araba died. Do you still have it?"

"Yeah," Peter said. "It's still there, at the Trasacco security post. When the guys came to install the new DVR, I asked them about the old one. They didn't really look at it in detail because they weren't there for that, but they told me that most of the time it's not worth it to try to repair it. Then, I asked management if they wanted me to keep the old machine around. They said as far as they were concerned, I could throw it out or give it away."

"I'm glad you didn't," Jojo said. "My friend works at a second-hand electronics store. He's an expert at computers and stuff. He asked me if you would like him to check the DVR to see if it can be fixed."

"Oh, really?" Peter said, sounding interested. "You mean to use it here as a backup?"

"If you like, but better than that, if my friend manages to sell it to someone, he says he can give you and me a small commission."

"Oh," Peter said, laughing. "I won't say no to that. I'll be on duty tomorrow, so he can come to Trasacco in the morning. What is his name?"

"Gideon," Jojo said. "We will come together, okay?"

FIFTY-ONE

Twelve months after

CLEO LARYEA MET WITH DS Isaac Boateng at a relatively secluded area in a shady car park outside the Department of Parks and Gardens. They sat in Laryea's car with the windows down and the front doors cracked open in the hope of catching a decent cross-breeze on an oppressive afternoon.

Boateng was clearly nervous about this meeting. "Am I in trouble, sir?"

Laryea shook his head, "Not at all. To the contrary, I need your help."

"Sir?"

"The forensic doctor spoke with you a couple of days ago about the evidence sent to the CID property room instead of to the FSL."

"That's correct, sir."

"If the blood on the metal clip or clasp, or whatever it is, contains DNA other than Lady Araba's, it could be a potential breakthrough."

"I agree, sir, but as you know, I'm no longer—"

"I'm aware you were taken off the case. We have no choice but to work with that, but here and now is an opportunity to redirect the investigation. We all know that the driver, Kweku-Sam, didn't kill Lady Araba. The fact is, evidence has been suppressed, and we cannot allow that to happen. I know it matters to you."

Boateng nodded, "Yes, sir," but he sounded tentative.

"There aren't that many people in the force like you and me," Laryea continued. "I'll be retiring soon, but you are the up-and-coming generation who can make things better. You have a science degree and care about your work. But it's tough to be an island of integrity when sneaky crocodiles are all around, circling you."

Boateng sighed. "That's the thing, sir."

"Bottom line," Laryea continued, "is we must find out whose DNA is on the piece of metal found on Lady Araba's bed, but we can't surrender it to Thomas to get it done, because in all likelihood, nothing will happen. So, we have to do something else. To start, I have signed the evidence out of the property room."

Boateng was startled. "Sir?"

"My name is now on the chain of custody form."

"Then, what's going to happen?"

"I want you to do the DNA testing."

Boateng let out a long breath and dropped his head as if guillotined. "Sir . . ."

Laryea shifted so he was looking directly at Boateng. "I know it feels like I'm putting your job on the line, but I'm not going to allow anything to happen to you. I will have your back. I promise you that."

His gaze down, Boateng chewed on his lower lip for a moment. Finally, he lifted his head. "Okay. I trust you, sir."

JOJO AND GIDEON arrived midmorning, well into Peter's shift. He shook hands warmly with both men, expressing that he appreciated Gideon's coming.

"Come in and take a look at the DVR," Peter said, steering them into the sentry room, which was smaller than it had seemed to Jojo from the exterior. On a small counter next to the window, a large security record book lay open next to a monitor screen, which showed a paneled image feed from the cameras at the front and rear gates. On the back wall was a shelf piled with miscellaneous junk, from which Peter extracted a clunky, dusty, black-and-chrome DVR.

"This is the old machine," Peter said, resting it on the counter. He pointed to a much sleeker model mounted on a bracket over the counter. "That's the new one we got a week after Lady Araba was murdered."

Gideon bent forward to peer at the DVR's front panel, and then the back. "So, how was the machine behaving when it started to go bad, and when was that?"

"I want to say about a month before Lady Araba was killed," Peter responded. "Sometimes it made a kind of whining noise, and the picture on the monitor was bad."

"Did anyone ever drop the machine?"

Peter shrugged. "Not that I know of."

"And you didn't have a backup system?" Gideon asked casually. "Like an external drive?"

Peter shook his head. "Not then. We do now. You know how it is—people learn their lesson after the fact."

"Yes, that's always the way it is," Gideon said with a knowing smile.

"So," Peter continued, "when the detective who was investigating the case asked us to try playing the video from the night Araba died, nothing showed on the monitor except some strange flashing and zigzag patterns."

"Did someone check that the cameras and the connecting cables were working at that time?" Gideon asked.

Peter nodded. "All that was fine. As soon as the new system was connected, everything worked." He tapped the DVR with his finger. "It's this thing that's the problem."

Gideon nodded, leaning against the wall and studying the machine like a doctor running through possible diagnoses.

"Do you think you can repair it?" Peter asked, sounding hopeful.

"It depends on how bad the damage is," Gideon said. "The trouble is the hard drive—either the actuator arm or the reader head or the platters, maybe all of them."

Peter looked at Jojo and said, "I have no idea what he's talking about."

Jojo laughed. "Yeah, and don't ask him to explain because you'll be even more confused. He always shows off like this. Very annoying."

Gideon grinned at Peter. "Don't mind him. Anyway, bottom line is, I won't know until I open up the hard drive to check it."

"Can you do that here?" Peter asked.

"Oh, no," Gideon replied, laughing. "I have to take it to the shop, if that's okay with you."

"Of course. No problem."

"I'll call you and let you know the verdict after I've examined it," Gideon said.

FIFTY-TWO

Twelve months after

A METRO TV REPORTER spoke with Cleo Laryea in an exclusive interview broadcast on the six o'clock evening news.

> **Reporter:** Can you confirm that new evidence has surfaced regarding the murder of Lady Araba from about a year ago, sir?
>
> **Laryea:** We have discovered evidence our investigators were not previously aware of, and it might—I repeat, *might*—throw new light on the case. What I can tell you is that it is an object from the crime scene at Lady Araba's home.
>
> **Reporter:** The murder weapon, perhaps?
>
> **Laryea:** I can't comment on that. What I would like, however, is to appeal to members of the public with any knowledge relating to the murder of Lady Araba to come forward to the authorities on a completely anonymous basis.
>
> **Reporter:** We've put the number to call at the bottom of the screen.
>
> **Laryea:** Thank you.
>
> **Reporter:** You're welcome, sir. One question I had, though: Why, in the initial days after the death of Lady

Araba, did the press have access to updates from the CID, including from the director-general, Madam Tawiah, but not after even a few days? What exactly happened to the investigation, sir?

Laryea: Well, the case was considered closed on the arrest of Lady Araba's driver. But now that new evidence has been introduced, thanks to the wisdom and steady hand of the director-general, we are now able to resume our investigation with full force. We value the backing of our leader tremendously, and I am confident that she wants to get to the bottom of this just as much as I do.

Reporter: With this new information you have unearthed, are you confident you will find the person who killed Lady Araba, sir?

Laryea: We are going to put every effort behind it, yes.

Reporter: Because, sir, as I don't need to tell you, the CID's record of solving major murder cases has been less than satisfactory.

Laryea: We want to change that, and I think I can safely say on the director-general's behalf that she wants that as well.

Reporter: Deputy Commissioner Laryea, thank you very much.

AFTER THE INTERVIEW was over, Laryea expected at least a couple of people to call. Director-General Tawiah, who was away in the Brong-Ahafo Region at the time, came first. "Laryea," she said, "good evening. How are you?"

"Evening, madam. I'm well, thank you, and you?"

"I'm confused," she said. "I haven't seen this TV news segment everyone has been telling me about, but is it true there is new evidence in the Araba Tagoe case? What is going on, and why wasn't I informed of it?"

"I apologize that I didn't contact you earlier, madam," Laryea said. "Had you not been away, I would have come directly to you in your office at CID Headquarters, but with you dealing with issues in B-A, I felt I should get things settled before troubling you."

"Okay, okay," Tawiah said impatiently, "but what is this new development?"

"On the day evidence was collected from the scene of Lady Araba's murder, one item was accidentally sent to the CID property room instead of the FSL, and it has been there all this time—"

"How did that happen?" Tawiah interrupted.

"It's a long story that I will not burden you with at the moment, madam, but the bottom line is that the item must be tested for DNA because it might give us an important lead."

"Well, yes, of course," Tawiah said, but Laryea sensed hesitancy in her voice. "Nevertheless, I don't like that you went on TV and gave an unauthorized interview."

"Actually, madam, it wasn't quite that way. I didn't go to them. They came to me. Someone must have leaked the news of this possible new piece of evidence to Metro TV. They got in touch with me, and at first, I was going to refuse any comment, but then I thought I could use the interview as an opportunity to appeal to the public for information about the murder and also send out a positive message about what we are doing at CID. As you know, madam, the public's trust in us is spotty, which is one of the reasons I praised the support you have steadfastly given the investigation."

Tawiah cleared her throat. "Yes, that is true—"

"And because of that support, madam—excuse me for interrupting—I would like to make a humble request of you, please."

"What is that?"

"I request that you put me entirely in charge of this investigation from now on."

"I think you already are," Tawiah said dryly. "Clearly, you have established yourself as the new lead on this, Laryea. I leave it to you."

"Thank you very much, madam."

Laryea hung up with a smile. The next call, which hit six minutes later, was from his friend Bob Agyekum, the general manager of Metro TV.

"I think your interview went very well," he said. "The way you built Madam Tawiah up was magnificent. You put her on a pedestal from which she cannot now climb down. Has she called you?"

"Yes," Laryea replied. "She's agreed to put me in charge of the case."

"Well done, my friend. Even Adam Kyei, our station owner, called me to congratulate me on the scoop, since none of the competing news outlets have it. So, he's happy."

"Also, I would say," Laryea added, "it puts a feather in your cap as the general manager."

"Thank you. So, what is next?"

"DS Boateng and I will go to the FSL tomorrow with the evidence, and he'll begin analysis on it. He will also be sending a second sample by courier to the forensics lab at Cape Coast University. That way, we'll have an independent evaluation."

"Did you tell Madam Tawiah that?"

"No, but she'll soon find out."

FIFTY-THREE

Twelve months after

As DCOP Laryea and DS Boateng walked into the FSL office, Thomas looked up in surprise.

"Good morning," Laryea said.

Thomas leapt to his feet and stiffened briefly in salute. "Morning, sir." He sent a questioning glance at Boateng. What was going on here?

The two visitors took their seats opposite Thomas's desk.

"Let me explain why we're here," Laryea said. "It came to my notice a few days ago that a piece of evidence taken from the scene of Lady Araba's murder was accidentally sent to the CID property room instead of to the FSL. It has been sitting there since then."

"Oh?" Thomas said in apparent surprise.

"You weren't aware of that, I don't suppose?"

"No, sir. I didn't know anything about it."

"Madam Tawiah has authorized me to take over the Lady Araba case," Laryea continued bluntly. "I have signed out the evidence from the property room, and I will now officially sign it over to DS Boateng here to maintain the chain of custody. DS Boateng will then begin to process the DNA here in the lab. Do you have any problems with that?"

"Not at all, sir."

"We'll also send samples to Prof. Kingsley's lab at Cape Coast University. I will put you in charge of that."

"No problem, sir," Thomas said, still looking nervous.

"Now, the other pieces of evidence from the crime scene—do you still have those?"

"Yes, sir," Thomas said. "One hair sample and two swabs of blood evidence, which are in the freezer. Should I get them for you?"

"Not yet," Laryea replied. "Keep them safely under lock and key. Sergeant Boateng will let you know when he's ready to proceed." He stood up. "I think a tour of your fine facility is in order. I've never been here before, if you can believe that."

IN THE REAR of the electronics shop at which he had once worked, Gideon watched over the shoulder of his friend and store owner, Jacob, who was carefully removing the lid from Trasacco's security hard drive. Inside the device were two stacked, polished discs with a spindle in the middle. At the end of a two-pronged arm were tiny heads that wrote and read the data on the discs.

Jacob grunted. "Stuck head. The arm should be parked to the side in the off position, but it's jammed in the middle of the disc."

"Yeah," Gideon agreed. "The platters look okay, though."

"Yup. Spinning well, and I don't see any obvious scratches."

"So?" Gideon said. "What do you think? Try for me, eh?"

"If you really want me to, no problem. I'll switch out the heads and then we'll try our data recovery software. If I find anything, I'll put it on a thumb drive for you. Only thing is I don't have a donor hard drive right now, but I think I can get one in two or three days. I'll let you know."

"Thank you, my man," Gideon said. He could barely wait to see the outcome, but he tempered his eagerness. It was quite possible that the hard drive would reveal nothing.

FIFTY-FOUR

Twelve and a half months after

"WE HAVE A LOT to discuss," Sowah said at the morning briefing. "Let's first address the DNA reports from DS Boateng at the FSL and Prof. Kingsley's CCU lab. Boateng's analysis finds the DNA of the strand of hair consistent with Lady Araba's, so that doesn't add any useful information to the case.

"Now, Boateng also finds the DNA on the bloody metal clip and on the two blood swabs in Thomas's freezer are consistent with Lady Araba's. DS Boateng didn't detect any other DNA on either the swab or the metal clip.

"On the other hand, Prof. Kingsley says he believes there's DNA from at least two different sources on the metal clip. He studied more than one area of the clip, and he's getting a DNA profile from the edge of the clip that is different from the body of it, where most of the blood was. But it's a very small amount, and he says he will have to carry out further processes to amplify it. That's going to take a few days. So, at the moment, we're in holding position as far as the DNA is concerned. Next, we come to the DVR findings, and here I'll let Gideon take over—"

Emma put up her hand. "Sorry, sir, before we go on—remember we were debating whether the metal clasp was engraved with some letters? Did either Boateng or Kingsley comment on that?"

Sowah shook his head. "No mention of that. Text him to

ask—he could have missed it or forgotten to mention it. Go, Gideon."

"I took the hard drive to Jacob, my friend who runs an electronics store," Gideon began. "He had a tough time recovering the data, and only some of what he obtained was of good quality. Anyway, he and I took turns watching for hours looking for relevant footage. A lot of it was corrupted data, so we couldn't see much or sometimes anything at all, but whenever there was something that looked significant, we made a screen recording and transferred it to a pen drive, which I have here." He plugged it into the company laptop and then looked quizzically at his still-seated colleagues. "What, are you made of stone? Do you want to see this or are you just going to sit there, staring at my face?"

Laughing sheepishly, the rest of the team got to their feet and gathered around Gideon.

"Jojo and Emma, I'm hoping you can help us here," he said. "We found this portion of the video where we see someone opening up the shed near the rear gate and taking out two large flowerpots. The image is not that clear, but take a look."

After a few seconds, Jojo said, "That's Ismael. He's the only one who has the key to the shed, and I recognize his physique."

"I agree," Emma said. "That's him, for sure."

"Good," Gideon said. "I was hoping you would say that, because the time stamp says Monday, third of July, at six fifty-five in the morning, and he said he took two planters like these to Lady Araba's upstairs terrace around that time. So, we can assume the time stamp is fairly accurate."

The others murmured agreement.

"Having settled that question," Gideon said, "we looked at the footage of the night before, starting from about nine o'clock, because we know that's when Kweku brought Lady Araba home from the event. One of the cameras at the front entrance briefly captured a man leaving at nine thirteen. The image cuts off, but that's probably Kweku-Sam, who told us he left around that time after bringing Lady Araba home.

"Then, at nine fifty-six, we see someone dressed in black come into view and walking pretty quickly toward the rear gate, followed by a dark-colored car that appears from the lower right corner of the screen, and then the person in black gets in the front passenger seat."

Everyone instinctively leaned forward for a better look.

"The car then moves toward the gate," Gideon went on, "which takes a little while to open automatically by the sensor mechanism, and then the car leaves."

"Was that a man or a woman who got in the car?" Sowah said. "The image is blurry."

"Let me try freezing it for a better look," Gideon said.

They all stared at the image, humming and hawing as they tried to make up their minds.

"I say a man," Jojo said. "The way he moves seems more masculine."

"Maybe," Emma said, "but it could be a large woman too."

"Who walks like a man?" Jojo asked with amusement.

"So?" Emma retorted. "It happens."

"Well," Walter came in, "what's the significance of the footage, though? Two people are going out somewhere, one picks up the other, and off they go."

"Why at the back gate?" Emma questioned. "If I lived at Trasacco and I was waiting for a friend to pick me up, the logical spot would be at the front gate, not the rear where the exit is. This looks as though the person didn't want to be seen."

Walter shrugged. "So, let's say he or she is having an affair with whoever the driver of the vehicle is. What's the big deal?"

"Perhaps," Gideon said. "Still, I was curious about the vehicle. Had it been parked to the side of the gate somewhere? So, I went back earlier than nine o'clock and found this at eight thirty-six. Looks like that same car approaches the rear exit from inside the complex, the gate slides open, and the man or woman in black we saw in the previous footage walks *into* the complex and continues out of the camera field."

"So, he or she was waiting for the driver to get the gate open," Walter said.

"I've just noticed he's wearing a backpack," Jojo observed.

"But watch what happens," Gideon said. "After this person in black comes in, the vehicle doesn't exit the complex. Instead, it backs up out of the camera's view."

"So the driver," Emma said, "whoever he or she is, waited there until the person in black came back out at nine fifty-six?"

"It appears so," Gideon said.

"What about the vehicle?" Walter asked. "It looks like a nice car like a Benz, or something like that."

"For sure, it's no Daewoo Matiz," Gideon said, referring to the matchbox-sized taxi-driver favorite because of its unbeatable gas mileage.

"Is there footage of the vehicle entering the complex from the front entrance?" Sowah asked.

"I've looked for it, sir," Gideon said. "Can't find it, and earlier than about eight o'clock the footage is practically nonexistent."

"Okay," Sowah said. "Then, Jojo, what you need to do today is take the video to Peter to see if he recognizes the vehicle or knows who was driving it."

"I'll do that, boss."

"Was there anything else of significance on the hard drive recovery?" Sowah asked Gideon.

"That's all I have, sir."

"It's a great job you've done," Sowah said warmly. "Round of applause, everyone."

They obliged as Gideon looked bashful but pleased.

Emma's phone buzzed and she checked the notification. It was a reply from DS Boateng with an image of the metal clasp attached. Emma smiled. "Who said there was no writing on the metal clip? Walter, I seem to remember—"

"You're saying there is?" Walter said, wrinkling his brow.

"Yes, sir," Emma said. "It says 'Prestige.'"

They all exchanged glances.

"What's 'Prestige?'" Jojo asked. "Is that whoever manufactured the metal thing?"

"Or maybe the object belongs to an Ewe person," Emma said. "You know how they love those names—Grace, Charity, Faith, Wisdom. My Ewe boyfriend's name is Courage."

"Someone, please google 'Prestige,'" Sowah said impatiently, "to see if it's some kind of metal company, and if so, maybe it has a picture of this metal device and what it's for. It's driving me to distraction."

Gideon was, of course, the fastest to reach the first results page. "There's Prestige Metal Products. Their products are brackets, sheet metal containers, hooks . . ."

Jojo moved over to peek at Gideon's screen. "Ah, but this looks like heavy-duty merchandise for the metal industry."

"And besides," Gideon observed, "this company doesn't engrave the brand name into its products."

"Keep searching," Sowah urged. "If there's a connection between this piece of metal and the murder of Lady Araba, we need to find it."

FIFTY-FIVE

Twelve and a half months after

"MORNING, MY BROTHER," JOJO said as he approached Peter at the beginning of the morning shift at Trasacco.

"Hey, morning! How are you?"

"I'm good. I have something to show you."

"Okay, I'm coming just now. You can go inside the security booth." Peter gave some instructions to the junior guards and then returned to Jojo.

Jojo rested his laptop on the counter. "Gideon recovered some footage from the Sunday night of Lady Araba's death, and I wanted you to see it."

"Good, good," Peter said eagerly.

Jojo popped in the thumb drive and launched the footage of the dark car approaching the rear gate, which automatically opened and let the figure in black in.

"Do you recognize that vehicle?" Jojo asked. "Or the person who entered the complex?"

Peter brought his eyes closer to the screen and shook his head. "Not really, no. Hold on."

He pulled down a large security register from the shelf behind them and plonked it on the counter. "This is the record for last year." Muttering dates, Peter turned the pages until he came to the right spot. "Second of July, right? Evening shift, seven fifty-five—one vehicle, a Mazda, entered; eight-oh-five, a Toyota Camry; and then something at eight thirty-three . . ." He peered at notes, moving his finger across the page. "What does that even say? I know who made this entry." Peter leaned out of the sentry room and yelled, "*Sako!*"

Gangly Sako came trotting up. "Yes, boss?"

"What is this you wrote here?" Peter demanded. "Why is your handwriting so bad?"

Sako stared at the entry, apparently having difficulty deciphering his own scribble. "Okay, the type of vehicle was a BMW, black in color; name of the driver, Ansong; purpose of visit, I wrote 'Doctor.'"

"What does that mean, exactly?" Peter asked.

"That's what I'm trying to figure out," Sako said, rubbing the back of his head as he tried to recall.

"And where is the plate number?" Peter asked sharply, "I've told you several times, Sako, you have to make your entries clear and complete. Just noting it's a black BMW isn't enough. We need more information about it."

"Sorry, boss," Sako said, looking down. He snapped his fingers. "Please, I remember now. It was a guy driving—no passengers— and he told me he was a doctor making a house call to one of the residents."

"Doctor? House call?" Peter said. "Which house?"

Sako shook his head. "He didn't say. I remember thinking he seemed strange because he was wearing a cap pulled down over his face and didn't really look like a doctor—from the way he was dressed, I mean."

"And because of the cap," Jojo said, "you couldn't get a good look at his face, right?"

"Yes please," Sako responded.

"Is it common for doctors to make house calls here?" Jojo asked.

"Not common, but it does happen sometimes," Peter said. He shrugged. "These rich people can afford it."

"You were on duty too that night," Jojo said to him. "You don't remember seeing this vehicle or the driver?"

Peter shook his head. "I was probably in the other booth and not paying attention to vehicles entering. We take turns in the booths."

"I see," Jojo said, thinking that was plausible. "And you said you did a patrol of the complex at ten thirty?"

"Yes," Peter said, "and I didn't spot that vehicle anywhere at that time."

"Yes," Jojo said, "because, by then, it had left. Let me show you."

The trio watched the 9:56 P.M. footage in which the car appeared and the dark figure got in. After some delay and back-and-forthing of the car, it drove out of the rear gate.

Peter shook his head. "I don't know who that might be, but the whole thing is suspect. This so-called doctor proceeded directly to the back gate to let in the second person, who then went somewhere in the complex and returned at nine fifty-six to where the guy in the car was waiting." His voice shook a little. "Do you have any footage showing the driver also getting out of the vehicle?"

"No," Jojo admitted, "but that doesn't mean he didn't."

The three men looked at each other for a moment, and then Peter said, "Okay, Sako, you may go."

"Thanks, brother Sako," Jojo said, smiling at him.

"Can you send the video to me?" Peter asked Jojo. "I want to look at it carefully again at home."

"No problem."

Peter clenched his fist. "We have to get these people."

FIFTY-SIX

Twelve and a half months after

IN THE BRIEFING ROOM, Sowah had an assignment for the team. "All of us, including myself, will again watch the CCTV footage with the figure in black, and then try to match it to our suspects. Gideon? Explain our little experiment."

"Okay," Gideon said, "I have photos of all our suspects. Those of the Tagoe and Seeza families are ones that we took ourselves, while others, like the pic of Bertha Longdon, Samson, and Susan Hayford, I got from the Internet. I turned their images into silhouettes so you won't know who you're looking at, and I also reduced the dimensions to approximately the size of the mystery person in the footage. The silhouettes are numbered, so all you have to do is rank them in the order you think they most match the mystery person."

For a moment, everyone simply stared at Gideon. Then Walter said, "I feel like I'm back in secondary school and about to take a test."

Jojo put up his hand. "Please, teacher, may I ask a question? How many hours do we have for this exam?"

"*Kwasea*," Gideon said, laughing as he passed around sheets of paper for the exercise. Then, with the whole team standing behind him, he brought up the silhouette pattern on the left side of the laptop screen as the footage played on the right.

"My advice," Sowah said, "is not to think too hard about your answers. Write your very first impressions, and then put your responses on the table."

Quietly, everyone wrote down their choices and dropped them on the pile. Sowah gathered them up and scanned them for a moment. "Very interesting. We have most votes for silhouette number four. Who is that, Gideon?"

"Susan Hayford," Gideon responded, referring to his key.

"*What?*" Jojo exclaimed.

"Seriously?" Emma said in surprise. "Come on, now."

"In second place," Sowah continued, "number six."

"That's Father Tagoe," Gideon said.

"More like it," Emma muttered.

After that, there was little unanimity among the choices.

"Boss," Jojo grumbled, "I'm sorry, but this is not a good test at all. It hasn't gotten us anywhere."

"Why do you say that?" Walter objected. "Maybe it means we should look more closely at people like Susan Hayford and Bertha Longdon."

"We knew that already," Jojo pointed out.

"This could reinforce it," Walter said valiantly.

Sowah raised a hand. "If anything, this exercise has taught us that it isn't what we see that matters, it's how our brains process it. We're all looking at the same images, yet we interpret them differently."

"Oh," Jojo said, with sudden enlightenment. "I see what you're saying."

Emma was curious about something else. "Gideon, how did you change the photos to silhouettes?"

"Oh, easy," he said. "Let me show you. I can use the photo I took of Dr. Caroline Seeza when she accompanied Augustus into the room the day we interviewed him."

Emma, who had never met Caroline Seeza, thought the doctor looked both eye-catching and professional with a teal stethoscope draped around her neck, a pale-yellow pants suit, and pearl earrings.

"I just use a software called Silhouette. Watch."

With a few clicks, Gideon turned the doctor into a dark shape and then sized it down.

"I think *she* looks like the mystery person," Emma declared.

"Not at all," Gideon said, laughing. "Not even close."

Sowah's phone rang. "Yes, good morning, Professor Kingsley. I'm fine, and you? You have the results?" He glanced up at the others, who had turned silent and were watching him intently. "Oh, really! Fantastic. Yes . . . okay. Thank you so much."

He hung up and looked around at the team members. "There are two sets of DNA on the metal clip. One is Lady Araba's, which we were expecting, but the other belongs to someone else. That someone is a woman."

FIFTY-SEVEN

One day before

AS JULIUS ENJOYED AN afternoon doze in his favorite chair, Caroline and Augustus watched TV in the sitting room. Out of the corner of her eye, Caroline saw her son frequently check his cell phone. Then it rang, and he leapt up to leave the room while answering. "Hello? Hey, how are you?"

Caroline glanced at her husband, who was safely snoring away, and got up quietly to peep into the hallway, where Augustus was speaking in hushed tones into his phone. Caroline stayed out of his sight but within earshot.

"Where are you now?" Augustus was saying. "Oh, okay. So, Monday is the big day, eh? What time is your show? So, you'll need to leave at around seven." He paused for a while, and then, "Araba, it's so good to hear your voice. Honestly, baby, I've tried to stop thinking about you, but I can't—no, wait, hear me out. I'm not thinking about sex. I . . . I just want to see you . . . but why did you call me, then? Because of my text? You could have ignored it, right?"

There was another pause, and Caroline could faintly hear Araba's voice on the other end.

"What time will you be home tomorrow night after the party?" Augustus asked. "No, I'm just asking. I just mean, well, don't stay too long. You need to be fresh for Monday . . . Yes, that sounds good. If you leave the party around nine, you can get home and go to bed early. I just wish you could do that with me." He laughed. "I'm kidding. I'll call you later, okay? I love you."

When Augustus returned to the sitting room he started as he saw Caroline waiting in the doorway with her arms folded.

"What is the spell this woman has on you?" she said coldly.

Augustus glowered at her. "I don't know what you're talking about."

"You and Araba are still talking. I don't believe this. After all we've said, all the progress we've made."

"You were eavesdropping?" Augustus said angrily. "I'm a grown man, Mama. Stop treating me like a child."

He sat down in sullen silence for a few minutes, then got up to leave. Caroline heard his bedroom door slam upstairs. *Then stop acting like a child.*

THAT NIGHT, AS they prepared for bed, Caroline said to Julius, "He's been talking to Araba."

Julius turned to her. "What?"

"Augustus. I overheard his conversation with Araba this afternoon." Caroline curled her lip in distaste. "'I love you, baby, I can't stop thinking about you,' and on and on. Ugh." She shook her head in disgust.

Julius heaved a long sigh, got into bed, and closed his eyes to think. He opened them again. "I give up. I don't know what to do with him."

Caroline sat at the edge of the bed, staring at the floor. "There's nothing the matter with Augustus. The trouble—*all* of it—is Lady Araba. She keeps manipulating him, twisting him around, stretching him to the limit, and soon he's going to snap."

FIFTY-EIGHT

Thirteen months after

DR. JAUREGUI WELCOMED EMMA into her office with a warm smile. "Come in, come in. Welcome."

"Thank you, Doctor. I was in the neighborhood, so I thought I would stop by. I hope you're not too busy?"

"The medical students will be here in a moment," Jauregui said, "but we have a little time. Have a seat. Water?"

"Yes, please. Thank you, Doctor."

Jauregui handed her a bottle of water from the small refrigerator in the corner of the room. She sat down. "So, how are things? Did you complete the radio program?"

"Um, well, that's partly why I'm here today," Emma said sheepishly. "I want to make a confession and also apologize."

Emma told the doctor the truth. No, she wasn't Jasmine Ohene, a reporter with Citi-FM, she was a private investigator who worked for the Sowah Detective Agency.

Jauregui began to laugh. "Why didn't you just say so? I still would have tried to help."

"Well, I know that now," Emma said, "but before I got here, I didn't. Some people don't like the sound of 'private investigator.'"

"Some don't like radio reporters either," Jauregui pointed out.

"True," Emma conceded. "But anyway, that's all irrelevant now because I found you here instead of someone who would've put obstacles in my way, so I want to thank you for that."

"You are most welcome, Emma," Jauregui said. "It was a delight meeting you. Do you have any updates?"

Emma gave her the follow-up on the metal clip and the DNA findings.

"A woman, huh?" Jauregui asked. "Intriguing. Of course, that still doesn't mean the murderer was a woman. We don't know if the metal clip is directly connected to the murder or just happened to be there."

"That's a good point," Emma said. She then related the saga of the mysterious CCTV footage that Gideon and his friend had managed to recover.

"You're all doing very good work," Jauregui said. "Keep at it. You're going to solve this."

"Thank you, Doctor."

They heard the clamor of voices outside in the vestibule.

"My students are here now, so I should get going," Jauregui said, rising from her seat. "But please, stop by again whenever you have time. Or maybe we can get a drink one of these days. Do you drink?"

"No please, Doctor."

"Agh," she said, pulling a face of regret. "Maybe I can change your mind on that. Nothing like a good, cold beer."

Emma laughed and was still smiling as she made her way to the front entrance through the powerful odor of formaldehyde and a crowd of fresh-faced, excited medical students, some of them in their short white jackets and all of them wide-eyed and innocent looking.

Emma got to the door and left. Fifty meters along, something struck her. She returned to the building, trying to spot one of the students she had noticed. There he was. She circled around to him. He was an impossibly tall young man with a light beard that didn't seem to want to grow out fully. He wasn't bad looking, Emma thought.

"Hello," she said. "Please, do you mind if I look at the stethoscope around your neck?"

"Sure," he said, taking it off and handing it to her. "It's brandnew—I've hardly used it."

Emma could see that. It was shiny, black, and free of any signs of wear and tear.

"You like it?" the medical student asked.

"Yes, but I'm curious. Why are there two tubes instead of one?"

"One tube goes to the right ear, the other to the left—like stereo channels," he explained. "It's a better system than one tube."

"And these two metal clips," Emma said, "one high up and another one almost at the tip where this thing is, whatever it's called."

"The diaphragm and the bell," he said. "For listening to different heart sounds and all that. And the clips are to keep the two tubes separated and prevent them from knocking against each other, which would prevent you from hearing well."

"I see." Emma peered at one of the clips and read off what was written on the side. "Littmann. Is that the make of the stethoscope?"

"Yes," the student said, his eyes fixed on her face. "It's one of the best-known brands."

"You realize you won't have much use for it in here, right?" Emma said with a wink. "None of the bodies here have beating hearts."

He laughed. "I know, but I just bought it, and I'm guarding it with my life."

"Got it," Emma said.

"My name is Robert," the student said, extending a hand. "And you?"

"Emma."

"Would you like to go out with me, Emma?"

"Thank you, but I have a boyfriend," she told him with a neutral expression.

"Oh," he said, clearly disappointed.

"Have you ever heard of Prestige stethoscopes?"

"No," Robert said, "but I can google it for you." He whipped out his phone and typed it in. "Hey, you're right! How did you know?"

He showed her the screen display of multiple Prestige stethoscope styles.

Emma fingered Robert's stethoscope. "Very strong material," she observed.

"Yes, the thicker the tubing, the better the quality. I can tell you more if you give me your number."

Nice try, she thought. "Sorry, I don't think my boyfriend would be very happy with that. But thank you. You've no idea how helpful you've been."

FIFTY-NINE

Hours before

"It's eight o'clock," Caroline whispered to Julius. "Time to get going."

As they passed by Augustus's room, they heard his TV blasting an action movie, his favorite genre—the bloodier, the better.

Outside, Julius took in his wife's appearance—black jeans, a black hoodie, and a backpack were decidedly not her style. She did own such clothing, but she rarely wore it.

As they settled into the BMW, Julius cleared his throat. "What are you going to do?"

"The less you know, Julius, the better," she replied.

"What's in the backpack?"

"Quiet," she said. "I'm thinking."

He shut up.

About five minutes away from their destination, Caroline said, "You remember Trasacco Valley, right?"

"I've been a few times, but not recently," he said.

"I've been there on quite a few occasions to make house calls," Caroline said, "so I know it well. There's a back entrance to the complex. I want you to drop me there. Then drive around to the front. At the gate, tell them you're a doctor making a house call. They never question that. Don't forget—wear your cap low. Then follow the signs to the rear gate. Approach it slowly and it will slide open by a sensor mechanism. I'll enter and proceed from there. There's a large tree next to the shed on the right-hand side. Park your car behind it and wait for me to come back. Got it?"

"Yes." Julius heaved a troubled sigh. Caroline glanced at him and saw how on edge he looked.

She reached out and squeezed his arm. "Don't worry, it will be okay. This is something we must do."

WHEN CAROLINE GOT into the complex, she checked her watch. Eight thirty-seven. She hoped that Araba would indeed stay at her event until about nine, as she had discussed with Augustus. Caroline kept her head down and adopted a gait she imagined to be masculine. She knew about the CCTV cameras, but Augustus had once told her the system was antiquated and practically useless.

As many times as Augustus had been at Araba's home, Caroline had never had the pleasure. Once, just out of curiosity while on a house call to the complex, she had asked one of the landscapers which unit was Araba's.

Caroline was tense, constantly on the lookout for patrolling security guards and at the same time assessing the risk-benefit of having Julius wait out there by the gate. The longer he was there, the greater the chances of his being seen loitering, though the car was mostly concealed behind the tree and shed.

Araba's house was dark except for a couple lights downstairs. The garage was open with a single vehicle parked there, almost certainly confirming that Araba was still out, since she owned two cars.

The gate at the bottom of the driveway was something of an impediment to Caroline's getting in, but the adjoining wall wasn't impossibly high. Nevertheless, scaling it was not so easy, and Caroline stumbled and fell as she dropped to the ground on the other side. She dusted herself off and hurried across the lawn to the front door, where the porch light was on. She dug in her pocket for Augustus's keys, which he had left carelessly lying on the coffee table at home. She knew he had a spare key to Araba's house and Caroline had no reason to believe he would have taken it off the ring.

She had already donned blue nitrile gloves. Her hand trembling somewhat, she tried each key in the lock. The first, second, third, and fourth ones all failed and Caroline cursed. She prayed the fifth would work. It did.

BEFORE SHE HEARD Araba's vehicle pull up, Caroline didn't have much time to decide where to hide. The master bedroom was out of the question, since there wasn't a single item of furniture that could conceal her presence. She went along the hall to the guest bedroom and hid in the closet, which was empty except for some naked hangers.

She heard two voices from downstairs, one belonging to Araba and the other to a male—her chauffeur, no doubt. After four or five minutes, the male bid Araba good night. Soon after that, Araba came up the stairs humming a tune. Then she went into her bedroom and out of Caroline's earshot.

She wasn't sure what to do next. She had contemplated waiting until Araba fell asleep, but that would take far too long. Caroline didn't have all night. She heard the sound of the bathroom shower starting up and waited a few seconds. This was the time to move.

She reached into the backpack and removed her stethoscope. The irony of using an instrument of healing for her mission wasn't lost on her. Caroline padded down the hall, grateful to the carpet for muffling her footsteps. Before entering the bedroom, she peeped around the doorjamb to be sure Araba was in the bathroom. She was, and she had put on some music—R&B, which Caroline acknowledged as a tasteful choice.

She entered the room, marveling at the huge walk-in closet with more clothes than she had ever seen in one place. Should she hide in here? Where was the best location from which to surprise her victim?

• • •

WITH ONE EYE peeping out from the closet entrance, Caroline watched Araba come out of the bathroom, toweled off and naked. Almost immediately, Araba's attention was drawn to a backpack to her left. Caroline had deliberately left it there. Araba started and turned to stare at it. It was within that precise moment that Caroline came up from behind and looped the stethoscope over Araba's head. Crossing her forearms behind Araba's neck, she pulled the stethoscope tubing tight. Araba gasped and gurgled, grabbing at her throat.

Caroline had anticipated a struggle, but she had underestimated Araba's pound-for-pound strength. She kicked out and twisted her body like a thrashing reptile, struggling both to breathe and pull the ligature away. Caroline staggered back toward the bookshelf, Araba with her. They both fell, and Caroline lost her grip. Araba let out a hoarse scream and staggered to her feet.

Caroline heard the screaming of her adrenaline-drenched brain inside her skull. Araba turned to face her, and Caroline had the sense she was losing control, a feeling to which she was not accustomed as a physician. She thought she said aloud, *I'll kill you before you kill my son*, but perhaps she only thought it. With heightened clarity, she saw the silver vase within reach, grabbed it, and struck Araba hard against the side of her head. Araba went down immediately as blood flashed on the white carpet. For a moment, she was still, and Caroline stood there out of breath, her energy depleted.

Araba moved and sat up, disoriented. Caroline, still breathing heavily, watched her struggle up the side of the bed until she was able to climb upon it and begin to crawl away. Caroline felt both pity and anger. *Where does she think she's going?*

She climbed onto Araba's back at an almost leisurely pace. Again, she looped the stethoscope over Araba's head, crossed the tubes behind her neck, and tightened surely and steadily. This time, Araba didn't struggle much. Caroline realized that one of the two clips holding the double tubing of her stethoscope was biting into her glove and the skin of her right hand, but she ignored it. The most important thing at this point was to not let up the pressure for at least four minutes. There was a ringing in her ears, and she was just beginning to realize how much Araba's scalp had bled and what a mess it had made.

Araba had stopped moving for some time now. Her hands shaking violently, Caroline checked for a carotid pulse. Nothing. She staggered off the bed, exhausted. She felt sick, but willed herself not to throw up. She looked at her blood-smeared gloves. The right one had a tear in it, and Caroline realized the stethoscope clip must have bitten into it. She carefully took both gloves off using the physician's one-touch technique and bundled them up into a plastic bag in her backpack. Then, she put on a new pair of gloves.

With a burst of panic, Caroline realized she was taking too long. She dropped the stethoscope and vase into her backpack and left quickly, giving one final backward glance at Araba sprawled on the bed. Halfway down the stairs, Caroline remembered what she had meant to do: stage it like a burglary homicide. Annoyed by her lapse, she returned to the bedroom, making a beeline for the dresser. She found jewelry in the second drawer, grabbed several pieces, and left the drawer open before departing once more.

AT NINE FIFTY-SIX, Julius saw his wife heading his way, switched on the ignition, and moved out from behind the tree and the shed.

Caroline opened the front passenger door and dropped in. "Drive out. Hurry."

Julius turned the BMW toward the exit and moved forward. The gate didn't budge.

"*Shit!*" Julius said, his voice cracking. "It won't open."

"Don't be stupid," Caroline said. "Of course it will open. Move up some more."

Julius did, but nothing happened. He gasped in desperation. "We're going to have to leave by the front."

"We're not doing that," Caroline said through gritted teeth. "Back up a little and try again."

Julius did as he was told, and this time the gate, albeit sluggishly, creaked open.

SIXTY

Thirteen months after

IN THE OFFICE, EMMA told Gideon, "Show me the pic of Dr. Caroline Seeza again."

"Okay," he said, leaning back and languidly working his laptop touch pad. "Here it is."

Emma looked at it for a moment, and then down at her phone screen, which she scrolled through to the image she wanted. It was a teal-colored stethoscope. "Take a look," she said, handing her phone to Gideon.

"Yeah, it looks similar to the one the doctor is wearing," he said. "Same color and all that. But lots of stethoscopes look alike. What's your point?"

"Look at the manufacturer, though."

Gideon drew in his breath sharply. "*Prestige.*"

"Exactly. The name on the side of the metal clip that Boateng took from the crime scene. And you see those two metal clips on the double tubing of the stethoscope? One at the top and one at the bottom end?"

Gideon was looking at her with a smile and light in his eyes that seemed to brighten his whole face. "Like the one at the crime scene."

"You got it."

Gideon's expression changed again. "But wait, I'm confused.

You can't be saying Dr. Caroline had anything to do with Lady Araba's murder. Or are you?"

Emma pointed at Gideon's laptop screen. "Well, look at her stethoscope. What's missing?"

"Shit," he whispered. "One of the metal clips—the one on the end. So, you're saying she went to Lady Araba, strangled her to death with her stethoscope—"

"Which would explain the double ligature marks listed in the autopsy."

"Okay, true too. And while Dr. Caroline was strangling Lady Araba, the metal clip rubbed against her finger and she transferred some DNA onto it."

"Precisely."

"Let's go talk to the boss," Gideon said, excitement in his voice.

"Hold on," Emma said. "We should build an airtight case first. I need to talk to DS Boateng."

He answered on her second attempt and Emma asked him if he knew the make of car Dr. Caroline drove.

"I've seen her in a Jaguar, but I think he has a BMW. Why, what's up?"

"We're just checking on routine stuff," she said cryptically, not wanting to be derailed. "Thank you, DS Boateng."

She ended the call and said to Gideon, "Justice Seeza has a BMW."

They stared at each other.

"He drove her there," Gideon said.

"He's the one who opened the gate for her," Gideon said.

"Then she went to Araba's house, killed her, came back to the car, and they drove away."

Jojo and Walter walked in from lunch.

"What are you two guys plotting?" Jojo asked.

"Sit down and listen, both of you," Gideon said. "We have something to tell you."

SIXTY-ONE

Thirteen and a half months later

AT THE CLINIC RECEPTION late in the afternoon, Sowah asked to see Dr. Caroline Seeza.

"Please, do you have an appointment?" the receptionist asked.

"No, but tell her I might have found something she's missing."

The receptionist looked puzzled, but he made the call to the back office anyway. "Please, have a seat," he told Sowah. "Someone will come for you."

Sowah waited for about ten minutes, and then a pretty nurse in a highly starched green-and-white uniform emerged from the inner sanctum. "Mr. Sowah?"

"Yes."

"Please, come with me."

CAROLINE SEEZA, M.D. was embossed on her door in gold letters. The nurse knocked and ushered Sowah in.

Dr. Seeza was busy with medical charts, of which there were quite a few.

"Good afternoon, Doctor," Sowah said.

She looked up. "Yes, what is it?"

"May I sit down?"

"Yes, yes, of course," she said irritably, waving at a seat. "I must say, Mr.—"

"Sowah." He noticed Dr. Seeza's teal stethoscope curled on her desk. Minus one of its metal clips.

"Mr. Sowah, this is not a good time for me. What is this about?"

"I'm a private investigator looking into the case of Lady Araba's murder."

"Okay, and?"

"We're following up on a number of pieces of evidence, trying to figure out their significance. By the way, is that a Prestige stethoscope you have?"

"Yes," she said. "Yes, it is. Why do you ask? Mr. Sowah, what is the purpose of this visit, exactly?"

From his pocket, Sowah removed a color print of the metal clip Boateng had found at the crime scene and laid it on the table next to Dr. Seeza's stethoscope.

She stared at it. "What is that?" Her voice had turned husky.

"Do you recognize it?"

"I don't know anything about it," Dr. Seeza snapped. "And I don't know why in the hell you've come here to interrupt my day with nonsense I know nothing about. Please leave."

Sowah got up, but for a moment, he moved the photo close to the metal clip on the doctor's stethoscope, as if to compare the two. "You're missing a clip from your stethoscope, Doctor. Could this be it?"

Dr. Seeza snatched the stethoscope off the table. "I told you to get out. Hurry up, before I call security."

"Thank you, Doctor. Have a blessed day."

Outside again, Sowah called Laryea. "She reacted. She's primed."

HAVING HAD HER staff cancel the rest of her appointments for the day, Caroline hurried home, where she found Julius working in his office.

"They know," Caroline said as she entered.

Julius turned to look at her. "Who knows? What are you talking about?"

"Someone came to the clinic," she said, hyperventilating. "A Mr. Sawyer, or Sowah, was his name. A private investigator."

Julius got up. "Caroline, sit down. You look as though you're about to faint."

"No, no, I'm fine. He had a picture of the clip, this Sowah guy."

"What clip?"

"It came off my stethoscope. I didn't realize it until we got home."

"What? You never mentioned this to me. I didn't realize that was what you used. And the stethoscope? You threw it out, I presume?"

Caroline was indignant. "Why would I do that? It still works perfectly well and it cost me a mint."

"But it might have trace evidence on it," Julius said, his voice rising in dismay.

"I know that," Caroline retorted sharply. "I'm not stupid. I cleaned it off thoroughly with bleach."

"Not good enough," Julius said, shaking his head. "You have to destroy the entire thing now. Where is it?"

"In the car."

"Go get it. Right now."

Caroline hurried out, but as she reached the sitting room, she heard a knock on the door.

OUTSIDE, CLEO LARYEA knocked a second time. It was Julius who answered, but he opened the door only a crack. "Yes?"

"I'm Deputy Commissioner of Police Laryea, CID. I'm here with my constable. May we speak for a moment?"

"Um, yes, but can you hold on one second? I'm not decent."

"Of course."

Julius shut the door. Without a word, Laryea signaled to the constable to go around to the other side of the house.

Julius returned. "Come in, please, Commissioner."

"Thank you." Laryea entered and followed the justice to the sitting room.

"Have a seat," Julius said. "How can I help?"

"Is Dr. Seeza at home?"

Julius shook his head. "No, she's out at the moment. Is there anything I can do for you?"

"I see two vehicles outside—the BMW belongs to you. To whom does the Jaguar belong?"

"To Doctor Seeza, but she's not using it at the moment. She's out with friends."

For a judge, Laryea thought, *he's a terrible liar.*

Julius started as shouts and sounds of a struggle came from outside. Laryea jumped up and pushed open the sliding glass door that led to the back patio. He ran around to the right side of the house, where he found Dr. Caroline Seeza writhing and screaming on the ground as the constable tried to handcuff her.

"What happened?" Laryea asked.

"Found her in the bushes," the constable said. "She was trying to hide something."

With his chin, the constable pointed at an object on the ground beside them: a silver vase.

"Aha," Laryea said with satisfaction.

"What are you doing?" Julius screamed, coming up from behind Laryea. "Leave her alone!"

He launched himself at the constable, fists flailing. Laryea pulled Julius off and wrestled him to the ground. Julius roared with fury.

"Justice Seeza," Laryea said, raising his voice above the din, "I'm arresting you for assaulting a police officer, for conspiracy to murder Araba Tagoe, and aiding and abetting the murder of same."

The constable got Caroline to her feet and brought her over to where Laryea was.

"Cuff him too," he said to the constable, and they switched places.

Caroline had gone limp now, weeping pathetically with her head bowed.

"Dr. Caroline Seeza, you are under arrest for the murder of Araba Tagoe."

"But I didn't do it," she wailed.

Two arrests in one night, Laryea thought. *Not bad at all.*

SIXTY-TWO

Fourteen months after

THE NEXT TIME EMMA saw Dele Tetteyfio, there were packed boxes piled high inside and outside the house, and a group of young men had started to load them up into a truck.

"Auntie, are you moving?" Emma asked in surprise.

"Hi, Emma," Dele said, smiling and sweating somewhat. "Yes, I'm getting a bigger place and a larger shop."

"Congrats," Emma said.

"Thank you. Oh, have a seat, or I should say, a box. Any one is fine."

The two women sat down beside each other.

"So," Emma said, "how are you feeling these days?"

"Now that the mystery of my niece's death has been solved," Dele said, "I sleep much better. But . . ."

"But?"

Dele shook her head. "I still don't understand why she did it—Dr. Caroline, I mean. How could she hate Araba so much?"

Emma thought about that for a moment. "I think it was less of a hatred for Araba than a consuming love she had for her son. I don't think a lot of people realized just how much she cared. He was her only child and the apple of her eye. In her view, Lady Araba was a malevolent force bent on destroying Augustus's life. Of course, we know that wasn't true. It was Caroline's imagination at work."

"Araba never wanted to hurt anyone," Dele said, her eyes brimming. "It was always people hurting her, and I just don't understand it. Look at what her father, my brother, did to her. I still feel guilty about not doing more to save her."

Emma nodded. "I know you do, Auntie. I only hope that with time, you'll come to terms with it and forgive yourself a little."

Dele smiled at her. "Thanks. You lift me up."

"Of course."

"Is the case against the Seezas strong?" Dele asked. "I keep worrying they'll wriggle out of it, especially with Julius being a judge—or ex-judge, I should say."

"The trace DNA on the weapon, Dr. Seeza's stethoscope, is consistent with Araba's DNA. The DNA on the metal clip at the crime scene, which was dislodged from the stethoscope during the act, is consistent with both Araba's and Dr. Seeza's DNA. Those two things alone put her at the scene. Then there are other things: the BMW, the fact that Augustus realized that Sunday night around eight-twenty that his parents weren't home. Interrogated separately, they gave alibis that didn't match up. So yes, the case is strong."

"Thank God for that."

Emma's phone buzzed and she took it out of her pocket. "That's Courage. We're meeting for lunch. Auntie Dele, I have to go now."

The two women embraced.

"When I'm settled into my new place," Dele said, "I'll invite you over for a good meal. And a beer." She laughed. "Only joking. I know you don't drink."

Emma walked away with mixed feelings. Sometimes, the solving of a murder brought a sort of peace to those left behind. That was the case with Auntie Dele. She would rest easier now. But as far as Augustus and the Tagoes were concerned, Emma's guess was that they would be working through their pain for a long time to come.

GLOSSARY

Asem (ah-SEM): trouble, drama (Twi)

Ashawo (ah-shah-WOH): prostitute

Awurade (Eh-woo-rah-DAY): God

Ayekoo! (ah-YAY-koh): well done, nice job

Banku (bang-KU): proportionate mixture of fermented corn and cassava dough in hot water mashed into a smooth, whitish paste and formed into balls

Batakari (ba-ta-ka-REE): plaid or striped smock

Bola (BOH-lah): trash, rubbish

Cedi (SEE-dee): Ghanaian monetary unit

Chaley (cha-LAY): bro, dude, buddy

Ete sen (eh-tih SENG): how are you? (Twi)

Fufu or *fufui* (*foo-FOO*): starchy food such as yam, cassava, or plantain pounded into a glutinous mass and eaten with a variety of soups

Ga: language and peoples of many coastal regions of Ghana, including the Greater Accra Region

Kontomire (*kohn-tohm-ee-ray*): stew prepared with cocoyam leaves, palm oil, dried fish, and other ingredients

Kwasea (*kwa-se-YAH*): fool, idiot

Maate (*mah-TIH*): Got it, I hear you; literally, "I have heard" (Twi)

Medaase (*mih-dah-sih*): Thank you (Twi)

Nyame adom (*Nyah-mih Ah-dohm*): [by] God's grace, [I am fine] in response to *ete sen* (Twi)

Oburoni (*oh-boo-roh-NEE*): white person

Pesewa (*PEH-swah*): monetary unit, 100 p = 1 *cedi*

Red-red: black-eyed peas cooked in palm oil and spices with fried ripe plantain

Tro-tro (*traw-traw*): minivan transportation for the masses

Twi (*chwee*): Akan language spoken by a large majority of Ghanaians

Wahala (origin Nigeria): trouble, drama

Yaaey! (*yah-AY*): response to *ayekoo!*

PRONUNCIATION GUIDE

Ghanaian languages contain combinations of vowels and consonants unfamiliar to the English language.

Dz, dj, or *gy*: "J" sound, as in *just* (e.g. *Djan, Gyan*)

Ei: "Ay" sound, as in *hay* (e.g. *Kyei*)

Ky: "Ch" sound, as in *church* (e.g. *Kyei*)

Oa: "Wa" sound, as in *whack* (e.g. *Boateng*)

ACKNOWLEDGMENTS

I'M DEEPLY GRATEFUL TO Bronwen, Juliet, Amara, Rachel, and all the crew at Soho Press, where I have found my literary home. I would be nothing without their skill and support in the writing and editing process. I applaud Soho's dedication to the discovery of the global voices out there, which have much to say.

Thanks to Trasacco Valley and its realtors for giving me a tour of their beautiful community and impressive mansions.

I'm also grateful to Jordan Sakre for introduction to Accra's clubs and Ghanaian celebrities; and to Writers Project of Ghana, and Vidya Bookstore in Accra, for their continued support.